The Best
AMERICAN
SHORT
STORIES
1978

The Best
AMERICAN
SHORT
STORIES
1978

Selected from
U.S. and Canadian Magazines
by Ted Solotaroff
with Shannon Ravenel
With an Introduction by Ted Solotaroff
Including the Yearbook of the
American Short Story

 1978

Houghton Mifflin Company Boston

Library of Congress Catalog Card Number: 16-11387
ISBN 0-395-27104-5

Printed in the United States of America

V 10 9 8 7 6 5 4 3 2 1

For Hal Scharlatt, 1935–1974

Publisher's Note

THIS 1978 EDITION OF *The Best American Short Stories* is the first volume in thirty-seven years that has not been edited by Martha Foley. The series started in 1915 under the editorship of Edward J. O'Brien and its very title reflects the naive optimism of a period when people assumed that a generally accepted "best" could be identified, even in fields of human endeavor that can't be measured in units of time, weight, or size.

Martha Foley took over as editor of the series in 1942 after Mr. O'Brien was killed during the World War II blitz of London. She and her husband, Whit Burnett, had edited *Story* magazine from 1931 to 1942, and in later years she taught creative writing at the Columbia School of Journalism. She died in September 1977, at the age of eighty.

Looking back over the thirty-six years of Miss Foley's editorship, one is struck by the unfailingly high standards of the collections she assembled and by the sustained admiration of those who reviewed the annual volumes. It's hard to believe that an editor wouldn't become jaded or lose touch with the times, after so many years, and begin to lose the respect of the critics. To the end of her life Martha Foley maintained a personal enthusiasm and critical integrity that commanded enviable attention in the literary world. We salute her achievement and mourn her passing.

Ted Solotaroff, editor of the *American Review* and currently an editor at Bantam Books, has chosen the stories that appear in this 1978 volume and provided a candid and discerning introduction. We had asked him to become associated with the series on a permanent basis but he wisely suggested that perhaps the time had come to modify the arrangements by inviting a different writer or critic to edit each new annual volume. A variety of fresh points of view should add liveliness to the series and provide a new dimension to the title. "Best" thereby becomes a sequence of informed opinions that gains reliability from its very diversity.

Also beginning with this volume, the annual editor will receive the support of Shannon Ravenel, whose role is to read, throughout the year, an enormous number of stories from the host of U.S. and Canadian magazines that publish short fiction, to screen out all but 150 or so for the editor's consideration, and to select the stories that make up the list of Distinguished Short Stories, which has become an important feature of these volumes. Ms. Ravenel is a former Houghton Mifflin editor who worked with Martha Foley in the past. Magazines wishing to make sure that their contributors are considered for *The Best American Short Stories* should see that Ms. Ravenel is on their subscription list.

Contents

Introduction

DURING THE PAST TEN YEARS of editing *American Review* I have seen and published a good deal of short fiction. This experience has been valuable in putting me in touch with a wide range of narrative writing and also with my own standards and prejudices of judgment. At the same time, though, what I've learned tends to complicate and, as I can't help feeling, mock the enterprise of putting together an anthology billed as "The Best American Short Stories" of the year. First of all, I have watched the definition of what makes a piece of writing a short story, or even fiction, pretty much collapse before my eyes and within my own mind. To give just a few examples, I have published a narrative monologue in which the speaker is a story that is trying to find its identity and to stay alive, and another which is based on an imaginary story by Borges. There was also an essay on the implications of the film *King Kong* as seen by a kind of idiot-savant, another which links all manner of material — fictional, historical, personal — into a series of responses to a two-part examination on "The Death of the Russian Novel," and another whose narrative line is a recipe for baking bread. *American Review* also published short fiction in the form of meditations and memoirs and vice versa, as well as chronicles in which the real and the imaginary freely mingle, an interview, an unsigned letter, or the liner notes to an album of songs by a country blues singer. In time I not only gave up trying or even wanting to distinguish the short story from these and other innovations in narrative writing, but also gave up even drawing a line between fiction and nonfiction, simply billing whatever wasn't poetry as "prose." So, in first taking up the task of choosing fiction for this collection that distinctly and defensibly restricts itself to the category of the "short story," not to mention "the best," I felt rather like a polymorphous perverse sensualist whose new bedmate practices only the missionary position.

But so be it. Better, as time went on, I found I wanted to construe the problem as an opportunity: i.e., to choose genuine short stories and nothing else, and hence do something for the most beleaguered of our literary forms and the waif of the magazine and publishing industry, by showing just how good and interesting and, yes, relevant (the regnant value of our perplexed age) it can be. Walter Benjamin in his magisterial essay "The Story Teller" argued that the art of storytelling was dying out, that it was being superseded by the modern media of information and by the story's younger and more topical relative, the novel. There are reasons to believe that, writing in 1935, Benjamin was gloomily prophetic, but there are other reasons, embodied in this collection, to believe his prognosis was premature. Or even wrong.

In an interview a few years back, the novelist John Barth speculates that it may be the novel, as we know it, which is passing out of literary history, but this "doesn't mean the end of narrative literature, certainly. It certainly doesn't mean the end of storytelling." Arguing against that article of the modernist literary faith which holds that plot — the constitutive element of storytelling — is a retrograde device, Barth says that there are "ways to be quite contemporary and yet go at the art in a fashion that would allow you to tell complicated stories simply for the aesthetic pleasure of complexity, of complication and unravelment, suspense, and the rest." One can add that beyond the writer's pleasure, there still lies the reader's, however sophisticated he may be, in the well-told story — a pleasure that may have become distracted, displaced, and undernourished, but one that is programmed into his nature as surely as gazing meditatively into a log fire (and not unrelated to it), a pleasure that can be so quickly and powerfully revived by a true storyteller like García Márquez. And no less basic in the human creature is the pleasure of telling stories. Indeed, the need to do so, as any bartender will tell you.

So, in behalf of the lingering interest in and significance of the short story, I have restricted my selection to those that are intended and identifiable as such. No excerpts from novels-in-progress, which such annual anthologies as this one often fall back upon, no

memoirs, lyrical meditations, or involuted narratives or monologues that enigmatically smile at the reader as if to say, "Boo-hoo,
where's the story," no experiments in the nonlinear story, the
antiplot story, the characterless character story. This has meant
leaving out of consideration a number of first-rate or otherwise
impressive pieces of narrative writing and, in several cases, a certain wrenching of my own heart. Three of my favorite fictional
pieces in the final issue of *American Review,* published last year,
were Robert Stone's "A Hunter in the Morning," Max Apple's
"Disneyad," and the late Meyer Liben's "The Garden." The first
two, however, were taken from forthcoming novels, and though
each stands very well on its own, and though they can readily be
read as stories, I had to pass them by. On the other hand, Liben's
account of his initiation to literature through the magic of Marvell's
poem, and his love for the high school English teacher who both
summoned and embodied its glory, seemed to me finally a beautifully rendered sketch rather than a story, lacking a strong complicating element that keeps the issue of the narrative open and
charges its resolution.

There were other painful exclusions on these grounds in which
pride of editorship wasn't involved. Cynthia Ozick's "Puttermesser," which appeared in *The New Yorker,* is a brilliant portrait of a
young woman lawyer, an x-ray, as it were, of a buried spirit, but
one whose material and pace seemed to me to anticipate a fuller
development of the narrative, so that it appeared to stop rather
than end, as though the beginning of a longer work. Or again,
there was an arrestingly original narrative by Janet Lindquist Black
in the *Northwest Review* — "Poika: 1929" — about a boy struggling
with his fear in a primitive Finnish enclave in Massachusetts that
again left me leaning eagerly in the direction of its continuation,
rather than with the settled feeling of a completed tale. I could be
less uncertain but was still regretful about ruling out other notable
pieces that were presented as excerpts or adaptations from novels,
such as Don DeLillo's "Players" in *Esquire,* Ralph Ellison's "Back-
whacking" in *Nimrod,* and Lee Smith's "Black Mountain Breakdown" in *The Carolina Quarterly.* Another difficult exclusion was
Elizabeth Bishop's "Memories of Uncle Neddy," which, though
imaginatively told, seemed to me to belong to the literature of
remembrance rather than of the story.

In the end, though, I have less trouble and remorse about the

"Short Stories of 1978" (really, of course, 1977) part of the title than I do about the front part — "The Best American . . ." Actually, it should read "North American," since one of the stories selected for the volume and some nine others listed among the distinguished ones of the year come from Canadian journals. But that's just a detail; it's the phrase "the best" that casts the more dubious shadow on the enterprise. First, there's the matter of coverage. The Coordinating Council of Little Magazines has some 600 periodicals as members and estimates there are at least another 400 each year that are not. Assuming, very conservatively, that only half of them publish some fiction, there are roughly 500 periodicals from which to choose this collection. And this is not to take into account the short fiction published by the myriad small presses in their collections. All of which is also in a kind of Heraclitean flux from year to year, as the little magazines and small presses come and go, emerge and fold. From a list of the periodicals that had been regularly sent to Martha Foley, and from her own diligent research in libraries, my colleague, Shannon Ravenel, was able to track down 123 periodicals and to go through a total of 500 issues containing well over 1000 stories. But, despite her best efforts, she was able to read perhaps one fourth of the stories published last year. From these she screened out some 150 for me to consider, to which I added another 50 or so that I heard about or that I had liked, two of which made it into the collection itself. So, across my mind stretches the shadow of the hundreds of stories that did not reach Shannon, as well as those she did not select (our tastes are reasonably close but hardly identical), or that I did not chance upon on my own.

I am not being unduly sedulous, merely realistic. After a decade of receiving stories for *American Review,* and of traveling around the country, and having unknown magazines, chapbooks of stories, even sheaves of mimeographed sheets thrust into my hands, in which, now and then, a gem of a narrative was hidden away amid otherwise mawkish writing or defiant scribbling — I know how farflung and often obscure are the places where genuine talent can be found in this ever-expanding and localizing literary culture of ours. I'm also aware of the testy indifference among literary editors, having shared it, toward sending issues to this collection, since for many years none of the stories I published in *American Review* were selected, which is what I mean, in part, about the self-irony and mockery of being set up now as the judge of "The Best." (We hope that the policy of choosing a different editor from year to year, which will broaden and vary the standpoints of editorial choice, will encourage many more editors to put Ms. Ravenel on their mailing list: (P.O. Box 3176, University City, Missouri 63130.)

2

Before I take up my own standpoint and give examples of it from the stories I've chosen and some of the ones I haven't, a few words seem in order about the subjectivity, and hence the vicissitudes, of editorial judgment, which also contributes to the sardonic side of my response to the idea of "The Best." Lionel Trilling once remarked to the effect that while we are reading a work of literature, it is also reading us, locating the kinds of experience that interest us, the styles and tones of writing we are responsive to, our specific areas of educated feeling, as well as the blind spots and dead spots in our taste, sensibility, and our competence to judge. A literary editor is particularly conversant with this reflective process. In most cases, you know fairly quickly, sometimes even in the first paragraph, whether you're going to be drawn to a manuscript or not. There is that stirring of your imagination by an immediacy of detail or statement or situation, or of encountering a tone that quickly evokes a responsive chord in your being and produces that simple, intimate sense of settling in. Some manuscripts that last for you may be slower in asserting the terms of their appeal, but even so, there is usually a kind of rightness and personal pleasure from the start — an authority in the voice, a weightedness to the materials, that generates interest. If you have to go through a large pile of fiction in a short time — say 200 stories in two weeks or so — you depend a great deal on this rather remorseless process of singling out your type of story (not very different from "my type of woman" or "my type of guy"), for you know that a story that hasn't begun to make its mark after a few pages is not likely to come even close to being one of the "keepers."

But where Trilling's point becomes particularly germane is with the stories that carry you firmly along to the end but leave you cooler than you'd expected, or critical, or otherwise unconfident of their staying power — it's lucid and potent all right, you say to yourself, but perhaps a bit contrived, or crude, or simplistic, or the ending doesn't quite work — or with those indirect stories that keep you willingly working hard by their skillfulness and intelligence, their subtlety of implication, the depth at which their point is being kept, but in the end somehow haven't yet jelled into a distinctive and reliable response. Clearly something significant is going on here, you say, it moves me but I finally don't get the point, or else, I think I get the point but it doesn't finally move me. But there is also the possibility that either of these problematic types of story is mainly just going past you, reading you and finding you faked out by your own fussiness or willfulness or finding you impatient, banal, provincial, obtuse.

There have been a number of occasions in the past where I have found myself to be a living proof of this possibility. A story that has left me in one of the above states of being of two minds turns up months or a year or two later in another magazine; I read it to confirm my judgment and instead find myself now completely in its thrall, except for that corner of my heart that is sinking in chagrin. I have even found a rejected work turning up in my conversation or contemplation two or three years later with a vividness and depth of recall that would impel me, my mouth full of crow, to write to the author and ask if that story (or essay or poem) I had turned down was still available. If it was, more times than not the mark it had left on my consciousness, and, no doubt, my unconscious, turned out to be a true one, contributing to the alteration of sensibility that would eventually welcome it wholeheartedly and, conversely, find me to have become a suitable medium for its terms of appeal. On the other hand, now and then I've eagerly bought a narrative which has turned cold or cloudy in my mind by the time I read it in galleys.

After such knowledge, what forgiveness, as Eliot asks; what enables you to go on trusting your judgment? Well, what you should learn from these cases of self-embarrassment is to try to read, as much as possible, for keeps. So, you arrange things as propitiously as possible, particularly for those manuscripts that make an unmistakable claim on your attention, that already have begun to matter. If you happen to be tired, distracted, or for some other reason less than fully present to it, you stop, put it aside, and take it up again later when you can pay close attention, open yourself, weigh its effect more justly. Sometimes you end up perplexed, ambivalent, or still a touch uncertain, and so you wait some more, return to it in a few days or a week and read it again, possibly even wait some more for its force to establish itself or not, once and for all, at that juncture where memory and sensibility provide the ground of a final judgment. In other words you try to let the work read you as propitiously as possible, as well as to imitate, in your small personal way, the selective process of history.

Among those sent to me was a story by Eleanor Clark called "Zoysia Grass" that I read three times. It's a beautifully felt narrative of the slow decline into senility of a gallant old widow, the narrator's stepmother, Maddy. It is told from a complex, highly compressed point of view, a memory image of her twirling a stick of asparagus and bent over, looking for something, as she comes down a garden path. But this image is made four-dimensional by the flow of time through it that renders the moment remembered as a commingling of her odd but rich marriage, her frustrations in the present, and the pathetic failing that lies beyond in her future. The device makes the story difficult, at first, to follow, though not to feel. By the second reading I had at least partly caught on, at least enough to grasp the rightness of the device for portraying both the way time exists in an aging mind, and also the associative processes of memory as they well up in the narrator's mind.

Still, the import of the story itself remained unclear to me, particularly because there was another element — the planting and then uprooting of a lawn of zoysia grass which had turned out to be ugly, lethal to all other forms of plant and possibly animal life, and virtually ineradicable. The narrator and her husband finally excavate to a depth of four feet to try to get rid of it and even so . . . But what did this zoysia grass have to do with the narrator and Maddy, her devotion to her husband, an unsuccessful scholar, her succession of ever more unpleasant residences after her husband's death? So I read it a third time, moved no less than before, but also still left searching for the elusive meaning in the story's controlling metaphor. I turned it this way and that. The inexorable ravages of time? Far too simple and banal. A marriage so intimate that its "root system" left the rest of Maddy's life barren? But the grass was hideous as well as rapacious and apparently permanent — so that didn't exactly check out, much less glow with significance. And after a few days more, Maddy with her snow-white hair, her faith in Matthew Arnold, the framed portrait of her husband which she took with her even on visits, all of this was still there amid the genteel squalor of a nursing home, but so was the mist of ambiguity around it. So, I finally gave up, though by the time this anthology is published . . .

Or again, to take a different kind of perplexity. There was a story by Susan Sontag called "Unguided Tour," which is a kind of debriefing of a veteran traveler through Europe after a recent trip, which, as she remarks at the outset, was taken to say goodbye to "the beautiful things," as well as to come to some kind of terms with her own *wanderlust*. It, too, is hard to follow, being told in a medley of voices — that of the woman, of a companion she left behind who also seems to double at times as an alter ego (or perhaps vice versa), and that of the man she took along to give a change of scenery to their fatigued relationship, as well as a comely young waiter she seduced, as well as the voices of curators, guides, guidebooks. Except for the last group, set off in quotes, the other voices are identified by pronouns; though only the "I" has a fixed identity and the "you"s, "he"s, and even "we"s require close attention. Moreover, the present conversation, after the trip, fades in and out of moments from the trip itself that are also often told in the present. Finally, the story is a mosaic of random remarks, impressions, memories, introspections, puns, as well as external details: "Mornings of departure. With everything prepared. Sun rising over the most majestic of bays (Naples, Rio, or Hong Kong) . . ." "That's the prison where they torture political suspects. Terror incognita." And so forth. The tone is grounded in ennui but fans out across a full range of rapidly conveyed emotions from deliriums of sensual pleasure to what I take to be the note of despair on which it ends. But there was the rub for me. For after a couple of readings I could pretty well work out the patterns of implication — travel as a kind of ultimate model of the transience of life and of the world, and of the intransigences of the self, but I did not feel them with any force, which is another way of saying I couldn't grasp the force of the experience for the writer. So I went back still again, recognizing now that the fluid, impressionistic, often monotonous flow worked precisely against the dramatizing of the material, while being perfectly in keeping with the theme, as I understood it, indeed reinforcing and charging it, style shaping content, seeding meaning — that was the risk the author had taken to guarantee the narrative's integrity. I could admire that but still the lack of any developing, complicating, resisting emotion of loss made the work seem psychologically unsigned, brilliant pithy writing that hadn't managed to deliver the poignancy of its subject.

3

No doubt my own standpoint is beginning to emerge, so let me fill it out more explicitly. I shall draw heavily on Benjamin, who is both a mentor and an adversary, and perhaps even more important to me in the latter role. He is also quite arbitrary at times and enigmatic at others, so bear with me.

Benjamin's use of the term "story" corresponds more closely to what we would call a "tale": i.e., it has its roots in the oral tradition, its favorite domicile was the hearth or the work-room, its archetypal artists were the peasant, the seafarer, the artisan; for "it combined the lore of faraway places, such as a much-traveled man brings home, with the lore of the past, as it best reveals itself to natives of a place." Thus its province was not the here and now but the more philosophical one of the there and then. For its principal distinguishing feature, in Benjamin's view, was its heuristic value. It dramatized a moral, practical instruction, or the illustration of a proverb or maxim. In other words, the tale was spun into a useful fabric, one that provided counsel for its audience, "counsel" being understood, as Benjamin puts it, less as "an answer to a question than a proposal concerning the continuation [and significance] of a story which is just unfolding." And because such stories were typically drawn from the ways of the world, from shared or readily communicable experience, their counsel becomes "the epic side of truth," namely wisdom, which, like storytelling itself, Benjamin believes is dying out.

As I read Benjamin, then, the story is less an evolving art form than a continuing if fading cultural resource: a vehicle for communicating and passing on the wisdom of the race by evoking "astonishment and thoughtfulness." Though open to individual embellishment its nature is to be repeatable: hence the narrative line is clear and distinct: it introduces a situation, complicates it, and then resolves it. It does not depend upon psychological explanation for its coherence, its psychology is characteristically simple, uninflected, and it withholds explanation, part of its art, to allow the listener or reader to grasp its import by means of his own imagination and insight. Further, it is the lack of dependency on psychological nuance that contributes to, in Benjamin's lovely phrase, the "chaste compactness" of the story and enables it to be remembered and retold.

This "chaste compactness" is achieved by the craft with which the storyteller hews to the axial lines of a person's character, tracing them through situations which test and illuminate them, thereby casting a glow on the manners, mores, and attitudes of the tribe, animated by a man's life process flowing through them. Benjamin frequently relates the story to "natural history," the disparate, variable, mutable ingredients and events of the world that nonetheless draw ineluctably if fortuitously on to a predetermined end, which is, of course, death.

The storyteller is conversant most of all with death: his art — layer upon layer of transparent incidents moving both indeterminately (suspense) and inexorably toward a fixed ending — is derived from his feeling for natural history. Indeed the older the storyteller, whether historically or personally, the more likely he is to identify his vision of life with nature and the "great inscrutable course of the world," and hence the more conversant he will be in communion with the transitory and the mortal. But whether he is as early as Herodotus or as late as Nikolai Leskov, the nineteenth-century Russian writer whom Benjamin uses as his principal touchstone and source of examples, the signature of the true storyteller is found in the movement of his tale toward *completeness,* the sense it leaves of an earned definitiveness of experience, however open its meaning to speculation and mystery. In a remarkable passage Benjamin associates death and storytelling as follows:

> *It is characteristic that not only a man's knowledge or wisdom, but above all his real life — and this is the stuff that stories are made of — first assumes transmissible form at the moment of his death. Just as a sequence of images is set in motion inside a man as his life comes to an end — unfolding the views of himself under which he has encountered himself without being aware of it — suddenly in his expressions and looks the unforgettable emerges and imparts to everything that concerned him that authority which even the poorest wretch in dying possesses for the living around him. This authority is at the very source of the story.*

Part of Benjamin's explanation for the decline of storytelling is that death has been pushed from the realm of domestic, lived fact to the periphery of our awareness by the ways in which we isolate ourselves from the dying and the dead. The point is typical of Benjamin's approach to the problem of the story. He does not concern himself with the arguments, familiar by 1935, that the conventions of plot are falsified by the random, provisional, indeterminate aspects of reality, that the free-standing, solid, explicable characters, more or less bereft of an unconscious, are belied by psychology as well as our own inner life, that fiction with a moral in tow or designed to illustrate a maxim is immediately suspect of simplifying experience and subverting art. Since virtually all didactic fiction today is a form of propaganda for authoritarian systems, the form is doubly dubious. Of course, Benjamin would say he is talking about "counsel," not thought control. And he would attribute the decline of counsel and wisdom to the fallen value of experience itself, whether of the person or community or the race, its supercession by the bewilderment of man in the face of his incessantly changing society, of a world that has gotten out of hand and has passed beyond the human scale of understanding and judgment. Hence the story is dying because of the incommunicability and incommensurability of being-in-the-world. He points out that the men returning from the First World War were silent rather than full of stories, and the novels that were later produced were "anything but experience that goes from mouth to mouth." What they communicated instead was mostly the enormity of modern warfare, the overwhelment of the person. As he puts it,

> *A generation that had gone to school on a horse-drawn street car now stood under the open sky in a countryside in which nothing remained unchanged but the clouds, and beneath these clouds, in a field of force of destructive torrents and explosions, was the tiny, fragile, human body.*

What are we to say forty-odd years further into the maelstrom that hardly requires war to reduce persons to social atoms? The mass society does that very readily, while its culture further undermines the communicability of experience by its various modes of pseudo-communication, the more pseudo, the better, as the TV ratings testify. Benjamin, who died in 1940, did not live to see his military image expand across the social spectrum, but he was already well aware of the media of information as a conquering adversary of the story. The product of the up-and-doing middle class with its preference for the factual and the explicable, the daily flood of information, works directly against the function and value of the traditional story. Though drawing upon the ways of the world, Benjamin's storyteller is indifferent to the verifiability of his account and offers no explanations for life in the there and then. Like man himself, the imaginative interest on which his story does depend has diminished to the meagerness of the "news story."

One can see how the primacy of information over genuine narrative has penetrated and altered our reading habits by comparing the child's to the adult's way of taking in a story. Still relatively innocent of the penchant for news, the child's request to "tell me a story" is qualitatively different from his parents' "Let's see what's in *The New Yorker* or *Ms.* this week." Like Benjamin's weavers at their looms, in which the rhythm of the work induces a receptivity to narrative — Benjamin calls it "self-forgetfulness" — the child, relaxed in his bed, creates a special state of attentiveness in which the story provides a passage from the day's activities through contact with otherness, preferably with a touch of the miraculous, that takes over his imagination and plays it toward sleep and redemption. The process is perhaps similar to the much more abbreviated, out-of-the-blue imaginings in an adult that presage that he is about to drop off.

But though adults also typically use bedside reading to put the day behind them and prepare for sleep, they do not open themselves to story in the way the child does. If an adult is reading a magazine and comes to a story, his mind-set does not alter and prepare to receive the rich and strange, but rather slightly adjusts itself to assimilate a more indirect kind of information, presented in a more personal but often no more imaginative form than the articles: the way we live now, etc. Most magazines most of the time reinforce this tendency by providing stories that do not come from afar, whether in time or place, but are rather news from the private sector, usually in keeping with the magazine's characteristic interests and tone, and the class-image of its editors and readers. A few popular magazines such as *Esquire* and *The New Yorker* which are responsive to literature will sometimes publish stories that have little or nothing to do with the rest of the magazine, but the fictions of Barthelme, Borges, or Bashevis Singer no doubt seem esoteric to most of its readers and have the air of distant relatives or uninvited guests of the family. The fallen value of fiction for its own sake is particularly apparent when a writer's stories are brought together, published, and quickly sink without a trace, rivaled only by collections of poetry in their predictable lack of appeal to today's common reader.

The media are not, however, the only lethal impediments and adversaries to Benjamin's notion of the story. There is also the novel. It departs from the story at its very outset, its roots being not in the oral tradition but in the printed word. The effect of this medium is, typically, to distance the writer from his audience: instead of a man among men, who "takes what he tells from experience — his own or that reported by others . . . and in turn makes it the experience of those who are listening to the tale," the novelist keeps his narrative to himself and has to be his own audience until he is finished. Anyone who has successfully told a story to a circle of people, and then, encouraged by his performance and their responsiveness, has tried to write it, is aware of how the spontaneity and intimacy of the oral turns into the self-consciousness and loneliness of the written. It is partly this difference that Benjamin has in mind when he goes on to write about the novelist in what seems to be a rather arbitrary and extreme way:

> *The novelist has isolated himself. The birthplace of the novel is the solitary individual, who is no longer able to express himself by giving examples of his most important concerns, is himself uncounseled, and cannot counsel others. To write a novel means to carry the incommensurable to extremes in the representation of human life. In the midst of life's fullness, and through the representation of this fullness, the novel gives evidence of the profound perplexity of the living.*

Defoe? Fielding? Or, even more notably, Dickens? — the writer whose novels took their place at the hearthside of countless Victorian households, who was so much the counselor that he loomed as the secretary and conscience of his society, whose fullness of presented life was so securely organized and intuitively understood that it provided his readers with intelligence rather than bewilderment: Benjamin's storyteller with endless staying power. But if one thinks about it, the further Dickens traveled in his career, the more his figure begins to take on the lineaments of Benjamin's novelist.

In the later novels like *Little Dorrit, Great Expectations,* and *Our Mutual Friend,* the fullness of life burdens rather than elates, as it

did the younger Dickens, while his faith in its center — the enter-
prising middle-class — collapses and turns into despair and contempt. His later protagonists and spokesmen, such as Arthur
Clennam, Pip, Bradley Headstone, far from being counseled, are
respectively stifled, bewildered, consumed by hate. Instead of the
élan of curiosity, wit, and broad imagination, the relish in oddity,
the confidence in the natural, the decent, the just, whose figures by
and large win out, the later novels are driven by darker energies, a
welling-up of the destabilizing, destructive, and perverse elements
of society and character that lead toward the study of the demonic
that was beginning to take form in the unfinished *Romance of Edwin
Drood.* Instead of the sense of intimacy between Dickens and his
characters, in the later novels he seems to stand alone, brooding
over individual conditions and social forces that denature his people, isolate them, imprison them. Once his animal faith in progress,
nurtured by the course of his own life as well as by the age, declined
and turned mordant, he increasingly found life to be, in Benjamin's term, "incommensurable" — and his main recourse if he was
to go on writing was precisely in developing an increasingly complex and centrally placed psychology. It is also interesting that as
this development was carrying him beyond and against the expectations of his audience, Dickens developed a need that became
obsessive to appear before them in public readings, as though sensing that while he was losing his hold on them through his published
words, he might still regain it through his actual voice, reinvoking
the mutual spell of intimacy through recourse to the oral.

And yet, and yet . . . Dickens continued to write stories to the
end, short ones as well as the elaborately plotted late novels which
remained his only way to organize and to some extent comprehend
life's fullness and perplexity.

4

For Benjamin the term "short story," which he uses only once, is
less a development of the traditional story than another example
of the various abbreviations of the forms and processes of the past
by the modern means of productivity. Rather than carrying on the
craft of the tale, the short story is, to his mind, an abbreviated
novel. In any case, he writes about the story as though Chekhov,
Mann, Kafka did not exist, though he also wrote perhaps the best

single essay on Kafka and was, I suspect, haunted by him. He even begins his essay with a story about Potemkin, who was once undergoing one of his paralyzing depressions and paralyzing the state as well. A pretty clerk, Shuvalkin, decided to attack the problem directly, entered Potemkin's room with a sheaf of documents, and emerged triumphantly with them signed, only to discover they had been signed "Shuvalkin . . . Shuvalkin . . . Shuvalkin." The story, Benjamin writes, "is like a herald racing two hundred years ahead of Kafka's work. The enigma which beclouds it is Kafka's enigma." He uses several other stories to illustrate the range of the doomed transactions of Kafka's cosmically burdened characters with the world and its authorities, but he does not deal with Kafka as a storyteller so much as the creator of a theater in which, like the classical Chinese, happenings are reduced to gestures, though in Kafka's case generally incongruous, enigmatic, confused, or futile ones.

But certainly Kafka was a storyteller of the there and then, and there is probably no better illustration of Benjamin's favorite kind of story in which the elements of myth and fairy tale interpenetrate the natural than his "Metamorphosis." To be sure, Kafka is without counsel and there is no more perfect witness than his protagonists to the profound perplexity of the living in the midst of life's fullness, no author who has carried the incommensurable to a further extreme. And yet Kafka was full of stories, and even parables, myths, and fables.

I agree with Benjamin about the humanistic usefulness he finds to be the story's defining ingredient, but I believe that it can be conveyed by other means than the counsels of the there and then. The contemporary short story is typically concerned with the here and now, particularly in cultures like ours in which the new, the perplexing, the ominous, the random constitute our central universal. It is no accident that the storytellers of the there and then are largely found today in Latin America, where the past still flows through and shapes the present, often tragically so. I believe that the usefulness of the comtemporary American story lies precisely in fighting for the human scale of experience and its communication against the forces that seek to diminish and trivialize it. I find that most stories that interest me accept the incommensurability of experience and struggle against it to make sense of the otherwise senseless, to locate the possibilities of coherence (in both senses of the term) in the otherwise incoherent flux of a society whose members are dazed by its mutability and by the babbling of its media about this "event," that "trend," who offer not knowledge of life but its momentary, abbreviated version — knowingness.

From this faith in the use of the story derives most of the standpoint from which I have selected the following stories. Though I try to remain open to innovation, I am more likely to respond to it as content — the opening up of fresh areas of common experience or the reclamation of banal ones through a strongly felt and rendered point of view — than as new ways of telling a story. The nonlinear antinarrative generally leaves me cold and impatient, since for all of its air of defiance, it is usually playing society's game, refragmenting what contemporary life is already tearing asunder — the delicate membranes that join body, mind, heart, spirit — and dining out, as it were, on the incoherent. I am also skeptical of surrealism, "irrealism," "surfiction," unless it has discernible lines of wit and emotion that ground it in shareable experience. Otherwise it becomes as banal and arbitrary as any other form of writing that offers no resistance to its own assumptions, and as tedious as listening to other people's dreams: consciousness without a context. I also have an indisposition to elaborately wired narratives that do not have much of the current of life at a critical point running through their circuits, and to obliquely told stories that cleverly chart a series of thematic coordinates and leave you to draw the line of meaning between them. I think the human situation is too interesting and urgent to turn it into literary games. By the same token, I am also skeptical about narratives that wish to be admired for their reticence, their decorum, that are squeamish about risking the unruliness of emotion and evasive about their convictions.

Hence I am disposed toward stories with a strong narrative movement that clearly gets somewhere, preferably to a point that is both unpredictable and right — a bullseye at 400 yards rather than at 40 feet. Whether a story deals with a subject as large as the Holocaust, such as Leslie Epstein's "Skaters on Wood," or as small as the mute grief of a salt-of-the-earth working man, such as Mary Ann Malinchak Rishel's "Staus," I want the writer to do justice to it and not dirt, to enrich my awareness of the life he or she is writing about and not cheapen or twist it into some reductive or inflated meaning. If it deals in perversity, as does Ian McEwan's "Psychopolis" or Gilbert Sorrentino's "Decades," I don't want to settle for still another bit of dabbling in the kinkiness of the age — but insist that the story earn its keep by its complexity of interest. Just as I do with a "positive" story, like Tim McCarthy's "The Windmill Man," which affirms the life of a straight-arrow builder by his devotion to the skills and integrity of his labor that lead to his death.

Confronted by a story whose material is as seemingly banal as Lynne Sharon Schwartz's "Rough Strife," which deals with the rifts in a marriage occasioned by a first pregnancy, or L. Hluchan Sintetos's story "Telling the Bees," in which a country woman tells about her affair with a sociology professor, I want to be made to feel that I haven't, more or less, been here before, not because the writing is particularly "experimental," but because its freshness of perception and depth of feeling are. On the other hand, if a story comes in from left field, as does Jonathan Baumbach's "The Return of Service," a fantasy of a man playing tennis against his father who is also the umpire, I ask that its inventiveness not absorb the content — leaving me dazzled but empty — but the other way around — leaving me struck by a new way of examining an old truth. As Benjamin would be, I am particularly impressed by stories such as Robert Sorrells's "The Blacktop Champion of Ickey Honey," Mark Helprin's "The Schreuderspitze," Elizabeth Cullinan's "A Good Loser," Joyce Carol Oates's "The Translation," or Stanley Elkin's "The Conventional Wisdom," whose situations are so interesting in themselves and whose issues are so distinctly dramatized that I can retell the story to a friend in attenuated form and still see his or her eyes light up with interest.

In general, as you may have gathered, my approach to a story is usually dialectical. If it is as gorgeously lyrical as Harold Brodkey's "Verona: A Young Woman Speaks," a young girl's account of the happiest time of her life, I want that lyricism to be tested by its opposite, in this instance the shakiness of her parents' marriage, the canker already forming in the rose. Similarly, I was impressed and moved by the way Joy Williams plays off the instability of a young mother against the steadfastness of her parents, the one reinforcing and illuminating the other, while leaving the psychological disparities open to speculation about the mysteries of parenting. Similarly, I was bowled over by Peter Taylor's "In the Miro District," in which the steadily mounting antipathy between two members of a family — a boy cast in the mold of the Southern gentry, and his maverick grandfather — and its eventual resolution, both centers and charges a study of manners and their effect on character, which for all of its leisurely storytelling tone is as hard and multifaceted and luminous as a diamond.

Well, that's about what I have to say in defense of the contemporary short story and the examples of it I have chosen. They have been arranged in an order which I hope will provide what little continuity an anthology can have, and part of the reader's interest may lie in finding connections and resonances between them as he goes along. But mainly they should be read on their own terms. And if I have only touched on the stories themselves, and only on some of them, this also is because each of them speaks articulately and forcefully and justly for itself. That is why I have chosen it.

TED SOLOTAROFF

The Best
AMERICAN
SHORT
STORIES
1978

LESLIE EPSTEIN

Skaters on Wood

(FROM ESQUIRE)

ON ASSISI STREET, inside the House of Culture, a number of boys and girls were skating. At least, from the orchestra seats, from the balcony and boxes, it looked as if the stage must have been covered with ice. That's how smoothly the children moved across it. They kept their hands behind their backs, the way skaters do, and glided about on bent knees. These were the students from the vocational school. The girls wore red mufflers and plaid, pleated skirts. The boys were in black — black trousers, black cutaway coats, but with white shirts and, at the neck, white ruffles. From one side of the stage to the other they went, hand in hand, or alone. Sometimes a girl would throw up her arms and start rapidly to spin, or a boy would loop or leap; but mostly the whole group just skated along, swaying a little, with serious faces.

In the orchestra pit, Mister Smolenskin played marches from *Aida* on the Gramophone machine.

When the children were done, they ran off the stage to tremendous applause. The Jews were stamping their feet on the floor. They whistled and shouted. They wouldn't stop. It's hard to say why the performance appealed so much to our citizens. Of course, they knew it was an illusion. There could not be, in Poland, in the month of July, any ice. You could see that the boys and girls were wearing regular shoes. Still, the applause got louder and louder. The crowd was frantic, almost. So the vocational students appeared once again. They slid forward on one foot and held the other one up behind. They leaned into the wind. This time Smolenskin was not playing a tune. The feet of the skaters went *shhh-shhh* over the wooden boards. In the audience, no one spoke a word. It's hard to say why. Perhaps because they were reminded of other times? Perhaps it was because the pantomime was so carefree and the bright skirts, the ruffles, so gay? The girls from the vocational school had their hair done in braids, which swung across their faces. How red their cheeks were! It was exactly as if the children were crossing the surface of a frosty pond.

Down from the rafters descended the Szapiro & Son chandelier. There was a light bulb inside it, and this, with the other house-lights, came on. The Jews sat for a moment, staring quietly at the empty stage. Then more Jews pushed in. They came through the back doors and milled in the aisles. These men and women were wearing elegant clothes — jackets and trousers that matched and, in spite of the heat, shawls and long dresses. No one could remember seeing so many jewels, such tiaras! It was a stunning gala. "We want the skaters, too!" the latecomers shouted. The rest of the crowd took up the cry. "Encore! Encore!" But the skillful students did not reappear; the big purple curtain swung shut instead.

That's when a disturbance broke out. From the balcony over-head, sheets of white paper came slipping and sliding down. There were dozens and dozens of these. The first-nighters stood on their seats to snatch them. There was something written on each. ONE DOESN'T PUT ON SHOWS IN A CEMETERY! That was the message on one. Another one went like this: NO DANCING ON THE GRAVES OF THE DEAD! In short, it was a boycott of the House of Culture! There was a sudden silence. People were staring upward, to see where the agitators might be. No one knew whether or not there would be a stampede. A plumpish man with black hair parted in the middle — his name was Luftgas — folded one of the broadsides in half and in half again. Then he threw it scornfully over his shoulder.

"We've heard all that before," he said.

True, true. These same documents had been dropped from all the rooftops. They showed up beneath doorways and on the benches of the spinning mills. TRANSPORT=DEATH, they said. Or: DON'T GO LIKE SHEEP. Still and all, the Jews paid little attention. What did it mean, exactly — *transport equals death*? Didn't the people who went off in the trains mail back postcards and letters saying that they were alive? And what if, just for the sake of argument, it was true that the Jews were being killed — what were the rest of them to do? What? Better to put it out of your mind. There were cafés to go to, and casinos. And here was a great event:

the grand premiere of the House of Culture! Eat, drink and be merry, that's what people wanted. Ladies and gentlemen, wouldn't you?

Meanwhile, on Assisi Street, someone had jumped to the lip of the stage. It wasn't a pamphleteer. It was — in a tux, in a top hat — the Master of Ceremonies, Mister Schotter. The crowd sighed. They clapped, rhythmically, impatiently. They wanted to see the show.

"Look," cried Schotter. "It's Baggelman! And Urinstein and Verble and Mordechai Kleen!" The audience twisted around. There, in a bunch, just inside the door, were the members of the Council. They were dressed in special frock coats and black polished shoes. The bigwigs, rabbis like Nomberg, and Chill, and Krautwirt of the Devout Buchers, were standing there, too. With Margolies in front, they came down the center aisle. Nobody cheered. But there weren't any catcalls, either. The procession went slowly, to the fancy stuffed chairs in the very front row.

Suddenly, there was a gasp, then a lot of buzz-buzzing. The Chairman and Madame Trumpeldor had appeared in the aisle!

A flash lamp went off. *Bing-bing* — it went off two more times. Young Krystal, the journalist, was taking pictures. The couple walked into the glare. Madame Trumpeldor clutched her husband's arm, through his cloak, with both of her hands. Her veil was down, at the line of her lower lip, which was unpainted. She was as thin, in her tight, shiny gown, as a silver fork or a spoon. The Elder himself wore a black cape, with gold trimming, and a hat just as black on his head. He was stooped, and his spectacle frames had slipped partway down the bend of his nose. There were lines on his cheeks that made him look like a man aged one hundred years. The Trumpeldors reached the end of the aisle. All by themselves they sat in the two biggest chairs.

Then the chandelier speedily rose up and up, and Schotter, hands in his armpits, spoke once again: "Our show is ready to start! It's by a world-famous author. It takes place hundreds of years ago, before there were clocks or gas lamps or engines for steam. Here we are in a faraway land. This is a country without any Jews. A place where it's always misty. What a fog! If you put your hand up, you can't see your fingers! Look! It's like the smoke from a fire! Seed of Abraham, close your eyes! You have to imagine these

things, like little children do!" And, taking one edge of the curtain
in his hand, the Master of Ceremonies walked across the stage: like
magic, the great purple sheet parted behind him.

At first the stage was dark, like a pitch-black box. But an owl, or
something like an owl, was hooting. Then a yellow light came on,
and you could see the fog. It was yellow, too, and looked like
clouds of sulfur. In the middle of the stage was a large, leafless
tree. Its limbs were black and twisted. The branches of other trees
stuck out from both wings. Were we in a forest? Suddenly, from
either side of the stage, two really frightening figures trotted out.
The members of the audience asked themselves: *Are these men or
women?* For both creatures wore ragged gowns and sandals with
heels, which suggested the female sex, as did the long curls of hair
that came from under their conical caps. But the beards on their
chins were just like a man's. These marvels met at the center of the
stage and, from under the palms of their hands, peered anxiously
about. What nails they had on their fingers! How the fogbank
swirled about their tattered clothes! Yet neither of these strange
beings was as tall as a half-grown child.

All at once, from behind the trunk of the gnarled tree, a third
crone came leaping. Smolenskin cranked the Gramophone handle
and the three witches — what else could such fiends be? — linked
arms and danced in a circle. They went, as they hopped, *hee-hee-
hee!* The latecomer jumped so wildly that his hat dropped off.
Some people — by his close-cropped hair, by the shape of his skull
— recognized him. It was the pinhead! The gardener boy! Grinning, his head lolling, he loomed over his partners. These two
began to speak, piping:

> *Fair is foul, and foul is fair.*
> *Hover through the fog and filthy air.*
> *The weird sisters, hand in hand,*
> *Posters of the sea and land.*

The voices belonged to Tushnet, with his face blackened, in a wig,
and to Leibel Shifter, in the same disguise. The children of the
Hatters' Asylum were putting on a show! What a sensation! No one
could remember when the orphans, the Elder's favorites, had last
left their mansion's walls. And why had they kept everything —

the long preparations, the months of effort — such a secret? Was it to give Trumpeldor and Madame Trumpeldor a wonderful surprise?

From some spot overhead, a thunderclap sounded. A bright light — the forks of lightning — lit up the stage. An orphan, standing where no one could see him, was shaking a piece of tin. People knew that, but they shivered anyway. The rumble and roar echoed like cannonballs rolling in a chute. And the arc of white light spilled over the crowd's upturned, frightened faces. The slave dance from *Aida* had stopped. The three demons, in the wind and rain, cupped their hands to their ears. *A drum, a drum! Macbeth does come.*

Two warriors, holding swords, moved from the back of the platform to the front. The furious storm broke about them. The lightning glanced off their breastplates and shields. It was as if young Krystal were setting off all of his flash lamps at once. One soldier took a step forward. He wore something like an airman's helmet, with leather flaps for his ears. Fixed to his face was a curly black beard. "So foul and fair a day," he shouted into the *boom-booming* blasts, "I have not seen!"

The other soldier was looking at the withered sisters. His mouth opened and closed. From fear his knees knocked together. He had a beard, too, but you could tell it was really Iza Flicker, who ten years before was just being born. He hugged his comrade-in-arms. The two warriors stared, trembling, agape; "Hail! Hail!" cried the hags, capering this way and that. At last, one swordsman, holding his weapon skyward, addressed the apparitions: "Speak, if you can. What are you?"

The gardener boy — he was supposed to be a deaf-mute, without any tongue at all — put his hand on top of his head. Then he said, in the same fancy Polish that everyone else was speaking, "All hail, Macbeth, that shalt be King hereafter!"

The sword fell out of the warrior's hand. He got to one knee and lowered his head, so that the audience knew he was thinking. The second soldier, played by the Flicker lad, screwed his courage up. "Speak then to me," he told the three witches.

FIRST WITCH: *Lesser than Macbeth, and greater.*
SECOND WITCH: *Not so happy, yet much happier.*
THIRD WITCH: *Thou shalt get kings, though thou be none.*

ALL TOGETHER: *So all hail, Macbeth and Banquo! Banquo and Mac-*
       beth, all hail!

No sooner had the creatures spoken than a whoosh of fog rose up
about them and, to thunder, to sizzling lightning, they vanished
inside it. Banquo ran here and there, slashing at the mist with his
sword. But when the clouds lifted, the weird sisters were gone.
The storm was over. Everything was clear and calm. Macbeth,
resting on one kneecap, never moved.

"Look how our partner's rapt," said Flicker. He walked over and
put his hand on the shoulder of the kneeling man.

BANQUO: *Were such things here?*
        Or have we eaten on the insane root
        That takes the reason prisoner?

There was no response. The green eyes of the owl — there it was,
sitting on a tree limb — began to glow. Softly it hooted. Banquo
leaned by the ear of his friend. Even though he whispered, you
could hear him in the farthest row: *You shall be King.*

Do you want to know who it was kneeling down? It was only the
left-handed Mann Lifshits. The clue was that the sheath for his
sword was on his right side. He was like a rock, not moving, not
speaking. Banquo, baffled, turned his back and leaned against the
tree. Then all the lights on the stage began to fade. The eyes of the
owl stood out, bright and green. Just before the whole theater was
swallowed up in fresh darkness, Lifshits, still kneeling, raised both
his hands. His fists were balled up at the sky. Then — it was almost
as if we were hearing his thoughts — he spoke these words: *Stars,
hide your fires. Let not light see my black and deep desires.*

That's when the curtains closed.

The Manchester of Poland — that's what people called our
town. It wasn't a cultural center like Bialystok. Sarah Bernhardt
never acted here in a play. Therefore, don't be surprised if hardly
anyone in the audience understood what was going on. They didn't
know about the great author Shakespeare. They had never heard
of *Macbeth.* What impressed them was how lifelike the storm was,
and the thick rolls of cottony fog. They also wanted to know how
the owl's eyes lit up, with electrical wires or what? Naturally, there

were many disputes about the witches. Did such harpies really exist? Some people took one side and some people another. Finally, someone said that in his opinion the three spirits were something that the kneeling soldier had dreamed. In dreams it's not only possible for women to wear beards, but the worst things you fear come true.

All of a sudden, a gypsy, or maybe it was a Negro woman, came out of the wings. She walked up and down in front of the curtains. All of her hair went into a rope-thick braid, which came down to her waist. Her tight dress had buttons on the front, from top to bottom. Lipstick, wet-looking, was on her lips. With both hands she held a letter, which she was reading out loud. *Bang-bang, thump-thump* — those were the sounds that kept coming from behind the shut curtain. As for the letter, it was all about meeting the witches, and told what we already know.

Suddenly the brown-skinned woman turned and faced the crowd. She talked to the letter writer, even though he wasn't there:

> *Thou shalt be*
> *What thou art promised. Yet do I fear thy nature.*
> *It is too full o' the milk of human kindness*
> *To catch the nearest way.*
> *Hie thee hither,*
> *That I may pour my spirits in thine ear,*
> *And chastise with the valor of my tongue*
> *All that impedes thee from the golden crown.*

At that moment, a little boy — he was squinting as if he had a headache — ran onto the lip of the stage. He had round shoulders, like all of our city-born Jews. His mouth opened up, but he didn't say a word.

"What is your tidings?" demanded the woman with the buttons.

But the boy from the Hatters' Asylum just stood on his heels. He was wearing hip boots, like a fisherman.

"What is your tidings? Your tidings?"

Alas, the poor fellow was stumped. His eyes screwed tightly shut. The crowd wanted to help him, but no one knew the right words. There was an awful silence; even the backstage noises ceased. In the front row, Trumpeldor, in an irritated way, slapped his knee. It was as if it were the boy's face he'd struck. For the child opened his eyes and finally spoke: *The King comes here tonight!* So saying, the messenger whirled about and ran off in the direction he'd come from.

All eyes, however, were on the woman in front of the purple curtain. Her face, which had been so smooth, so calm even, was now strained and twisted. She spoke through her flashing teeth, making a hissing sound:

> *The raven himself is hoarse*
> *That croaks the fatal entrance of Duncan*
> *Under my battlements. Come, you spirits*
> *That tend on mortal thoughts, unsex me here,*
> *And fill me from the crown to the toe, topful*
> *Of direst cruelty!*

What happened next created a sensation in the House of Culture. There had never been anything like it in the whole history of Poland. The woman on the stage undid her four top buttons and pulled her green gown away from her chest. What a tremendous shock! This wasn't, after all, an anonymous actress, a stranger. It was our little Gutta Blit, all grown up. And you could practically see her bosom! *Come to my woman's breasts and take my milk for gall!*

"My dearest love, Duncan comes here tonight!" Someone else, speaking those words, was coming onto the stage. A man! The breast-plated soldier! And the shameless woman simply remained there, with her wide-shouldered gown half undone. In the eyes of the crowd, this topped what had gone before. Worse still: she stooped down so that he, who was shorter, would be able to kiss her. Yes, he kissed her. He was still wearing his leather headgear. And the kiss did not stop. It went on. She bent over him, drooped over him. She wrapped him up. With his stiff armor he strained against her. On the curtain, the lights were dimming and dimming. The little soldier faded in her arms, and both players in turn disappeared into near darkness. Out of that gloom, there came the soldier's muffled voice: *If we should fail?* And her reply:

> *We fail!*
> *When Duncan is asleep*
> *What cannot you and I perform upon him.*
> *We'll not fail!*

Then the light was gone completely. No one could see a thing. Yet the Jews, to a man, gave a shudder. They thought that the soldier was still there, with his head on the bosom of the awful witch.

Presto! The lights blazed on again, the double drapes of the curtain parted, and the Jews saw before them something more astounding still. For what had been, only minutes before, a forest, with a single gnarled and blasted tree, was now — one-two-three! — the great hall of an ancient castle! Real torches were fixed on the massive chunks of wall, and battle flags hung from the ceiling. On the left, there was a big wooden door; on the right, a staircase, a high one, with a normal-size door at the top. Without thinking, people applauded. Everything was so well done. There was even moss on the stones.

Mister Smolenskin played the part of *Aida* where the elephants and catapults start to arrive. The wooden door swung open, and a half dozen Hatters' orphans, in Scottish kilts and hats with feathers, stepped into the vaulted room. They were pretending to blow on oboes. Then more crowded in, carrying dressed duck on platters, and realistic beef. How good the meat looked! How tasty! Through the door next came a row of archery experts, with their big bows strapped over their shoulders. In the middle of this crowd — they were lads and lassies — stood Nathan Hobnover. He had the same bare knees as all the others; the difference was, on top of his head, glittering, glistening, there sat a round golden crown. The Gramophone music stopped. The retainers and so forth held still. Hobnover, the King, pointed across the stage to the shadowy spot beneath the wooden stairs. His little blond goat's beard waggled when he talked: *See, see, our honored hostess!*

Out stepped Lady Macbeth. She had on a sort of nightgown that fit tightly around her neck and swept all the way to the floor. Only her brown head and black braid were showing. "Your servant ever," she said.

"Give me your hand," said King Duncan, holding his head so that the band of gold would not slip. But Lady Macbeth's hands remained inside the folds of her gown. The two actors walked side by side up the staircase. Something was squeaking: Hobnover's leather shoes. At the top, the King went through the door; she followed. Then the lights got so dim that, try as you might, you couldn't see the red beef, you couldn't see the duck.

A bell rang. A pause. It rang again. It was sounding the hour.

The eyes of the Jews got used to the lack of light. Mann Lifshits, in armor, was standing by the foot of the stairs. He was breathing loudly, like a runner. When the bell rang a third time, he took a step. Then he stretched out his hand. "Is this a dagger which I see before me?" These were the soldier's exact words. He staggered upward, clutching at the empty air. "I have thee not, and yet I see thee still. Art thou but a dagger of the mind? A false creation?" The knife he meant was right there in his hand. That's what was so strange about his behavior. He held the blade outward, staring at it, talking to it, as if it belonged to a different person. Raving that way, he went up the rest of the stairs.

There he waited, while the bell continued to toll. Suddenly — it made people gasp — the door swung open and Gutta Blit came rushing out. She ran by her husband and said, though more to herself than to him: *Had he not resembled my father as he slept, I had done it.* Then she hurried down the staircase and vanished into the shades. The bell struck for the twelfth time. Midnight. "The bell invites me," said the black-bearded soldier. Then he made a rhyme — *Hear it not, Duncan, for it is a knell that summons thee to heaven, or to hell* — and went into the room where his wife had been.

Time went by. Maybe, after all, it would be a peaceful night. But the audience of Jews was stirring. Something was going to happen, but they didn't know what. All of a sudden, there was a dreadful scream, a real shriek. It alarmed many people. Some of the play-goers wanted to leave. "It's just an owl, an owl," shouted Councilman Popower from his seat in the front row. Sure enough, the green eyes of the bird — perched on a beam in the rafters—started to glow.

Mann Lifshits came out of the sleeping chamber. He dragged himself like an old man down the well-worn stairs. "I have done the deed," he said.

His partner materialized out of the somber light. "My husband!" Gutta Blit declared. They stood together whispering:

MACBETH: *I am afraid to think what I have done.*
LADY MACBETH: *Got get some water*
                         And wash this filthy witness from your hand.
MACBETH: *This is a sorry sight.*

The warrior raised both his hands. They were a bright red.

LADY MACBETH: *A little water clears us of this deed.*
MACBETH: *Hark! Whence is that knocking?*

There was indeed a knocking, a loud pounding noise. The actors turned toward the large door. But the sound was not located there. It came from over their heads, from where the King named Duncan was sleeping. Lifshits, Gutta Blit — they hugged each other from fear.

The banging got louder. It was as if something were being hurled against the wood. *Boom! Boom!* Then the noise stopped. All by itself the door swung open, and Nathan Hobnover walked out. He streamed with the same red that covered the hands of his host. His skin, his nightdress, were drenched in the liquid — it came out of his body in spouts. He held his arms up, the way a sleepwalker does; the gold crown stayed on his head. Slowly he began to descend the stairs. On the way down, the strength of his heart failed him: he clasped his hands to it and opened his mouth. He looked like a tenor singing a song. Then, in a spray, he tumbled all the way down.

What chaos then! Everybody seemed to wake up at once. The servants and archers ran about, rubbing their eyes. Banquo, the second soldier, came in and turned on the lights. "O horror!" he cried. "Horror, horror!" The whole cast was shouting:

> *Awake, awake!*
> *Ring the alarm bell. Murder and treason!*
> *Ring the bell.*

But no one in the audience heard these words. If anything, the bedlam there was worse than on the stage. The Jewesses who were not gasping, weeping, were sitting there as if stunned senseless. Many of the men were pointing at Macbeth and his mate, as if to say, *There he is! They did it! Catch them!* Even the Councilmen were thrown into confusion. "Assassins!" they shouted. "Anarchists!" None paid the slightest attention to Popower. He was pulling the sleeves of his colleagues and saying, "But Verble, but Kleinweiss, it's only a play!"

It's an interesting point that Popower raised. Every day the Jews saw things more frightening than witches and fogbanks and hooting owls. Was there a man or woman in the House of Culture who had not lost, one way or another, a person he loved? Could any spectator know for sure that he, himself, would not be transported before the week was out? No! No! Not likely! Here people walked around as thin as sticks, with their bones practically showing. In the winter, our citizens froze. They choked from the smell in the summer. You could always hear a mad person shouting, *An English tailor!* or some other irrational phrase. It was as if hell had been moved to the surface of the earth. And the worst thing, the horror of horrors, was that the Jews got used to their lives. Sometimes the newspapers would blow off the corpses: there would be the green face or the blue face of a person you knew. This is what everyone saw, even the young, living children. No one thought twice about it.

In the House of Culture, however, the Jews were frantic. They pulled on the roots of their hair. Impossible to think these people didn't know they were seeing a play. Those were rubber daggers! It was a story from a hundred years ago! No, the crowd knew perfectly well that in a moment or two, Nathan Hobnover would jump up from his pool of bogus blood; yet they wept as if he had been an actual King.

Has there ever been a better illustration of the wonderful power of art?

By the time things calmed down, the stage was almost deserted. The actors had run off in opposite directions — the archers in search of the supposed plotters, the retainers carrying Lady Macbeth, who, in all the excitement, had fainted. Mann Lifshits, and poor Hobnover, of course, were alone in the castle hall. The former put his boot on the latter's chest, and the purple walls of the curtain began jerkily to close on them both. Then — it was the last thing the crowd was able to see — the murderer stooped, plucked the bright crown from the head of his victim, and, carefully, using both hands, set it down upon his aviator's helmet. The curtains snapped shut. The audience sat in their seats, dumbfounded. They could hardly take it in: he *was* the King, then, just as the witches predicted. But one person was applauding. It made a small sound in the cavern of the room. In her long gloves, gloves that went past her elbow, Madame Trumpeldor was beating her palms together. When they saw that, the Jews began applauding, too.

*

Ladies and gentlemen, the Manchester of Poland is one thing, America is another. In the New World, even schoolchildren knew this famous drama by heart. There's no need to spend so much time on details. Here's what happens next: Macbeth orders some people to kill General Banquo, and before you know it, it's done. All this took place, with swords and clubs and daggers, in front of the curtain, a terrible thing to see. One of the killers ran at Banquo with a sword. It went into his chest, right through his armor, and came out the other side. But Iza Flicker did not fall down. He staggered toward his assassin, who, in terror, let go the weapon. Then a second killer stabbed him in the throat. Bright-colored blood came out of the General's mouth. Yet, amazingly, even with the sword blade still running through him, Flicker stood his ground. That's when a third murderer, in a cloak, with a mask on, struck him over the head with a spike-filled club. The brave General plunged down. They dragged him away by the arms and the legs.

You can imagine how our local Jews responded to this! The murder of Duncan was bad enough, but at least it had taken place behind closed doors. Flicker was killed before their very eyes. No doubt about it! How could it be a trick? The people in the front rows saw the dagger go in to the hilt. So the uproar began. It didn't last long, though. For no sooner had the cries of outrage started to swell than the retainers, Lifshits' now, no longer Hobnover's, marched in a line across the front of the stage. They carried the roast beef and the duck on platters. There was fruit, too: melons and apples and oranges and pears. And more: a golden-scaled fish, a pike, probably, with its head and its tail attached; round red and round yellow cheeses; and a whole tray of cakes and pastries and — could it be! — butter-crumb tarts. The Jews were suddenly speechless. One after the other, the servants disappeared inside the center crack of the curtain; as the last orphan, the one with the sweetmeats, stepped through, these draperies parted. The drama within the castle went on.

The scene was just the same now, except that a large wooden table, fully set, with chairs all around, had been pulled into the center of the hall. The rest of the Hatters' Asylum population were seated around it, drinking goblets of wine. They were Lords and Ladies. The Queen was at the far end of the table, her white teeth, her white eyes, flashing in her dusky face. The King walked cheerfully about. He slapped his guests' backs, he slapped their shoulders. He carved the meat with a knife. Everyone was talking and laughing at once. What a hubbub! What a jolly feast! The crowd in the House of Culture could actually smell — that's how realistic it was — the smoked fish. After a time, Macbeth stood before his place at the table. Before sitting down, he picked up a silver cup. "Now good digestion wait on appetite," he loudly proposed, "and health on both!"

The company raised their goblets in response; they gulped down the wine. But the King thrust his fingers, wet with grease, into his curly beard. He gasped. He croaked: "Behold! Look! Lo!" If such a thing were possible, his hair, where it was not weighted down with the yellow crown, was rising from his head. Young Lifshits stared, with bulging eyes, at his chair. Two servants, who had been standing before it, now stepped aside, and everyone in the theater saw there was something propped up there. At first glance, it appeared to be a white laundry sack. But the thing moved. A sack with something inside it? A Lord sitting nearby then spoke to the King: *May't please Your Highness, sit.* Mann Lifshits was now chewing his fingers; he mumbled: *The table's full.* On the top of this seated object was something like a head, which began to twist back and forth. It was as if a person were wearing a sheet, one with cut-out holes for the eyes. Yes! It was exactly like a child dressed up as a ghost! But a second Noble did not seem to see it. He gestured toward the spot:

NOBLE: *Here is a place reserved, sir.*
MACBETH: *Where?*
NOBLE: *Here, my good Lord.*

Was the goblin invisible? The Noble was practically touching it with his hand, yet not a single guest showed the slightest sign of surprise. It was then that the figure in the sheet — perhaps just to call attention to its presence — rose from the chair and stood on its rubber-soled shoes. What was terrible, awful, unspeakable, really, was the sword handle stuck into one side of its body and the sword blade that came out the other side. Ladies and gentlemen! This was the ghost of Iza Flicker!

All of the food previously mentioned was still on the table, practically untouched. The juicy red meat was there, and the pike fish with scales like gold leaf, and the crisp duck! But feast or no feast, the Jews were upset. A golem! A ghost! This time, however, the front row — the Council — was staying calm. The reason for this was that, at the center, in her comfortable chair, Madame Trumpeldor was not shouting like the others. Instead of going *eeeeeee!* she went *hee! hee!*

Of all things, she was laughing. And bit by it, her point of view spread to the people around her. After all, there *was* something funny about what was happening on the stage. To see a grown man, a man with a beard, trembling, shaking, and popping his eyes, was amusing to start with. But the real humor came when young Lifshits cried out such things as "Hence, horrible shadow!" and "Never shake thy gory locks at me!" and not a soul at the banquet could tell what he was talking about. For all they knew, the man was raving at air. What a good joke!

The guests at the party seemed to be making light of the matter, too. "Oh, proper stuff!" scoffed Gutta Blit, and her husband sheepishly smiled. The Lords and Ladies chuckled and made witty remarks. Macbeth himself, fully recovered, proposed a new toast. "I drink to the general joy o' the table!" Everyone cheered. They were having a good time again. But the white specter returned. The sword was gone from its body. Instead, there was a red splotch, a wound, at its throat. It was actually dripping! At this horrible sight, the Jews began loudly sighing. Macbeth staggered backward, white as a dish, and threw out his arms. The Nobles, alarmed now, stood up from the table. But Madame Trumpeldor laughed harder than ever. She bent double inside of her sparkling gown. On the stage, Gutta Blit took her husband by the collar. She hissed into his ear: *Why do you make such faces? You look but on a stool.*

Onstage, the guests fled in confusion. But in the front row, Madame Trumpeldor was laughing harder than ever. She was gasping. She bubbled over. She lifted the veil from her face. "Ha! Ha! Don't you see? Trumpeldor! Madame Trumpeldor! On the stage! It's us they're playing! Ha! Ha! Ha! Him and me!"

The next thing that happened, the curtains were closed and some sort of hag appeared in front of them. "Look!" exclaimed Madame Trumpeldor. "A witch! We'll learn our fortune!"

This creature — she wore a conical hat and a blue robe stuck over with yellow stars — was dancing and skipping to the music

Mister Smolenskin made. The chains around her neck, her arm bracelets, her bangles — all these clinked and chinked together. Finally, she stopped and leaned forward. You could see the paint on the lids of her eyes. She smiled at the spot where Trumpeldor and his wife were sitting and crooked her finger at him: *Meet me in the morning; thither he will come to know his destiny.*

Quick as a flash, the hag slipped through the seam in the curtain. There was a hooting noise. A hoot again. And the purple cloths parted on the same scene with which the *Tragedia Makbeta* had begun. Thunder. More thunder. The identical black, leafless tree. Only this time, the fog — or smoke it was, or steam — seemed to be coming out of a big metal pot in the center of the stage. Near this kettle hopped Tushnet and the pinhead and Leibel Shifter, each with a tuft of beard on his chin. They were throwing awful-looking things into the stew.

> FIRST WITCH: *Fillet of a fenny snake,*
> *In the caldron boil and bake.*
> *Eye of newt and toe of frog,*
> *Wool of bat and tongue of dog.*
> SECOND WITCH: *Scale of dragon, tooth of wolf,*
> *Witch's mummy, maw and gulf*
> *Of the ravin'd salt-sea shark,*
> *Root of hemlock digg'd in the dark.*

The Jews couldn't help groaning. What feast was this? And only a moment before, they had been serving real duck! The gardener boy, skipping wildly around, holding his hat on, was even worse. He gave them the shivers:

> THIRD WITCH: *Liver of blaspheming Jew,*
> *Gall of goat, and slips of yew!*

Then they all joined hands and, like regular boys, danced around the boiling, bubbling broth: *Double, double, toil and trouble, fire burn and caldron bubble.* The child with the tin shook it mightily. The thunder cracked. Lightning flickered. The cellophane strips under the pot writhed like snakes, like bright tongues of flame.

Into this scene came King Macbeth, looking lost. He had his crown on his head and wore his short leather skirt. But his shoulders, under the weight of his armor, were drooping. He demanded that the fiends make more predictions. Immediately, the hag, the big witch, told him what to be afraid of and what not to fear. And it was good news, too! Macbeth could never be beaten until the forest of Birnam — an absolute impossibility — marched up Dunsinane Hill. But the tyrant was not satisfied. "Yet my heart throbs to know one thing," Mann Lifshits declared.

> *Tell me, if your art*
> *Can tell so much. Shall Banquo's issue ever*
> *Reign in this kingdom?*

It was as if he'd told a joke. The witches laughed and laughed. They pointed to the kettle, which just sat there boiling over. Suddenly a child, a boy, hardly more than a toddler, climbed out of the caldron and began to wander around. A second child, no older than the first, popped up in his place. And then a third one appeared. Mann Lifshits knew how to make his eyes bug out of their sockets. He did this now and staggered backward as well.

> *A fourth! Start, eyes!*
> *What, will the line stretch out to the crack of doom?*
> *Another yet! A seventh!*

It was true. One after the other, children were hauling themselves over the top of the kettle and dropping to the ground. The amazing part was this: that vessel wasn't big enough to hold them all; three could have fit in at the most. Yet they kept materializing — a sixth, a seventh, an eighth — as if they had been woven out of the wisps of steam.

How these gay children appealed to our poor citizens! How fat their little legs were! *Come, chickee,* the audience cried. They were cooing and cooing. Even Macbeth seemed affected. He held his arms out to the tots. But they ran by him to where Iza Flicker, on piano wires, was coming out of the sky. This ghost of Banquo hovered a moment, then set on each upturned head a paper crown, gold-colored, that tied with elastic under the chin. That is how Macbeth learned the answer to his question. He stared, child-

less, empty-handed, at the little Kings. How they romped! They
were having a wonderful party.

"Ha! Ha!"

It wasn't the witches laughing. It wasn't Madame Trumpeldor.
This time it was Trumpeldor himself.

"I'm not upset!" the Elder shouted. "Don't look so scared, Jews!
I'm not angry. Look, I'm smiling. Don't think a play can frighten
me!"

It was silent inside the theater now. No one knew whether the
show was over or not. The Szapiro & Son chandelier started down
from the ceiling; Trumpeldor looked at it, glared at it, and slowly
it rose again.

"Relax! Don't worry!" Trumpeldor yelled. "There's only one
thing I want to know. A little thing. Who is responsible for this
production? Tell me! Give me his name! Don't say the children did
it! Don't make me laugh! They were tricked into this job. They
didn't know what they were doing. I forgive them. I kiss you,
children! I am blowing you kisses! My dears! My sons! I am not a
bad man!"

At that moment, the owl hooted again. Everyone looked for the
bird, for its lit-up eyes. It wasn't there. Not on its perch. Not on the
stage. Not anywhere. But the hoot-hooting continued, louder than
ever. It seemed to be coming from far off, perhaps from outside
the theater completely. And drawing nearer, too. The audience
stirred. People who had pocket watches took them out. From either
side of the stage, the curtain was coming together. Still no sign of
the bright green eyes! What could it mean?

Then someone in the House of Culture announced: "The
train!"

"Not possible!" another Jew shouted.

"It's only three o'clock in the afternoon!"

Then the whistle rang sharply from the direction of the Rado-
goszcz Station.

"Maybe," said Councilman Popower, "we should go home."

From the benches, from the balcony, from the expensive, upholstered chairs, the whole audience rose together. But Trumpeldor
held up his hands.

"Jews! Jewesses!" he shouted. "Don't go! Sit! The play isn't over!
Let's find out what happens next!"

And the result was, everybody sat down.

*

From then on, the performance switched back and forth, from one place to another. First we would be in England, where the forces of law and order, led by little Krystal, the dead King's son, were preparing to attack the despot's kingdom. England! Imagine! The next moment we would be in that dark, smoky land itself. Crowds of orphans dragged over the stage, crying for a piece of bread. Blind people fumbled about, bumping into the scenery. Worst were the killers, who trotted this way and that, stabbing anybody they saw. It was a charnel house.

Finally we came back to the hall of the villain's castle. Night. Always night. At the top of the stairs, someone appeared holding a candle. It was Gutta Blit. Her hair was loose and full of electrical charges. Shoeless. Her nightdress half undone. A sleepwalker! The beams from the candle glistened on her open eyes. What struck the Jews was the little jerks her head made, just a few centimeters at a single time. They heard her sniffling at something. "Here's the smell of the blood still!" she said. Then she began to glide down the flight of stairs.

"Crazy woman!" said Popower.

"Witch!" said Krautwirt, the Devout Buchers' rabbi.

The Queen of Scotland, so dark, so dusky, was by then halfway down. She tossed her head. It was like a horse reacting to flies. "Who would have thought the old man to have had so much blood in him?" she said.

"Poor thing! Poor thing!" Madame Trumpeldor murmured. "How she's suffering!"

Young Miss Blit went the rest of the way down the stairs. In her bare feet, in her dragging gown, she walked to the entranceway. "To bed, to bed, to bed" was what she was saying. But she did not go to bed. She threw off the bolt of the gigantic door. It swung open. Immediately, wind from a machine blew the hair back from her head. *Whoosh!* The candle went out in her hand.

Trumpeldor and Madame Trumpeldor were leaning against each other. They held each other up. She was stroking the cloth that his cape was made of. "Chaim, sweet Chaim. I see into the future. Like a witch does. Like a gypsy. There will be Jews in this future, honey Chaim. Not so many. Not nearly so many. But the same kind of Jews that are living now."

"Look!" Trumpeldor responded.

Everyone did. The Scottish Queen, so distracted, was stepping out of the castle, into the sudden blast of the wind. It whistled about her. On this sad scene the two sides of the curtain, like a pair of shutters, drew closed.

Right away, something that looked like a palm tree came tripping across the front of the stage and — it's the only way to describe it — sat down. This was from right to left. Then, from left to right, a healthy bush darted out and crouched down next to the palm. A pine tree with needles came after, and then two or three little shrubs. Before you knew it, there was a line of vegetation across the whole front part of the stage. Their branches were trembling. They shook their green leaves.

Then the curtains parted. The scene was in an open place. There were some rocks and, here and there, an evergreen tree. The wind was still blowing from some spot offstage. It shook the dark curls of Mann Lifshits' beard. "Come, put mine armor on," he said. He was already wearing his metal breastplate, and his tight leather helmet was pulled onto his head. Nonetheless, he wanted more protection. "My armor!" he repeated. A Hatters' Asylum orphan ran about, tying on extra layers of padding and new pieces of mail. Lifshits was swelling. It looked as if, under such a load of metal, he could hardly stand. But he left-handedly drew his sword out. Then he laughed. A long, loud laugh that made, inside his armor, a hollow sound: *I will not be afraid of death and bane till Birnam Forest come to Dunsinane!* At that moment, one of the evergreens came a step closer. It had feet on the bottom! It moved! So did another one of the firs! One little plant, ragged and windblown, dashed almost to the tyrant's elbow, and then held perfectly still. All the foliage at the edge of the stage began to shake and stir. The twigs were nudging each other.

Someone walked onto the stage. It was the messenger again. He was, in his hip boots, rooted to the ground. "I-I-I-I" — he said, and Macbeth said: *Thou comest to use thy tongue. Thy story, quickly.* At last this poor fellow spoke: *I looked toward Birnam, and anon methought the wood began to move.* Mann Lifshits gaped and raised his blade. "Liar and slave!" he shouted. But already the whole of the forest was closing upon him. New trees ran in from left and right. Not trees! Children holding branches! With leaves glued onto their backs! This was young Krystal's army! The English troops had arrived!

"Hurrah!" cried the Jews, tremendously excited. "Kill him! Kill the tyrant!"

In an instant, the children surrounded the King completely. Snarling, sneering, he waved his sword: *I'll fight till from my bones my flesh be hacked.*

No hope for Macbeth. Wherever the Jews looked, even in the aisles of the House of Culture and along the theater walls, they saw the forces of order. But then the poor Jews had to look twice. For those in the aisles were not orphans but, in their leaf-green uniforms, grown-up men. They had rubber clubs in their hands. And caps on! Caps! The theater was filled with policemen!

And still more were pouring through the Assisi Street door. The whistle blew. So the train *had* come into the transfer station! But there wasn't the pandemonium that you would expect. The players stood there in one position or another. The audience just sat. They could not believe such a thing could happen. So it was really rather quiet in the House of Culture when Trumpeldor, with his back to the stage, started to speak.

"I know there are Jews who hate me and want to kill me. Some of these so-called Jews are in this theater now. Well, here I am! Here's my bare breast! Anyone can shoot me who wants to! From the balcony! The way they shot Abraham Lincoln! Or stab me, like Caesar!"

Now people were starting to whimper and groan. Mister Smolenskin played more *Aida* to restore the calm. But Trumpeldor continued shouting: "I, Trumpeldor, come to you like a robber to rob you of your dearest ones. I, Trumpeldor, take you by the hand and lead you to death. *What a monster!* That's what you're thinking. You, with your jewels, your gloves, your nice soft seats in a theater. But it is a cage we are in! You and I together! And in this cage with us, there is a hungry lion! He wants to spring! To devour us all! And I? I? I am the lion tamer. I stuff his mouth with meat! It's the flesh of my brothers and sisters! The lion eats and eats! He roars! But he does not spring! Thus, with ten Jews, I save a hundred. With a hundred, I save a thousand. With a thousand, ten thousand more. My hands are bloody. My feet are bloody. My eyes are closed with blood. I have no conscience! But that's why your conscience is clear!"

Suddenly the Elder of the Jews started forward. He took long steps up the orchestra aisle. "Save us! Save us!" our citizens cried, trying to touch him, to hold him. But Trumpeldor strode straight to the Assisi Street door. The policemen made a barrier out of their batons, but the Elder went through it, like a knife through grass. Behind him, in the House of Culture, the Jews were wailing and holding on to each other. On the stage, machines made a wind that shook the actors' beards and made the pasted leaves toss and tremble. Macbeth threw his warlike shield in front of his body. Above his head he raised his wooden sword.

The Rumkowski Geyser had been taken over by the Trainmasters. They used it now as their own private spa. But it looked the same as it always had, with its brick walls holding up the great whitewashed dome. Steam still came from a hole in the top, and sunshine, in the shape of a moving yellow ball, came in. It was to the front of this municipal bath that Trumpeldor's carriage, with Trumpeldor inside it, came quickly trotting.

Even before the coach's big wheels stopped turning, Trumpeldor had hopped down and was striding toward the steam-bath entrance. Guards were there too, but the Elder, gripping his cane, swept by. Even this far away, you could hear the whistling at the transfer station. A high sound. A low one. That meant two locomotives, both of them keeping up steam. It would be a long train, then.

Just inside the Geyser was a big curving hallway where you took off your clothes. Trumpeldor walked straight through it. With his hat on, and his cloak, with the whole outfit from the gala performance, he pushed into the chamber of steam.

How hot it was! How hard to breathe! Impossible to see through the droplets on his glasses. Then a voice he knew — it was the Chief Trainmaster's — echoed about him.

"It is the Jew, Trumpeldor! Born from two other Jews!"

The Elder looked around. Nothing but steam clouds. Hot blasts of air. Below him, in a pit, at the center of the rotunda, he could barely make out the flaming beech logs, the glow of the flat, heated rocks. Water, dripping from water pipes, snarled and crackled over the stones, like the whites of cooking eggs.

"Yes! Just a Jew. But he acts like a King!"

Something moved above Trumpeldor's head. He took off his blurred spectacles. A left leg, giant-size, with moles, was crossed over a right one. The steam parted a second. The Elder saw the Warrior, his bright lips, his wet chest.

"Herr Trainmaster, I am talking to you as the Elder of the Jews.

As a high official! An emergency happened! Something must be done!" Trumpeldor's hair was already sticking to the back of his neck. He squinted into the mists. "Policemen have invaded the House of Culture! They are there at this moment! How dare they do it! What nerve! To threaten citizens' lives! Important people! Influential Jews!"

"Lives? What lives? Today there will be a big transport. That's so. But the Jews on it will become farmhands and milkmaids and such."

Trumpeldor started shouting. He banged the tip of his cane on the sodden boards. "Don't insult me! I'm not a shit-wagon puller! This is no rabbi with a nose in a book! I know all about it! I know what goes on in the forest! I know about those mattresses with ladies' hair! You can't fool the Elder of the Jews the way you can a needle threader! He's smart! He knows everything!"

The Chief Trainmaster folded his ivory arms. "What forest?"

Then a different voice rolled off the rounded walls. "Why continue the charade? Obviously he knows."

Trumpeldor could not figure out which way to look. The benches in the steam bath went around the entire room. They rose, one ring above the other, like the seats in an ancient theater. This speaker could be anywhere.

"In my opinion, we should let the whole world in on it. Do you think anyone will object? They'll thank us. They'll applaud. A thousand years from now, people will remember us precisely for this, the way they remember Pasteur."

"Please!" cried the Elder. "Cancel the transport! I beg you to call it off! My children! My little Jews!"

But the voice went on, the same as before. "Here's an idea! With every corpse we bury a bronze tablet, on which is carved: *In such and such a place, on such and such a date, we alone had the courage to deal with Mister Feinberg or Steinberg or Weinberg, whatever the name of the Jew.*"

Trumpeldor wrung his hands. "But this was our grand premiere!"

The voice was silent. The Elder stared upward, into the swirling mists. Just for a moment that steam parted. Way up, in the highest place, under the dome top, someone was sitting. A red-skinned person. Boiled-looking. He was beating himself with twigs, like a Finn. Then the steam clouds closed in again.

Everything on Trumpeldor was already wilting. The brim of his hat drooped down. His cane felt rubberized. Dizzily, he reached out his hand for something to hold to, but nothing was there. Would someone tell him why the whole world was spinning? He knew that outside, to the west of the city, the sun was going down. But why did it seem to be stuck over the top of the Rumkowski Geyser? Its light kept pouring in. It made the steam whiter and whiter, blinding him.

"Our job takes toughness! Toughness!" It was the same voice still. "Toughness like Genghis Khan!"

Who was this? Who? Trumpeldor lifted his head. He peered once more into the leaping light. He blinked against the dazzle, the glare. Instantly, as if all the steam had been sucked out of the rooftop, he saw the bare pink body plain. It was him! Him! The one who thought up the trains!

The Elder shuddered. It wasn't from fear. Proudly, he threw his wet cloak around himself. "The dog!" he said, his wide lips curling. "Uncircumcised!" And Trumpeldor fell with a thump to the floor.

The Jews are a desert people. Dry. Arid. Always moving around. Not like these warriors, a forest folk, deeply rooted, used to mists and dampness and fogs. This is to say that Trumpeldor had only fainted: perhaps from too much steam?

When he at last opened both eyes, everything was quiet and shadowy and still. The fire in the fire pit was out. There was no one up there on the benches. No one on the benches below. The municipal bath was deserted. Had anyone ever been there?

Outside, the Elder's coach and his coach horse were missing. That meant he had to walk all the way back to where he had started.

There were some people inside the House of Culture, but only a few. The Jews from the Council, and the big rabbis, were sitting together, near the orchestra pit. Mister Smolenskin was missing. So was Schotter. Luftgas, up until then an important person, was likewise gone. It turned out that hardly anyone had been left out of the train. Maybe, out of hundreds and hundreds, two or three dozen at most. The vocational-school students, the wonderful skaters, were passengers, too. But the orphans from the Hatters' Asylum had not left the stage. Some of them still had the fir branches glued to their clothes.

Trumpeldor walked down the aisle and sat in his special chair.

Madame Trumpeldor's seat was empty. Undoubtedly, she had one on the train. The Elder put his hat on the unoccupied cushion, as if he intended to reserve it.

There were more hours left of that night. Sooner or later, everyone inside the House of Culture started to doze. Let us leave them there, just sleeping. Never mind about dreams.

JOYCE CAROL OATES

The Translation

(FROM TRIQUARTERLY)

WHAT WERE THE WORDS for woman, man, love, freedom, fate? — in this strange land where the architecture and the countryside and the sea with its dark choppy waters and the very air itself seemed to Oliver totally foreign, unearthly? He must have fallen in love with the woman at once, after fifteen minutes' conversation. Such perversity was unlike him. He had loved a woman twenty years before; had perhaps loved two or even three women in his lifetime; but had never fallen in love, had never been *in love;* such melodramatic passion was not his style. He had spoken with her only for fifteen minutes at the most, and not directly: through the translator assigned to him. He did not know her at all. Yet that night he dreamed of rescuing her.

"I am struck and impressed," he said politely, addressing the young woman introduced to him as a music teacher at the high school and a musician — a violist — herself, "with the marvelous old buildings here . . . the church that is on the same street as my hotel . . . yes? . . . you know it? . . . and with the beauty of the parks, the trees and flowers, everything so well-tended, and the manner of the people I have encountered . . . they are friendly but not effusive, they appear so very . . . so very healthy," he said, hearing his voice falter, realizing that he was being condescending — as if it surprised him, the fact that people in this legendary, long-suffering nation were not very different from people anywhere. But his translator translated the speech and the young woman appeared to agree, nodding, smiling as if to encourage him. Thank God he had not offended her. "I am very grateful to have been allowed a visa," he said. "I have never visited a country that has struck me in such a way . . . an immediate sense of, of . . . how shall I put it? . . . of something like nostalgia . . . do you know the expression, the meaning? . . . nostalgia . . . emotion for something once possessed but now lost, perhaps not now even accessible through memory . . ."

If he was making a fool of himself with this speech, and by so urgently staring at the woman, Alisa, the others did not appear to notice; they listened intently, even greedily, as Oliver's young translator repeated his words, hardly pausing for breath. He was a remarkable young man, probably in his early twenties, and Oliver had the idea that the translator's presence and evident goodwill toward him were freeing his tongue, giving him a measure of happiness for the first time since he had left the United States. For the first time, really, in many years. It was marvelous, magical, to utter his thoughts aloud and to hear, then, their instantaneous translation into a foreign language — to sit with his translator at his left hand, watching the effect of his words upon his listeners' faces as they were translated. An eerie, uncanny experience . . . unsettling and yet exciting, in a way Oliver could not have explained. He had not liked the idea of relying upon a translator; one of his failings, one of the disappointments of his life, had always been a certain shyness or coolness in his character, which it was evidently his fate not to alter, and he had supposed that travel in a country as foreign as this one, and as formally antagonistic to the United States, would be especially difficult since he knew nothing of the language. But in fact the translator was like a younger brother to him, like a son. There was an intimacy between them and a pleasurable freedom, even an unembarrassed lyricism in Oliver's remarks, that he could not possibly have anticipated.

Of course his mood was partly attributable to the cognac, and to the close, crowded, overheated room in which the reception was being held, and to his immediate attraction for the dusky-haired, solemn young woman with the name he could not pronounce — Alisa was as close as he could come to it; he would have to ask the translator to write it out for him when they returned to the hotel. It would not last, his mood of gaiety. But for the present moment he was very happy merely to hear these people speak their language, a melodic play of explosive consonants and throaty vowels; it hardly mattered that his translator could manage to translate only a fraction of what was being said. He was happy, almost euphoric. He was intoxicated. He had to restrain himself from taking one of Alisa's delicate hands in his own and squeezing it, to show how taken he was by her. *I know you are suffering in this prison state of yours,* he wanted to whisper to her, *and I want, I want to do something for you . . . want to rescue you, save you, change your life . . .*

The director of the Lexicographic Institute was asking him a courteous, convoluted question about the current state of culture in his own nation, and everyone listened, frowning, as if with anxiety, while, with one part of his mind, Oliver made several statements. His translator took them up at once, transformed them into those eerie, exquisite sounds; the director nodded gravely, emphatically; the others nodded; it seemed to be about what they had anticipated. One of the men, white-haired, diminutive, asked something in a quavering voice, and Oliver's translator hesitated before repeating it. "Dr. Crlejevec is curious to know — is it true that your visual artists have become artists merely of the void — that is, of death — that they are exclusively morbid, that they have turned their backs on life?" The translator blushed, not quite meeting Oliver's gaze, as if he were embarrassed by the question. But the question did not annoy Oliver. Not in the least. He disliked much of contemporary art anyway and welcomed the opportunity to express his feelings, warmly, knowing that what he said would endear him to these people. It pleased him most of all that Alisa listened so closely. Her long, nervous fingers toyed with a cameo brooch she wore at her throat; her gray eyes were fixed upon his face. "Art moves in a certain tendril-like manner . . . in many directions, though at a single point in history one direction is usually stressed and acclaimed . . . like the evolutionary gropings of nature, to my way of thinking. Do you see? The contemporary pathway is but a tendril, a feeler, an experimental gesture . . . because it is obsessed with death and the void and the annihilation of self, it will necessarily die . . . it pronounces its own death sentence."

The words were translated; the effect was instantaneous; Oliver's pronouncement seemed to meet with approval. The director, however, posed another question. He was a huge man in his fifties, with a ruddy, beefy face and rather coarse features, though his voice seemed to Oliver quite cultured. ". . . But in the meantime, does it not do damage? . . . to the unformed, that is, to the young, the susceptible . . . does it not do irreparable damage, such deathly art?"

Oliver's high spirits could not be diminished. He only pretended
to be thinking seriously before he answered, "Not at all! In my part
of the world, serious art is ignored by the masses; the unformed,
the young, the susceptible are not aware of its existence!"

He had expected his listeners to laugh. But they did not laugh.
The young woman murmured something, shaking her head.
Oliver's translator said to him, "She says she is shocked . . . unless,
of course, you are joking."

The conversation shifted. Oliver was taken to other groups of
people, was introduced by his translator, was made to feel important, honored. From time to time he glanced back at the young
woman — when he saw her preparing to leave, he was stricken; he
wanted to tell his translator to stop her; but of course that would
have been indecorous. *I want to do something for you. Anything. I want
. . .* But it would have been indecorous.

"She is a fine person, very hardworking, very trustworthy," Liebert was saying slowly. "Not my friend or even acquaintance, but
my sister's . . . my older sister, who was her classmate. She is a very
accomplished violist, participated in a festival last spring in Mos-
cow, but also a very fine teacher here, very hardworking, very
serious."

"Is she married?" Oliver asked.

They were being driven in a shiny black taxicab along an avenue
of trees in blossom — acacia, lime — past buildings of all sizes,
some very old, some disconcertingly new, of glass and poured
concrete and steel, and from time to time the buildings fell back
and a monument appeared, sudden, grandiose, rather pompous
— not very old either, Oliver noted. Postwar.

"There is some difficulty, yes," the translator said, "with the
husband . . . and with the father as well. But I do not know, really.
I am not an acquaintance of hers, as I said. She lives her life, I live
mine. We meet a few times a year, at gatherings like the one last
night . . . she too does translations, though not into English. Into
Italian and German exclusively."

"Then she is married? You mentioned a husband? . . ."

Liebert looked out the window, as if embarrassed by Oliver's
interest. He was not unwilling to talk about the young woman, but
not willing either. For the first time in their three days' acquaintance, Oliver felt the young man's stubborn nature. "They have
not been together in one place for many years, as I understand it,"

he said. "The husband, not an acquaintance of my own, is some years older than she . . . a doctor, I believe . . . a research specialist in an area I know nothing of. He is in another city. He has been in another city, and Alisa in this city, for many years."

"I'm sorry to hear that," Oliver said sincerely. "She struck me as sweet, vulnerable . . . possibly a little lonely? I don't like to think that she may be unhappy."

Liebert shrugged his shoulders.

"Unhappy, so?" he murmured.

They drove through a square and Oliver's attention was drawn to an immense portrait of a man's face, a poster three stories high.

"Amazing!" he said without irony.

"It is not amazing, it is ordinary life," Liebert said. "We live here."

". . . She isn't unhappy, then? No more than most?"

"There is not the — what is the word? — the compulsion to analyze such things, such states of mind," Liebert said with a vague air of reproach. "It is enough to complete the day — working hard, doing one's obligations. You understand? Leisure would only result in morbid self-scrutiny and the void, the infatuation with the void, which is your fate."

"My fate?" Oliver said. "Not mine. Don't confuse me with anyone else."

Liebert mumbled an apology.

They drove on in silence for a few minutes. They were approaching a hilly area north of the city; in the near distance were mountains of a peculiar magenta color, partly obscured by mist. Oliver felt, still, that uncharacteristic euphoria, as if he were in a dream, a kind of paradise, and on all sides miracles ringed him in. He had not been prepared for the physical beauty of this place, or for the liveliness of its people. And his translator, Liebert, was quite a surprise. He spoke English with very little accent, clear voiced, boyish, attentive to Oliver's every hesitation or expression of curiosity, exactly as if he could read Oliver's thoughts. He took it as his solemn duty, evidently, to make Oliver comfortable in every way. His manner was both shy and composed, childlike and remarkably mature. He had a sweet, melancholy, shadowed face with a head of thick, dark, curly hair and a widow's peak above a narrow forehead; his cheekbones were Slavic; his complexion was pale but with a faint rosy cast to it, as if the blood hummed warmly

him before the visit came to a conclusion. It seemed
fact of life that he, Oliver, had money, had a certain
estige, however lightly he valued it, and had, most of
reedom to travel anywhere he wished. The vast earth
much of it as he cared to explore. Other cultures,
life were open to his investigation. Even the past was
ld visit places of antiquity, could assemble countless
uable objects, could pursue any interest to its culmi-
editor and publisher of a distinguished magazine,
essays on international culture with as little empha-
upon politics, Oliver was welcome nearly anywhere;
ral languages — French, German, Italian, Spanish
did not know a country's language a skillful inter-
signed to him and there was rarely any difficulty.
as accustomed to think of himself as colorless, as a
had wanted to be a poet and a playwright, as a young
nevertheless true that he was a success and that he
amount of power. Alisa and Liebert, however, were
a sense they were prisoners.

hey proclaimed their great satisfaction with postwar
azis had been driven back, another world power had
aid, the government under which they now lived was
rfection as one might wish. Compared to their tumul-
able past, how sunny their present seemed! — of
were happy. But they were prisoners just the same.
ot leave their country. It might even be the case that
t leave this particular city without good cause. Oliver
know that nearly one third of the population was
one level or another, in espionage — neighbors re-
eighbors, relatives on relatives, students on teachers,
upervisors, friends on friends. It was a way of life. As
said one day, it was nothing other than ordinary life

w. He knew. The two of them were fortunate just to
t weren't manual; they were fortunate to be as free as
lking with an American. He believed he could gauge
he abstract, in the collective, no matter that the two of
ally strangers to him. He knew and he did sympathize
of his better judgment, he wished that he could help

close beneath the skin. Large brown eyes, a long nose, ears too
large for his slender face . . . something about him put Oliver in
mind of a nocturnal animal, quick, furtive, naturally given to
silence. In general he had an ascetic appearance. No doubt he was
very poor, in his ill-fitting tweed suit and scuffed brown shoes, his
hair crudely cut, so short that it emphasized the thinness of his
neck and the prominence of his Adam's apple. Not handsome,
perhaps, but attractive in his own way. Oliver liked him very much.

"If you would like, perhaps another meeting could be arranged,"
he said softly. "That is, it would not be impossible."

"Another meeting? With her?"

"If you would like," Liebert said.

Love: loss of equilibrium. Imbalance. Something fundamental to
one's being, an almost physical certainty of self, is violated. Oliver
had loved women in the past and he had felt, even, this distressing
physical urgency, this anxiety before; but it had never blossomed
so quickly, based on so little evidence. The night of the reception
at the Institute he had slept poorly, rehearsing in his sleep certain
phrases he would say to Alisa, pleading with her, begging her. For
what? And why? She was a striking woman, perhaps not beautiful;
it was natural that he might be attracted to her, though his experiences with women in recent years had been disappointing. But the
intensity of his feeling worried him. It was exactly as if something
foreign to his nature had infiltrated his system, had found him
vulnerable, had shot his temperature up by several degrees. And
he rejoiced in it, despite his worry and an obscure sense of shame.
He really rejoiced in it. He woke, poured himself some of the
sweet-tasting brandy he had left on his night table, lay back upon
the goose-feather pillows, and thought of her. Was it possible he
could see her again? Under what pretext? He was leaving in four
days. Possibly he could extend his visit. Possibly not.

He recalled her bony, broad cheekbones, the severity of her
gaze, her rather startled smile. A stranger. One of many strangers.
In this phase of his life, Oliver thought, he met only strangers; he
had no wish to see people he knew.

I love you. I want, what do I want? . . . I want to know more about you.

A mistake, but he could not resist pouring more brandy into the
glass. It tasted like sweet, heavy syrup at first and then, after a few
seconds, like pure alcohol, blistering, acidic. One wished to obliter-

ate the strong taste with the sweet — the impulse was to sip a little more.

According to his clock in its small leather traveling case, it was three-fifteen.

I want . . . what do I want? he murmured aloud.

Liebert translated for Oliver: "She says that the 'extravagance' you speak of in Androv's chronicles . . . and in our literature generally . . . is understood here as exaggeration . . . metaphors? . . . metaphors, yes, for interior states. But we ourselves, we are not extravagant in our living."

"Of course I only know Androv's work in translation," Oliver said quickly. "It reads awkwardly, rather like Dreiser . . . do you know the name, the novelist? . . . one of our distinguished American novelists, no longer so popular as he once was . . . I was enormously impressed with the stubbornness, the resiliency, the audacity of Androv's characters, and despite his technique of exaggeration they seemed to me very lifelike." He paused, in order to give Liebert the opportunity to translate. He was breathing quickly, watching Alisa's face. They were having a drink in the hotel lounge, a dim, quiet place where morose potted plants of a type Oliver did not recognize grew more than six feet high, drooping over the half-dozen marble tables. Oliver was able to see his own reflection in a mirror across the room; the mirror looked smoky, webbed as if with a spider's web; his own face, there, hovered indistinct and pale. His constant, rather nervous smile was not visible.

In the subdued light of the hotel lounge, Alisa seemed to him more beautiful than before. Her dark hair was drawn back and fastened in an attractive French twist; it was not done carelessly into a bun or a knot, the way many local women wore their hair; it shone with good health. She wore a white blouse and, again, the old-fashioned cameo brooch, and a hip-length sweater of some coarse dark wool, and a nondescript skirt that fell well below her knees. Her eyes were slightly slanted, almond shaped, dark, glistening; her cheekbones, like Liebert's, were prominent. Oliver guessed her to be about thirty-five, a little older than he had thought. But striking — very striking. Every movement of hers charmed him. Her mixture of shyness and composure, her quick contralto voice, her habit of glancing from Oliver to Liebert to

Oliver again, almost flirt[...] at her but he could not l[...]

"She says: Of course w[...] could we have survived? [...] the bizarre tall tales . . . '[...] with the allusion? . . . no[...] of *The Peasants*," Liebert [...] following all this. In fact, [...] woman fascinated him; h[...] seen her somewhere bef[...] . . . And he had read only [...] work. "From the early fif[...] country has been under f[...] Turks . . . centuries of o[...] alone there were two mill[...] travagance' and even the [...] survived?"

"I know, I understand, [...] once.

He could not relax, th[...] noon. Something was urge[...] could not quite comprehe[...] eler, not really a tourist, p[...] merit the designation of "[...] ment's term, not his own —[...] predictable words with a [...] strange, charming countr[...] himself over a forty-three[...] shallow, superficial, hypoc[...] pretend knowledge and sy[...] tor; he had not suffered ex[...] early, failed marriage, a sa[...] sion, the stray, undefined di[...] listened to the woman's low, [...] translator's voice; he observ[...] shabby clothing, and judg[...] would not notice. Liebert, [...] with him, must sense by n[...] have some awareness of the [...] hoped the young man wo[...]

bitterly agains[...] to him an ugl[...] measure of p[...] all, complete [...] was his — as [...] other ways of [...] his, for he co[...] books and va[...] nation. As th[...] which feature[...] sis as possible[...] he knew sev[...] — and if he [...] preter was a[...] Though he [...] failure — he [...] man — it wa[...] had a certain[...] powerless; in[...]

Of course [...] events. The [...] come to thei[...] as close to p[...] tuous, mise[...] course they [...] They could [...] they could n[...] happened t[...] involved, on[...] porting on [...] teachers on [...] Liebert had [...] for them.

Oliver kn[...] have jobs th[...] they were, [...] their fate in[...] them were [...] and, in spit[...] them.

At dusk they walked three abreast along the sparsely lit boule-vard, the main street of the city. Oliver was to be taken to a workingman's café; he was tired of the hotel food, the expensive dinners. They spoke now of the new buildings that were being erected south of the city, along the sea cliff; they told Oliver that he must take time to visit one of the excavations farther to the south — he would see Roman ornaments, coins, grave toys, statu-ary. "Alisa says the evidence of other centuries and other civiliza-tions is so close to us," Liebert murmured. "We are unable to place too much emphasis upon the individual, the ephemeral. Do you see? I have often thought along those lines myself."

"Yes, I suppose so — I suppose that's right," Oliver said slowly.

Alisa said something to him, looking up at him. Liebert, on his right side, translated at once: "Future generations are as certain as the past — there is a continuity — there is a progress, an evolu-tion. It is clear, it is scientifically demonstrable."

"Is it?" Oliver said, for a moment wondering if it might be so. "Yes — that's possible — I'm sure that's possible."

Liebert translated his words and Alisa laughed.

"Why is she laughing? What did you say?" Oliver asked, smiling.

"I said — only what you said. I translated your words faithfully," Liebert said rather primly.

"She has such a ready, sweet laugh," Oliver said. "She's so charm-ing, so unconscious of herself . . . Ask her, Liebert, where she's from . . . where she went to school . . . where she lives . . . what her life is like."

"All that?" Liebert asked. "So much!"

"But we have all evening, don't we?" Oliver said plaintively. ". . . All night?"

That day he had been a guest at the district commissioner's home for a two-hour luncheon. He had been driven to the village where the poet Hisjak had been born. Along with another guest of honor, an Italian novelist, he had been shown precious documents — the totally illegible manuscripts of an unknown writer, unknown at least to Oliver — kept in a safe in a museum. The first two evenings of his visit had been spent at endless dinners. He had witnessed a troupe of youthful dancers in rehearsal; he had admired the many statues of heroes placed about the city; he had marveled over the Byzantine domes, the towers and vaulting roofs and fountains. But his hours with Alisa and Liebert were by far the most enjoyable; he knew he would never forget them.

They ate a thick, greasy stew of coarse beef and vegetables, and many slices of whole-grain bread and butter, and drank two bottles of wine, of a dry, tart nature, quite unfamiliar to Oliver. The three of them sat at a corner table in an utterly unimpressive restaurant; like a diner, it was, crude and brightly lit and noisy as an American diner. At first the other patrons took notice of them, but as time passed and the restaurant grew noisier, they were able to speak without being overheard. Oliver was very happy. He felt strangely free, like a child. The food was delicious; he kept complimenting them and asking Liebert to tell the waitress, and even to tell the cook; the bread, especially, seemed extraordinary — he insisted that he had never tasted bread so good. "How can I leave? Where can I go from here?" he said jokingly. They were served small, flaky tarts for dessert, and Oliver ate his in two or three bites, though he was no longer hungry and the oversweet taste, apricots and brandy and raw dark sugar, was not really to his liking.

"You are all so wonderful . . ." he said.

Alisa sat across from him, Liebert sat to his left. The table was too small for their many dishes and glasses and silverware. They laughed together like old friends, easily, intimately. Alisa showed her gums as she laughed — no self-consciousness about her — utterly natural, direct. Her eyes narrowed to slits and opened wide again, sparkling. The wine had brought a flush to her cheeks. Liebert too was expansive, robust. He no longer played the role of the impoverished, obsequious student. Sometimes he spoke to Oliver without feeling the necessity to translate his English for Alisa; sometimes he and Alisa exchanged remarks, and though Oliver did not know what they were saying, or why they laughed so merrily, he joined them in their laughter. Most of the time, however, Liebert translated back and forth from Oliver to Alisa, from Alisa to Oliver, rapidly, easily, always with genuine interest. Oliver liked the rhythm that was established: like a game, like a piece of music, like the bantering of love. Oliver's words in English translated into Alisa's language, Alisa's words translated into Oliver's language, magically. Surely it was magic. Oliver asked Alisa about her background, about the village she had grown up in; he asked her about her parents; about her work. It turned out that her father had been a teacher also, a music teacher at one of the colleges — "very distinguished and well loved" — but he had become ill, there was no treatment available, he had wanted to return to his home district to die. Oliver listened sympathetically. There was more to it, he supposed, there was something further about it . . . but he could not inquire. And what about the husband? But he could not inquire, he did not dare.

"You are all so remarkably free of bitterness," he said.

Liebert translated. Alisa replied. Liebert hesitated before saying: "Why should we be bitter? We live with complexity. You wish simplicity in your life . . . good divided sharply from evil, love divided from hate . . . beauty from ugliness. We have always been different. We live with complexity; we would not recognize the world otherwise."

Oliver was staring at Alisa. "Did you really say that?" he asked.

"Of course she said that. Those words exactly," Liebert murmured.

"She's so . . . she's so very . . . I find her so very charming," Oliver said weakly. "Please don't translate! Please. Do you see? It's just that I find her so . . . I admire her without reservation," he said, squeezing Liebert's arm. "I find it difficult to reply to her. Central Europe is baffling to me; I expected to be meeting quite different kinds of people; your closed border, your wartime consciousness that seems never to lift, your reputation for . . . for certain inexplicable . . ." Both Liebert and Alisa were watching him, expressionless. He fell silent. Absurdly, he had been about to speak of the innumerable arrests and imprisonments, even of the tortures reported in the West, but it seemed to him now that perhaps these reports were lies. He did not know what to believe.

"Freedom and constraint cannot be sharply divided, the one from the other," Liebert said coldly. "Freedom is a relative thing. It is relative to the context, to the humanity it . . . serves? . . . shelters. For instance, your great American cities, they are so famed, they are 'free,' you would boast, citizens can come and go as they wish . . . each in his automobile, isn't that so? But, in fact, we know that your people are terrified of being hurt by one another. They are terrified of being killed by their fellow citizens. In this way," Liebert said, smiling, "in this way it must be judged that the nature of freedom is not so simple. But it is always political."

"There's a difference between self-imposed restrictions and . . . and the restrictions of a state like yours," Oliver said, obscurely hurt, blinking. He had no interest in defending his nation. He did not care about it at all, not at the moment. "But perhaps you are correct; the issue is always political, even when it is baffling and obscure . . . In America we have too much freedom and the individual is free to hurt others, this is an excess of . . . am I speaking too quickly? . . . this is an excess rather than . . . But I don't wish to talk of such things," he said softly. "Not tonight. It is more important, our being together. Do you agree? Yes? Ask Alisa — does she agree?"

They agreed. They laughed together like old friends.

"Alisa says we must live our lives in the interstices of the political state," Liebert said slyly, "like sparrows who make their nests on window ledges or streetlamps. They are happy there until the happiness stops. We are happy until it stops. But perhaps it will not stop for many years — who can predict? Political oppression is no more a disaster than an accident on the highway or a fatal disease or being born crippled . . ."

"Disaster is disaster," Oliver said thickly. "What do we care? There isn't time. I must leave in a few days . . . I admire you both so very, very much. You're noble, you're brave, you're attractive . . . she is beautiful, isn't she? . . . beautiful! I've never met anyone so intelligent and beautiful at the same time, so vivacious, good-natured . . . Will you tell her that? Please?"

Liebert turned to her and spoke. she lowered her head, fussed with her hair, reddened slightly, frowned. A long moment passed. She glanced shyly at Oliver. Seeing the desperation in his eyes, she managed to smile.

"Thank you," Oliver whispered. "Thank you both so very much."

Something was stinging him.

Bedbugs?

His arms were curiously leaden; he could not move; he could not rake his nails against his sides, his abdomen, his buttocks, his back. He groaned but did not wake. The stinging became a single sweeping flame that covered his body, burned fiercely into his eyes.

"Alisa?" he said. "Are you here? Are you hiding?"

He was in the Old City, the City of Stone. Much of it had been leveled during the war, but there were ancient buildings — fortresses, inns, cathedrals. The weight of time. The weight of the spirit. On all sides, voices were chattering in that exquisite, teasing language he could not decipher. They were mocking him, jeering at him. They knew him very well. He was to be led to their shrine, where a miracle would be performed. The holy saint of Toskinjevec, patron saint of lepers, epileptics, the crippled and the insane and the fanatic . . . He was being hurried along the cobblestone streets. There were heavy oak doors with iron hinges; there were rusted latches and locks; walls slime green with mold, beginning to crumble. Footsteps rang and echoed. Liebert held his hand, murmured words of comfort, stroked his head. He wanted only to obey. "Where is she? Is she already there?" he whispered. Liebert told him to be still — he must not speak! Someone was following them. Someone wished to hurt them. Oliver saw, in a panic, the greenish copper steeple of an old church; he could take refuge in its ruins; no one would find them there. The main part of the building had been reduced to rubble. A wall remained, and on this wall were posters of the great president — charmingly candid shots that showed the man with one of his children, and in a peasant's costume, with a rifle raised to his shoulder and one eye squinted shut, and on the ledge above a waterfall, his arm raised in a salute to the crowd gathered below. Oliver hurried. Someone would stand guard for them — one of the men he had seen in the restaurant, had seen without really considering; a young black-haired man who had been playing chess with a friend, and who had not glanced up a single time at Oliver and his friends. But now he would stand guard. Now he was to be trusted.

They descended into a cellar. Everywhere there were slabs of stone, broken plasterboard, broken glass. Weeds grew abundantly in the cracks. "Hurry," Liebert urged, dragging him forward. Then Oliver was with her, clutching at her. By a miracle they were together. He kissed her desperately, recklessly. She pretended to resist. "No, there isn't time, there isn't enough time," he begged. "No, don't stop me . . ." She went limp; she put her arms around his neck; they struggled together, panting, while the young translator urged them on, anxious, a little annoyed. Oliver's entire body stung. Waves of heat swept over him and broke into tiny bits so that he groaned aloud. He wanted her so violently, he was so hungry for her, for her or for something . . . "How can I bring you with me?" he said. "I love you, I won't surrender you." She spoke in short, melodic phrases. He could not understand. Now she too was anxious, clutching at him, pressing herself against him. Oliver could not bear it. He was going mad. Then, out of the corner of his eye, he happened to see someone watching them. The police! But no, it was a poorly dressed old man, a cripple, peering at them from behind a broken wall. He was deformed; his legs were mere stumps. Oliver stared in a panic. He could not believe what he saw. Behind the old man were two or three others, half crawling, pushing themselves along through the debris by the exertions of their arms, their legs cut off at the thigh. They were bearded, wide-eyed, gaping, moronic. He understood that they were moronic. Oliver tried to lead Alisa away, but she resisted. Evidently the men were from a nearby hospital and were harmless. They had been arrested in an abortive uprising of some sort years before, and punished in ways fitting their audacity; but now they were harmless, harmless . . .

His sexual desire died at once. The dream died at once.

He could not sleep. The dream had left him terrified and nauseated.

During the past few years, life had thinned out for Oliver. It had become insubstantial, unreal, too spontaneous to have much value. Mere details, pieces, ugly tiny bits. Nothing was connected and nothing made sense. Was this life? — this idle, pointless flow? He had watched it, knowing that one must be attentive, one must be responsible. But he had not really believed in it. There was no internal necessity, no order, only that jarring spontaneity, a world of slivers and teasing fragments. Ugly and illusory.

Here, however, things seemed different. He could breathe here. There were travelers who could not accept the reality of the countries they visited and who yearned, homesick, for their own country, for their own language; but Oliver was not one of them. He would not have cared — not for a moment! — if the past were eradicated, his home country destroyed and erased from history.

He poured brandy into a glass, his fingers steady.

"Would I mourn? . . . Never."

The dream had frightened him but it was fading now. It was not important. He had had too much to eat, too much to drink. His emotional state was unnatural. Love was an imbalance: he was temporarily out of control. But he would be all right. He had faith in himself.

The woman lived in a one-room apartment, Liebert had informed him. She shared it with another teacher at the high school, a woman. Should Oliver wish to visit her there — how could it be arranged? She could not come to the hotel. That was out of the question. Liebert had muttered something about the possibility of the other woman's going to visit her family . . . though this would involve some expenses . . . she would need money. It would be awkward but it could be arranged. If so, then Alisa would be alone and Oliver would be welcome to visit her. There might be danger, still. Or was there no danger? Oliver really did not know.

"And what of her husband?" Oliver had asked hesitantly.

"Ah — there is no risk. The man is in a hospital at Kanleža, in the mountains . . . he is receiving treatment for emotional malad-justment . . . a very sad case. Very sad. It is tragic, but he is no risk; do not worry about him," Liebert said softly.

They looked at each other for a moment. Oliver warmed, red-dened. He did not know if he was terribly ashamed or simply excited.

"I love her," he whispered. "I can't help it."

Liebert might not have heard, he had spoken so softly. But he did not ask Oliver to repeat his words.

"How much money would the woman need?" Oliver asked help-lessly.

They had been here, in this room. The money had changed hands and Liebert had gone and Oliver had undressed at once, exhausted from the evening, from all the eating and drinking and talking. He had wanted only to sleep. His fate was decided: he would meet Alisa the following day, he would extend his visit for another week, perhaps, in order to see her every day. But now he must sleep, he was sick with exhaustion. And so he had slept. But dreams disturbed him; in them he was trying to speak, trying to make himself understood, while strangers mocked and jeered. The last dream, of Alisa and the deformed old men, was the most violent of all, a nightmare of the sort he had not had for years. When he woke he felt debased, poisoned. It was as if a poison of some sort had spread throughout his body.

He sat up, leafing through a guidebook in English, until dawn.

"But I don't understand. Where is Mr. Liebert?"

His new translator was a stout, perspiring man in his fifties, no more than five feet four inches tall. He wore a shiny black suit with a vest and oversized buttons of black plastic. Baldness had enlarged his round face. His eyebrows were snarled and craggy, his lips pale, rubbery. With a shrug of shoulders he dismissed Liebert. "Who knows? There was important business. Back home, called away. Not your concern."

He smiled. Oliver stared, thinking, he's a nightmare, he's from a nightmare. But the man was real, the bright chilly morning was real. Oliver's dismay and alarm were real. He tried to protest, saying that he had liked Liebert very much, the two of them had understood each other very well; but the new translator merely smiled stupidly, as before. "I am your escort now and your translator," he repeated.

Oliver made several telephone calls, but there was nothing to be done.

"I do not have the acquaintance of Mr. Liebert," he said as they walked out together. One eyelid descended in a wink. "But there is no lack of sympathy. It is all the same. A nice day, isn't it? That is acacia tree in blossom; is lovely, eh? Every spring."

The man's accent was guttural. Oliver could not believe his bad luck. He walked in a trance, thinking of Alisa, of Liebert — Liebert, who had been so charming, so quick. It did not seem possible that this had happened.

That day he saw the posters of his dream. He saw a tarnished coppery green steeple rising above a ruined church. He saw, in the distance, long, low, curiously narrow strips of cloud or mist rising from the sea, reaching into the lower part of the city. Beside him the squat, perspiring man chattered in babyish English, translated signs and menus, kept asking Oliver in his mechanical chirping voice, "It is nice, eh? Spring day. Good luck." From time to time he winked at Oliver as if there were a joke between them.

˙Oliver shuddered.

The city looked different. There was too much traffic — buses, motorbikes, vans of one kind or another — and from the newer section of the city, where a number of one-story factories had been built, there came invisible clouds of poison. The sky was mottled; though it was May 15, it was really quite cold.

"Where is Liebert?" Oliver asked, more than once. "He and I were friends . . . we understood each other . . ."

They went to a folk museum where they joined another small group. Oliver tried to concentrate. He smiled, he was courteous as always, he made every effort to be civil. But the banalities — the idiotic lies! His translator repeated what was said in a thick, dull voice, not passing judgment as Liebert would have done, slyly — and Oliver was forced to reply, to say something. He stammered, he heard his voice proclaiming the most asinine things — bald, blunt compliments, flattery. Seven or eight men in a group for an endless luncheon, exchanging banalities, hypocritical praise, chatter about the weather and the blossoming trees and the National Ballet. The food was too rich, and when Oliver's came to him it was already lukewarm. The butter was unsalted and tasteless. One of the men, a fat, pompous official, exactly like an official in a political cartoon, smoked a cigar and the smoke drifted into Oliver's face. He tried to bring up the subject of his first translator but was met with uncomprehending stares.

Afterward he was taken, for some reason, to the offices of the Ministry of Agriculture; he was introduced to the editor of a series of agricultural pamphlets; it was difficult for him to make sense of what was being said. Some of these people spoke English as well as his translator did, and he had the idea that others merely pretended not to know English. There was a great deal of chatter. He thought of Alisa and felt suddenly exhausted. He would never get to her now — it was impossible. Beside him, the fat sweating man kept close watch. What was being said? — words. He leaned against a gritty windowsill, staring absently out at the innumerable rooftops, the ugly chimneys and water tanks, the banal towers. He remembered the poison of his dream and could taste it in the air now; the air of this city was remarkably polluted.

"You are tired now? Too much visit? You rest, eh?"

"Yes."

"You leave soon, it was said? Day after tomorrow?"

"Yes. I think so."

There were streetcars, and factory whistles. Automobile horns. In the street someone stared rudely at him. Oliver wondered what these people saw — a tall, sandy-haired man in his early forties, distracted, haggard, rather vain in his expensive clothes? They looked at his clothes, not at him. At his shoes. They did not see him at all; they had no use for him.

"You are maybe sick? . . ."

"A little. I think. Yes."

"Ah!" he said, in a parody of sympathy. "You go to room, rest.

Afterward perk up. Afterward there is plan for evening — yes?
All set?"

"Evening? I thought this evening was free."

The man winked. "She is friend — old friend. Sympathizes
you."

"I don't understand," Oliver stammered.

"All understand. All sympathize one another," the man said
cheerfully.

"Is wealthy? Own several automobiles? What about house —
houses? Parents are living? How many brothers and sisters? Is
married, has children? How many? Names?"

The three of them sat together, not in Alisa's room but in another café. Oliver was paying for their drinks. He was paying for
everything. The woman's curt, rude questions were being put to
him in clusters and he managed to answer, as succinctly as possible,
trying not to show his despair. When his translator repeated
Oliver's answers, Alisa nodded emphatically, always the same way,
her eyes bright, deliberately widened. Wisps of hair had come loose
about her forehead; it annoyed Oliver that she did not brush them
away. She was a little drunk, her laughter was jarring, she showed
her gums when she laughed — he could hardly bear to watch
her.

"Say like our country very much? Good. New place going up —
there is new company, Volkswagen — many new jobs. When you
come back, another year, lots new things. You are friendly, always
welcome. Very nice. Good to know . . ."

The conversation seemed to rattle on without Oliver's interven-
tion. He heard his voice, heard certain simpleminded replies. Alisa
and the fat man laughed merrily. They were having a fine time.
Oliver drank because he had nothing else to do; whenever he
glanced at his watch, the other looked at it also, with childish, open
avarice. Time did not pass. He dreaded any mention of the room,
of the alleged roommate who had left town, but he had the idea
that if he refused to mention it, the others would not mention it
either. They were having too good a time, drinking. They murmured to each other in their own language and broke into peals of
laughter, and other patrons, taking notice, grinned as if sharing
their good spirits.

"Is nice place? All along here, this street. Yes? Close to hotel. All close. She says: Is wife of yours pretty? Young? Is not jealous, you on long trip, take airplane? Any picture of wife? Babies?"

"No wife," Oliver said wearily. "No babies."

"No —? Is not married?"

"Is not," Oliver said.

"Not *love?* Not once?"

"Not," he said.

The two of them exchanged incredulous looks. Then they laughed again and Oliver sat silent, while their laughter washed about him.

Being driven to the airport he saw, on the street, a dark-haired cyclist pedaling energetically — a young long-nosed handsome boy in a pullover sweater — Liebert — his heart sang: *Liebert.* But of course it was not Liebert. It was a stranger, a boy of about seventeen, no one Oliver knew. Then again at the airport he saw him. Again it was Liebert. A mechanic in coveralls, glimpsed in a doorway, solemn, dark-eyed, with a pronounced widow's peak and prominent cheekbones: Liebert. He wanted to push his way through the crowd to him. To his translator. He wanted to touch him again, wanted to squeeze his hands, his arm. But of course the young man was a stranger — his gaze was dull, his mouth slack. Oliver stared at him just the same. The plane was loading, it was time for him to leave, yet he stood there, paralyzed.

"What will I do for the rest of my life?" he called to the boy.

ELIZABETH CULLINAN

A Good Loser

(FROM THE NEW YORKER)

WHEN I was twenty-six I went to Ireland and lived there for two years. I did this on the strength of a day and a half I'd once spent driving from Cork to Dublin on a three-week vacation in Europe. I was taken with the plain-looking Irish villages, the simple cities, with the modest beauty of the people and the extravagant beauty of the countryside. At home in New York, where I worked for an advertising agency, I began saving money and when I had enough I went back to study at the College of Art in Dublin. Afterwards the time I spent there struck me as the most interesting thing I had to say about myself, and I was always bringing it into the conversation, with the result that eventually I came to disbelieve in those years. I also became reluctant to go back. From year to year I'd decide I couldn't afford the time or the money to go over for a visit, and the years added up to ten when last summer I was offered the use of a house in Booterstown. A friend of a friend was coming to New York for the month of July. Her name was Hope Hazlitt, and she was a transplanted American such as I'd been, though unlike me she'd taken root. She had some sort of job and she had this house, which she rented furnished and didn't want to leave empty. Hope Hazlitt was also rich, a purebred Presbyterian from Seattle, divorced and with a young son, who was to be enrolled in an American summer camp. I had my doubts about returning under these conspicuously alien auspices, but still, a whole house for a month, rent-free — it seemed too good to pass up. I consulted the map of Dublin that hangs on the wall behind my sofa and located Booterstown on the south side of the city, roughly between Ballsbridge and Blackrock, which meant that it was at least a suburb, not some godforsaken spot, and so I took the plunge.

In a recurrent dream I used to have, pure, classical Dublin had been reconstructed along lines that my sleeping mind must have lifted from forgotten pictures of Mussolini's Italy. All the streets were the width of the New England Thruway, all the buildings were massive blocks of stone, in all the statues the men were muscle-bound. Dreams have a way of affecting conscious life, and gradually this one took on an authority that I felt less and less able to question, and so I was in a state of joyful relief that day last summer as I rode in from the airport and discovered, street by street, that there were really no changes to speak of. I'd arranged to spend my first night at Buswell's, an inexpensive hotel in the center of town. My room was on the Kildare Street side, and the maid had opened the window to let the place air. I went and looked out. There were gulls roosting on top of the National Museum across the street — I'd forgotten the Dublin gulls. I'd forgotten just how low the Dublin roofscape is, and how low-key the sounds of a business day are in that capital city — how non-chalantly people there go about their business. As I took all this in, the gray city that I'd been carrying around in my head faded into thin air. The real city, incomparably gay and unfathomably care-less, was mine once again. I was starting to unpack when the phone rang. It was Hope Hazlitt. She said, "Can you come on out and see the house?" For "on" she said "an," and I was impressed — she still had her American accent, whereas half an hour in Dublin and I was already rushing my words in the Irish way.

I said, "I'm free anytime."

"How about now?" she suggested firmly. "We're leaving first thing in the morning, and I'd like to get things settled."

I said, "Give me an hour or so."

"We'll say half past one." It was then about noon. "You can take the 6, the 7, the 7A, the 8, or the 45 bus. When you get to Booterstown, look on the right-hand side for a big pub called The Punch Bowl. That's the corner of Booterstown Avenue, where you get off. Castle Court is just off Booterstown Avenue."

I'd waited ten years to come back to Dublin and I wasn't going to wait another couple of hours to touch home base. I dashed over to Grafton Street and wandered up and down there in an ecstasy of recognition. I bought an Irish *Times,* I stopped and had bacon and egg at Bewley's; then I walked down to College Green and caught a No. 6 bus. As I swung on board I had a powerful sense of going away from where I wanted to be, but I was happy, too, riding past the noble Georgian squares, then on into Ballsbridge, where the dark-red brick houses look like small orphanages or reformatories. Ballsbridge is a rich neighborhood; soon it gave way to lesser suburbs. Dublin Bay came into view on the left. Merrion Road expanded to four lanes and became Rock Road. I was unfamiliar with this stretch, and I became distracted and missed the big pub Hope Hazlitt had told me to look out for. By the time I realized my mistake and got off, I was close to Blackrock and I had a long walk back and then another long walk the length of Booterstown Avenue, in both directions, for there was no street marked Castle Court. Not that I minded this walk. Booterstown was everything I could have asked for — a small place, hardly more than one long street lined with gray stone bungalows set close to the curb behind strips of garden where the occasional stunted palm or monkey-puzzle tree grew among purple and pink snapdragons.

Back on Rock Road, I went into The Punch Bowl and asked the barman where Castle Court was. "That's the place off Beech Road," he said, smoothing his hair with one hand and then with the other. "Take the first turn to your right off Booterstown Avenue." He gave me these directions with a look of distrust, which I understood after I'd followed them. Castle Court was a development, a group of twelve identical, brand-new two-story whitewashed brick houses that belonged in suburban Long Island or New Jersey. I was bitterly disappointed, half an hour late, angry at having been misdirected, and ready to make light of all this as I rang Hope Hazlitt's doorbell, but Hope wasn't in a light mood. "You're late," she said as she opened the door.

I said, "I got lost. Castle Court isn't marked."

She said, "Yes, it is."

"Not on Booterstown Avenue," I said.

She said, "Come an in." As I stepped inside, two things hit me simultaneously: The house was grotesque, and I was stuck there. "I haven't finished cleaning up yet," said Hope.

"You don't have to bother," I assured her. What I felt was something like "Why waste energy cleaning a place as ugly as this?" But if Hope Hazlitt read my mind or if she noticed the dismay behind my politeness she didn't let on.

"Shall we have a look around?" she said.

What impressed me most about that house was the carpeting, which was mercilessly wall-to-wall — the front hall, the living room, the staircase, the upstairs hall, and the dining room were all covered in sleazy red nylon pile with a design that looked like a lot of fat gold snakes. Then there was the living-room furniture: two chairs, sofa, and hassock upholstered in light-tan imitation leather. In the dining room, a spindly drop-leaf table was opened out and surrounded by six heavy chairs of vaguely ecclesiastical and definitely secondhand appearance. There was also an upright piano. A wrought-iron chandelier hung from the low ceiling, and there were French windows facing a walled square of lawn. The kitchen was presentable, but as we stepped onto the orange plaid linoleum I was filled with homesickness for the bed-sitter in Fitzwilliam Square where I'd lived ten years before. The kitchen there had been a sort of shed built into a corner, though in no way detracting from that beautiful room with its ornate marble fireplace, one tall window, and high carved and gilded ceiling.

"How did you happen to choose this place?" I asked Hope Hazlitt.

She said, "It was exactly midway between Bobby's school and my job in town. Come an upstairs."

On the second floor there were four small bedrooms and a pale-yellow bath. Hope opened the first door on the left and said, "This is Bobby's room." The walls were covered with pictures of English pop singers and American baseball players. She said, "I'm not going to bother doing any cleaning in here. I figured it wouldn't appeal to you." She was absolutely right. We crossed the hall to a much smaller room — suitable, I thought, for the maid. Hope said, "I thought this would suit you."

I said, "What about the others?"

She said, "I use the little room next door as a kind of study." It contained a desk, a file cabinet, and a couple of folding chairs. "Then there's my room." She was ready to pass it by, but I stopped, and so she opened the door. "I won't be cleaning this up, either, so don't bother coming in here. Just leave everything the way it is." This was spoken peremptorily, as much as to say "Keep out." And so after I moved in I made a point, every couple of days, of going in and walking around Hope Hazlitt's bedroom. It was a real boudoir and, true to her word, she hadn't done a thing in the way of tidying up there. Clothes were piled on the red velvet boudoir chair. Shoes stuck out from under the bed, which, beneath a pink satin comforter, was obviously unmade. A hair dryer trailed its cord from the open drawer of an antiqued white night table, and the table itself was covered with curlers. The wastebasket was overflowing.

I was amused by all this. Or rather, it amused me to turn the emotional cartwheel it took to go from Hope Hazlitt's vulgar boudoir in that ghastly house in Castle Court out into the sober charm of Booterstown with its gray stone cottages, its vivid gardens. Being a seaside suburb, the place had a holiday air. There was no beach, but people would climb the steps at one end of the seawall to sit on the rocks and sun themselves or go swimming in the shallow water. That was an exceptional July — at least, it would have been exceptional anywhere else. For Ireland it was miraculous. Day after day, the sky was blue, the sun was strong, and there was a wonderful breeze. The pleasure I took in all this, the bliss I felt at being back in Ireland, soon permeated the house in Castle Court. After a couple of days I was quite content there.

When I lived in Dublin before, I made no friends at the College of Art — that is, not among the girls. Love can develop under almost any conditions, but friendship, in its beginnings, requires the right medium, and for me the College of Art was all wrong. I wasn't a full-time student, which set me apart to begin with, and my nationality finished the job. I used to feel that the girls in my classes had an image of me that corresponded to what an old woman I'd met in Mayo must have had in mind when she addressed me as "Yank."

If the boys at the College of Art thought me Yankish, it didn't seem to matter, and I didn't lack boyfriends in Ireland. Dublin social life was democratic and it flourished after hours. When the pubs closed, word would go out that someone's flat was available, and at the subsequent "party" you'd come across anyone from members of the Dail to fiddlers up from the country for the day. But the nicest Irishman I met came my way by a roundabout route. One day toward the end of my second year, a letter arrived from someone named Stephen Cronin, who said he was just back from New York, where a girl we both knew had told him to look me up. I didn't particularly like the girl and so I ignored the letter. Two weeks later my doorbell rang; when I answered it, a tall, very thin young man with curly gray hair introduced himself and said, "You didn't answer my note, so I thought I'd come round."

Stephen worked in the publicity office of Aer Lingus. He was appalled at how little I knew of Irish life, apart from the pubs and parties and the College of Art, and he set out to correct the situation; in his little white sports car, we went flying in every direction along the empty Irish roads. He was an ideal guide — well informed, funny, tireless, and above all cultured. He had a passion for Georgian furniture and silver, old Waterford glass, English pictures, Indian carpets, all of which he collected and stored in the basement of his parents' house in Dalkey. I began to envision life among these things, and the vision appealed to me. I'd been in love a lot and always found it harrowing; I was ready for something more civilized. Then one evening Stephen came by in a terrible state. "Forgive me, Ann," he said, "but I must talk to someone."

It's doubly flattering to be chosen as a confidante; you feel both important and on the verge of becoming more so. I said, "Come on in. I'll make some tea."

Laughing with embarrassment, groaning with real misery, he sat down and launched into a story that floored me. "I've been in love with someone for three years — a Spanish girl who worked in the Embassy here. I was never so involved with anyone, but she was very neurotic and used to throw terrible scenes."

I wasn't in love with Stephen but I hadn't ruled out this possibility, and as I listened to him what was uppermost in my mind was covering myself. "What sort of scenes would she make?" I asked.

"She'd quite literally beat her head against the wall."

"What would you do then?"

"Simply walk out."

"What would set her off in the first place?"

"It was mostly that she wanted to live with me and try it out, but I wanted to get married. Otherwise I knew I'd be left high and dry."

"What finally happened?"

"She transferred to London. Now she's come back and says she wants to marry me."

I said, "Do you still want to marry her?"

He didn't. The Spanish girl went home to Barcelona, and Stephen and I continued to go out, but things weren't the same. The illusion was gone, and we spent most of our time together analyzing his previous love affairs: the Norwegian, the Belgian, the Venezuelan, the Israeli — they were all more or less the same type, a little disturbed and very determined. When I came back to New York, we exchanged a few letters, and occasionally he flew over on Aer Lingus business; I'd wonder then whether something mightn't yet develop between us but I felt that in the light of the Spanish girl I struck him as a bit tame — that was how I struck myself, compared to her — and so I held back. When one Christmas he wrote that he was getting married (surprisingly — for him — to a girl with an Irish surname), I was relieved, though I got the impression that he felt guilty with respect to me. He seemed bent on establishing the image of us as having a unique kind of friendship and after the marriage he kept me posted on his affairs. They bought a house in Monkstown. He wrote, "I hope you'll come over and stay with us. There's plenty of room." Soon there was a baby. "You wouldn't believe what a frightful business it is," he wrote. And then, "Stephen George has a sister, Bianca." In the end I did feel some sort of connection with this unknown family; when I agreed to take Hope Hazlitt's house I wrote and told Stephen, and after I was installed in Castle Court he was the first person I called.

"Ann," he said, "I was delighted to get your letter. When will you come to supper?"

I said, "When would you like?"

There was a high-pitched scream at his end. "No, no, Bianca," he said off to one side, and then to me, "Hang on, will you? Let me talk to Suzanne."

With the toe of my shoe I traced one of the gold snakes on the Castle Court carpet, imagining the sort of carpet where Stephen would be standing and the sort of room — a perfect sort of room.

He came back on the line and said, "How would Wednesday suit you?"

I said, "Wednesday's fine."

"I'll pick you up. Will we say half six?"

"Fine," I said. "Wait'll you see this house."

When he did, he frowned and smiled and shook his head, like someone bearing up well under bad news. I said, "Isn't it awful?"

"It's pretty bad," he said. "All the same, I expect you're comfortable."

I said, "In a horrible sort of way I am."

He looked at his watch. "Can I tear you away?" He no longer had a sports car — he drove a small station wagon now. The weight of family life had fallen on him, and he bore it with a touching mixture of gravity and lightheartedness. "Suzanne is looking forward to meeting you," he said as he turned carefully into the traffic on Rock Road.

I said, "I'm looking forward to meeting her." It would have been truer to say I was curious. I wondered how he'd made out — whether his story had a happy ending or one that was merely acceptable. "I was surprised that you married an Irish girl."

"Suzanne's not typical," he said. "She has a mind of her own."

In my experience, Irish girls always had minds of their own — quick, canny, sometimes generous, usually critical minds. I'd never been particularly comfortable with those girls and I felt in no great hurry to meet another, but Monkstown was practically on top of Booterstown, and it took about three minutes to get to Stephen's house. As we drove up, the front door opened, and two women and four children came out onto the doorstep. One woman was rather matronly. The other was a short, thin girl with the blue eyes, rosy cheeks, and curly black hair that are traditionally called Irish beauty. She proved to be Stephen's wife, which meant that the little girl who looked just like her was Stephen's daughter; the little boy with the long blond bob turned out to be Stephen's son. The two other children were strikingly overweight, and when they and the matronly woman had gone and we'd stepped inside, I for some reason — as a rule I'm not outspoken — brought this up. "I'm glad Stephen George and Bianca are who they are," I said. "Those other children were awfully —"

"Fat!" said Suzanne. "That's all I can think of when they're around. I never get used to it."

"It's my one prejudice, fatness," said Stephen. "I loathe it."

The ice was broken. We were of one mind and off to a good start. Suzanne said, "I've got a couple of things still to do for our supper, Ann. Would you like to help Stephen get the kids ready for bed?"

Stephen George was four and a half, Bianca just three. They were beautiful and full of energy and they took complete advantage of their father as he struggled to get them undressed. "You

see what it's like," he said to me, helpless with love and exasperation.

Finally Suzanne came upstairs. "Are you being very bold?" she
asked the children. This set off a fresh struggle, but it was the last.
Stephen George and Bianca were exhausted. The covers were
drawn up over their beds, the light was put out, and we left the
room. Suzanne said, "Come see the house, Ann."

I have an impression of that house now rather than a clear image
of any part of it. I remember rooms painted wonderful colors —
rose red, deep Wedgwood, bright yellow. I see marvellous chests
and chairs, the fruits of Stephen's long, profitable bachelorhood
— his carpets, his interesting objects, his pictures. One thing stands
out in my mind, a series of paintings of some big, serious, creamy-
looking sheep shown close up in a dark meadow. They're as clear
to me now as if I'd lifted my eyes to them again and again, but in
fact I got only a glimpse of those creamy sheep, for they hung in
the dining room, and we didn't eat there. A small table had been
set up in the drawing room, and this was where we spent the
evening, though I can't describe the drawing room, either — probably because I was distracted. We had a good time; we three hit it
off. In the middle of dinner, Suzanne put down her fork and said,
"I can't believe how different you are from what I expected."

I said, "What did you expect?"

"Someone sort of pale and serious." Stephen blushed and pro-
tested. She said to him, "I suppose you were trying to make me
jealous — jealous and not jealous. Tearing poor Ann down but
letting me know she was in the picture."

I said, "Shame on you, Stephen," but I didn't really mind. That
I'd made a contribution to this happy household seemed to entitle
me to share the happiness, which is something I don't often feel.
I'm not someone who's comfortable as a third, or a fifth, or a
fifteenth. I believe people are meant to pair off and I accept the
corollary to this: that people who don't pair off, for whatever
reason — bad judgment, or bad luck, or some quirkiness of mind
or heart — must suffer the consequences. But there was nothing
to suffer that night at the Cronins'.

Suzanne said, "Anyway, I'm glad you're not pale and serious."

"But I am," I said. "Serious, anyway."

Stephen said, "The trouble with most people is they're not serious enough."

"Or personal enough, I think," said Suzanne.

I said, "It's a question of technique, isn't it? Knowing when to be one thing or the other and how much."

"One's constantly readjusting," said Suzanne. "God, I hate it! Have some more lasagna, Ann." I passed my plate; she gave me a second helping and said, "Why haven't you got married?"

Stephen laughed in embarrassment, but I wasn't embarrassed. I said, "That's a good question."

"A good question that I suppose doesn't have an answer," said Suzanne.

She needn't have let me off the hook; I had an answer. "Somebody once said to me that when a man isn't married you can't help wondering why, but with a woman it just means she didn't like the people who asked her, and the people she'd have liked didn't ask."

Stephen said, "Do you think that's true today?"

I said, "I think it'll always be true, more or less."

"I wonder," said Suzanne. "We have a friend who's a doctor and has two children, and she positively refuses to marry their father. She says she has quite enough to handle."

"Well," I said, "it's true of me."

"Still and all," said Suzanne, "you should be married."

Stephen said, "You really should, Ann."

"I know. It's odd," I said, "not being. Sometimes it feels a bit like never having been a child."

Suzanne nodded vigorously. "There's that whole area missing."

I said, "I seem to attract the wrong sort of men."

"What sort?" she asked.

"Oh," I said, "people who for some reason think I'm going to give them a bad time. And then I don't."

She shook her head from side to side, slowly, several times. "I know, I know," she said. "I was the same. By the time I met Stephen I was so fed up that I said I'd only just try the marriage and only for three months."

"So you see how lucky I am," said Stephen.

I saw this and something else: To the extent that his happiness was hard-won it was still threatened. Happiness is at best a day-to-day affair, but this was a lucky day, and the luck had something to do with my not being pale and serious. I felt like a piece of missing evidence — the proof that Stephen had had a real choice, which, in turn, enhanced the choice he'd made. I think this was why the three of us got on so well — we had a common interest.

"Look," Suzanne said, "are you doing anything this Saturday?"

I said, "I'm not sure."

"A friend of ours, a cellist, is giving a recital. If you're free, why don't you come along?"

"To be perfectly honest," I said, "things like that — quartets and things — put me to sleep." I wasn't being honest at all. I was hedging, reluctant to wear out my welcome, but the welcome was real and not to be backed away from.

Suzanne said, "What about Sunday? We could do something in the afternoon. Were you ever to the Botanic Gardens?"

Stephen said, "I think I took you there, Ann — just before you left."

I said, "That was the zoo."

"The zoo! What was I thinking of?" He'd been thinking of the Spanish girl. He was probably thinking of her again. I know I was — of her and of the evenings in my flat spent talking out his past and talking away the then present. I really didn't regret any of this but I recognized that possibly the time could have been better spent.

"Anyway, it was a very nice zoo," I said.

"And it's a very nice Botanic Gardens," said Suzanne. "Come for Sunday lunch; then we'll all go off. It's a while since we took the kids to the Gardens."

The kitchen in the Cronins' house was small and it had an old-fashioned look. Doing the dishes there was as pleasant as dinner in the drawing room had been, and when the dishes were finished there was pleasantness left over. "Shall we go for a walk?" Stephen suggested.

Suzanne said, "We could take the dogs over to the strand and give them a run."

I said, "What dogs?"

"Dora and Margo," she said. "They live in the garden."

I said, "Is it all right to leave the children?"

"Oh sure," she said. "We'll only be a minute."

Stephen let himself out the kitchen door and met us in front with a sheepdog and an Airedale. Monkstown strand was only a couple of blocks away, but we drove there with the dogs panting and whining and trying to pace in the back of the station wagon.

When they were let loose they began racing up and down the promenade, but Dora, the sheepdog, soon got tired and settled down to a melancholy trot alongside us. Stephen patted her and said, "Poor Dora — she's too old to keep up with Margo, and it drives her mad."

I was struck by that remark. It seemed to me to contain a world of sympathy and understanding — that is to say, sympathy and understanding beyond the requirements of family life — which was the great thing about the Cronins. They weren't as closed off in their intimacy as married couples usually seem to me to be.

On Friday I went down to the country to visit friends who have a farm in Monaghan. I've always lived in the city — I'm happy and at home there — but at that farm I'm happier and more at home than I've ever been anyplace else. You can practically taste the air there; you can hear the stillness. I was supposed to stay one night but I stayed two. Sunday morning I took the bus back to Dublin, stopped in at Castle Court to change my clothes, heard Mass at the big, homely Booterstown church, and then went straight to the Cronins'. This quick succession of drastically different perspectives left me keyed up — in contrast to Stephen, who looked a bit played out when he answered the door. "The children have been outrageous," he said. "It took us half an hour, but we finally got them down for their naps."

I said, "I thought things seemed awfully calm." Things, in fact, seemed not so much calm as cool. Inside, in the hall, I felt as if I were receiving the house's equivalent of a blank look but I told myself it was my imagination. When we walked into the kitchen, I changed my mind again and decided I'd been right the first time.

Suzanne said, "Forgive us if we're a bit droopy, Ann. We were at the most dreadful party last night. It went on and on and got more and more boring. Both of us drank too much and slept badly."

States of grace or of mere congeniality don't often survive a change of scene or additions to the cast of characters. The events of a couple of days had been bound to bury our pleasant evening, and I blamed myself for not bearing this in mind. "Then today you had to have me," I said.

"Not at all," said Stephen. "We were looking forward to it."

Suzanne said, "Yes. You can put it all out of our minds."

The third person is often called on to provide distraction, to smooth over rough places or otherwise ease family pressures. I set about this task willingly and with a confidence based on long experience and the proven compatibility of the Cronins and myself. "I have a foolproof routine for parties," I said. "You stay in one place and talk to anyone who happens to come up to you, no matter who. You'd be surprised at all the people you meet that way."

Suzanne said, "That'd be the trouble."

"It beats dodging around, picking and choosing," I said.

"I suppose you don't feel so morally empty afterward," said Stephen. He had a nice way of sharpening your point without turning it against you.

I said, "Exactly."

Suzanne said, "Stephen, will you open the wine?" She went to the refrigerator and took out a salmon salad, molded in the shape of a fish and decorated with sliced olives and strips of pimento; it seemed the only thing we could have eaten in that pretty kitchen. "That's your place, Ann." She indicated the middle chair.

I sat down and rested my elbows on the inlaid beechwood table. "You can't imagine how good it feels to be in a house like this," I said. "After Castle Court."

"What exactly's wrong with the place?" asked Suzanne.

"For one thing, it's too done up." I helped myself to the salad and passed the plate to Stephen.

He smiled and said, "Ann had a great liking for dilapidation."

"I wasn't happy unless the stuffing was coming out of the furniture."

"Well, we all get a bit sentimental that way, don't we?" said Suzanne.

I'd always admired Irish hardheadedness, the national determination to call a heart a bleeding heart even, or maybe especially, when the heart was my own. I said, "I suppose that's what it amounts to."

"The next time you come to Ireland you must stay with us," Stephen said.

At the moment I was glad I hadn't taken him up on that old invitation. It's the hostess who ends up with the guest on her hands, and I'd begun to suspect that Suzanne Cronin and I might have also ended up getting on each other's nerves. I said, "I'm not a very good guest, even with people I'm close to."

Suzanne said, "I don't believe that." She spoke not deprecatingly but in a positive way, as if I'd exaggerated. It occurred to me then that there was something more than tiredness in the air. I wondered if the Cronins had quarrelled, and in the interest of winning myself immunity, even at the cost of my pride, I offered a dreary bit of autobiography. "We lived with my grandmother when I was a child. We couldn't ever have company of our own, and I never really got over it. I'm still self-conscious in other people's houses."

"Families," said Stephen. "My grandfather lived with us when I was a kid. He used to take snuff, and I was so ashamed that I'd tell the other kids it was medicine."

"My grandparents died before I was born," said Suzanne. "I was always jealous of people who had them. Have some bread, Ann." She passed me the board; I cut myself a slice and passed it to Stephen.

"Do you find Dublin much changed?" he asked.

This was a subject I could throw myself into, having thought of little else for days. Watching the bathers at Booterstown, gazing up at my old house in Fitzwilliam Square, mingling with the lunchtime crowd in Stephen's Green, wandering among the shoppers at Brown Thomas, standing on O'Connell Bridge, walking the quays, I'd turned the past and the present over and over in my mind and come to a rather complicated and idiosyncratic conclusion which I was very pleased with and more than happy to air: "Different but not really changed."

"Explain yourself," said Stephen. He loved this kind of talk.

I said, "I get a real sense of how things have kept on going. I mean ordinary things — people having birthdays and getting sick and getting better, or getting mad at each other and making up or holding a grudge; and the whole time everyone running into everyone else on Grafton Street or in the Green. Somehow it all adds up to something that looks practically the same and feels totally different."

"But not changed," said Stephen. He looked puzzled but interested. Suzanne looked bored.

I said, "Maybe it's me. In a lot of ways I've been standing still."

Stephen said, "Some people should. Some people are right the way they are."

I saw then what was wrong. After I'd left the other night, they'd talked about me. Suzanne had said, "Ann's really awfully nice," and Stephen had gone on from there, for that was the trouble with him — he was injudicious. He always had been. He was open and enthusiastic and truthful and he didn't know when to keep quiet. He'd gone on about the Spanish girl with me and he'd undoubtedly gone on about me with his wife. Suzanne would have said, "Why didn't it come off between you two?"

And instead of "We weren't in love," he'd probably answered, "I don't know," or words to that unnecessarily honest and ambiguous effect.

Suzanne got up and put the salad plate on the counter, replacing it with a bowl of fruit. "We stayed up talking about you the other night," she said as she sat down again. "Stephen is awfully fond of you, Ann."

It made me sad and it made me furious. I said, "The truth is, I was always too odd for Stephen's taste."

"But that's what we like about people, isn't it?" she said. "The thing that makes them different is the thing that attracts us."

"I was a little too different." I turned to Stephen for corroboration of what he must have at some point acknowledged to himself.

He said, "I think of you whenever I go down Fitzwilliam."

Into this conversational dead end walked Bianca, crying to herself and rubbing her eyes. Behind her came Stephen George, who looked at the remains of the salad and said, "I want some lunch."

Stephen said, "I think we'll ignore that."

"I want lunch!" said Bianca.

"We're all finished," their mother said. "Besides, you had yours before, you and Stephen George. You had your lovely eggs. Remember?"

Stephen George said, "I don't remember." Bianca began to scream.

I took a pear from the bowl, pushed my chair away from the table, and said to the children, "Take me outside and show me the garden."

Of all the good things about that house, the garden was possibly the best. It was a long stretch of level ground surrounded by a high hedge, with borders of flowers on the two sides and a vegetable garden at the back. There were trees — an apple, a handsome chestnut, a laburnum, and a young elm with a swing attached to one of the branches. Two wooden deck chairs were set up near the house; when my eyes adjusted to the sunlight I noticed croquet wickets sticking up in the grass. The dogs ran up and jumped all over us and then ran off again. Stephen George said to me, "Do you want to see the game?"

I thought he probably wanted to play croquet and I said, "Sure."

He led me to the back of the garden, where a short, sturdy flight of wooden stairs stood against the hedge; we climbed the stairs to what was a small private grandstand looking out on a playing field. A cricket match was in progress. Stephen George and I watched for a minute or two; then he said, "Would you like to swing?"

I translated this as "I'd like to swing," and said, "Sure." But Bianca had got there first. I said, "How about a push, Bianca?" She stood up and sat down again, but the swing was slightly off balance, and my first hesitant push made it zigzag; Bianca began to scream. I steadied the swing, and she jumped off and ran into the house.

"Now it's my turn," Stephen George said with innocent satisfaction.

I'd sent him up half a dozen times when his father came out into the garden and strolled over to us. Stephen looked preoccupied and a little sheepish, and so the change of plan he proposed came as no surprise, though I was irritated by the way he put it: "Do you feel like going to the Botanic Gardens?" It was as if it were a brainstorm he'd just had, and from this I gathered that the plan had already been rejected. I felt a little left out, a little in the way, and no less so for the recognition that the feeling was unreasonable, since I no longer had any desire to go to the Botanic Gardens.

"Why don't we skip it?" I said.

"It's difficult with the children," he explained. "When they start acting up, there's not much you can do."

I said, "Don't be silly. They're fine children."

"We might sit out here and relax," he suggested.

"That's just what I feel like doing." Sunbathing is conducive to silence, and I was tired of making conversation, tired of being taken the wrong way.

Suzanne came out in a bikini. "Would you like to borrow one?" she asked. I declined, feeling overly fastidious, which I probably am. Stephen brought out another deck chair and set it up; then he inflated and filled a plastic wading pool for the children, who took off their clothes and began to dash in and out of the water. "Watch me!" they cried as they bellyflopped or lay on their stomachs splashing each other. The dogs retreated to the far end of the

garden and lay down under the trees, though every so often
Margo, the Airedale, would get up and make a frantic circuit of
the yard, while poor Dora looked on, her rheumy old eyes full of
despair. In this desultory but slightly hectic fashion, an hour
passed, then another hour. Finally the sun went behind the trees,
and I sat forward.

"I'd better be going," I said.

Suzanne said, "Won't you stay for tea?"

The offer was a formality, a way of keeping up the appearance
of friendship, when in fact we'd had more than enough of each
other's company. For the same reason and also for the sake of my
self-respect, I made an offer of my own. "Why don't you come
back and have tea with me? You could see the famous house." This
plan offered activity, distraction, and a change of scene, which
made it seem, at that point, like a good idea, or at least the better
one. The children were dressed, Suzanne changed into a skirt and
blouse, Stephen put on a sweater, and we climbed into the car and
drove to Castle Court. In the strong late-afternoon light the twelve
white houses stood out like twelve sore thumbs.

"My God!" said Suzanne.

"The last one on the right," I reminded Stephen. He circled the
development and came to a stop at the end house.

Suzanne said, "It's all very mock Georgian."

"More like mock Levittown," I said. Stephen, knowing something of America, laughed.

"Well, anyway, it's very mock," said Suzanne.

She began to rub me the wrong way. It wasn't as if I were to
blame for the flareup of Stephen's interest in me. It wasn't even as
if that interest meant anything — it was a simple reflex, as incon-
sequential as the blink of an eye. Still, I could see her side of it —
balance is crucial to marriage, and if I'd tipped the balance then I
had to go. It was cut and dried and had nothing to do with me
personally. The recognition of this revived something in me — my
sense of proportion, my sense of humor. I said, "Ta-da!" and
opened the front door and let them in.

Suzanne turned in a circle, took everything in, and said, "How
hideous!" In her, too, something had suddenly revived — the authority that was hers by virtue of the beautiful house in Monkstown. She led the way into the Castle Court living room, turned
another circle, and said, "It's perfectly hideous." The children,

running from room to room, found the piano and began to bang on the keyboard; the noise drew us to the dining room. Suzanne looked out the French windows at the neat patch of grass and shook her head in disbelief. "You'd think there'd at least be a few marigolds."

I said, "You would, wouldn't you?"

She shuddered. "I couldn't live in a place like this."

I said, "I think of it as just a place I'm staying."

She said, "I couldn't *stay* in a place like this. I'd be too depressed."

I said, "I can't afford to get depressed. I'm stuck here."

"I'd get out of it somehow," she insisted. "I'd go to a hotel."

"I can't afford that, either." My sense of humor began to give way again. I said, "You don't want to go upstairs, do you?"

"Let's," she said.

And so I led them up to the second floor and showed them my little cell, Bobby's bedroom, the pale-yellow bath, Hope Hazlitt's study. The boudoir door was closed. "What's in there?" asked Suzanne.

I said, "The master bedroom." She opened the door and gave a little gasp.

"More of a mistress's bedroom," said Stephen.

Suzanne said, "It's positively decadent."

"It is, isn't it?" I said.

Stephen stepped over the threshold and surveyed the room, mentally taking its measure. "It's a good size," he concluded and stepped back out into the hall.

"Yes," said Suzanne. "Why aren't you using this one?"

I said, "I was told not to." I closed the door on the pink satin comforter, the unmade bed, the boudoir chair, the dirty clothes, the curlers. "What about tea?" I asked them.

Suzanne said, "Thank you, Ann, but I think we'll move along — though I'd love a glass of water."

We went back downstairs to the kitchen, where Stephen George and Bianca had got hold of a bag of mints I'd left on the table. "Please put those back," said their father.

"Can't they have one?" I asked.

Suzanne and Stephen exchanged a look that was both discreet and thoroughly intimate — the house had done the trick. They'd begun to remember what they meant to each other and what they'd done for each other — she, thanks to him, and he, thanks to her, would in all probability never be faced with so desolate a prospect as that house in Castle Court. "Maybe just one mint apiece," Stephen said. Stephen George took a mint for himself and one for his sister, unwrapped them, and threw the papers on the floor.

"Pick up the sweet papers," Stephen said. Bianca dropped her mint and began to cry. "May she have another, Ann?" asked Stephen.

I said, "Sure."

Bianca grabbed the bag and threw the mints on the floor. Mortified and amused, Stephen said, "We'd best be going."

I walked them to the door. "How much longer will you be here?" asked Suzanne.

I said, "Another three weeks."

"We must see each other again," she said. "We might have lunch in town one day."

I said, "Yes," but I doubted that we'd be having lunch in town or anything else. It would only be a repetition of the afternoon we'd just spent together — another skirmish in an undeclarable war of which I had to end up the loser, as I was the loser now. But if you're going to be a loser you might as well be a good one, you might as well play the part. I followed them outside and stood on the doorstep with my arms folded across my chest, my head slightly tilted. I made a pathetic picture, standing there alone in front of that awful house, but I wasn't as pathetic as I looked. Nor were the Cronins, as they slammed and locked their car doors, so very safe. For, with all the resources it has to command, happiness remains a shaky fortress. Sorrow is the stronghold.

HAROLD BRODKEY

Verona: A Young Woman Speaks

(FROM ESQUIRE)

I KNOW a lot! I know about happiness! I don't mean the love of
God, either: I mean I know the human happiness with the crimes
in it.

Even the happiness of childhood.

I think of it now as a cruel, middle-class happiness.

Let me describe one time — one day, one night.

I was quite young, and my parents and I — there were just the
three of us — were traveling from Rome to Salzburg, journeying
across a quarter of Europe to be in Salzburg for Christmas, for the
music and the snow. We went by train because planes were erratic,
and my father wanted us to stop in half a dozen Italian towns and
see paintings and buy things. It was absurd, but we were all three
drunk with this; it was very strange: we woke every morning in a
strange hotel, in a strange city. I would be the first one to wake;
and I would go to the window and see some tower or palace; and
then I would wake my mother and be justified in my sense of
wildness and belief and adventure by the way she acted, her sense
of romance at being in a city as strange as I had thought it was
when I had looked out the window and seen the palace or the
tower.

We had to change trains in Verona, a darkish, smallish city at
the edge of the Alps. By the time we got there, we'd bought and
bought our way up the Italian peninsula: I was dizzy with shopping
and new possessions: I hardly knew who I was, I owned so many
new things: my reflection in any mirror or shopwindow was re-
splendently fresh and new, disguised even, glittering, I thought. I
was seven or eight years old. It seemed to me we were almost in a

movie or in the pages of a book: only the simplest and most light-filled words and images can suggest what I thought we were then. We went around shiningly: we shone everywhere. *Those clothes.* It's easy to buy a child. I had a new dress, knitted, blue and red, expensive as hell, I think; leggings, also red; a red loden-cloth coat with a hood and a knitted cap for under the hood; marvelous lined gloves; fur-lined boots and a fur purse or carryall, and a tartan skirt — and shirts and a scarf, and there was even more: a watch, a bracelet: more and more.

On the trains we had private rooms, and Momma carried games in her purse and things to eat, and Daddy sang carols off-key to me; and sometimes I became so intent on my happiness I would suddenly be in real danger of wetting myself; and Momma, who understood such emergencies, would catch the urgency in my voice and see my twisted face; and she — a large, good-looking woman — would whisk me to a toilet with amazing competence and un-stoppability, murmuring to me, "Just hold on for a while," and she would hold my hand while I did it.

So we came to Verona, where it was snowing, and the people had stern, sad faces, beautiful, unlaughing faces. But if they looked at me, those serious faces would lighten, they would smile at me in my splendor. Strangers offered me candy, sometimes with the most excruciating sadness, kneeling or stooping to look directly into my face, into my eyes; and Momma or Papa would judge them, the people, and say in Italian we were late, we had to hurry, or pause, and let the stranger touch me, talk to me, look into my face for a while. I would see myself in the eyes of some strange man or woman; sometimes they stared so gently I would want to touch their eyelashes, stroke those strange, large, glistening eyes. I knew I decorated life. I took my duties with great seriousness. An Italian count in Siena said I had the manners of an English princess — at times — and then he laughed because it was true I would be quite lurid: I ran shouting in his *galleria*, a long room, hung with pictures, and with a frescoed ceiling: and I sat on his lap and wriggled: I was a wicked child, and I liked myself very much; and almost everywhere, almost every day, there was someone new to love me, briefly, while we traveled.

I understood I was special. I understood it *then.*

I knew that what we were doing, everything we did, involved money. I did not know if it involved mind or not, or style. But I knew about money somehow, checks and traveler's checks and the clink of coins. Daddy was a fountain of money: he said it was a spree; he meant for us to be amazed; he had saved money — we weren't really rich but we were to be for this trip. I remember a conservatory in a large house outside Florence and orange trees in tubs; and I ran there too. A servant, a man dressed in black, a very old man, mean-faced — he did not like being a servant anymore after the days of servants were over — and he scowled but he smiled at me, and at my mother, and even once at my father: we were clearly so separate from the griefs and wearinesses and cruelties of the world. We were at play, we were at our joys, and Momma was glad, with a terrible and naïve inner gladness, and she relied on Daddy to make it work: oh, she worked too, but she didn't know the secret of such — unreality: is that what I want to say? Of such a game, of such an extraordinary game.

There was a picture in Verona Daddy wanted to see; a painting; I remember the painter because the name Pisanello reminded me I had to go to the bathroom when we were in the museum, which was an old castle, Guelf or Ghibelline, I don't remember which; and I also remember the painting because it showed the hind end of the horse, and I thought that was not nice and rather funny, but Daddy was admiring; and so I said nothing.

He held my hand and told me a story so I wouldn't be bored as we walked from room to room in the museum/castle, and then we went outside into the snow, into the soft light when it snows, light coming through snow; and I was dressed in red and had on boots, and my parents were young and pretty and had on boots too; and we could stay out in the snow if we wanted; and we did. We went to a square, a piazza — the Scaligera, I think; I don't remember — and just as we got there, the snowing began to bellow and then subside, to fall heavily and then sparsely, and then it stopped: and it was very cold, and there were pigeons everywhere in the piazza, on every cornice and roof, and all over the snow on the ground, leaving little tracks as they walked, while the air trembled in its just-after-snow and just-before-snow weight and thickness and grey seriousness of purpose. I had never seen so many pigeons or such a private and haunted place as that piazza, me in my new coat at the far rim of the world, the far rim of who knew what story, the rim of foreign beauty and Daddy's games, the edge, the white border of a season.

I was half mad with pleasure, anyway, and now Daddy brought

five or six cones made of newspaper, wrapped, twisted; and they held grains of something like corn, yellow and white kernels of something; and he poured some on my hand and told me to hold my hand out; and then he backed away.

At first there was nothing, but I trusted him and I waited; and then the pigeons came. On heavy wings. Clumsy pigeony bodies. And red, unreal bird's feet. They flew at me, slowing at the last minute; they lit on my arm and fed from my hand. I wanted to flinch, but I didn't. I closed my eyes and held my arm stiffly; and felt them peck and eat — from my hand, these free creatures, these flying things. I liked that moment. I liked my happiness. If I were mistaken about life and pigeons and my own nature, it didn't matter *then*.

The piazza was very silent, with snow; and Daddy poured grains on both my hands and then on the sleeves of my coat and on the shoulders of the coat, and I was entranced with yet more stillness, with this idea of his. The pigeons fluttered heavily in the heavy air, more and more of them, and sat on my arms and on my shoulders; and I looked at Momma and then at my father and then at the birds on me.

Oh, I'm sick of everything as I talk. There is happiness. It always makes me slightly ill. I lose my balance because of it.

The heavy birds, and the strange buildings, and Momma near, and Daddy too: Momma is pleased that I am happy and she is a little jealous; she is jealous of everything Daddy does; she is a woman of enormous spirit; life is hardly big enough for her; she is drenched in wastefulness and prettiness. She knows things. She gets inflexible, though, and foolish at times, and temperamental; but she is a somebody, and she gets away with a lot, and if she is near, you can feel her, you can't escape her, she's that important, that echoing, her spirit is that powerful in the space around her.

If she weren't restrained by Daddy, if she weren't in love with him, there is no knowing what she might do: she does not know. But she manages almost to be gentle because of him; he is incredibly watchful and changeable and he gets tired; he talks and charms people; sometimes, then, Momma and I stand nearby, like moons; we brighten and wane; and after a while, he comes to us, to the moons, the big one, and the little one, and we welcome him, and he is always, to my surprise, he is always surprised, as if he didn't deserve to be loved, as if it were time he was found out.

Daddy is very tall, and Momma is watching us, and Daddy anoints me again and again with the grain. I cannot bear it much longer. I feel joy or amusement or I don't know what; it is all through me, like a nausea — I am ready to scream and laugh, that laughter that comes out like magical, drunken, awful and yet pure spit or vomit or God knows what, that makes me a child mad with laughter. I become brilliant, gleaming, soft: an angel, a great bird-child of laughter.

I am ready to be like that, but I hold myself back.

There are more and more birds near me. They march around my feet and peck at falling and fallen grains. One is on my head. Of those on my arms, some move their wings, fluff those frail, feather-loaded wings, stretch them. I cannot bear it, they are so frail, and I am, at the moment, the kindness of the world that feeds them in the snow.

All at once, I let out a splurt of laughter: I can't stop myself and the birds fly away but not far; they circle around me, above me; some wheel high in the air and drop as they return; they all returned, some in clouds and clusters driftingly, some alone and angry, pecking at others; some with a blind, animal-strutting abruptness. They gripped my coat and fed themselves. It started to snow again.

I was there in my kindness, in that piazza, within reach of my mother and father.

Oh, how will the world continue? Daddy suddenly understood I'd had enough, I was at the end of my strength — Christ, he was alert — and he picked me up, and I went limp, my arm around his neck, and the snow fell. Momma came near and pulled the hood lower and said there were snowflakes in my eyelashes. She knew he had understood, and she wasn't sure she had; she wasn't sure he ever watched her so carefully. She became slightly unhappy, and so she walked like a clumsy boy beside us, but she was so pretty: she had powers, anyway.

We went to a restaurant, and I behaved very well, but I couldn't eat, and then we went to the train and people looked at us, but I couldn't smile; I was too dignified, too sated; some leftover — pleasure, let's call it — made my dignity very deep, I could not stop remembering the pigeons, or that Daddy loved me in a way he did not love Momma; and Daddy was alert, watching the luggage, watching strangers for assassination attempts or whatever; he was on duty; and Momma was pretty and alone and *happy*, defiant in that way.

And then, you see, what she did was wake me in the middle of the night when the train was chugging up a very steep mountainside; and outside the window, visible because our compartment was dark and the sky was clear and there was a full moon, were mountains, a landscape of mountains everywhere, big mountains, huge ones, impossible, all slanted and pointed and white with snow, and absurd, sticking up into an ink-blue sky and down into blue, blue shadows, miraculously deep. I don't know how to say what it was like: they were not like anything I knew: they were high things: and we were up high in the train and we were climbing higher, and it was not at all true, but it was, you see. I put my hands on the window and stared at the wild, slanting, unlikely marvels, whiteness and dizziness and moonlight and shadows cast by moonlight, not real, not familiar, not pigeons, but a clean world.

We sat a long time, Momma and I, and stared, and then Daddy woke up and came and looked too. "It's pretty," he said, but he didn't really understand. Only Momma and I did. She said to him, "When I was a child, I was bored all the time, my love — I thought nothing would ever happen to me — and now these things are happening — and you have happened." I think he was flabbergasted by her love in the middle of the night; he smiled at her, oh, so swiftly that I was jealous, but I stayed quiet, and after a while, in his silence and amazement at her, at us, he began to seem different from us, from Momma and me; and then he fell asleep again; Momma and I didn't; we sat at the window and watched all night, watched the mountains and the moon, the clean world. We watched together.

Momma was the winner.

We were silent, and in silence we spoke of how we loved men and how dangerous men were and how they stole everything from you no matter how much you gave — but we didn't say it aloud.

We looked at mountains until dawn, and then when dawn came, it was too pretty for me — there was pink and blue and gold, in the sky, and on icy places, brilliant pink and gold flashes, and the snow was colored too, and I said, "Oh," and sighed; and each moment was more beautiful than the one before; and I said, "I love you, Momma." Then I fell asleep in her arms.

That was happiness then.

MARK HELPRIN

The Schreuderspitze

(FROM THE NEW YORKER)

IN MUNICH are many men who look like weasels. Whether by genetic accident, meticulous crossbreeding, an early and puzzling migration, coincidence, or a reason that we do not know, they exist in great numbers. Remarkably, they accentuate this unfortunate tendency by wearing mustaches, Alpine hats, and tweed. A man who resembles a rodent should never wear tweed.

One of these men, a commercial photographer named Franzen, had cause to be exceedingly happy. "Herr Wallich has disappeared," he said to Huebner, his supplier of paper and chemicals. "You needn't bother to send him bills. Just send them to the police. The police, you realize, were here on two separate occasions!"

"If the two occasions on which the police have been here had not been separate, Herr Franzen, they would have been here only once."

"What do you mean? Don't toy with me. I have no time for semantics. In view of the fact that I knew Wallich at school, and professionally, they sought my opinion on his disappearance. They wrote down everything I said, but I do not think that they will find him. He left his studio on the Neuhausstrasse just as it was when he was working, and the landlord has put a lien on the equipment. Let me tell you that he had some fine equipment — very fine. But he was not such a great photographer. He didn't have that killer's instinct. He was clearly not a hunter. His canine teeth were poorly developed; not like these," said Franzen, baring his canine teeth in a smile which made him look like an idiot with a mouth of miniature castle towers.

"But I am curious about Wallich."

"So is everyone. So is everyone. This is my theory. Wallich was never any good at school. At best, he did only middling well. And it was not because he had hidden passions, or a special genius for some field outside the curriculum. He tried hard but found it difficult to grasp several subjects; for him mathematics and physics were pure torture.

"As you know, he was not wealthy, and although he was a nice-looking fellow, he was terribly short. That inflicted upon him great scars — his confidence, I mean, because he had none. He could do things only gently. If he had to fight, he would fail. He was weak.

"For example, I will use the time when he and I were competing for the Heller account. This job meant a lot of money, and I was not about to lose. I went to the library and read all I could about turbine engines. What a bore! I took photographs of turbine blades and such things, and seeded them throughout my portfolio to make Herr Heller think that I had always been interested in turbines. Of course, I had not even known what they were. I thought that they were an Oriental hat. And now that I know them, I detest them.

"Naturally, I won. But do you know how Wallich approached the competition? He had some foolish ideas about mother-of-pearl nautiluses and other seashells. He wanted to show how shapes of things mechanical were echoes of shapes in nature. All very fine, but Herr Heller pointed out that if the public were to see photographs of mother-of-pearl shells contrasted with photographs of his engines, his engines would come out the worse. Wallich's photographs were very beautiful — the tones of white and silver were exceptional — but they were his undoing. In the end, he said, 'Perhaps, Herr Heller, you are right,' and lost the contract just like that.

"The thing that saved him was the prize for that picture he took in the Black Forest. You couldn't pick up a magazine in Germany and not see it. He obtained so many accounts that he began to do very well. But he was just not commercially minded. He told me himself that he took only those assignments which pleased him. Mind you, his business volume was only about two-thirds of mine.

"My theory is that he could not take the competition, and the demands of his various clients. After his wife and son were killed in the motorcar crash, he dropped assignments one after another. I suppose he thought that as a bachelor he could live like a bohemian, on very little money, and therefore did not have to work more than half the time. I'm not saying that this was wrong. (Those accounts came to me.) But it was another instance of his weakness and lassitude.

"My theory is that he has probably gone to South America, or thrown himself off a bridge — because he saw that there was no future for him if he were always to take pictures of shells and things. And he was weak. The weak can never face themselves, and so cannot see the practical side of the world, how things are laid out, and what sacrifices are required to survive and prosper. It is only in fairy tales that they rise to triumph."

Wallich could not afford to get to South America. He certainly would not have thrown himself off a bridge. He was excessively neat and orderly, and the prospect of some poor fireman handling a swollen bloated body resounding with flies deterred him forever from such nonsense.

Perhaps if he had been a Gypsy he would have taken to the road. But he was no Gypsy, and had not the talent, skill, or taste for life outside Bavaria. Only once had he been away, to Paris. It was their honeymoon, when he and his wife did not need Paris or any city. They went by train and stayed for a week at a hotel by the Quai Voltaire. They walked in the gardens all day long, and in the May evenings they went to concerts where they heard the perfect music of their own country. Though they were away for just a week, and read the German papers, and went to a corner of the Luxembourg Gardens where there were pines and wildflowers like those in the greenbelt around Munich, this music made them sick for home. They returned two days early and never left again except for July and August, which each year they spent in the Black Forest, at a cabin inherited from her parents.

He dared not go back to that cabin. It was set like a trap. Were he to enter he would be enfiladed by the sight of their son's pictures and toys, his little boots and miniature fishing rod, and by her comb lying at the exact angle she had left it when she had last brushed her hair, and by the sweet smell of her clothing. No, someday he would have to burn the cabin. He dared not sell, for strangers then would handle roughly all those things which meant so much to him that he could not even gaze upon them. He left the little cabin to stand empty, perhaps the object of an occasional hiker's curiosity, or recipient of cheerful postcards from friends travelling or at the beach for the summer — friends who had not heard.

He sought instead a town far enough from Munich so that he would not encounter anything familiar, a place where he would be unrecognized and yet a place not entirely strange, where he would have to undergo no savage adjustments, where he could buy a Munich paper.

A search of the map brought his flying eye always southward to the borderlands, to Alpine country remarkable for the steepness of the brown contours, the depth of the valleys, and the paucity of settled places. Those few depicted towns appeared to be clean and well placed on high overlooks. Unlike the cities to the north — circles which clustered together on the flatlands or along rivers, like colonies of bacteria — the cities of the Alps stood alone, *in extremis*, near the border. Though he dared not cross the border, he thought perhaps to venture near its edge, to see what he would see. These isolated towns in the Alps promised shining clear air and deep-green trees. Perhaps they were above the tree line. In a number of cases it looked that way — and the circles were far from resembling clusters of bacteria. They seemed like untethered balloons.

He chose a town for its ridiculous name, reasoning that few of his friends would desire to travel to such a place. The world bypasses badly named towns as easily as it abandons ungainly children. It was called Garmisch-Partenkirchen. At the station in Munich, they did not even inscribe the full name on his ticket, writing merely "Garmisch-P."

"Do you live there!" the railroad agent had asked.

"No," answered Wallich.

"Are you visiting relatives, or going on business, or going to ski?"

"No."

"Then perhaps you are making a mistake. To go in October is not wise, if you do not ski. As unbelievable as it may seem, they have had much snow. Why go now?"

"I am a mountain climber," answered Wallich.

"In winter?" The railway agent was used to flushing out lies, and when little fat Austrian boys just old enough for adult tickets would bend their knees at his window as if at confession and say in squeaky voices, "Half fare to Salzburg!," he pounced upon them as if he were a leopard and they juicy ptarmigan or baby roebuck.

"Yes, in the winter," Wallich said. "Good mountain climbers thrive in difficult conditions. The more ice, the more storm, the greater the accomplishment. I am accumulating various winter records. In January, I go to America, where I will ascend their highest mountain, Mt. Independence, four thousand metres." He blushed so hard that the railway agent followed suit. Then Wallich backed away, insensibly mortified.

A mountain climber! He would close his eyes in fear when looking through Swiss calendars. He had not the stamina to rush up the stairs to his studio. He had failed miserably at sports. He was not a mountain climber, and had never even dreamed of being one.

Yet when his train pulled out of the vault of lacy ironwork and late-afternoon shadow, its steam exhalations were like those of a man puffing up a high meadow, speeding to reach the rock and ice, and Wallich felt as if he were embarking upon an ordeal of the type men experience on the precipitous rock walls of great cloud-swirled peaks. Why was he going to Garmisch-Partenkirchen anyway, if not for an ordeal through which to right himself? He was pulled so far over on one side by the death of his family, he was so bent and crippled by the pain of it, that he was going to Garmisch-Partenkirchen to suffer a parallel ordeal through which he would balance what had befallen him.

How wrong his parents and friends had been when they had offered help as his business faltered. A sensible, graceful man will have symmetry. He remembered the time at youth camp when a stream had changed course away from a once gushing sluice and the younger boys had had to carry buckets of water up a small hill, to fill a cistern. The skinny little boys had struggled up the hill. Their counsellor, sitting comfortably in the shade, would not let them go two to a bucket. At first they tried to carry the pails in front of them, but this was nearly impossible. Then they surreptitiously spilled half the water on the way up, until the counsellor took up position at the cistern and inspected each cargo. It had been torture to carry the heavy bucket in one aching hand. Wallich finally decided to take two buckets. Though it was agony, it was a better agony than the one he had had, because he had retrieved his balance, could look ahead, and, by carrying a double burden, had strengthened himself and made the job that much shorter. Soon, all the boys carried two buckets. The cistern was filled in no time, and they had a victory over their surprised counsellor.

So, he thought as the train shuttled through chill half-harvested fields, I will be a hermit in Garmisch-Partenkirchen. I will know no one. I will be alone. I may even begin to climb mountains. Perhaps I will lose fingers and toes, and on the way gather a set of wounds which will allow me some peace.

He sensed the change of landscape before he actually came upon it. Then they began to climb, and the engine sweated steam from steel to carry the lumbering cars up terrifying grades on either side of which blue pines stood angled against the mountainside. They reached a level stretch which made the train curve like a dragon and led it through deep tunnels, and they sped along as if on a summer excursion, with views of valleys so distant that in them whole forests sat upon their meadows like birthmarks, and streams were little more than the grain in leather.

Wallich opened his window and leaned out, watching ahead for tunnels. The air was thick and cold. It was full of sunshine and greenery, and it flowed past as if it were a mountain river. When he pulled back, his cheeks were red and his face pounded from the frigid air. He was alone in the compartment. By the time the lights came on he had decided upon the course of an ideal. He was to become a mountain climber, after all — and in a singularly difficult, dangerous, and satisfying way.

A porter said in passing the compartment, "The dining car is open, sir." Service to the Alps was famed. Even though his journey was no more than two hours, he had arranged to eat on the train, and had paid for and ordered a meal to which he looked forward in pleasant anticipation, especially because he had selected French strawberries in cream for dessert. But then he saw his body in the gently lit half mirror. He was soft from a lifetime of near-happiness. The sight of his face in the blond light of the mirror made him decide to begin preparing for the mountains that very evening. The porter ate the strawberries.

Of the many ways to attempt an ordeal perhaps the most graceful and attractive is the Alpine. It is far more satisfying than Oriental starvation and abnegation precisely because the European ideal is to commit difficult acts amid richness and overflowing beauty. For that reason, the Alpine is as well the most demanding. It is hard to deny oneself, to pare oneself down, at the heart and base of a civilization so full.

Wallich rode to Garmisch-Partenkirchen in a thunder of proud Alps. The trees were tall and lively, the air crystalline, and radiating beams spoke through the train window from one glowing range to another. A world of high ice laughed. And yet ranks of competing images assaulted him. He had gasped at the sight of Bremen, a port stuffed with iron ships gushing wheat steam from their whistles as they prepared to sail. In the mountain dryness, he remembered humid ports from which these massive ships crossed a colorful world, bringing back on laden decks a catalogue of stuffs and curiosities.

Golden images of the north plains struck from the left. The salt-white plains nearly floated above the sea. All this was in Germany, though Germany was just a small part of the world, removed almost entirely from the deep source of things — from the high lakes where explorers touched the silvers which caught the world's images, from the Sahara where they found the fine glass which bent the light.

Arriving at Garmisch-Partenkirchen in the dark, he could hear bells chiming and water rushing. Cool currents of air flowed from the direction of this white tumbling sound. It was winter. He hailed a horse-drawn sledge and piled his baggage in the back. "Hotel Aufburg," he said authoritatively.

"Hotel Aufburg?" asked the driver.

"Yes, Hotel Aufburg. There is such a place, isn't there? It hasn't closed, has it?"

"No, sir, it hasn't closed." The driver touched his horse with the whip. The horse walked twenty feet and was reined to a stop. "Here we are," the driver said. "I trust you've had a pleasant journey. Time passes quickly up here in the mountains."

The sign for the hotel was so large and well lit that the street in front of it shone as in daylight. The driver was guffawing to himself; the little guffaws rumbled about in him like subterranean thunder. He could not wait to tell the other drivers.

Wallich did nothing properly in Garmisch-Partenkirchen. But it was a piece of luck that he felt too awkward and ill at ease to sit alone in restaurants while, nearby, families and lovers had self-centered raucous meals, sometimes even bursting into song. Winter took over the town and covered it in stiff white ice. The unresilient cold, the troikas jingling through the streets, the frequent snowfalls encouraged winter fat. But because Wallich ate cold food in his room or stopped occasionally at a counter for a steaming bowl of soup, he became a shadow.

The starvation was pleasant. It made him sleepy and its constant physical presence gave him companionship. He sat for hours watching the snow, feeling as if he were part of it, as if the diminution of his body were great progress, as if such lightening would lessen his sorrow and bring him to the high rim of things he had not seen before, things which would help him and show him what to do and make him proud just for coming upon them.

He began to exercise. Several times a day the hotel manager knocked like a woodpecker at Wallich's door. The angrier the manager, the faster the knocks. If he were really angry he spoke so rapidly that he sounded like a speeded-up record: "Herr Wallich, I must ask you on behalf of the other guests to stop immediately all the thumping and vibration! This is a quiet hotel, in a quiet town, in a quiet tourist region. Please!" Then the manager would bow and quickly withdraw.

Eventually they threw Wallich out, but not before he had spent October and November in concentrated maniacal pursuit of physical strength. He had started with five each, every waking hour, of pushups, pull-ups, sit-ups, toe-touches, and leg-raises. The pull-ups were deadly — he did one every twelve minutes. The thumping and bumping came from five minutes of running in place. At the end of the first day, the pain in his chest was so intense that he was certain he was not long for the world. The second day was worse. And so it went, until after ten days there was no pain at all. The weight he abandoned helped a great deal to expand his physical prowess. He was, after all, in his middle twenties, and had never eaten to excess. Nor did he smoke or drink, except for champagne at weddings and municipal celebrations. In fact, he had always had rather ascetic tendencies, and had thought it fitting to have spent his life in Munich — "Home of Monks."

By his fifteenth day in Garmisch-Partenkirchen he had increased his schedule to fifteen apiece of the exercises each hour, which meant, for example, that he did a pull-up every four minutes whenever he was awake. Late at night he ran aimlessly about the deserted streets for an hour or more, even though it sometimes snowed. Two policemen who huddled over a brazier in their tiny booth simply looked at one another and pointed to their heads, twirling their fingers and rolling their eyes every time he passed by. On the last day of November, he moved up the valley to a little village called Altenburg-St. Peter.

There it was worse in some ways and better in others. Altenburg-St. Peter was so tiny that no stranger could enter unobserved, and so still that no one could do anything without the knowledge of the entire community. Children stared at Wallich on the street. This made him walk on the little lanes and approach his few destinations from the rear, which led housewives to speculate that he was a burglar. There were few merchants, and, because they were cousins, they could with little effort determine exactly what Wallich ate. When one week they were positive that he had consumed only four bowls of soup, a pound of cheese, a pound of smoked meat, a quart of yogurt, and two loaves of bread, they were incredulous. They themselves ate this much in a day. They wondered how Wallich survived on so little. Finally they came up with an answer. He received packages from Munich several times a week and in these packages was food, they thought — and probably very great delicacies. Then as the winter got harder and the snows covered everything they stopped wondering about him. They did not see him as he ran out of his lodgings at midnight, and the snow muffled his tread. He ran up the road toward the Schreuderspitze, first for a kilometre, then two, then five, then ten, then twenty — when finally he had to stop because he had begun slipping in just before the farmers arose and would have seen him.

By the end of February the packages had ceased arriving, and he was a changed man. No one would have mistaken him for what he had been. In five months he had become lean and strong. He did two hundred and fifty sequential pushups at least four times a day. For the sheer pleasure of it, he would do a hundred and fifty pushups on his fingertips. Every day he did a hundred pull-ups in a row. His midnight run, sometimes in snow which had accumulated up to his knees, was four hours long.

The packages had contained only books on climbing, and equipment. At first the books had been terribly discouraging. Every elementary text had bold warnings in red or green ink: "It is extremely dangerous to attempt genuine ascents without proper training. This volume should be used in conjunction with a certified course on climbing, or with the advice of a registered guide. A book itself will not do!"

One manual had in bright-red ink, on the very last page: "Go back, you fool! Certain death awaits you!" Wallich imagined that, as the books said, there were many things he could not learn except by human example, and many mistakes he might make in interpreting the manuals, which would go uncorrected save for the critique of living practitioners. But it didn't matter. He was determined to learn for himself and accomplish his task alone. Besides, since the accident he had become a recluse, and could hardly speak. The thought of enrolling in a climbing school full of young people from all parts of the country paralyzed him. How could he reconcile his task with their enthusiasm? For them it was recreation, perhaps something aesthetic or spiritual, a way to meet new friends. For him it was one tight channel through which he would either burst on to a new life, or in which he would die.

Studying carefully, he soon worked his way to advanced treatises for those who had spent years in the Alps. He understood these well enough, having quickly learned the terminologies and the humor and the faults of those who write about the mountains. He was even convinced that he knew the spirit in which the treatises had been written, for though he had never climbed, he had only to look out his window to see high white mountains about which blue sky swirled like a banner. He felt that in seeing them he was one of them, and was greatly encouraged when he read in a French mountaineer's memoirs: "After years in the mountains, I learned to look upon a given range and feel as if I were the last peak in the line. Thus I felt the music of the empty spaces enwrapping me, and I became not an intruder on the cliffs, dangling only to drop away, but an equal in transit. I seldom looked at my own body but only at the mountains, and my eyes felt like the eyes of the mountains."

He lavished nearly all his dwindling money on fine equipment. He calculated that after his purchases he would have enough to live on through September. Then he would have nothing. He had expended large sums on the best tools, and he spent the intervals between his hours of reading and exercise holding and studying the shiny carabiners, pitons, slings, chocks, hammers, ice pitons, axes, étriers, crampons, ropes, and specialized hardware that he had either ordered or constructed himself from plans in the advanced books.

It was insane, he knew, to funnel all his preparation into a few months of agony and then without any experience whatever throw himself alone onto a Class VI ascent — the seldom climbed *Westgebirgsausläufer* of the Schreuderspitze. Not having driven one piton, he was going to attempt a five-day climb up the nearly sheer western counterfort. Even in late June, he would spend a third of his time on ice. But the sight of the ice in March, shining like a faraway sword over the cold and absolute distance, drove him on. He had long passed censure. Had anyone known what he was doing and tried to dissuade him, he would have told him to go to hell, and resumed preparations with the confidence of someone taken up by a new religion.

For he had always believed in great deeds, in fairy tales, in echoing trumpet lands, in wonders and wondrous accomplishments. But even as a boy he had never considered that such things would fall to him. As a good city child he had known that these adventures were not necessary. But suddenly he was alone and the things which occurred to him were great warlike deeds. His energy and discipline were boundless, as full and overflowing as a lake in the mountains. Like the heroes of his youth, he would try to approach the high cord of ruby light and bend it to his will, until he could feel rolling thunder. The small things, the gentle things, the good things he loved, and the flow of love itself were dead for him and would always be, unless he could liberate them in a crucible of high drama.

It took him many months to think these things, and though they might not seem consistent, they were so for him, and he often spent hours alone on a sunny snow-covered meadow, his elbows on his knees, imagining great deeds in the mountains, as he stared at the massive needle of the Schreuderspitze, at the hint of rich lands beyond, and at the tiny village where he had taken up position opposite the mountain.

Toward the end of May he had been walking through Altenburg-St. Peter and seen his reflection in a store window — a storm had arisen suddenly and made the glass as silver-black as the clouds. He had not liked what he had seen. His face had become too hard and too lean. There was not enough gentleness. He feared immediately for the success of his venture if only because he knew well that unmitigated extremes are a great cause of failure. And he was tired of his painful regimen.

He bought a large Telefunken radio, in one fell swoop wiping out his funds for August and September. He felt as if he were paying for the privilege of music with portions of his life and body. But it was well worth it. When the storekeeper offered to deliver the heavy console, Wallich declined politely, picked up the cabinet himself, hoisted it on his back, and walked out of the store bent under it as in classic illustrations for physics textbooks throughout the industrialized world. He did not put it down once. The storekeeper summoned his associates and they bet and counterbet on whether Wallich "would" or "would not," as he moved slowly up the steep hill, up the steps, around the white switchbacks, onto a grassy slope, and then finally up the precipitous stairs to the balcony outside his room. "How can he have done that?" they asked. "He is a small man, and the radio must weigh at least thirty kilos." The storekeeper trotted out with a catalogue. "It weighs fifty-five kilograms!" he said. "Fifty-five kilograms!," and they wondered what had made Wallich so strong.

Once, Wallich had taken his little son (a tiny, skeptical, silent child who had a riotous giggle which could last for an hour) to see the inflation of a great gas dirigible. It had been a disappointment, for a dirigible is rigid and maintains always the same shape. He had expected to see the silver of its sides expand into ribbed cliffs which would float over them on the green field and amaze his son. Now that silver rising, the sail-like expansion, the great crescendo of a glimmering weightles mass, finally reached him alone in his room, too late but well received, when a Berlin station played the Beethoven Violin Concerto, its first five timpanic D's like grace before a feast. After those notes, the music lifted him, and he riveted his gaze on the dark shapes of the mountains, where a lightning storm raged. The radio crackled after each near or distant flash, but it was as if the music had been designed for it. Wallich looked at the yellow light within a softly glowing numbered panel. It flickered gently, and he could hear cracks and flashes in the music as he saw them delineated across darkness. They looked and sounded like the bent riverine limbs of dead trees hanging majestically over rocky outcrops, destined to fall, but enjoying their grand suspension nonetheless. The music travelled effortlessly on anarchic beams, passed high over the plains, passed high the forests, seeding them plentifully, and came upon the Alps like waves which finally strike the shore after thousands of miles in open sea. It charged upward, mating with the electric storm, separating, and delivering.

To Wallich — alone in the mountains, surviving amid the dark massifs and clear air — came the closeted, nasal, cosmopolitan voice of the radio commentator. It was good to know that there was something other than the purity and magnificence of his mountains, that far to the north the balance reverted to less than moral catastrophe and death, and much stock was set in things of extraordinary inconsequence. Wallich could not help laughing when he thought of the formally dressed audience at the symphony, how they squirmed in their seats and heated the bottoms of their trousers and capes, how relieved and delighted they would be to step out into the cool evening and go to a restaurant. In the morning they would arise and take pleasure from the sweep of the drapes as sun danced by, from the gold rim around a white china cup. For them it was always too hot or too cold. But they certainly had their delights, about which sometimes he would think. How often he still dreamed, asleep or awake, of the smooth color plates opulating under his hands in tanks of developer and of the fresh film which smelled like bread and then was entombed in black cylinders to develop. How he longed sometimes for the precise machinery of his cameras. The very word "*Kamera*" was as dark and hollow as this night in the mountains when, reviewing the pleasures of faraway Berlin, he sat in perfect health and equanimity upon a wicker-weave seat in a bare white room. The only light was from the yellow dial, the sudden lightning flashes, and the faint blue of the sky beyond the hills. And all was quiet but for the music and the thunder and the static curling about the music like weak and lost memories which arise to harry even indomitable perfections.

A month before the ascent, he awaited arrival of a good climbing rope. He needed from a rope not strength to hold a fall but lightness and length for abseiling. His strategy was to climb with a short self-belay. No one would follow to retrieve his hardware and because it would not always be practical for him to do so himself, in what one of his books called "rhythmic recapitulation," he planned to carry a great deal of metal. If the metal and he reached the summit relatively intact, he could make short work of the descent, abandoning pitons as he abseiled downward.

He would descend in half a day that which had taken five days to climb. He pictured the abseiling, literally a flight down the mountain on the doubled cord of his long rope, and he thought that those hours speeding down the cliffs would be the finest of his life. If the weather were good he would come away from the Schreuderspitze having flown like an eagle.

On the day the rope was due, he went to the railroad station to meet the mail. It was a clear, perfect day. The light was so fine and rich that in its bath everyone felt wise, strong, and content. Wallich sat on the wooden boards of the wide platform, scanning the green meadows and fields for smoke and a coal engine, but the country-side was silent and the valley unmarred by the black woolly chain he sought. In the distance, toward France and Switzerland, a few cream-and-rose-colored clouds rode the horizon, immobile and high. On far mountainsides innumerable flowers showed in this long view as a slash, or as a patch of color not unlike one flower alone.

He had arrived early, for he had no watch. After some minutes a car drove up and from it emerged a young family. They rushed as if the train were waiting to depart, when down the long trough-like valley it was not even visible. There were two little girls, as beautiful as he had ever seen. The mother, too, was extraordinarily fine. The father was in his early thirties, and he wore gold-rimmed glasses. They seemed like a university family — people who knew how to live sensibly, taking pleasure from proper and beautiful things.

The littler girl was no more than three. Sunburned and rosy, she wore a dress that was shaped like a bell. She dashed about the platform so lightly and tentatively that it was as if Wallich were watching a tiny fish gravityless in a lighted aquarium. Her older sister stood quietly by the mother, who was illumined with consideration and pride for her children. It was apparent that she was overjoyed with the grace of her family. She seemed detached and preoccupied, but in just the right way. The littler girl said in a voice like a child's party horn, "Mummy, I want some peanuts!"

It was so ridiculous that this child should share the appetite of elephants that the mother smiled. "Peanuts will make you thirsty,

Gretl. Wait until we get to Garmisch-Partenkirchen. Then we'll
have lunch in the buffet."

"When will we get to Garmisch-Partenkirchen?"

"At two."

"Two?"

"Yes, at two."

"At two?"

"Gretl!"

The father looked alternately at the mountains and at his wife
and children. He seemed confident and steadfast. In the distance
black smoke appeared in thick billows. The father pointed at it.
"There's our train," he said.

"Where?" asked Gretl, looking in the wrong direction. The father picked her up and turned her head with his hand, aiming her
gaze down the shimmering valley. When she saw the train she
started, and her eyes opened wide in pleasure.

"Ah . . . there it is," said the father. As the train pulled into the
station the young girls were filled with excitement. Amid the noise
they entered a compartment and were swallowed up in the steam.
The train pulled out.

Wallich stood on the empty platform, unwrapping his rope. It
was a rope, quite a nice rope, but it did not make him as happy as
he had expected it would.

Little can match the silhouette of mountains by night. The great
mass becomes far more mysterious when its face is darkened, when
its sweeping lines roll steeply into valleys and peaks and long impossible ridges, when behind the void a concoction of rare silver
leaps up to trace the hills — the pressure of collected starlight.
That night, in conjunction with the long draughts of music he had
become used to taking, he began to dream his dreams. They did
not frighten him — he was beyond fear, too strong for fear, too
played out. They did not even puzzle him, for they unfolded like
the chapters in a brilliant nineteenth-century history. The rich explanations filled him for days afterward. He was amazed, and did
not understand why these perfect dreams suddenly came to him.
Surely they did not arise from within. He had never had the world
so beautifully portrayed, had never seen as clearly and in such
sure, gentle steps, had never risen so high and so smoothly in
unfolding enlightenment, and he had seldom felt so well looked

after. And yet, there was no visible presence. But it was as if the mountains and valleys were filled with loving families of which he was part.

Upon his return from the railroad platform, a storm had come suddenly from beyond the southern ridge. Though it had been warm and clear that day, he had seen from the sunny meadow before his house that a white storm billowed in higher and higher curves, pushing itself over the summits, finally to fall like an air avalanche on the valley. It snowed on the heights. The sun continued to strike the opaque frost and high clouds. It did not snow in the valley. The shock troops of the storm remained at the highest elevations, and only worn gray veterans came below — misty clouds and rain on cold wet air. Ragged clouds moved across the mountainsides and meadows, watering the trees and sometimes catching in low places. Even so, the air in the meadow was still horn-clear.

In his room that night Wallich rocked back and forth on the wicker chair (it was not a rocker and he knew that using it as such was to number its days). That night's crackling infusion from Berlin, rising warmly from the faintly lit dial, was Beethoven's Eighth. The familiar commentator, nicknamed by Wallich Mälzels Metronom because of his even monotone, discoursed upon the background of the work.

"For many years," he said, "no one except Beethoven liked this symphony. Beethoven's opinions, however — even regarding his own creations — are equal at least to the collective pronouncements of all the musicologists and critics alive in the West during any hundred-year period. Conscious of the merits of the F-Major Symphony, he resolutely determined to redeem and . . . ah . . . the conductor has arrived. He steps to the podium. We begin."

Wallich retired that night in perfect tranquillity but awoke at five in the morning soaked in his own sweat, his fists clenched, a terrible pain in his chest, and breathing heavily as if he had been running. In the dim unattended light of the early-morning storm, he lay with eyes wide open. His pulse subsided, but he was like an animal in a cave, like a creature who has just escaped an organized hunt. It was as if the whole village had come armed and in search of him, had by some miracle decided that he was not in, and had left to comb the wet woods. He had been dreaming, and he saw his dream in its exact form. It was, first, an emerald. Cut into an octagon with two long sides, it was shaped rather like the plaque at the bottom of a painting. Events within this emerald were circular and never-ending.

They were in Munich. Air and sun were refined as on the station platform in the mountains. He was standing at a streetcar stop with his wife and his two daughters, though he knew perfectly well in the dream that these two daughters were meant to be his son. A streetcar arrived in complete silence. Clouds of people began to embark. They were dressed and muffled in heavy clothing of dull blue and gray. To his surprise, his wife moved toward the door of the streetcar and started to board, the daughters trailing after her. He could not see her feet, and she moved in a glide. Though at first paralyzed, as in the instant before a crash, he did manage to bound after her. As she stepped onto the first step and was about to grasp a chrome pole within the doorway, he made for her arm and caught it.

He pulled her back and spun her around, all very gently. Her presence before him was so intense that it was as if he were trapped under the weight of a fallen beam. She, too, wore a winter coat, but it was slim and perfectly tailored. He remembered the perfect geometry of the lapels. Not on earth had such angles ever been seen. The coat was a most intense liquid emerald color, a living light-infused green. She had always looked best in green, for her hair was like shining gold. He stood before her. He felt her delicacy. Her expression was neutral. "Where are you going?" he asked incredulously.

"I must go," she said.

He put his arms around her. She returned his embrace, and he said, "How can you leave me?"

"I have to," she answered.

And then she stepped onto the first step of the streetcar, and onto the second step, and she was enfolded into darkness.

He awoke, feeling like an invalid. His strength served for naught. He just stared at the clouds lifting higher and higher as the storm cleared. By nightfall the sky was black and gentle, though very cold. He kept thinking back to the emerald. It meant everything to him, for it was the first time he realized that they were really dead. Silence followed. Time passed thickly. He could not have imagined the sequence of dreams to follow, and what they would do to him.

*

He began to fear sleep, thinking that he would again be sub-
jected to the lucidity of the emerald. But he had run that course
and would never do so again except by perfect conscious recollection. The night after he had the dream of the emerald he fell
asleep like someone letting go of a cliff edge after many minutes
alone without help or hope. He slid into sleep, heart beating wildly.
To his surprise, he found himself far indeed from the trolley tracks
in Munich.

Instead, he was alone in the center of a sunlit snowfield, walking
on the glacier in late June, bound for the summit of the Schreuderspitze. The mass of his equipment sat lightly upon him. He was
well drilled in its use and positioning, in the subtleties of placement
and rigging. The things he carried seemed part of him, as if he
had quickly evolved into a new kind of animal suited for breathtaking travel in the steep heights.

His stride was light and long, like that of a man on the moon. He
nearly floated, ever so slightly airborne, over the dazzling glacier.
He leaped crevasses, sailing in slow motion against intense white
and blue. He passed apple-fresh streams and opalescent melt pools
of blue-green water as he progressed toward the Schreuderspitze.
Its rocky horn was covered by nearly blue ice from which the
wind blew a white corona in sines and cusps twirling about the
sky.

Passing the bergschrund, he arrived at the first mass of rock. He
turned to look back. There he saw the snowfield and the sun turning above it like a pinwheel, casting out a fog of golden light. He
stood alone. The world had been reduced to the beauty of physics
and the mystery of light. It had been rendered into a frozen state,
a liquid state, a solid state, a gaseous state, mixtures, temperatures,
and more varieties of light than fell on the speckled floor of a great
cathedral. It was simple, and yet infinitely complex. The sun was
warm. There was silence.

For several hours he climbed over great boulders and up a range
of rocky escarpments. It grew more and more difficult, and he
often had to lay in protection, driving a piton into a crack of the
firm granite. His first piton was a surprise. It slowed halfway, and
the ringing sound as he hammered grew higher in pitch. Finally, it
would go in no farther. He had spent so much time in driving it
that he thought it would be as steady as the Bank of England. But
when he gave a gentle tug to test its hold, it came right out. This
he thought extremely funny. He then remembered that he had

either to drive it in all the way, to the eye, or to attach a sling along its shaft as near as possible to the rock. It was a question of avoiding leverage.

He bent carefully to his equipment sling, replaced the used piton, and took up a shorter one. The shorter piton went to its eye in five hammer strokes and he could do nothing to dislodge it. He clipped in and ascended a steep pitch, at the top of which he drove in two pitons, tied in to them, abseiled down to retrieve the first, and ascended quite easily to where he had left off. He made rapid progress over frightening pitches, places no one would dare go without assurance of a bolt in the rock and a line to the bolt — even if the bolt was just a small piece of metal driven in by dint of precariously balanced strength, arm, and Alpine hammer.

Within the sphere of utter concentration easily achieved during difficult ascents, his simple climbing evolved naturally into graceful technique, by which he went up completely vertical rock faces, suspended only by pitons and étriers. The different placements of which he had read and thought repeatedly were employed skillfully and with a proper sense of variety, though it was tempting to stay with one familiar pattern. Pounding metal into rock and hanging from his taut and colorful wires, he breathed hard, he concentrated, and he went up sheer walls.

At one point he came to the end of a subtle hairline crack in an otherwise smooth wall. The rock above was completely solid for a hundred feet. If he went down to the base of the crack he would be nowhere. The only thing to do was to make a swing traverse to a wall more amenable to climbing.

Anchoring two pitons into the rock as solidly as he could, he clipped an oval carabiner on the bottom piton, put a safety line on the top one, and lowered himself about sixty feet down the two ropes. Hanging perpendicular to the wall, he began to walk back and forth across the rock. He moved to and fro, faster and faster, until he was running. Finally he touched only in places and was swinging wildly like a pendulum. He feared that the piton to which he was anchored would not take the strain, and would pull out. But he kept swinging faster, until he gave one final push and, with a pathetic cry, went sailing over a drop which would have made a mountain goat swallow its heart. He caught an outcropping of rock on the other side, and pulled himself to it desperately. He hammered in, retrieved the ropes, glanced at the impassable wall, and began again to ascend.

As he approached great barricades of ice, he looked back. It gave him great pride and satisfaction to see the thousands of feet over which he had struggled. Much of the west counterfort was purely vertical. He could see now just how the glacier was riverine. He could see deep within the Tyrol and over the border to the Swiss lakes. Garmisch-Partenkirchen looked from here like a town on the board of a toy railroad or (if considered only two-dimensionally) like the cross-section of a kidney. Altenburg-St. Peter looked like a ladybug. The sun sent streamers of tan light through the valley, already three-quarters conquered by shadow, and the ice above took fire. Where the ice began, he came to a wide ledge and he stared upward at a sparkling ridge which looked like a great crystal spine. Inside, it was blue and cold.

He awoke, convinced that he had in fact climbed the counterfort. It was a strong feeling, as strong as the reality of the emerald. Sometimes dreams could be so real that they competed with the world, riding at even balance and calling for a decision. Sometimes, he imagined, when they are so real and so important, they easily tip the scale and the world buckles and dreams become real. Crossing the fragile barricades, one enters his dreams, thinking of his life as imagined.

He rejoiced at his bravery in climbing. It had been as real as anything he had ever experienced. He felt the pain, the exhaustion, and the reward, as well as the danger. But he could not wait to return to the mountain and the ice. He longed for evening and the enveloping darkness, believing that he belonged resting under great folds of ice on the wall of the Schreuderspitze. He had no patience with his wicker chair, the bent wood of the windowsill, the clear glass in the window, the green-sided hills he saw curving through it, or his brightly colored equipment hanging from pegs on the white wall.

Two weeks before, on one of the eastward roads from Altenburg-St. Peter — no more than a dirt track — he had seen a child turn and take a well-worn path toward a wood, a meadow, and a stream by which stood a house and a barn. The child walked slowly upward into the forest, disappearing into the dark close, as if he had been taken up by vapor. Wallich had been too far away to hear footsteps, and the last thing he saw was the back of the boy's bright blue-and-white sweater. Returning at dusk, Wallich had expected to see warmly lit windows, and smoke issuing efficiently from the straight chimney. But there were no lights, and there was no smoke. He made his way through the trees and past the meadow only to come upon a small farmhouse with boarded windows and no-trespassing signs tacked on the doors.

It was unsettling when he saw the same child making his way across the upper meadow, a flash of blue and white in the near darkness. Wallich screamed out to him, but he did not hear, and kept walking as if he were deaf or in another world, and he went over the crest of the hill. Wallich ran up the hill. When he reached the top he saw only a wide empty field and not a trace of the boy.

Then in the darkness and purity of the meadows he began to feel that the world had many secrets, that they were shattering even to glimpse or sense, and that they were not necessarily unpleasant. In certain states of light he could see, he could begin to sense, things most miraculous indeed. Although it seemed self-serving, he concluded nonetheless, after a liftime of adhering to the diffuse principles of a science he did not know, that there was life after death, that the dead rose into a mischievous world of pure light, that something most mysterious lay beyond the enfolding darkness, something wonderful.

This idea had taken hold, and he refined it. For example, listening to the Beethoven symphonies broadcast from Berlin, he began to think that they were like a ladder of mountains, that they surpassed themselves and rose higher and higher until at certain points they seemed to break the warp itself and cross into a heaven of light and the dead. There were signs everywhere of temporal diffusion and mystery. It was as if continents existed, new worlds lying just off the coast, invisible and redolent, waiting for the grasp of one man suddenly to substantiate and light them, changing everything. Perhaps great mountains hundreds of times higher than the Alps would arise in the sea or on the flatlands. They might be purple or gold and shining in many states of refraction and reflection, transparent in places as vast as countries. Someday someone would come back from his place, or someone would by accident discover and illumine its remarkable physics.

He believed that the boy he had seen nearly glowing in the half-darkness of the high meadow had been his son, and that the child had been teasing his father in a way only he could know, that the child had been asking him to follow. Possibly he had come upon great secrets on the other side, and knew that his father would join him soon enough and that then they would laugh about the world.

When he next fell asleep in the silence of a clear windless night in the valley, Wallich was like a man disappearing into the warp of darkness. He wanted to go there, to be taken as far as he could be taken. He was not unlike a sailor who sets sail in the teeth of a great storm, delighted by his own abandon.

Throwing off the last wraps of impure light, he found himself again in the ice world. The word was all-encompassing — *Eiswelt*. There above him the blue spire rocketed upward as far as the eye could see. He touched it with his hand. It was indeed as cold as ice. It was dense and hard, like glass ten feet thick. He had doubted its strength, but its solidity told that it would not flake away and allow him to drop endlessly, far from it.

On ice he found firm holds both with his feet and with his hands, and hardly needed the ice pitons and étriers. For he had crampons tied firmly to his boots, and could spike his toe points into the ice and stand comfortably on a vertical. He proceeded with a surety of footing he had never had on the streets of Munich. Each step bolted him down to the surface. And in each hand he carried an ice hammer with which he made swinging cutting arcs that engaged the shining stainless-steel pick with the mirror-like wall.

All the snow had blown away or had melted. There were no traps, no pitfalls, no ambiguities. He progressed toward the summit rapidly, climbing steep ice walls as if he had been going up a ladder. The air became purer and the light more direct. Looking out to right or left, or glancing sometimes over his shoulders, he saw that he was not truly in the world of mountains.

Above the few clouds he could see only equal peaks of ice, and the Schreuderspitze dropping away from him. It was not the world of rock. No longer could he make out individual features in the valley. Green had become a hazy dark blue appropriate to an ocean floor. Whole countries came into view. The landscape was a mass of winding glaciers and great mountains. At that height, all was separated and refined. Soft things vanished, and there remained only the white and the silver.

He did not reach the summit until dark. He did not see the stars because icy clouds covered the Schreuderspitze in a crystalline fog which flowed past, crackling and hissing. He was heartbroken to have come all the way to the summit and then be blinded by masses of clouds. Since he could not descend until light, he decided to stay firmly stationed until he could see clearly. Meanwhile, he lost patience and began to address a presence in the air — casually, not thinking it strange to do so, not thinking twice about talking to the void.

He awoke in his room in early morning, saying, "All these blinding clouds. Why all these blinding clouds?"

Though the air of the valley was as fresh as a flower, he detested it. He pulled the covers over his head and strove for unconsciousness, but he grew too hot and finally gave up, staring at the remnants of dawn light soaking about his room. The day brightened in the way that stage lights come up, suddenly brilliant upon a beam-washed platform. It was early June. He had lost track of the exact date, but he knew that sometime before he had crossed into June. He had lost them in early June. Two years had passed.

He packed his things. Though he had lived like a monk, much had accumulated, and this he put into suitcases, boxes, and bags. He packed his pens, paper, books, a chess set on which he sometimes played against an imaginary opponent named Herr Claub, the beautiful Swiss calendars upon which he had at one time been almost afraid to gaze, cooking equipment no more complex than a soldier's mess kit, his clothing, even the beautifully wrought climbing equipment, for, after all, he had another set, up there in the *Eiswelt*. Only his bedding remained unpacked. It was on the floor in the center of the room, where he slept. He put some banknotes in an envelope — the June rent — and tacked it to the doorpost. The room was empty, white, and it would have echoed had it been slightly larger. He would say something and then listen intently, his eyes flaring like those of a lunatic. He had not eaten in days, and was not disappointed that even the waking world began to seem like a dream.

He went to the pump. He had accustomed himself to bathing in streams so cold that they were too frightened to freeze. Clean and cleanly shaven, he returned to his room. He smelled the sweet pine scent he had brought back on his clothing after hundreds of trips through the woods and forests girdling the greater mountains. Even the bedding was snowy white. He opened the closet and caught a glimpse of himself in the mirror. He was dark from sun and wind; his hair shone; his face had thinned; his eyebrows were now gold and white. For several days he had had only cold pure water. Like soldiers who come from training toughened and healthy, he had about him the air of a small child. He noticed a certain wildness in the eye, and he lay on the hard floor, as was his habit, in perfect comfort. He thought nothing. He felt nothing. He wished nothing.

Time passed as if he could compress and cancel it. Early-evening darkness began to make the white walls blue. He heard a crackling fire in the kitchen of the rooms next door, and imagined the shadows dancing there. Then he slept, departing.

On the mountain it was dreadfully cold. He huddled into himself against the wet silver clouds, and yet he smiled, happy to be once again on the summit. He thought of making an igloo, but remembered that he hadn't an ice saw. The wind began to build. If the storm continued, he would die. It would whittle him into a brittle wire, and then he would snap. The best he could do was to dig a trench with his ice hammers. He lay in the trench and closed his sleeves and hooded parka, drawing the shrouds tight. The wind came at him more and more fiercely. One gust was so powerful that it nearly lifted him out of the trench. He put in an ice piton, and attached his harness. Still the wind rose. It was difficult to breathe and nearly impossible to see. Any irregular surface whistled. The eye of the ice piton became a great siren. The zippers on his parka, the harness, the slings and equipment, all gave off musical tones, so that it was as if he were in a place with hundreds of tormented spirits.

The gray air fled past with breathtaking speed. Looking away from the wind, he had the impression of being propelled upward at unimaginable speed. Walls of gray sped by so fast that they glowed. He knew that if he were to look at the wind he would have the sense of hurtling forward in gravityless space.

And so he stared at the wind and its slowly pulsing gray glow. He did not know for how many hours he held that position. The rape of vision caused a host of delusions. He felt great momentum. He travelled until, eardrums throbbing with the sharpness of cold and wind, he was nearly dead, white as a candle, hardly able to breathe.

Then the acceleration ceased and the wind slowed. When, released from the great pressure, he fell back off the edge of the trench, he realized for the first time that he had been stretched tight on his line. He had never been so cold. But the wind was dying and the clouds were no longer a great corridor through which he was propelled. They were, rather, a gentle mist which did not know quite what to do with itself. How would it dissipate? Would it rise to the stars, or would it fall in compression down into the valley below?

It fell; it fell all around him, downward like a lowering curtain. It fell in lines and stripes, always downward as if on signal, by command, in league with a directive force.

At first he saw just a star or two straight on high. But as the mist departed a flood of stars burst through. Roads of them led into infinity. Starry wheels sat in fiery white coronas. Near the horizon were the few separate gentle stars, shining out and turning clearly, as wide and round as planets. The air grew mild and warm. He bathed in it. He trembled. As the air became all clear and the mist drained away completely, he saw something which stunned him.

The Schreuderspitze was far higher than he had thought. It was hundreds of times higher than the mountains represented on the map he had seen in Munich. The Alps were to it not even foothills, not even rills. Below him was the purple earth, and all the great cities lit by sparkling lamps in their millions. It was a clear summer dawn and the weather was excellent, certainly June.

He did not know enough about other cities to make them out from the shapes they cast in light, but his eye seized quite easily upon Munich. He arose from his trench and unbuckled the harness, stepping a few paces higher on the rounded summit. There was Munich, shining and pulsing like a living thing, strung with lines of amber light — light which reverberated as if in crystals, light which played in many dimensions and moved about the course of the city, which was defined by darkness at its edge. He had come above time, above the world. The city of Munich existed before him with all its time compressed. As he watched, its history played out in repeating cycles. Nothing, not one movement, was lost from the crystal. The light of things danced and multiplied, again and again, and yet again. It was all there for him to claim. It was alive, and ever would be.

He knelt on one knee as in paintings he had seen of explorers claiming a coast of the New World. He dared close his eyes in the face of that miracle. He began to concentrate, to fashion according to will with the force of stilled time a vision of those he had loved. In all their bright colors, they began to appear before him.

*

He awoke as if shot out of a cannon. He went from lying on his back to a completely upright position in an instant, a flash, during which he slammed the floorboards energetically with a clenched fist and cursed the fact that he had returned from such a world. But by the time he stood straight, he was delighted to be doing so. He quickly dressed, packed his bedding, and began to shuttle down to the station and back. In three trips, his luggage was stacked on the platform.

He bought a ticket for Munich, where he had not been in many many long months. He hungered for it, for the city, for the boats on the river, the goods in the shops, newspapers, the pigeons on the square, trees, traffic, even arguments, even Herr Franzen. So much rushed into his mind that he hardly saw his train pull in.

He helped the conductor load his luggage into the baggage car, and he asked, "Will we change at Garmisch-Partenkirchen?"

"No. We go right through, direct to Munich," said the conductor.

"Do me a great favor. Let me ride in the baggage car."

"I can't. It's a violation."

"Please. I've been months in the mountains. I would like to ride alone, for the last time."

The conductor relented, and Wallich sat atop a pile of boxes, looking at the landscape through a Dutch door, the top of which was open. Trees and meadows, sunny and lush in June, sped by. As they descended, the vegetation thickened until he saw along the cinder bed slow-running black rivers, skeins and skeins of thorns darted with the red of early raspberries, and flowers which had sprung up on the paths. The air was warm and caressing — thick and full, like a swaying green sea at the end of August.

They closed on Munich, and the Alps appeared in a sweeping line of white cloud-touched peaks. As they pulled into the great station, as sooty as it had ever been, he remembered that he had climbed the Schreuderspitze, by its most difficult route. He had found freedom from grief in the great and heart-swelling sight he had seen from the summit. He felt its workings and he realized that soon enough he would come once more into the world of light. Soon enough he would be with his wife and son. But until then (and he knew that time would spark ahead), he would open himself to life in the city, return to his former profession, and struggle at his craft.

PETER TAYLOR

In the Miro District

(FROM THE NEW YORKER)

WHAT I most often think about when I am lying awake in the night, or when I am taking a long automobile trip alone, is my two parents and my maternal grandfather. I used to suppose, after I had first got to be a grown man and had first managed to get away from Tennessee, that those two parents of mine thrusting my grandfather's company upon me as they did when I was growing up, and my company upon him when he was growing very old, and their asking the two of us to like it, though we possessed the very opposite natures, was but that couple's ruthless method of disposing of the two of us, child and aging parent, in one blow. But I can see now — from the vantage point of my own late middle age — that there was really no ruthlessness in it on their part. Because I realize that living their busy, genteel, contented life together during the nineteen-twenties they didn't have the slightest conception of what that old man my grandfather was like. Or of what that boy, their son, was like either. They weren't people to speculate about what other people and other times were "like." They knew only that what they did was what everybody else still did about grandfathers and grandsons in or about the year 1925 — in and around Nashville, Tennessee.

The fact is, my two parents were destined to go to their graves never suspecting that they had put a grandfather and a grandson in so false a position with each other that the boy and the old man would one day have to have it out between them. Indeed, they would go to their graves never suspecting that long before either of them had ever given a serious thought to dying, Grandfather and I had already had it out between us quite brutally and fatefully and had it out, as a matter of fact, in the front hall of their house in Acklen Park, in Nashville. It happened the summer when my grandfather was seventy-nine and I had just turned eighteen. Any real pretense at companionship between the old man and me came to an abrupt and unhappy end that summer. It left me with complications of feeling that I had not known before. For my grandfather, of course, whose story this is meant to be — more than mine — it did something considerably worse than leave him with complications of feeling.

What actually happened was that he turned up at our house in Acklen Park one day in July, driving his Dodge touring car and wearing his gabardine topcoat and his big straw hat, arrived there unheralded and unannounced, as he himself was fond of saying, and let himself in our front door with his own key, the key that, despite his protests, my two parents always insisted upon his having. And what he found inside the house that day was not a clean-cut young boy whom he had watched growing up and whom his daughter and son-in-law — away then on a short summer trip — had left at home to see after the premises. He found, instead, a dishevelled, disreputable-looking young fellow of eighteen summers who was hardly recognizable to his own grandfather, a boy who had just now frantically pulled on his clothes and who instead of occupying his parents' house alone was keeping a young girl in the house with him, a girl whom he had hurriedly hidden at the first sound of his grandfather's tires in the driveway — hidden, as a matter of fact, in the big oak wardrobe of the downstairs bedroom which his visiting grandfather was always expected to occupy. The ensuing confrontation between the grandfather and the grandson seemed on its surface to be accidental and something that might finally be forgotten by both of them. But it was not quite so simple as that . . . The old man and his grandson were never quite the same after that day — not the same with each other and probably not the same within themselves. Whatever their old relationship had been, it was over forever.

To me it seems natural that I should think about all of this whenever I am lying awake at night or when I am behind the wheel of my car on some endless highway. The memory of it raises questions in my mind that there seem to be no answers to, and those are inevitably the questions one entertains at such times. I find myself wondering why, in that antediluvian Tennessee world

I grew up in, it was so well established that grandfathers and grandsons were to be paired off and held answerable to each other for companionship; why it was that an old graybeard and a tow-headed little boy, in that day and age, were expected to be more companionable even than fathers and sons are told today they ought to be. For it really is my recollection that anywhere one turned in that world one was apt to see a bent old man and a stiff-necked little boy trudging along a country road together or plodding along the main street of a town. The world I am speaking of isn't the hard-bitten, Monkey Trial world of East Tennessee that everybody knows about but a gentler world in Middle Tennessee and more particularly the little region around Nashville which was known fifty years ago as the Nashville Basin and which in still earlier times, to the first settlers — our ancestors — was known somewhat romantically perhaps, and ironically, and incorrectly even, as the Miro District.

My grandfather, who did not take Nashville so seriously as my parents did, was fond of referring to the city itself as the Miro District (because he said only an antique Spanish name could do justice to the grandeur which Nashvillians claimed for themselves). According to Grandfather, this region had originally been so called in honor of one Don Estevan Miro, last of the Spanish governors of Spanish Louisiana, and according to this same knowledgeable grandfather of mine, the entire state of Tennessee had once been claimed to be a rightful part of that province by both the French and the Spanish in their day as its rulers. He used often to say to me, all irony about grandeur aside, that knowing such odd pieces of history about the place where one lived made the life one lived there seem less boring. He didn't couch it quite that way. He would not of course have used the word "boring." It wasn't in his vocabulary. But there is no doubt that's what he meant. And I used to try to imagine why it was that when he was scouting through the low ground or hill country west of the Tennessee River during the Civil War, it had made the war seem less hateful to him at times and less scary and less boring for him to know — or to believe — that the Spanish and the French had once held title to what was by then his own country or that the Indians had once held that land sacred, or for him to realize whenever he came in to Nashville that the site of the old citadel itself, Fort Nashborough, had once actually been known merely as French Lick.

*

My grandfather, when I first remember him, lived over in the next county from us, forty miles west of Nashville. But he was always and forever driving over for those visits of his — visits of three or four days, or longer — transporting himself back and forth from Hunt County to Nashville in his big tan touring car, with the canvas top put back in almost all weather, and usually wearing a broad-brimmed hat — a straw in summer, a felt in winter — and an ankle-length gabardine topcoat no matter what the season was.

He was my maternal grandfather and was known to everyone as Major Basil Manley. Seeing Major Manley like that at the wheel of his tan touring car, swinging into our driveway, it wasn't hard to imagine how he had once looked riding horseback or muleback through the wilds of West Tennessee when he was a young boy in Forrest's cavalry, or how he had looked, for that matter, in 1912, nearly half a century after he had ridden with General Forrest, at the time when he escaped from a band of hooded night riders who had kidnapped him — him and his law partner (and who had murdered his law partner before his eyes, on the banks of Bayou du Chien, near Reelfoot Lake).

Even when I was a very small boy, I always dreaded the sight of him out there in our driveway in his old car when he was arriving for a visit. I hated the first sound of his tires in the gravel as he came wheeling up to the house and then suddenly bore down on the brakes at the foot of our front-porch steps. I dreaded him not because I was frightened by his coming or by the history of his violent exploits, which I knew about from an early time, but because I was aware always of the painful hours that he and I who had nothing in common and for whom all our encounters were a torture would be expected to put in together.

The old man had always had a way of turning up, you see — even when I was little more than an infant — just when it suited *me* least, when I had *other* plans, which might include almost anything else in the world but the presence of a grandfather with whom it was intended I should be companionable. Sometimes he would go directly into our back yard, if it were summertime, without even removing his hat or his gabardine coat. He would plant one of the canvas yard chairs on the very spot where I had been building a little airfield or a horse farm in the grass. Then he would throw himself down into the chair and undo his collar button and remove his starched collar — he seldom wore a tie in

those days — and next he would pull his straw hat down over his
face and begin his inevitable dialogue with me without our having
exchanged so much as a glance or a how-do-you-do. It used to
seem to me he only knew I was there with him because he knew I
was required to be there. "I guess you've been behaving yourself,"
he said from under his hat, "the way a Nashville boy ought to
behave himself." And, of course, I knew well enough what was
meant by that. It meant I was some kind of effeminate city boy
who was never willing to visit his grandfather alone in the country
and who could never comprehend what it would be to ride muleback through the wilds of West Tennessee — either in pursuit of
Yankee marauders or in flight from hooded night riders. Looking
up at the old man from the grass beside his chair (or from the
carpet beside his platform rocker if we were settled in his downstairs bedroom), I thought to myself — thought this, or something
like it — Someday you and I will have to have it out between us. I
shall have to show you how it is with me and how I could never be
what you are . . . I often looked up at him, wanting — I know now
— to say something that would insult him and make him leave me
alone or make him take his walking stick to me. The trouble was,
of course — and I seemed to have sensed this before I was school
age even — that we couldn't understand or care anything about
each other. Something in each of us forbade it. It was as though
we faced each other across the distasteful present, across a queer,
quaint world that neither of us felt himself a part of.

When I looked up at him while we were talking, often out in the
back yard but more often in his room, I could never think exactly
what it was about him that I hated or if I really hated him at all.
Yet many a time I had that shameful feeling of wanting to insult
him. And so I got into the habit of trying to see him as my two
parents saw him. That's the awful part, really. I would look at him
until I saw him as I knew they saw him: an old country granddaddy
who came to town not wearing a tie and with only a bright gold
collar button shining where a tie ought to have been in evidence. It
seems shocking to me nowadays how well I knew at that tender age
just how my parents did surely see such an old man and, indeed,
how they saw all else in the world about us. They saw everything in
terms of Acklen Park in the city of Nashville in the Nashville Basin
in Middle Tennessee in the old Miro District, as it had come to be
in the first quarter of the twentieth century. I suppose it was my

knowing how Mother and Father saw the other grandfathers, who did actually live with *their* families in the Acklen Park neighborhood, that made me know for certain how they saw Major Basil Manley. To them, those other grandfathers seemed all elegance while he seemed all roughness. Those others lived quietly with their sons and daughters while he insisted upon living apart and in a county that was only on the periphery of Middle Tennessee. Those other grandfathers were a part of the families who had taken them in. (They had managed to become so or perhaps had always been so.) When you saw one of those other grandfathers out walking with a little grandson along West End Avenue, it was apparent at once that the two of them were made of the same clay, or at least that their mutual aim in life was to make it appear to the world that they were. Sometimes the old man and the little boy walked along West End hand in hand or sometimes with their arms about each other, the old man's arm on the little boy's shoulder, the little boy's arm about the old man's waist. It is a picture that comes into my mind almost every day that I live.

This ancient and well-established practice of pairing off young with old so relentlessly and so exclusively had, I think, as one of its results the marvel that men over fifty whom one meets in Nashville nowadays are likely to seem much too old-fashioned to be believed in almost — much too formal in their speech for any modern man, much too stiff in their manner to be taken seriously at all. They seem to be putting on an act. It is as if they are trying to *be* their grandfathers. Either that or these grandsons of Confederate veterans are apt to have become pathetic old roués and alcoholics, outrageously profane and willing to talk your ear off in the country-club bar — usually late at night — about how far they have fallen away from their ideals, about how very different they are from the men their grandfathers were. To hear them talk, one would actually suppose none of them ever had a father. One gets the impression that they only had grandfathers — elegant grandfathers born before 1860.

What is more to the point, though, is that this business of pairing off bent old men with stiff-necked little boys plainly had its effect, too, upon the old men — the grandfathers themselves. For when finally they approached their last years they often became absurd martinets, ordering the younger men and boys in their families about in their quavery old voices (and often getting laughed at behind their backs). Or some among these very same old men who had once stood firm at Missionary Ridge or had fought in the trenches before Petersburg or, like Grandfather Manley, had ridden with General Forrest became toward the very end as thoroughly domesticated as any old woman — could be seen fussing about the house like some old spinster great-aunt, rearranging the furniture or washing up little stacks of dishes, forever petting and hugging the young people in the family or clucking and fretting and even weeping softly whenever the young people didn't behave themselves as they ought to do.

My Grandfather Basil Manley was an exception to all of this, and I had been fully aware of the fact long before the time he caught me and my girl staying in his room. He was an exception in the first place because he refused from the very start to move into the same house with my mother and father — at the time when he was widowed — or even, for that matter, to come and live in the same town with us. He had resisted making that fatal mistake that so many of his contemporaries made — of moving in with their children. He was clearly different from them in a number of other respects, too, but it must have been that first, firm refusal of his to move in with us that allowed him to think for a few years that he could altogether escape the ignominious fate — of the one kind or the other — which his contemporaries had to endure.

He did not turn into an old woman and he did not try to play the martinet. Except for those relatively brief visits of his, he was free of the rules and mores of my parents' Nashville life. After three or four days spent mostly in my company, he would be off again to his farm in Hunt County and to the "primitive" life he lived there. If it was hard for anyone to see why he insisted on living in Hunt County when he could have lived so comfortably in Nashville, I at any rate thanked God on my knees that he had made that choice and prayed that he would never change his mind. For the most part, he went on living in the drafty, unheated farmhouse that he and his father before him had been born in. And on a farm where both cotton and tobacco had once been the money crops, but where tomatoes, strawberries, and corn had now become more profitable. There was no prestige or tradition about the kind of farming he did over there. (It was somehow felt an embarrassment that he raised only tomatoes, strawberries, corn. It

amounted to *truck* farming, though we did not even say the word.)
And certainly there was no romance about the place itself. That is
to say, his farm and the county it was in were considered somewhat
beyond the pale, not being in the handsome, bluegrass, limestone
country where livestock farms — and particularly horse farms —
made the landscape a joy to look upon and where the people had
always held themselves well above other mortal Tennesseans. He
preferred to go on living over there even after my father had
bought our fine house in Acklen Park and set aside the room there
for his exclusive occupancy.

It will be useful at this point to explain that before that day when
I hid my girl in the wardrobe there actually had been two other
serious and quite similar face-offs between my grandfather and me
and useful that I give some account of those earlier confrontations.
They both took place when I was eighteen, in the very same year
as the fateful one. And on both of those occasions Grandfather
stayed on in the house afterward, just as if nothing out of the
ordinary had happened. This was so despite there having been
more violent interplay between us — verbal and otherwise — in
those two encounters than there was destined to be in the last.

The first of them was in April of that year. My parents were not
out of town that time. Rather, my father was in the hospital to
undergo an operation on his prostate gland. He went into the
hospital on the Sunday afternoon before the Monday morning
when the operation was scheduled. Possibly he and my mother
regarded the operation more apprehensively than they should
have. My mother managed to obtain a room next to his in the
hospital. She went in with him on Sunday in order to be near him
during that night. My grandfather had of course been notified of
the circumstances. Mother had even made a long-distance telephone call from Nashville to Huntsboro. And since Grandfather
declined still to have a telephone in his house or to let the lines to
other houses go across his land, he had had to be fetched by a
messenger from his farm to Central's office on the town square.

That was on Saturday afternoon, and Mother had hoped he
might come to Nashville on Sunday and stay in the house — presumably to keep me company — at least until Father was safely
through the operation. But the old man was offended by everything about the situation. He resented being sent for and brought

to the telephone office. He resented having to hear Mother's indelicate news in the presence of Central herself (a local girl and a cousin of ours). And the worst of it was, so he said on the telephone to Mother, he didn't believe in the seriousness of the operation. Actually, when Mother and Father had previously mentioned to him the possibility of such surgery he had insisted that no such operation "existed" and that the doctor was pulling Father's leg. I was told this afterward by my father — long afterward — who said the old man had clearly resented such an unseemly subject's being referred to in his presence by his daughter or even by his son-in-law.

Anyhow, my mother told me that Grandfather would not be coming to stay with me on Sunday. I don't know whether or not she believed it. And I cannot honestly say for sure whether or not *I* believed he wasn't coming. I know only that on that Sunday afternoon, after my parents had left for the hospital, I telephoned two of my friends, two Acklen Park boys who would be graduating with me from Wallace School that June, and invited them to come over and to bring with them whatever they could manage to filch from their fathers' liquor closets. Actually, it was only my way of informing them of what I had in mind for that Sunday afternoon and evening, because I knew where the key to Father's closet was and knew there was more than enough bourbon whiskey there to suffice for three boys on their first real binge. Since this was an opportunity we had all been contemplating for some time, my invitation was only a matter of form.

I heard Grandfather Manley in the driveway at about half past six. In fact, I had lost track of time by then. We had been gulping down our whiskey as though it were lemonade. I could hardly stand on my feet when he came into the breakfast room, where we were seated about the table. I had made a stab at getting up when I first heard his car outside. My intention was to meet him, as usual, in the front hall. But as soon as I had got halfway up I felt a little sick. I knew I would be too unsteady on my feet to effect my usual sort of welcome in the hall, which would have entailed my taking his bag to his room for him and helping him off with his topcoat. Instead, I was still seated at the table when he stepped into the breakfast-room doorway. I did manage to rise from my chair then, scraping it crazily along the linoleum floor, which, at any rate, was more than the other two boys managed. And I faced him across the gold pocket watch that he was now holding out in his open palm like a piece of incriminating evidence. Although I say I faced him across the watch, his eyes were not really on me when he spoke but on the other boys at the table. "It's more than half an hour past my suppertime," he said. "I generally eat at six." That is how I can account for the time it was. Drunk as my two friends assuredly were and difficult as they undoubtedly found it to rise, they did, when Grandfather said that about suppertime, manage to rise somehow from their chairs and without a word of farewell went stumbling out through the kitchen and out of the house.

Grandfather then turned and went to his room, giving me an opportunity to put away the liquor and the glasses. Or I suppose that was his purpose. Perhaps he had only gone to remove his topcoat and his hat. When he came back, I had not stirred but still sat there with one hand on the quart bottle, fully intending to pour myself another drink. I had waited, I think, with the intention of pouring it in his presence. Looking at me, he said, "It's a fine sort of company you are keeping nowadays here in Nashville." At that, I took up the bottle and began pouring whiskey into my glass.

"They're my friends," I said, not looking at him. He stepped over to the table, seized the bottle by its neck with one hand, and took hold of my glass with the other. But I held on firmly to each — did so for several moments, that is. Together we were supporting both glass and bottle in midair. And then it must have been simultaneously that each of us relinquished his hold on both. The glass fell to the table, crashing and breaking into small pieces and splashing its contents over the tabletop. The bottle landed sidewise on the table, spewing out whiskey on Grandfather Manley's trousers, then rolled onto the floor, coming to rest there, unbroken but altogether empty. Immediately Grandfather Manley said, "Now you get that mess cleaned up." And he went off through the house to his room again.

His command had literally a sobering effect upon me, as probably nothing else could have — more so, certainly, than the breakage and spillage had. Though I was feeling unsteady, I did clean up the tabletop and I wiped up the floor. I decided to take the fragments of glass and the empty bottle out to the garbage can in the alley. I didn't want my mother to see any of it and to raise questions when she came home on Monday. As I was returning from the garbage can to the house through the dark back yard, I had sudden guilt feelings about my mother and father, visualizing them in the hospital, Father lying in the white bed and Mother sitting in a straight chair beside him. I knew that I had to go to my grandfather's room and take whatever satisfaction I could from the scolding I fancied he would surely give me.

I found him in his room, seated in his platform rocker, which like all the other furniture in the room was made of golden oak, with caning in the seat and back. He sat in it as if it were a straight chair, with one of his long, khaki-clad legs crossed stiffly over the other and one high-topped brown shoe sticking out assertively into the room. All the furniture in the room was furniture that he had brought there, at my mother's urging, from his house in Hunt County. It was in marked contrast with the rest of the furniture in our house. Mother had said, however, that he would feel more comfortable and at home with his own things in the room, and that he would be more likely to take real possession of it — which, after all, was what she and Father hoped for. I suspect they thought that would be a first step toward moving him in to live with us. In the end, Mother was actually disappointed at the particular pieces he chose to bring. But there will be a time later on for me to say more about that.

Anyway, there he was in his rocker, already divested of his starched collar and of the vest he always wore under his gabardine coat. His suspenders were loosened and hanging down over the arms of the chair. And he had lit his first cigarette of the evening. (He had given up his pipe at the time of his escape from the night riders and had taken up cigarettes, instead, because he said they gave more relief to his nerves. He had given up his beard and mustache then, too, because he couldn't forget how awful they had smelled to him when he had been hiding in the swamp for days on end and under stagnant water for many hours of the time.) I came into the room and stood before him, my back to the great golden-oak folding bed, which, when it was folded away against the wall, as it was now, could easily be mistaken for a large wardrobe like the one I was facing on the other side of the room, matching it almost exactly in size, bulk, and color. I stood there in silence for several moments, waiting for him to begin the kind of dressing down which he had never given me and which if he could have given me then might have made all the difference in the world in our future relations — and perhaps our lives.

For a while, he said nothing. Then he said, "I don't want any supper tonight. If the cook left something, you'd better go eat it. Because if you *can* eat, it will likely do you good!" There was no note of sympathy in his voice — only an acknowledgment of my condition. But I could tell there was going to be no dressing down, either. It was going to be just like always before when we had been left alone together.

"I can't eat anything," I said. And I began to feel that I was going to actively ill. But somehow I was able to control and overcome that feeling. Then I began to feel drunk again, as drunk as I had been when he first came in on us. I slumped down onto a leather ottoman and sat with my elbows on my knees, still looking at him. It was just as it had always been before. We had nothing to say to each other — nothing we *could* say. And thinking about all the times we had been left together like this when I was a little boy, it seemed to me that I had always been somewhat drunk whenever he and I had had to talk, and had always been unable to make any sense at all.

"Tell me what it was like," I suddenly began now in a too loud voice. "Tell me what it was like to be kidnapped by those night riders . . . out in Lake County." He sat forward in his chair as if so astonished by what I had said that he would have to come to his feet. But still he didn't get up, and I went on. "And what it was like . . . to see Captain Tyree hanged before your very eyes." I was hesitating and stammering as I spoke. I had never before said anything like this to him. In the past, you see, when we had been wanting a topic, I had always pressed him to tell me about the Civil War — not because I cared much about the War but because, as I realize now but didn't understand then, it was what my parents cared about and were always telling me I ought to get him to talk about. But he didn't want to talk about the War. Not in a serious way. He would say, "There's little to tell, God knows," and put me off with a slapstick anecdote or two, about shooting a man's hat off outside the Gayoso Hotel during the raid on Memphis, or about meeting General Forrest on a backcountry road when, as a boy of sixteen and riding bareback on a mule, he was on his way to enlist in Forrest's own critter company, and how General Forrest and some other officers had forced him off the road and into a muddy ditch and didn't even look back at him until he yelled out after them every filthy kind of thing he could think of. "But since I was a mite small for my age," he would say, "they must have mistook me for some local farm boy. Only Forrest himself ever looked back — looked back with that sickly grin of his." And then he was sure to end that anecdote saying, "Likely I'm the onliest man or boy who ever called Bedford Forrest a son of a bitch and lived."

That was not the kind of war story I wanted, of course. My father, who read Civil War history, would, in my presence, try to draw the old man out on the subject, asking him about Forrest's strategy or whether or not the War might have been won if Jeff Davis had paid more attention to the "Western theatre." And all Grandfather Manley would say was: "I don't know about any of that. I don't know what it matters."

But that Sunday night in his room, instead of plaguing him to talk about the War, as I had always previously tended to do, I took the opposite tack. And I think I could not have stopped myself from going on even if I had wanted to. As I rattled on, I felt my grandfather looking at me uncertainly, as though he were not sure whether it was I or he that was drunk. "Tell me about your kidnapping," I said, actually wavering on the big leather ottoman as I spoke and my voice rising and lowering — quite beyond my control. "Or tell me about the earthquake in 1811 that your old daddy used to tell you about, that made the Mississippi River run upstream and formed Reelfoot Lake, and how you imagined when you were lost in the swamp, and half out of your head, that you could see the craters and fissures from the earthquake still there."

Suddenly Grandfather lit his second cigarette, got up from his chair, and went over and stood by a window. I suppose it occurred to him that I was mocking him, though I couldn't have said, myself, whether or not I was. "You're all worked up," he said. "And it's not just that whiskey in you. Your mother's got you all worked up about this damnable operation of your dad's."

"Tell me what it was like," I began again. In my confused and intoxicated state, my whole system seemed determined to give it all back to him — all the scary stories I had listened to through all the years about the night riders of Reelfoot Lake. I can hear myself clearly even now, sometimes speaking to him in a singsongy voice more like a child's voice than the ordinary man's voice I had long since acquired. "Tell me what it was like to wake up in the Walnut Log Hotel at Samburg, Tennessee . . . Tell me what it was like to lie in your bed in that shackly, one-story, backwoods hotel and have

it come over you that it was no dream, that hooded men on horseback filled the yard outside, each with a blazing pine-knot torch,
that there really was at every unglazed window of your room the
raw rim of a shotgun barrel."

As I babbled away, it was not just that night but every night that
I had ever been alone in the house with him. I had the sensation of
retching or of actual vomiting not the whiskey I had in my stomach
but all the words about the night riders I had ever had from him
and had not known how to digest — words I had not ever wanted
to hear. My confusion was such that some of the time I did not
know at all what I was saying. I knew only that this was the beginning of my freedom from him. And I had no notion of why it
should be so. Only now and then a vague thought or an image took
shape for me — of him as the young soldier on horseback or of the
war itself that he would not reveal to us, that he always substituted
talk about the night riders for. But now I would not have to have
any of the night-rider business again. I was giving it all back. And
as I did so, how nerve-racking my voice was, almost beyond endur-
ance — to me no less than to my grandfather, he who sat before
me in the bright light he had now put on in the room, wearing his
rough, country clothes, his blue shirt and khaki trousers, blinking
his veiny eyelids at me, not really listening any longer to what I
said. He was thinking then, as I knew he had always thought: *You
don't want to hear such stuff as that. Not from me, you don't. You just want
to hear yourself sketching in my old stories, giving them back to me. It makes
you feel good. It helps you hide your feelings or whatever it is you've always
wished to hide.* He sat before me blinking and thinking — or one
process; or one rhythm, at any rate. And not really listening to me
at all.

But I couldn't stop myself, any more than he could stop me with
his blinking or with the twisting back and forth of his weak chin
and lean jaw. The twisting was somehow offensive to me. It was
something I had seen him do to other people who troubled or
annoyed him in some way. It was almost as if he were chewing
tobacco and looking for a place spit — which was something he
liked to boast he had never done. And I heard my awful childlike
voice going on. It was as though it were not mine and as though I
were someone hidden on the far side of the room from us in the
big oak wardrobe where I would one day hide that girl. But my

voice persisted. I went on and on, so nervous as I looked into his white-blue eyes that I feared I would burst into tears or, worse still, into silly, little-boy laughter.

"Tell how they ordered you and Marcus Tyree out of your beds, though you each slept with a revolver at your side, ordered you up from your straw mattresses on those homemade bedsteads and required the two of you to get fully dressed, even to putting on your starched collars and your black shoestring ties, and then escorted you both on muleback, at gunpoint, out to the edge of the bayou."

But he said nothing. He only kept on blinking at me. And the bright light had little or nothing to do with it. In recent years, he had always blinked at me. (When I was fourteen, when I was sixteen, when I was eighteen. Those were the years when it got to be unbearable.) Each time we met, I pressed him to tell me tales about his war exploits and the suffering he had endured. ("Ask him!" my father had said to me. "Ask him!" my mother had said to me.) That was what set him blinking usually. He distrusted all garrulous young people. Most of all, those who asked questions. *Why have you never waited and allowed me to speak for myself?* I knew he was thinking but didn't say. *And why is it you've never opened your mouth to me about yourself?*

He had always thought I was hiding something. Tonight, his suspicion was so strong I could hear it in his breathing. I went on and on. "Tell me again how you, alone, escaped! How the night riders made a bonfire on the banks of the bayou and put a rope around Captain Tyree's neck, torturing him, pulling him up and letting him down until finally he said, 'Gentlemen, you're killing me.' And then one of the men said, 'That's what we aim to do, Captain.' And they yanked him up for the last time. How a moment later, when all eyes were on the strung-up body of your friend, your law partner, your old comrade-in-arms from the War days and with whom you had come there only as 'two friends of the court' to settle old land disputes made not by any man on earth but by an earthquake a hundred years before almost to the day, how at that moment, really in one of your wicked explosions of temper — afterward it was your rage you remembered most clearly — you vowed to survive (vowed it in your rage) and yourself bring to justice those squatters-turned-outlaws. And seeing your one chance to escape, you, in your saving rage, dived into the brackish water of the Bayou du Chien — you a man of sixty and more even then. Tell me how . . . you hid under the log floating in the bayou (somebody made a gavel from its wood for you later) and how in the predawn dark they filled the dead log you were under full of buckshot, supposing it was you that was dead out there, supposing it was your body they saw floating, drifting sluggishly in the Bayou du Chien toward Reelfoot Lake."

Before I finished, he had begun to laugh his sardonic courtroom laugh, which was more like an old piece of farm machinery that needed oiling than like most human laughter. It was a laugh that was famous for having destroyed the case of many a courtroom lawyer in Hunt County — more frequently than any argument or rhetoric he had ever employed. I had heard him laugh that way at our dinner table, too, when my father had expressed some opinion or theory that Grandfather had not agreed with but that he knew he could not refute with logic. And I went on long after I knew that any use there might have been in my performance that day was over. Long after I had realized that if my performance were going to have any effect it had already been had. At some point I could see that he was no longer listening and that, after all, the victory of this engagement was somehow his. Finally I was silenced by his silence. Now he had come back from the window and sat down in the chair again and was smiling his wickedest courtroom smile at me. His blue eyes seemed very bright, and I could tell that for a few moments at least my singsong recounting of his experiences had stirred his memory. I felt that if I encouraged him and if he permitted himself he would even now take up where I had left off and describe one more time his ten days of wandering in the swamp after his escape and then perhaps his finally reaching a logging road on high ground and there lapping up water like an Indian out of the hoofprints of horses, because he knew it was rainwater and pure, and then the ride to Tiptonville, concealed under the hay in a farmer's wagon bed. And at last the trial of the nine night riders.

He loved to dwell upon the fact that all nine men were proved to be previously convicted criminals, not downtrodden backwoodsmen whose livelihood in fishing and hunting the government and the big landowners of Lake County wished to take away. Perhaps he went over all that in his mind for a few moments, but what his wicked smile and the light in his eyes spoke of was a victory he was revelling in at that present moment. My long spiel about the night-rider trouble had reflected the many times I had had to listen to his account of it. And to him, I somehow understood in a flash of insight, it meant above all else what was perhaps dearest to his soul of all things during those years. It meant how many times he had successfully avoided reminiscing about the War. In retrospect, I can see that it had become almost mechanical with him to answer any requests I made for stories about the War with stories about his adventures at Reelfoot Lake. For a number of years, I think, he had tried to distract me with just any of his old stories about hunting bear or deer or about lawsuits he had had that took him into tough communities where he had sometimes to fight his way out of the courtroom and sometimes share a bed in a country hotel with a known murderer whom he was defending. But for a long time there had been no variations in his response.

I did not know then, and do not know now, at what moment he took a vow never to talk about the Civil War and his own experiences in it, or whether he unconsciously and gradually began to avoid the subject with members of his family — after he had already ceased talking about it with anybody else. But from his smile that day and his laughter, which I had only before heard him direct at my parents, I began to sense that he regarded me chiefly as their agent and that yielding to me in my pressing him to tell me about his war would be the first chink in his armor of resistance to my parents and could end with nothing less than their bringing him into Nashville and into our house to live.

At last, he got up from his chair again. He was no longer smiling at me but clearly he was no longer angry with me, either. And at the end, when he dismissed me from his room, it occurred to me that seeing an eighteen-year-old boy drunk was nothing new to a man of his experience in the rough sort of world he came along in and that my pilfering my father's whiskey while he was in the hospital seemed to him almost a natural and inevitable mistake for a boy my age to have made. "You've had a hard day," he said — rather sternly but not more so than if he had been correcting me about some show of bad manners. "Get yourself a night's sleep, and we'll go to the hospital tomorrow to see how your dad is making out. Seems to me he and your mama've got you so worked up there's no telling what you *might* have done if I hadn't shown up as I did, unheralded and unannounced."

*

It was hardly six weeks later that we had our second run-in. He came in to Nashville on Decoration Day, when, of course, the Confederate veterans always held their most elaborate services and celebrations out at the State Fairground. Father and Mother had gone to Memphis to visit Father's sister out there over the Decoration Day weekend. They wouldn't have planned to go, so they said, except that Grandfather as usual swore he was never again going to attend a Confederate Reunion of any kind. He had been saying for years that all the reunions amounted to were occasions to promote everybody to a higher rank. He acknowledged that once upon a time he had been a party to this practice. He had been so for many years, in fact. But enough was enough. It was one thing to promote men like himself who had been private soldiers to the rank of captain and major but quite another to make them colonels and generals. They had voted him his majority back in the years before his kidnapping by the night riders. But since the experience of that abduction by those murderous backwoodsmen he had never attended another Confederate Reunion. For more than a dozen years now he had insisted that it would not be possible for him to pass in through the Fairground gates on any Decoration Day without being sure to come out with the rank of colonel. He could not countenance that. And he could not countenance that gathering of men each year to repeat and enlarge upon reminiscences of something that he was beginning to doubt had ever had any reality.

From the first moment after I had put my parents on the train for Memphis, I think I knew how that weekend was going to go. I would not have admitted it to myself and didn't admit it for many years afterward. I suspect, too, that from the time some weeks earlier when he had heard of my parents' plans to go to Memphis — that is, assuming that he would not be coming in for the Reunion — Grandfather must also have had some idea of how it might go. Looking back, it seems almost as if he and I were plotting the whole business together.

It didn't of course seem that way at the time. Naturally, I can only speculate on how it seemed for him, but he had made more than one visit to Nashville since the day he found me there drinking with my friends, and I had observed a decided change in him — in his attitude toward me, that is. On one occasion he had offered me a cigarette, which was the next thing, it seemed to me then, to offering me a drink. I knew, of course, that Grandfather had, at one time or another, used tobacco in most of its forms. And we all knew, as a matter of fact, that when he closed the door to his room at night he nearly always poured himself a drink — poured it into a little collapsible tumbler that, along with his bottle of sour mash, he had brought with him in his Gladstone bag. His drinking habits had never been exactly a secret, though he seldom made any direct reference to them except in certain stories he told. And whatever changes there were in his style during his very last years, his drinking habits never changed at all — not, I believe, from the time when he was a young boy in the Confederate Army until the day he died.

It is true that I often smelled liquor on his breath when he arrived at our house for a visit, but I believe that was because he made a habit of having a quick one when he stopped along the way to rest and to relieve himself at the roadside. Moreover, that was only like the drink he had in his room at night — for his nerves. I believe the other drinking he had done in his lifetime consisted entirely of great bouts he had sometimes had with groups of men on hunting trips, often as not in that very region around Reelfoot Lake where he had witnessed the torture and strangulation of his old comrade-in-arms and law partner and where he had then wandered for ten nights in the swampy woodland thereabouts (he had regarded it as unsafe to travel by day and unsafe to knock on any cabin door, lest it be the hideaway of one of the night riders), wandered without food and without fresh water to drink, and suffering sometimes from hallucinations.

I feel that I must digress here in order to say a few things about those hallucinations he had, which must actually have been not unlike delirium tremens, and about impressions that I myself had of that country around the lake when I visited it as a child. As a very young child — no more than three or four years old — I had been taken on a duck-hunting trip to the lake with Father and Grandfather and a party of men from Hunt County. I didn't go with them, of course, when, attired in their grass hats and grass skirts and capes — for camouflage — they took up their positions in the marshlands. I was left in the hunting lodge on the lake's edge in the care of the Negro man who had been brought along to do the cooking. I don't remember much about the days or the nights of that expedition. I must have passed them comfortably and happily enough. All I remember very clearly is what seemed the endless and desolate periods of time I spent during the early-morning hours and the twilight hours of each day of our stay there, all alone in the lodge with Thomas, the cook. As I sat alone on the screened porch, which went all the way round that little batten-board lodge (of no more than three or four rooms and a loft), and listened to Thomas's doleful singing in the kitchen, all I could see was the dark water of the lake on one side and of the bayou on the other, with the cypress stumps and other broken trees rising lugu-briously out of the water and the mysterious, deep woods of the bottomlands beyond on the horizon. It seemed to me that I could see for miles. And the fact was, the lodge being built high upon wooden pilings, it was indeed possible to see great distances across the lake, which was five miles wide in places.

During those hours on the screened porch, I would think about the tales I had heard the men tell the night before when they were gathered around the iron stove and I was going off to sleep on my cot in a far corner of the room. I suppose the men must have been having their drinks then. But I can't say that I remember the smell of alcohol. All the smells there in that place were strange to me, though — the smell of the water outside, the smell of the white-wash on the vertical boarding on the lodge, and the smell of the musty rooms inside the lodge, which stood empty most of the year. The tales the men told were often connected with the night-rider trouble. Others were old tales about the New Madrid Earthquake that had formed the lake more than a hundred years before. Some of the men told old folktales about prehistoric monsters that rose up out of the lake in the dark of the moon.

I don't recall my father's contributing to this talk. My memory is that he sat somewhat outside the circle, looking on and listening appreciatively to the talk of those older men, most of whom had probably never been outside the state of Tennessee, unless it was to go a little way up into Kentucky for whiskey. But my Grand-father Manley contributed his full share. And everyone listened to him with close attention. He spoke with an authority about the lake, of course, that none of the others quite had. When those other men told their stories about prehistoric monsters rising from the lake, one felt almost that Grandfather when he emerged from his ten days in the swampland, according to his own account, must have looked and smelled like just such a prehistoric monster. To me the scariest of his talk was that about some of the hallucinations he had, hallucinations about the hooded men mounted on strange animals charging toward him like the horsemen of the Apocalpyse. But almost as frightening as his own reminiscences were the accounts he had heard or read of that earthquake that made the lake.

The earthquake had begun on December 16, 1811, and the sequence of shocks was felt as far away as Detroit and Baltimore and Charleston, South Carolina. Upriver, at New Madrid, Missouri, nearly the whole town crumbled down the bluffs and into the river. The shocks went on for many days — even for several months — and in between the shocks the earth vibrated and sometimes trembled for hours on end "like the flesh of a beef just killed." Men and women and children, during the first bad shocks, hung on to trees like squirrels. In one case, a tree "infested with people" was seen to fall across a newly made ravine, and the poor wretches hung there for hours, until there was a remission in the earth's undulation. Whole families were seen to disappear into round holes thirty feet wide, and the roaring of the upheaval was so loud that their screams could not be heard.

Between Memphis and St. Louis, the river foamed and in some places the current was observed to have reversed and run upstream for several hours. Everywhere, the quake was accompanied by a loud, hoarse roaring. And on land, where fissures and craters appeared, a black liquid was ejected sometimes to a height of fifteen feet and subsequently fell in a black shower, mixed with the sand that it had forced up along with it. In other places, the earth burst open, and mud, water, sandstone, and coal were thrown up the distance of thirty yards. Trees everywhere were blown up, cracking and splitting and falling by the thousand at a time. It was reported that in one place the black liquid oozed out of the ground to the height of the belly of a horse. Grandfather had heard or read somewhere that John James Audubon had been caught in some of the later, less violent shocks and that his horse died of fright with him sitting it. Numbers of people died, of course, on the river as well as on the land, and many of those who survived were never afterward regarded as possessing their right senses.

Among the hallucinations that my grandfather had while wandering in the low ground after his escape was that that earthquake of a hundred years before — almost to the day of the month — had recurred, commenced again, or that he was living in that earlier time when the whole earth seemed to be convulsed and its surface appeared as it must have in primordial times. And he imagined that he was there on that frontier in company with the ragged little bands of Frenchmen and Spaniards and newly arrived American settlers, all of whose settlements had vanished into the earth, all of them in flight, like so many Adams and Eves, before the wrath of their Maker.

My father told me more than one time — again, long after I was grown — that it was only after Grandfather Manley had had a few drinks and was off somewhere with a group of men that he would describe the time of wandering in the swamps and describe his hallucinations about the earthquake. And I myself heard him speak of those hallucinations, when I was at the lodge with them and was supposed to be asleep in my cot, heard him speak of them as though they were real events he had experienced and heard him say that his visions of the earthquake were like a glimpse into the eternal chaos we live in, a glimpse no man should be permitted, and that after that all of his war experiences seemed small and insignificant matters — as nothing. And it was after that, of course, that he could never bring himself to go back to those Reunions and take part in those reminiscences with the other old soldiers of events so much magnified by them each year or take part in their magnification of their own roles by advancing themselves in rank each year.

Grandfather could only confide those feelings of his to other men. He would only confide them when he had a little whiskey in him. And what is important, too, is that he only drank alone or in the company of other men. He abhorred what my father and mother had come to speak of in the nineteen-twenties as social drinking. Drinking liquor was an evil and was a sign of weakness, he would have said, and just because one indulged in it oneself was no reason to pretend to the world that there was virtue in it. *That,* to him, was hypocrisy. Drinking behind closed doors or in a secluded hunting lodge, though one denounced it in public as an evil practice, signified respect for the public thing, which was more important than one's private character. It signified genuine humility. And so it was, I must suppose, that he in some degree approved of the kind of drinking bout he had caught me in. And his approval, I suppose, spoiled the whole effect for me. It put me in the position, as I understand it now, of pretending to be like the man I felt myself altogether unlike and alien to.

And so it was that the circumstances he found me in were quite different on that inevitable Decoration Day visit of his. My parents were no sooner aboard the train for Memphis that Friday night than I had fetched a certain acquaintance of mine named Jeff Patterson — he was older than I and had finished his second year at Vanderbilt — and together we had picked up two girls we knew who lived on Eighth Avenue, near the Reservoir. We went dancing at a place out on Nine Mile Hill. We were joined there by two other couples of our acquaintance, and later the eight of us came back to Acklen Park. (I must say that I was much more experienced with girls by that age than I was with liquor.) We had had other, similar evenings at the houses of the parents of the two other boys who joined us that night, but until then I had never been so bold as to use my parents' house for such purposes.

The girls we had with us were not the kind of girls such a boy as I was would spend any time with nowadays. That is why this part of the story may be difficult for people of a later generation to understand. With one's real girl, in those days, a girl who attended Ward-Belmont School and who was enrolled in Miss Amy Lowe's dancing classes, one might neck in the back seat of a car. The girl might often respond too warmly. But it was one's own manliness that made one overcome one's impulse to possess her and, most of all, overcome her impulse to let herself be possessed before taking the marriage vow. I am speaking of decent boys and girls, of course, and I acknowledge that even among decent or "nice" young people of that day there were exceptions to the rule. One knew of too many seven-month babies to have any doubt of that. Still, from the time one was fourteen or fifteen in Nashville one had to know girls of various sorts and one had to have a place to take girls of "the other sort." No one of my generation would have been shocked by the events of that evening. The four couples went to bed — and finally slept — in the four bedrooms on the second floor of my parents' house in Acklen Park. I had never before brought such a party to our house, and I gave no thought to how I would clean up the place afterward or how I would conceal what had gone on there.

It was only a few minutes past seven the next morning when I heard Grandfather's car outside in the driveway. I was at once electrified and paralyzed by the sound. Lying there in my own bed with that girl beside me, and with the other couples still asleep in

the other rooms, I had a vision of our big, two-story brick house as
it appeared from the outside that May morning, saw the details of
the stone quoins at the four corners of the house, the heavy green
window blinds and the keystones above the windows, even the
acanthus leaves in the capitals of the columns on the front porch.
I saw it all through my grandfather's sharp little eyes as he turned
into the gravel driveway, and saw through his eyes not only my
parents' car, which I had carelessly left out of the garage, but the
cars also of the two other boys who had joined us, all three cars
sitting out there in the driveway on Sunday morning, as if to an-
nounce to him that some kind of party — and even *what* kind of
party, probably — was going on inside.

He didn't step into his room to set down his Gladstone bag. I
heard him drop it on the floor in the front hall and then I heard
his quick footsteps on the long stairway. Then I heard him opening
the doors to all the bedrooms. (We *had* had the decency to close
ourselves off in separate rooms.) He opened my door last, by design I suppose. I was lying on my stomach and I didn't even lift my
head to look at him. But I knew exactly how he would appear there
in the doorway, still wearing his long coat and his summer straw
hat. That was the last thought or the last vision I indulged in before
I felt the first blow of his walking stick across my buttocks. At last
he had struck me! That was what I thought to myself.

By the time I felt the second blow from his stick I had realized
that between the two blows he delivered me he had struck one on
the buttocks of the girl beside me. By the time he had struck the
girl a second time she had begun screaming. I came up on my
elbows and managed to clamp my hand over her mouth to keep
the neighbors from hearing her. He left us then. And over his
shoulder, as he went striding from the room, he said, "I want you
to get these bitches out of this house and to do so in one hell of a
hurry!" He went back into the hallway, and then when I had scram-
bled out of bed I saw him, to my baffling chagrin and unaccount-
able sense of humiliation, hurrying into the other rooms, first one
and then another, and delivering blows to the occupants of those
other beds. Some of the others, I suppose, had heard him crack
the door to their rooms earlier and had crawled out of bed before
he got there. But I heard him and saw him wielding his stick
against Jeff Patterson's backside and against the little bottom of the
girl beside him. Finally — still wearing his hat and his gabardine

coat, mind you — he passed through the hall again and toward the
head of the stairs. I was standing in the doorway to my room by
then, but clad only in my underwear shorts. As he went down the
stairsteps he glanced back at me and spoke again: "You get those
bitches out of your mother's house and you do it in one hell of a
hurry."

Even before I was able to pull on my clothes, all four of the girls
were fully dressed and scurrying down the stairs, followed immediately by the three boys. I came to the head of the stairs and stood
there somewhat bemused, looking down. The girls had gone off
into the front rooms downstairs in search of certain of their possessions. I heard them calling to each other desperately: "I left my
lipstick right here on this table!" And "Oh, God, where's my
purse?" And "Where in the world are my pumps?" I realized then
that one of them had gone down the stairs barefoot, and simultaneously I saw Grandfather Manley moving by the foot of the stairs
and toward the living room.

I descended slowly, listening to the voices in the front room.
First there had come a little shriek from one of the girls when
Grandfather entered. Then I heard his voice reassuring them. By
the time I reached the living-room doorway, he was assisting them
in their search, whereas the three boys only stood by, watching. It
was he himself who found that little purse. Already the four girls
seemed completely at ease. He spoke to them gently and without
contempt or even condescension. The girl who had been my date
left with the others, without either of us raising the question of
whether or not I might see her home. As they went out through
the wide front door the four girls called out "Goodbye!" in cheerful
little voices. I opened my mouth to respond, but before I could
make a sound I heard Grandfather answering, "Goodbye, girls."
And it came over me that it had been to him, not me, they were
calling goodbye. When he and I were alone in the hall, he said,
"And now I reckon you realize what we've got to do. We've got to
do something about those sheets."

It is a fact that he and I spent a good part of that day doing
certain cleanup jobs and employing the electric iron here and
there. I can't say it drew us together, though, or made any sort of
bond between us. Perhaps that's what he imagined the result would
be. But I never imagined so for a moment. Though he and I were
of the same blood, we had parted company, so to speak, before I

was born even, and there was some divisive thing between us that
could never be overcome. Perhaps I felt that day that it was my
parents, somehow, who would forever be a wall between us, and
that once any people turned away from what he was, as they had
done, then that — whatever it was he was — was lost to them and
to their children and to their children's children forever. But I
cannot say definitely that I felt anything so certain or grand that
day. I cannot say for sure what I felt except that when he spoke
with such composure and assurance to those girls in my parents'
living room, I felt that there was nothing in the world he didn't
know and hadn't been through.

As he and I worked away at cleaning up the bedrooms that
morning, I asked myself if his knowing so well how to speak to
those girls and if the genuine sympathy and even tenderness that
he clearly felt toward them meant perhaps that his insistence upon
living alone in that old house over in Hunt County suggested there
were girls or women in his life still. Whatever else his behavior that
day meant, it meant that the more bad things I did and the worse
they were, then the better he would think he understood me and
the more alike he would think we were. But I knew there must yet
be something I could do that would show him how different we
were, and saw that until I had made him grasp that, I would not
begin to discover what, since I wasn't and couldn't be like him, I
was like.

In July, Mother and Father went up to Beersheba Springs, on
the Cumberland Plateau, for a few days' relief from the hot
weather. Beersheba was an old-fashioned watering place, the resort
in past times of Episcopal bishops, Louisiana planters, and the
gentry of Middle Tennessee. By the nineteen-twenties only a select
few from the Nashville Basin kept cottages there and held sway at
the old hotel. It was the kind of summer spot my parents felt most
comfortable in. It had never had the dash of Tate Springs or the
homey atmosphere of Monteagle, but it was older than either of
those places and had had since its beginning gambling tables,
horses, and dancing. Behind the porticoed hotel on the bluff's
edge, the old slave quarters were still standing, as was also the
two-story brick garçonnière, reached by a covered walkway from
the hotel. There was an old graveyard overgrown with box and red
cedar, enclosed by a rock wall and containing old gravestones lean-

ing at precarious angles but still bearing good Tennessee-Virginia names like Burwell and Armistead. Farther along the bluff and farther back on the plateau were substantial cottages and summer houses, a good number of them built of squared chestnut logs and flanked by handsome limestone end chimneys. The ancient and unreconstructed atmosphere of the place had its attraction even for Grandfather Manley, and my parents had persuaded him to accompany them on their holiday there.

He drove in to Nashville and then, still in his own car, followed Mother and Father in their car to Beersheba Springs, which was seventy or eighty miles southeast of Nashville, on the edge of the plateau and just above what used to be known as the Highland Rim. It seemed a long way away. There was no question in my mind of the old man's turning up in Nashville this time. I looked forward with pleasure to a few days of absolute freedom — from my parents, from my grandfather, and even from the servants, who were always given a holiday whenever my parents were out of town. I was in such relaxed good spirits when Father and Mother and Grandfather Manley had departed that I went up to my room — though it was not yet noon — and took a nap on my bed. I had no plans made for this period of freedom except to see even more than usual of a Ward-Belmont girl whom I had been dating during most of that winter and spring and whom my parents, as an indication of their approval of my courting a girl of her particular family, had had to dinner at our house several times and even on one occasion when my grandfather was there. She was acknowledged by my family and by everyone else to be my girl, and by no one more expressly than by the two of us — by the girl herself, that is, and by me.

I was awakened from my nap just before noon that day by the ringing of the telephone in the upstairs hall. And it so happened that the person calling was none other than she whom I would have most wished to hear from. It was not usual for such a girl to telephone any boy, not even her acknowledged favorite. I have to say that as soon as I heard her voice I experienced one of those moments I used often to have in my youth of seeming to know how everything was going to go. I can't blame myself for how things did go during the next twenty-four hours and can't blame the girl, either. Since this is not the story of our romance, it will suffice to say that though our romance did not endure for long after that time, these events were not necessarily the cause of its failure. The girl herself has prospered in life quite as much as I have. And no doubt she sometimes speaks of me nowadays, wherever in the world she is living, as "a boy I went with in Nashville," without ever actually mentioning my name. At any rate, when she telephoned that day she said she was *very much* upset about something and wanted *very much* to see me at once. She apologized for calling. She would not have been so brash, she said, except that since I had told her of my parent's plans she knew I would probably be at home alone. The circumstance about which she was upset was that since her parents, too, were out of town, her two older sisters were planning "an awful kind of party" that she could not possibly have any part in. She wanted me to help her decide what she must do.

My parents had taken our family car to Beersheba, and so it was that she and I had to meet on foot, halfway between Acklen Park and her house, which was two or three miles away, out in the Belle Meade section. And it ended of course, after several hours of earnest talk about love and life — exchanged over milkshakes in a place called Candyland and on the benches in the Japanese Garden in Centennial Park — ended by our coming to my house and telephoning her sisters that she had gone to spend the night with a classmate from Ward-Belmont. The inevitability of its working out so is beyond question in my mind. At least, in retrospect it is. Certainly both of us had known for many days beforehand that both sets of parents would be out of town; and certainly the very passionate kind of necking which we had been indulging in that summer, in the darkness of my father's car and in the darkness of her father's back terrace, had become almost intolerable to us. But we could honestly say to ourselves that we had made no plans for that weekend. We were able to tell ourselves afterward that it was just something that happened. And I was able to tell myself for many years afterward—I cannot deny it categorically even today — that I would not have consented to our coming to my house if I had thought there was the remotest possibility of Grandfather Manley's turning up there.

And yet, though I can tell myself so, there will always be a certain lingering doubt in my mind. And even after it was clear to both of us that we would sleep together that night, her sense of propriety was still such that she refused to go up to the second floor of my house. Even when I led her into Grandfather Manley's room, she did not realize or did not acknowledge to herself that it was a bedroom we were in. I suppose she had never before seen anything quite like the furniture there. "What a darling room!" she exclaimed when I had put on the floor lamp beside the golden-oak rocker. And when I pulled down the great folding bed, even in the dim lamplight I could see that she blushed. Simultaneously almost, I caught a glimpse of myself in the mirror of the oak bureau and I cannot deny that I thought with a certain glee in that moment of my grandfather or deny that I felt a certain premonition of events.

My first thought when I heard his car outside the next afternoon was: We are in *his* room! We are in *his* bed! I imagined that that was what was going to disturb him most. The fact was that we had been in and out of his bed I don't know how many times by then. We had not only made love there in a literal sense, and were so engaged when he arrived, but we had during various intervals delighted each other there in the bed with card games and even checkers and Parcheesi, with enormous quantities of snacks which the cook had left for me in the refrigerator, and finally with reading aloud to each other from volumes of poetry and fiction which I fetched from my room upstairs. If there had been any sense of wrongdoing in our heads the previous afternoon regarding such preoccupations as would be ours during those two days, it had long since been dispelled by the time that old man my grandfather arrived.

When I told her there beside me that it was the tires of my grandfather's car she and I had heard skidding in the gravel and that it was now his quick, light step on the porch steps that I recognized, she seized me by the wrist and whispered, "Even if he knows I'm here, I don't want him to see me, and I don't want to see him. You have to hide me! Quickly!" By the time we had pushed up the folding bed, there was already the sound of his key in the front door. There was nothing for it, if she were to be hidden, but to hide her in the wardrobe.

"Over there," I said, "if you're sure you want to. But it's his room. He's apt to find you."

"Don't you let him," she commanded.

"You put on your clothes" was all I could say. I was pulling on my trousers. And now she was running on tiptoe toward the wardrobe, with nothing on at all, carrying all her clothing and a pillow and blanket from the bed, all in a bundle clutched before her. She opened the wardrobe door, tossed everything in before her, and then hopped in on top of it. I followed her over there, buttoning my trousers and trying to get into my shirt. As I took a last step forward to close the door on her, I realized that except for her and the bundle of clothing she was crouched on the wardrobe was entirely empty. There were no possessions of Grandfather's in it. I thought to myself, Perhaps he never opens the wardrobe even. And as I closed the door I saw to my delight that my brave girl, huddled there inside the wardrobe, wasn't by any means shedding tears but was smiling up at me. And I think I knew then for the first time in my life how wonderful it is to be in love and how little anything else in the world matters. And I found myself smiling back at her with hardly an awareness of the fact that she hadn't a piece of clothing on her body. And I actually delayed closing the door long enough to put the palm of my hand to my mouth and throw her a kiss.

Then, having observed the emptiness of the wardrobe, I glanced over at the oak bureau and wondered if it weren't entirely empty, too. I was inspired by that thought to quickly gather up my books, along with a bread wrapper and a jam jar, a kitchen knife, a couple of plates and glasses, and also my own shoes and socks, and to stuff them all inside a drawer of the bureau. On opening the heavy top drawer I found I was not mistaken. The drawer was empty and with no sign of its ever having been used by Grandfather — perhaps not since the day when the furniture had first been brought from Hunt County and Mother had put down the white paper in it for lining.

Already I had heard Grandfather Manley calling my name out in the front hall. It was something I think he had never done before when arriving at the house. His choosing to do so had given me the extra time I had needed. When I closed the big bureau drawer I looked at myself in the wide mirror above it, and I was almost unrecognizable even to myself. I was sweating profusely. My hair was uncombed. I had not shaved in two days. My trousers and shirt were all wrinkles. But I heard my grandfather calling me a second time and knew I had to go out there.

When I stepped, barefoot, into his view I could tell from his expression that he saw me just as I had seen myself and that I was barely recognizable to him. He was standing at the foot of the stairs, from which point he had been calling my name. No doubt my face showed him how astonished I was to have him call out to me on coming into the house — at the informality and open friendliness of it. No doubt for a minute or so he supposed that accounted wholly for my obvious consternation. He actually smiled at me. It was rather a sickly grin, though, like General Forrest's, the smile of a man who isn't given to smiling. And yet there was an undeniable warmth in his smile and in the total expression on his face. "I couldn't abide another day of Beersheba Springs," he said. "The swells over there are too rich for my blood. I thought I would just slip by here on my way home and see what kind of mischief you might be up to."

Clearly what he said was intended to amuse me. And just as clearly he meant that he preferred whatever low life he might find me engaged in to the high life led by my parents' friends at Beersheba. Presently, though, he could deceive himself no longer about my extraordinary appearance and my nervous manner's indication that something was wrong.

"What's the matter, son?" he said.

"Nothing's the matter," I said belligerently.

The very friendliness of his demeanor somehow made me resent more bitterly than ever before his turning up at so inconvenient a moment. This was my real life he had come in on and was interfering with. Moreover, he had intruded this time with real and unconcealed feelings of his own. I could not permit him, at that hour of my life, to make me the object of his paternal affection. I was a grown man now and was in love with a girl who was about to be disgraced in his eyes. How could there be anything between him and me? His life, whether or not it was in any way his fault, had kept him from knowing what love of our sort was. He might know everything else in the world, including every other noble feeling that I would never be able to experience. He might be morally correct about everything else in the world, but he was not morally correct about love between a man and a woman. This was what I felt there in the hall that afternoon. I was aware of how little I had to base my judgment on. It was based mostly on the nothing that had ever been said about women in all the stories he had told me. In the stories about the night riders, for instance, there was no incident about his reunion with his wife, my grandmother, afterward. And I never heard him speak of her by her first name. Even now I wonder how we ever know about such men and their attitude toward women. In our part of the world we were brought up on tales of the mysterious ways of Thomas Jefferson, whose mother and wife are scarcely mentioned in his writings, and Andrew Jackson and Sam Houston, whose reticence on the subject of women is beyond the comprehension of most men nowadays. Did they have too much respect for women? Were they perhaps, for all their courage in other domains, afraid of women or afraid of their own compelling feelings toward women? I didn't think all of this, of course, as I faced Grandfather Manley there in the hall, but I believe I felt it. It seemed to me that his generation and my own were a thousand years apart.

"What's the matter, son?" he said.

"Nothing's the matter," I said.

There was nothing more for either of us to say. He began to move toward me and in the direction of his room. "Why don't you wait a minute," I said, "before you go into your room?"

His little eyes widened, and after a moment he said, "It ain't my room, y'know. I only stay in it."

"Yes," I said, "but I've been reading in there. Let me go clear up my books and things." I had no idea but to delay him. I said, "Maybe you should go out to the kitchen and get something to eat."

But he walked right past me, still wearing his hat and coat, of course, and still carrying his little Gladstone bag. When he had passed into his room and I had followed him in there, he said, "I see no books and things."

"No," I said. "I hid them in the bureau drawer. I didn't know whether you would like my being in here."

He looked at me skeptically. I went over and opened the drawer and took out my books and my shoes and socks. Then I closed the drawer, leaving everything else in it. But he came and opened the drawer again. And he saw the plates and other things. "What else are you hiding?" he asked. No doubt he had heard the knives and the plates rattling about when I closed the drawer. Then he turned and walked over to the wardrobe. I ran ahead of him and placed myself against the door. "You've got one of those bitches of yours hidden in there, I reckon," he said.

"No, sir," I said, trying to look him straight in the eye.

"Then what is it?" he said. And he began blinking his eyes, not because I was staring into them but because he was thinking. "Are you going to tell me, or am I going to find out for myself?"

Suddenly I said, "It's my girl in there." We were both silent for a time, staring into each other's eyes. "And you've no right to open the door on her," I finally said. "Because she's not dressed."

"You're lying," he came back at me immediately. "I don't believe you for a minute." He left me and went to the folding bed and pulled it down. He set his bag on the bed and he poked at the jumble of sheets with his cane. Then he stood there, looking back at me for several moments. He still had not removed his straw hat and had not unbuttoned his coat. Finally he began moving across the room toward me. He stood right before me, looking me in the eye again. Then, with almost no effort, he pushed me aside and opened the wardrobe door.

She still hadn't managed to get into her clothes but she was hugging the pillow and had the blanket half pulled over her shoulder. I think he may have recognized her from the one time he had met her at dinner. Or maybe, I thought to myself, he was just such an old expert that he could tell what kind of girl she was from one glance at her. Anyway, he turned on me a look cold and fierce and so articulate that I imagined I could hear the words his look expressed: "So this is how bad you really are!" Then he went directly over to the bed, took up his bag and his cane, left the room, and left the house without speaking to me again.

When I had heard the front door close I took the leather ottoman across the room and sat on it, holding hands with that brave and quiet girl who, with the door wide open now, remained crouching inside the wardrobe. When finally we heard him drive out of the driveway, we smiled at each other and kissed. And I thought to myself again that his generation and ours were a thousand years apart, or ten thousand.

I thought of course that when Grandfather Manley left Acklen Park he would continue on his way to Hunt County. But that was not the case. Or probably he did go to Hunt County, after all, and then turned around and went back to Beersheba Springs from there. Because, according to the account which my parents gave me later, he arrived at Beersheba at about eleven o'clock that night, and it would be difficult to explain how he was dressed as he was unless he had made a trip home and changed into the clothes he arrived in. He left Acklen Park about four in the afternoon, and from that time through the remaining ten years of his life he was never again seen wearing the old gabardine coat or either of his broad-brimmed hats. When he arrived at Beersheba, Mother and Father were sitting on the front gallery of the hotel with a group of friends. They were no doubt rocking away in the big rockers that furnished the porch, talking about the bridge hands they had held that evening, and enjoying the view of the moonlit valley below Cumberland Mountain.

When they saw him drive up, the car was unmistakable of course. But the man who emerged from it was not unmistakable. Major Basil Manley was dressed in a black serge suit, and in the starched collar of his white shirt he wore a black shoestring tie. I can describe his attire in such detail because from that day I never saw him in any other. That is, except on Decoration Day in those later years, when he invariably appeared in Confederate uniform. And in which uniform, at his own request, he was finally buried, not at Huntsboro and not in the family graveyard but at Mount Olivet Cemetery, at Nashville. My father's account of his arrival on the hotel porch is memorable to me because it is the source of a great discovery which I felt I had made. My parents didn't recognize him for a certainty until he had passed along the shadowy brick walkway between the hovering boxwoods and stepped up on the porch. And then, significantly, both of them went to him and kissed him on the cheek, first my mother and then my father. And all the while, as my father described it, Major Manley stood there, ramrod straight, his cheeks wet with tears, like an old general accepting total defeat with total fortitude.

And what I understood for certain when I heard about that ceremony of theirs was that it had, after all, been their battle all along, his and theirs, not his and mine. I, after all, had only been the pawn of that gentle-seeming couple who were his daughter and son-in-law and who were my parents. His disenchantment and his eventual corruption had been necessary to their purposes, and I had been their means of achieving that end. It is almost unbelievable the changes that took place in Grandfather from that day. He grew his beard again, which was completely white now, of course. It hid his lean jaw and weak chin, making him very handsome, and was itself very beautiful in its silky whiteness against his black suit and black shoestring tie. The following year — the very next May

— he began attending the Confederate Reunions again. And of course he was immediately promoted to the rank of colonel. Yet he did hold out against ever wearing the insignia of that rank, until he was in his coffin and it was put on him by other hands. As far as I know, he never allowed anyone — not even the other veterans — to address him otherwise than as "Major Manley." And in the fall, after he had first appeared in his new role at Beersheba Springs, he began coming in to Nashville more often than ever. I was not at home that fall, since that was my first year away at college, but when I would go home for a weekend and find him there or find that he had been there, I would observe some new object in his room, an old picture of my grandmother as a girl, bare-shouldered and with dark curls about her face, the picture in its original oval frame. Other family pictures soon appeared, too. And there was a handsome washbasin and pitcher, and there were some of his favorite books, like Ramsey's "Annals of Tennessee," and lawbooks that had belonged to his father, my great-grandfather. And then, very soon, he began to bring in small pieces of furniture that were unlike the golden-oak pieces already there.

When my mother had first urged Grandfather Manley to come live with us, it was just after my grandmother died and before we had moved into the big house in Acklen Park. He had said frankly then that he thought he would find it too cramped in our little house on Division Street. But when they bought the new house, they had done so with an eye to providing accommodations that would be agreeable to an old man who might before many years not like to climb stairs and who, at any rate, was known to be fond of his privacy. They consulted with a number of their friends who had the responsibility for aging parents. It was a bond they were now going to share with those friends, or a bond which they aspired to, anyway. In those days in Nashville, having a Confederate veteran around the place was comparable to having a peacock on the lawn or, if not that, at least comparable to having one's children in the right schools. It was something anybody liked to have. It didn't matter, I suppose, what rank the veteran was, since he was certain to be promoted as the years passed. The pressure on Major Manley to move in with his daughter and son-in-law was gentle always, but it was constant and it was enduring. One of the most compelling reasons given him was that they wanted him to get to know his only grandson and that they wanted the grandson to have

the benefit of growing up in the house with him. Well, when the
new house was bought and he was shown that room on the first
floor which was to be reserved perpetually for him whenever he
might choose to come and occupy it, and when he was urged to
furnish it with whatever pieces he might wish to bring in from
Hunt County, he no doubt felt he could not absolutely reject the
invitation. And he no doubt had unrealistic dreams about some
kind of rapport that might develop between him and the son of
this daughter and son-in-law of his.

I don't remember the day it happened, of course, but it must
have come as a considerable shock and disappointment to Mother
when a truck hired in Huntsboro arrived bearing not the rosewood
half-canopied bed from her mother's room at home, or the cannonball fourposter from the guest room there, but the foldaway
golden-oak bed instead, and the other golden-oak pieces instead of
the walnut and mahogany pieces she had had in mind. Yet no
complaint was made to the old man. (His daughter and son-in-law
were much too gentle for that.) The golden oak had come out of
the downstairs "office" in the old farmhouse, which he had furnished when he first got married and brought his wife to live with
his own parents. No doubt he thought it most appropriate for any
downstairs bedroom, even in Acklen Park. The main object was to
get him to occupy the room. And, after his fashion, this of course
was how he had occupied it through the years.

But by Christmas of the year he and I had our confrontations he
had, piece by piece, moved all new furnishings into the room and
had disposed of all the golden oak. The last piece he exchanged
was the folding bed for the walnut cannonball bed. When I came
home at Christmas, there was the big fourposter filling the room,
its mattress so high above the floor (in order to accommodate the
trundle bed) that a set of walnut bed steps was required for Grandfather to climb into or out of it. And before spring came the next
year Grandfather had closed his house in Hunt County and taken
up permanent residence in Acklen Park. He lived there for the rest
of his life, participating in my parents' lively social activities, talking
freely about his Civil War experiences, even telling the ladies how
he courted my grandmother during that time, and how sometimes
he would slip away from his encampment, make a dash for her
father's farm, and spy on her from the edge of a wood without
ever letting her know he had been in the neighborhood.

Such anecdotes delighted the Nashville ladies and the Nashville gentlemen, too. But often he would talk seriously and at length about the War itself — to the great and special delectation of both my parents — describing for a roomful of people the kind of lightning warfare that Forrest carried on, going on late into the evening sometimes, describing every little crossroads skirmish from Between the Rivers to Shiloh, pausing now and then for a little parenthetical explanation, for the ladies, of such matters as the difference between tactics and strategy. Sometimes he would display remarkable knowledge of the grand strategy of the really great battles of the War, of Shiloh and Vicksburg and Stone's River and Franklin and Chickamauga, and of other battles that he had had no part in. When he had a sufficiently worthy audience he would even speculate about whether or not the War in the West might have been won if Bragg had been removed from his command or whether the whole War mightn't have been won if President Davis had not viewed it so narrowly from the Richmond point of view. Or he would raise the question of what might have happened if Lee had been allowed to go to the Mountains.

I heard my parents' accounts of all such talk of his. But I heard some of it myself, too. The fall after I had graduated from Wallace School, I went away to the University of the South, at Sewanee. My father had gone to Vanderbilt because he had been a Methodist, and Vanderbilt was the great Methodist university in those days. But he and Mother, under the influence of one of his aunts, had become Episcopalian before I was born even. And so there was never any idea but that I should go to Sewanee. I liked being at Sewanee and liked being away from Nashville for the first time in my life. The university was full of boys from the various states of the Deep South. I very soon made friends there with boys from Mississippi and Louisiana and South Carolina. And since Nashville was so close by, I used to bring some of them home with me on weekends or on short holidays. They of course had never seen Grandfather Manley the way he had been before. And they couldn't imagine his being different from the way he was then. He would gather us around him sometimes in the evening and talk to us about the War Between the States. The boys loved to listen to him. They really adored him and made over him and clamored for him to tell certain stories over and over again. I enjoyed it, too, of course. He seemed quite as strange and interesting an old character to me as he did to them. And sometimes when I would ask him a question, just the way the others did, he would answer me with the same politeness he showed them, and at those times I would have the uneasy feeling that he wasn't quite certain whether it was I or one of the others who was his grandson, whether I was not perhaps merely one of the boys visiting, with the others, from Sewanee.

ROBERT T. SORRELLS

The Blacktop Champion
of Ickey Honey

(FROM THE AMERICAN REVIEW)

I TRY HARD to be optimistic about life, but when Hoke Warble came to me and told me he had agreed to a $1000 grudge match with Newton Slock, I said, "Hoke, why don't you just go on and give Newton his money right now and save yourself and all of us, your friends, the embarrassment of having to sit out there on those splintery bleachers at the Ickey Honey Country Club under what will no doubt be a broiling August sun and watch you get your ass whipped?"

Or words to that effect.

But first, *Ickey Honey*. It's a hamlet in Punkin County, South Carolina, and though now called the Gateway to the Blue Ridge, it is not quite far enough up in the mountains to get more than one snow every four or five years that doesn't melt by noon. It's really more "out from" than "up toward."

Too — contrary to whatever those slack-jawed kids over in the college town of Clemson might say about it — the name is not what you might think. *Honey*, for instance, is a corruption of an old Indian word, *Honea*, which in the Cherokee means *Path*. The *Ickey* is another corruption from the Cherokee, *Ikeowaywa*, which, imperfectly translated, means *The Place From Which One Leaps Out*. So those Clemson people delighted in telling each other that Ickey Honey was the jumping-off place, the end of the earth. In fact, however, to the Cherokees Honea Ikeowaywa was the Point of Beginning, the place from which the hunters went to hunt, the warriors to make war, and so on, with the implication that they were the actual center of things, the place where all paths come together. Something like Rome, I gather.

But what can you expect from a corrupt people if not a corruption of language?

However, the old-line natives retained the history, after a fashion, and that is why our high school athletic teams call themselves the Warpathers. We kept our high school, by the way, because when all that consolidation got started about 20 years ago, we fell off the county superintendent's list. So by being lost we managed to keep our integrity, unlike most of those new schools which ended up in the middle of some junky hunk of land without even a dusting of topsoil: schools juxtaposed to nowhere and neighbored by nothing but parking lots for the buses.

In Ickey Honey, at least, you had to walk past the school every day of your life, and you knew it was where you had to put in your time, like it or not, and you knew it was a part of the whole Ickey Honey scene — just like the church you had to go to. I am not saying that everyone liked it. I am simply saying that *it* was there and so were *you,* and the result was you grew up with a very personal one-to-one relationship with things.

As to Hoke Warble, he was less what you'd call a *friend* than a part of me. Neither "Friend" nor "Enemy." Just always Hoke, the derivation of whose name I will spare you the complex though fascinating details. Hoke was as native to Ickey Honey as cones to our pines or red to our earth or shotguns to our weddings.

At the same time, though, it must be admitted that Hoke had certain desires in this world, one of which was To Rise. Hoke even wanted to excel. Now you must also understand this: coming from a place like Ickey Honey can do things *to* you as well as *for* you. If we grew up rich in deep and abiding relationships to our buildings and our people, we grew up poor in vocational models. A few gas station attendants, some feed store people, a grocer or so, and the preachers twice a week. That was it. When I was growing up we didn't even have any rednecks in town on Saturdays. *We* were the rednecks, and every Saturday you'd find most of Ickey Honey hunkered down chewing and whittling and staring bug-eyed on the sidewalks of such big towns as Six Mile and Ninety-Six.

So either you praised the virtues of living crimeless in Ickey Honey, or the minute you set eyes on a real town you started plotting your escape. But if you were Hoke, you dreamed on a grander scale. Where most of us decided to stay or leave for the wider world, Hoke decided he could both stay and leave by bringing the Wider World into Ickey Honey. After finding out that other places were far brighter and more inviting, and after dutifully toting his slide rule around Clemson for four years, Hoke wanted Ickey Honey to be worthier of him than he figured it was. He wanted Ickey Honey to improve.

So he established, subscribed, and built the Ickey Honey Country Club, the first step on Ickey Honey's forced march into Growth and Development. A disinterested observer, however, might have concluded that the Country Club was really something else. A city park, say, with an imposing gateway arch to belie what was on the other side: a pool, covered over after six drownings (though no people), a memorial plaque to Hoke, two outdoor basketball goals, their metal nets missing, and the tennis court.

The tennis court. Hoke built it 15 years ago, long before tennis, like golf in its time, had become a game of the masses. Hoke, some said, had always been a man of vision. As a matter of fact the last time I heard that said was the day Hoke came in to talk to me about the Best Two Out of Three Set Grudge Match. As another matter of fact, he said it himself.

"What do you mean, 'Get my ass whipped'? " He extended his head as far as he could from his neck and glared up at me. I am five feet ten.

"Of course I will beat him," he demanded, and swabbed his sweating face with a huge handkerchief. It was late June, but summer had come early.

"Huh!" he bullied further, a forefinger jabbing right between my eyes. "I will destroy him. Newton Slock. Yech! That's not even a name. What kind of name is that? You know all about weird things."

The implications of his questions fanned the fires of his own inventiveness.

"I'll tell you about weird. Newton Slock. *That's* weird. Do you know how big a freak he is? Let me tell you about Newton Slock . . ."

"No, Hoke," I interrupted. "You don't need to tell me about Newton Slock. I know about Newton Slock. Newton Slock attended Presbyterian College for Gentle Men, and in his four years there he was President or Editor of everything from the Minor Sports Club to their yearbook *The Guiding Light*."

"Huh!" Hoke said, his red face cracked by a sour smile. "Huh! It's easy to see you've been around him for a minute and a half. I'll de*stroy* him," he said by way of getting back to basics, and he wadded his handkerchief down into a pocket of his blue shorts.

"Listen, DB," I said. DB stood for *Drag Butt,* a nickname Hoke hadn't much cottoned to, but which stuck anyway because Hoke was built like . . . well, like a toad, maybe. Or a fireplug. A sack of corncobs?

"DB," I said, "first off, Newton Slock is your friend. You got him here to help 'improve' the town by making it into a subdivision — for which I don't much love either of you. And he has helped you make a passel doing it.

"Also," I went on quickly before he could stick his finger back between my eyes like the barrel of a Saturday-night special, "Newton Slock is a very competent tennis player who was captain of his team in college and who has played a lot of tennis since.

"And who," I hurried right on, "has not spent nearly so much of his leisure time as you sitting and *watch*ing tube tennis whilst drinking cases of beer and consuming plastic snack-slops by the crate."

"You don't understand a thing," Hoke said. I had run out of breath. "There is no way that weirdo can beat me."

"How about by playing better tennis?" Forthrightness compelled me at least to put it forward as a possibility.

"And he can't because first off," he shoved that salami-shaped thumb up at me, "he is a *Freak!* Second off," and he pulled his index finger up from his fist, "he is *wrong.* Third of all . . ."

Now it looked like a salami and two Vienna sausages. I wondered how he ever managed to hold a racket with a hand like that.

". . . I'm right."

His hand stayed bunched near my chin; so I had a chance to look at his fingers for a minute before I answered.

"Hoke, it occurs to me that all the Right in the world will not make you as good a tennis player as Newton Slock."

He looked crushed, not because it occurred to him my judgment might be sound, but because he must have suffered a sense of betrayal.

"Lookee," he said to me.

I looked at his hand. So did he. He even started to point at it before quickly stuffing it into his shorts pocket.

"You don't even know what he's done. How can you talk like that and not even know what he's done?"

I had wondered what had happened, but I knew Hoke well enough to know he would never answer a direct question.

"He cheated you," I said and turned as if to walk away.

He grabbed my arm.

"You're gonna hold the stakes," he said.

"Fine," I answered real quick, figuring I'd gotten off pretty light if that's all there was to it. But I smelled the rat when I looked at him.

"You're also gonna get me in shape," he said with what I took to be a leer.

"No way."

"Lotsa ways."

"Hoke, you idiot. I don't know a durned thing in the world about tennis or how to get in shape for playing the fool game."

"I'll teach you. There's nothing to it. Honest. All you have to do is keep your eye on the ball and return their shots. Let them wear themselves out. Simple."

"I'll tell you what's simple," I said. "What's simple is that I can't even be out in the field as a county agent nearly as much as I'd like because I got no knees, what with arthritis from old Warpathers football days. And that means I have to ply much of my trade in an office which doesn't keep me very even-tempered, which means in addition that there is no way I *can* go hoppitying around a macadam tennis court like some twenty-year-old. And neither can you because you'd drop dead from cardiac arrest and heat prostration — especially in this kind of weather."

"One more thing," he said, just like I'd never opened my mouth. "You're going to referee, too, so you might as well start boning up on the rules."

I did not respond. He knew I could be as hard-headed as anyone — including himself — and that when I clammed up he'd better talk fast because I never bothered to spend much time arguing cases. You get so you mean it or you don't in this world, and there's no point standing around jawing. Now Hoke, being what he called an entrepreneur, was nothing but a sack full of arguments.

"All right," he said. "I thought you were a friend. All right."

He looked like he always does when he busied his mouth to work his brain. I still wasn't going to ask him what all this mess was about.

"Then I'll tell you," he said. "Tell you short and sweet."

"All right," I said.

"It's really very simple," he said, giving all the appearance of being calm and in control under intense emotional pressure.

I gestured for him to please go on.

"He's a cheat."

"A cheat?" I said.

He looked confused. Then, "Land," he nearly whispered. "Land is the wealth of a nation."

I said nothing.

"He has been robbing me blind and I intend to beat the bastard at his own game, Lodi. Then I'm going to kill him."

It was the first time all day he had called me by my name.

As for myself, I'm a County Agent. An entomologist, really, who got into county agenting so I could eat regularly. Too, the job let me stay in or near home, which suited me just fine.

Lodi Poidle. I was drafted to fight the Korean War, but ended up in Austria, realized that *Poidle* was a corruption of *Peutl,* and that it was from Austria we came some hundred and fifty years ago. But that was through my father. Through my mother, a Scot, we have been here God only knows how long. Also through my mother we have been here more or less forever, since she was part Cherokee. When I was a child and asked which part, she only laughed, but when my father asserted at the dinner table that he knew which part was Indian, she would just smile sweetly and say, "The Princess part."

So in Salzburg, Austria, I learned to skate and ski, to speak a little German, and to be dissatisfied forever with American bread and beer. Then back home to finish school, take the county agenting job, marry, and accept my place as a stable member of the Ickey Honey community. And all because of bugs.

When I was little, I remember, I loved the pines: loblolly, slash, white. I remember sitting in a plantation of them once, listening.

Crunch, crunch.

I finally asked my father what it was I kept hearing. He sat down beside me, listened carefully, and said, "Pine borers. They are eating the trees. Look," and he showed me their holes, even got his knife and dug out a few of the varmints.

I said, "They are eating up all the trees?" He said, "Yes, Lodi." I wept, then spent years hating the pine borers with all the passion of my youth, determined to learn how to save the world from them. That's why I went to college in the first place. But there I learned to love bugs. The fruit fly, for instance. You have to admire him after a while. And nits and newts and mites and all the rest . . .

"Buggy!"

It was Hoke shouting at me. I rested my racket on my toes. He was unhappy with my play.

"Damn, Lodi. You got to go after the ball. You got to chase it to hit it back. Isn't anyone going to hit it right to your forehand every time. You're not giving me the first sign of a sweat."

"Sweat! All I have to do is stand here and I sweat."

"Well if you'd wear shorts and a T-shirt instead of those khaki trousers and shirts you wouldn't get so hot."

I pointed the racket at him. "Hoke, you're stupider than you look if you think I'm going to walk around this town in short pants that look like underwear."

"Get ready for another serve, Lodi. If I can get my power up for the serves I can take him."

"Hoke, if there's anything Newton can do it's return serves."

Hoke glared across the net at me. "Oh yeah? Well if there's anything else he can do it's foot fault." His face was a ball of red, wet hatred. "You got to watch him careful on that or he'll foot fault on me all day long if you don't catch him and call him on it."

I walked off the court toward the bench and started to button up my shirt.

"Hey!" Hoke yelled, racing around the net. "Where you going? You promised me two hours this morning. We only been out here thirty minutes."

"I think it probably isn't right for me to train you if I'm going to have to referee the match, Hoke, because I'll have to call your foot faults, too."

"I don't foot fault."

"You do."

"I don't."

"Do."

"Don't," he hollered.

I stood quietly and stared him down.

"Much?" he asked.

"Every time," I answered.

"Well hell, Lodi. You mean you'd call something like that on me after what he's done? Would you?"

I finished tucking in my shirt.

"Lodi?" he whined. "Man, I *need* you. You got to *help* me. You got to tell me things like how does he serve? And, how does he play the net? And stuff like that. Lodi?"

I faced him. "Hoke, how many years have you been playing tennis with Newton Slock?"

He shrugged. "Ten, maybe. Why?"

I could only shake my head. This was beginning to surpass wonder.

"Then you have probably played two thousand games with Newton Slock, since for the first five of those years he was the only other person in town who knew how to play."

"So?" he shrugged. "What's that got to do with foot faults?"

Even I was stunned. "It means I'm going to call them," I mumbled.

"Good!" he shouted, beaming at me like he meant it. "I just had to make sure you were still Mr. Incorruptible. Get your racket and let's go."

I did, too. I was a good example of how Hoke Warble — slide rule dangling jauntily from his hip, wearing his civil engineering degree on his sleeve like some wear their hearts — was able to borrow money enough to buy land, hire surveyors, rent bulldozers, and, by whispering the sweetest of honey into the ears of conservative builders, turn them into daring speculation contractors. He could talk people into things. Part wheedle, part bully, but mostly a playing on your own greed or whatever strength he knew he could grab you by and turn you with. And to give credit, the minute he knew that Clemson Agricultural College was going to stop being a military academy and start being a University with coeds, was the minute he understood the power of wide roads leading from Clemson direct to where the town I grew up in stood. No need to guess who owned the best rights of way when it all got started.

That was Hoke, but it was almost worth it to watch him play tennis. His serve, for instance, wasn't what you could call good, but it was hard to return. He held his racket in what at first appeared to be the ordinary way, only because his hands were so small, he had to chisel the grip down and then hold it about three inches up from the end. Also, he couldn't hold but one ball at a time in the other hand. But since all the pros had three balls, he did too — in his pockets. I mean you to understand he kept two or three balls in *each* pocket. As I have suggested, Hoke already filled out his clothes. So to stuff all those balls into the side pockets gave him the appearance of a hog with great wens on each hip.

Then he would peer steadfastly across the net at his opponent. With the ball held right up against the bottom of his racket, he would begin to rock his entire body forward and backward while at the same time he shoved his arms back and forth so you weren't sure what to watch. When he had gotten himself all wound up, he would lean way over toward the net, bring his racket to the ground in front of his left toes, rear back, and with a quick jerk and grunt serve the ball.

As a rule, he served three times. The first went into the net. The second ticked the top of the net. And the third he just pooped the ball into play. When the time came for *you* to do something, you were either worn out watching all that business or just exactly bored enough to be out of the notion to play.

But play we did: I would serve and serve so he could practice his returns. Then he would serve and serve while I shagged balls for him. It was wearing work, but Hoke went at it like a pro. Hours and hours and hours of it.

I thought once that he might lose 50 pounds working like he did with out-and-out hot weather already settled in like it was. But every time he finished sweating off eight pounds (he weighed in before and after each session) he'd drink about a quart of beer with his sandwiches and snack-slops. Plus his regular meals. So he ended up eating more than usual. And the more he trained, the bigger he got.

"But stronger, Lodi," he'd insist. "And quicker."

Which brings me to Newton Slock.

Newton wasn't a native. Newton was from what is called the Low Country, a section of our fair state thick with history, plague, cotton, a language called Gullah, and rich people who still can't stand the sight of someone from Up Country who can afford to drive his own car to work.

Now there are two ways for people like me to approach an out-sider like Newton. One is to say that at least he has seen the light and come to where God intended people instead of sand fleas and red bugs to live. The other is to remain always suspicious. Since he was a good friend of Hoke's, I was at least somewhat predis-posed toward the latter, but being me, I was also prepared for the former.

All of Newton's activities in Presbyterian College for Gentle Men were nothing but preparation for the Life of the Real World, as he phrased it. Committees, activities, meetings, clubs, organizations, Service to the Community . . . Lord, there was no end to it. He was Hoke's P.R. man, in short, and the volume of leaflets, letters, flyers, pamphlets, and advertisements he flooded into the mails was wor-thy of any government bureaucrat. Not to mention the number of dinners eaten or rounds of golf played with university deans, tex-tile mill executives, and editorial writers for the local newspapers — all to help turn Ickey Honey into a subdivision worthy of Hoke Warble.

"Not a subdivision," Newton gently said one day years ago. "What we are creating here is a Residential Community, Lodi," and he looked at me with those Gentle Man's sincere eyes.

"I see," I said back. "But what's it going to *do?*"

"Do, Lodi?" He never broke stride. "Why, it won't have to *do* anything. It will provide a restful place for people to live in. It will be a retreat where people can reintegrate themselves and so face the next day's challenges."

"It seems to me," I tried, "that people are already integrated if they live more or less where they work."

"Ah, Lodi," he smiled.

"It seems to me, Newton, that when you make a person live away from his work, or when you make him do work he hates so much that he feels he has to live away from it, then you have separated him out from himself so that he *has* to reintegrate. My father never needed any reintegrating because, being a forester and a farmer, he lived where the fruit of his labor was."

"Your father lived in another time, Lodi."

"Newton, I live right here in Ickey Honey where my work is."

"Hmmm," he said wisely. "Bugs are ubiquitous, yes, but not all of us in this modern world of today are able to do that. This nation isn't agricultural anymore, Lodi."

He said that very archly as though I probably hadn't heard the news yet. I was going to tell him that people had always lived in towns, and that in lots of places they lived happily and well-integrated right above their shops. But I figured it wouldn't help.

Besides, Newton was a nice enough person. He was not mean. He was not a beast. It's just that I didn't understand how someone who was supposed to be so smart could really believe the things he kept saying.

So we practiced, Hoke and I. We practiced the forehand return, the backhand return, lobs, serves, the serve return, the two-hand grip. He practiced doing like Arthur Ashe, or Jimmy Connors, or Ilie Nastase, or . . .

But through it all, Hoke remained largely his own man. When I had told him earlier that I couldn't go hoppitying around the court it was because Hoke was about the only player I had ever seen, and hop was what he did most. He always seemed to go up and down more than back and forth. That never changed much, either, though I must admit that as the match drew nearer Hoke was able to make his upping and downing more useful. And just a week before the match itself, he had a long and serious talk with me before our practice session.

"Lodi," he said, the sincerity nearly choking him. "You'll never know how much I appreciate your helping me this way."

I shrugged. "I've actually come to enjoy it, Hoke," I said. "I didn't think I would, but I have actually come to like the game. Sort of."

"I will tell you something," he went on. "I am going to beat him."

I waited for more, but there was silence. I looked up and damned if there weren't tears in his eyes.

"Well," I said. "Well, Hoke. I never thought you had a chance four weeks ago. But durned if I don't think you can give him a real run for his money now."

At that, the tears disappeared, and so, too, I think, did the era of good feeling that we had been sharing.

"Money!" he snorted, and it did not take a genius to gather he was not alluding to the $1000 bet. Had Newton been cheating him? I still couldn't believe it, couldn't believe, at any rate, that there was something illegal involved. I kept my own counsel and waited for Hoke to reveal himself.

He gave me a man-to-man stare and a professional little pat on my bottom as he said, "Let's hit it, Lodi," his voice quiet but firm with the sureness of a man who knows his destiny is soon to be fulfilled.

As for my own destiny, it was bouncing along innocently enough until the day I was driving back to my office after a visit to look at a garden club president's scaly azaleas. A sporty little Audi had nipped in front of me and on the left side of its bumper was a sticker. It pictured a hand clenched tightly around a tennis racket being held on high. The inscription read: TENNIS NOW! On the other side of the bumper was another sticker. It read: ALL POWER TO THE COURTS. Dawn glimmered slowly in my gut where a voice rumbled lowly unto me saying, *Lodi, Old Bean, someone has been very busy promoting this thing while you were out training Hoke.*

They came in from all around, the Natives did. They came in from places that hadn't even been crossroads for 30 years. They came in in their pickups and on their baled-together flatbeds. They came in with NeHis, R.C.s, little packets of salted goobers, peanut butter crackers, Cheez-Its, and dangerous-looking sacks worn soft from constant reusings. They came in in overalls, ankle boots, their sides sliced to give bunions ease, their little children barefoot and knobbly-ankled, their teenaged daughters slumpshouldered against maturity, their boys ballsy but stiff-necked against the alien feel of a town grown smooth and untouchable to the rough clutch of their snag-nailed hands; their sense of being forever excluded, as heavy and real to them as the heat that had hunkered down on us all for the past week.

They found places for their vehicles near the Ickey Honey Country Club, parked, and made their way to the tennis court. There were stands on both sides of the court, and for no reason other than that he had parked nearest it, the first arrival had stepped warily up on the closest set of plank bleachers; followed, then, by the others as they clanked and chugged into town and in their own turns parked near the vehicles they knew, the ones they understood to be like their own and thus peopled by their own kind. They climbed the seats, sat, looked around with care, not wanting to move fast enough to draw attention to themselves.

Across the way another crowd was taking its place: white trousers and shorts with deck shoes for sailing on the lake, smoothly tanned all over, lounging, at ease, relaxed and chatting with one another.

Yet they sedulously avoided eye contact with the people on my side. Except, that is, by flicking, darting little side glances. Their heads stayed averted. They were the Residents.

After not too long the principals arrived. From the Residents there came a polite pat-a-pat-a-pat of applause. From the others . . .

I would like to say that I heard groans when Hoke and Newton made their appearances. I would like to say they gasped . . . or snickered . . . or did something outrageous. But they didn't, and I loved them for holding their collective judgment in abeyance. And yet . . .

. . . and yet something went through them when they saw the two men, when they saw that *those* were to be the contestants they had lurched into town to see, were willing to sit on splintery planks under an already roasting sun to watch as the ancient rituals of man's pride in self and family and place were satisfied.

. . . something of wonder crossed their faces.

To their right was Newton Slock: six feet two inches, trim, dark-haired, fit looking; his tennis shoes were Adidas, a solid suede, a no-nonsense shade of blue with socks to match; his tennis shorts were lighter in color, more what you might call Bonnie Blue; his shirt — its rolled collar very precisely casual — was color-coordinated with the shorts and sneakers, a thin rim of maroon piping around the sleeves of the shirt and down the sides of the shorts. On his wrists were light blue sweatbands. Topping it off was a visor, blue on the underside, a rich, creamy off-white above. A take-charge guy, you could tell right off.

And to their left was Hoke. He too had chosen Adidas, but they were white trimmed in gold. His socks matched, as did his shorts and shirt, with its little alligator emblazoned over his heart. Not only did he have sweatbands on his wrists — bright gold ones — but a sweatband encircled his head as well, like a tight halo.

They were a sight indeed. Hoke did squat bends while Newton went through a complex routine of circular arm movements. Apparently they were not going to give each other any warm-ups like every other tennis player in the world does before a match; so the next move was mine. I stepped toward the net, careful not to get onto either side of the court lest one of them accuse me of favoring the other. I motioned them to come to me.

"Well," I began.

They glared at each other.

"Well, here we are. I reckon it's time to start."

Newton kept up his arm swinging while Hoke bounced up and down on his toes. They looked like two boxers.

"Hoke, Newton, this is a grudge match for one thousand dollars winner take all, best two out of three sets. The first two can be won on tie-breakers, but if it should go to the third, we play Old Rules and you have to win by two games. Right?"

"That's what we agreed to, Lodi," Newton said, and you could have slid to Heaven on the oil in his voice.

"All right, then," I said. "Newton, since you have been challenged, you serve first. Hoke, where are you going to start off?" He nodded to where he had been warming up. "All right, then . . ." I was about to tell them to shake hands now and come out fighting, but they had turned away and were heading to their respective positions.

What shall I say of that match? Newton served and scored. Served and scored. Served and scored. Served and won the first game. They swapped courts.

Then it was for Hoke to serve. He did, and the ball smashed into the net. He served again, and it bounced off the top of the net to land in the service area. He served once more, pooping the ball over the net toward Newton who returned it with a forehand smash that ripped by Hoke just as he was on a bounce up and thus unable to give chase.

His other three serves met much the same fate. Newton whapped them all back so hard poor Hoke could hardly see them coming, and I wondered why, after he served the ball, he didn't move instead of obstinately bouncing straight up and down where he was. Newton returned every single serve clear across the court from Hoke, who didn't seem to catch on to what was clear even to a gravelly voiced little native son behind me. "Poppa," he asked the puff-eyed, nine-fingered, frighty-looking man directly behind me, "oughten that there fat one to do something else?"

And that was pretty much the story of the first set — except for the two games Newton lost or gave away by playing left-handed. I breathed a little sigh of relief: at that rate it couldn't take too long.

However, I hadn't counted on temper. After Newton won the third game of the second set and was starting around to wipe his

face at the net before going to the other court, Hoke flung his
racket against the fencing behind him and loosed a terrible flow of
invective. I was startled, but Newton was stopped in his tracks, and
the crowd on my side loved it. A small but hearty bit of laughter
riffled through them to make its impact on Hoke, who by then had
stalked to the fence to retrieve his Wilson T 4000 "Pro" Frame with
Sensor Dome to Reduce Vibration from Contact. He stared hard
at it as though to make certain it had withstood the throwing it
presumably was made to withstand. Newton wiped his face and I
noticed him looking across at Hoke who swigged mightily several
times from a tennis-ball can filled with Crocodile Juice or some
such business. It was a green, mostly sweet liquid that Hoke seemed
to think would see him through life. I drank some once when I was
getting him in shape, but it tasted like Kool-Aid to me.

He drank mightily, I say, and glared unadulterated hate back at
Newton. They each finished their refreshments and ablutions and
took up their positions once more. It was Hoke's turn to serve, his
last serve having been broken, as they say in tennis circles, by
Newton.

Hoke may some day in his life be out, but he will never be down.
I think we'll have to bury him standing up. I not only had not
counted on bad temper, I had not counted on Hoke's basic, well,
sneakiness. He quick-served.

Instead of going through his usual folderol of a wind-up, he
took his preliminary stance but flipped the ball quickly and popped
it over the net. Newton stared at it as it bounced once, then twice,
then even a third time before his brain responded to what his eyes
so clearly saw.

"What was that?" Newton yelled.

"That was fifteen-love, Dummy," Hoke yelled back.

Newton straightened. Still in disbelief, he looked over at me.
Then I realized he wanted a ruling. There hadn't been anything
for me to do once the game got underway, and I had almost forgotten I was supposed to referee. But what did I know? Newton
had been ready. Hoke had been ready. They had both been where
they were supposed to be.

"Fifteen-love, Newton," I called back, and held my hands out to
let him know there was nothing personal in it from me.

"Serve it up like that again, DB," Newton dared. "Serve it like
that again." He looked ready for tigers.

Hoke was craftier than that, though, and what he did was to throw the ball up in the air. Then he gripped his weapon with both hands, and as the ball descended, he took aim on it like a batter would on a hugely arcing, slow Ephus pitch. The ball hung high in the air hardly rotating enough to have any kind of spin on it at all, floated so slowly you could count the puce hairs on its hide. Then at just the right moment, he slashed as viciously as ever any medieval knight slashed at the juncture of an enemy's neck and shoulder. It cleared the net by a fraction, hit just in the service area, and spun off the side of the court so hard and fast that even if Newton had been ready for it there was no way he could have gotten to it.

Hoke cackled, positively jumping up and down at the spectacle of Newton standing bug-eyed.

"That's thirty-love in case you were going to ask." He whickered and fairly danced into position for the next serve . . .

. . . which Newton returned out of bounds, losing for the moment the cool which was his hallmark in the tennis world of Ickey Honey.

So that for the next serve, Hoke was in a position to win his very first game of set two. He readied himself as Newton gripped and regripped the handle of his nylon-stringed, high-tensile, steel Wilson T 2000. Around came Hoke for the serve. *Smash!* into the net . . . *Pop!* off the top . . . and while Newton eased up to blitz the *Poop* that had to follow, Hoke himself, after pooping, rushed the net with a scream and a whoop that caught Newton unaware just enough for his return not to have very much on it. Hoke caught it on the run and blasted it with a leaping two-handed *Splat!* that sent it careening not only off the court but over the restraining fence behind Newton as well.

"No!" screamed Newton Slock, looking now again to me for official confirmation of his protest. "No fair. Foul. You can't scream like that."

I hadn't read that you couldn't scream like that. As a matter of fact as an old Warpather I had thought the scream pretty good, reminiscent of the times Hoke, a terrifying-looking but otherwise ineffectual linebacker, would leap feet first across the line of scrimmage warcrying all the way. It often got him kicked out of the game, but by that time it would have worked its purposes of scaring the opposition and getting him kicked out so he wouldn't have to play any more that afternoon.

"No fair," Newton kept insisting. "You're not allowed to distract your opponent that-a-way. It isn't cricket." His normally dulcet tones had become peculiarly shrill.

All the while Hoke cackled to himself and strutted up and down the backline of the court. He wiped a trickle of Crocodile Juice from his chin.

"Come off it, Newton Shlock," he called. "You're still ahead three games to my puny one. Can't you stand that? Heh heh heh," he finished. "Heh heh."

That seemed to calm Newton down a bit as he took up his position. He looked ready to serve, but then turned and walked away a few steps talking to himself.

Come on, baby, we could all hear him mutter. *Let's put this joker down and get on back home.*

He apparently did himself some good, because he got back to the line and served one of the most bully fast serves I ever saw.

The crowd on both sides *oohed* at it, but Hoke stood there calm as pie.

"Out," he said very politely and very softly.

"What? What do you mean out? That serve was fair by six inches." Newton looked over to me.

I was in for it.

"I didn't see it," I said, hoping it was loud enough for them to hear without being so loud as to let everybody know I hadn't watched where it hit.

"Better play it over," Hoke mewed.

"Play it over, hell!" Newton bellowed. "It was in."

"Rule says," Hoke went on calm as a sleeping cat, "you got to play it over if it is contested and the judge can't make a call. Heh heh heh."

It was, and I couldn't. I shrugged to say I was sorry. Newton talked to himself again for a little, then went back to the line, but Hoke had gotten to him and he double-faulted. Love-fifteen.

Newton started putting himself into it now. He wiped the sweat from his brow, blinked twice, and served again. Hoke held his racket out and let the ball return itself. Newton either hadn't expected him to be able to return that hard a serve, or was starting to wear down mentally a little, because he never tried to make a play on it.

Love-thirty.

With the next serve, he heaved mightily once more and got off another blistering serve, but just as last time Hoke got the racket out to it and let the ball return itself. Newton managed to return that return, but Hoke fed him a high, deep lob that Newton had to run back for. The sun was high by then and the sweat was rolling fast off everybody, so Newton didn't get as much string on the ball as he should have. It got back over the net, but Hoke pounced on it and placed it out of reach.

Love-forty.

Newton's first serve was laid in with great strength, but it caught the net for a fault. The second serve was milder. Hoke got to it and lobbed it high and deep again. Newton ran back and smashed a return, but Hoke caught it at the net and made Newton run up fast to get it back over. Another deep lob, another pop over the net, another run by Newton, another deep lob, another hard run to the net where he smashed it past Hoke for the score.

Fifteen-forty, but Hoke had worked very little and Newton had worked a lot.

Even I had to admire Hoke at that point. He was playing what's called a very smart game, and I started to wonder if maybe he had a chance after all. I also started to wonder whether Newton didn't understand what was going on yet. He lost the next point and the game on exactly the same kind of *I'll-hit-it-while-you-run-after-it* play of the point before.

They swapped courts once again, pausing longer at their rest areas to drink deep and sponge off. It was hot. I heard cans getting popped in the stands behind me, and the deep, soft sounds of slurped foam came trailing on the sweet smell of hot beer.

Score, Set Two: three games to two, Mr. Slock.

The Natives had finally warmed up to the game as well as to the day. Though they were even more ignorant about it than I had been, they began to understand the basic points, though in truth the thing they liked best was the way the players urged themselves on.

Newton's favorite routine was to wheel around from the net when he had made a particularly bad play and stalk away where he would set one hand on a hip and talk — actually to himself, though it looked like he was trying to reason with the fence. He would gesture and gesticulate, then shake his racket at it as if threatening to raise a lump on its mesh if it didn't start doing better.

But there were more violent moments, too. His standard form of mayhem was to stare across the net at Hoke after a goof, then swirl around and fling his racket at the fence. When he did that, a nicely large murmur of approval would well up from the stands on my side. Once, I heard someone whose voice came from very near where most of the beer popping came from holler out that he ought to have flang the racket at Hoke, heh-heh-heh. That brought even louder murmurs of approval from his friends, and I heard three cans pop nearly at once.

Hoke, on the other hand, was constantly in motion anyway, and his usual sign of disgust was to skim his racket across the court at the fence behind him. If that didn't do any good on the next point, he would take it in both hands and approach the post that held the net up, and there he would pop the strings on the top of the post as though not so much to see how really and truly well-built the Stratabow construction was (he had changed from his Wilson Sensor Dome to a Wilson Chris Evert), but more to let it understand that another bad miscue would bring it instant ruin. Beyond that, he would slam the flat of it against the top of the net, smash the edge of it into the fence behind him, or toss the whole thing up into the air as he walked away from whatever had disgusted him . . .

. . . such that when Newton and Hoke both were going hot and heavy at themselves, it sounded less like a tennis match than the preliminary clash and rattle of muskets as advance scouts began feeling for enemy pickets to discover the whereabouts and strengths of an entrenched foe.

The heat was getting ferocious. Each serve took more time. Each return required more effort. The stops at the refreshment areas between court swappings lasted longer. The cans popped more often behind me, and the paper sacks were getting plopped down under the stands, empty now of their contents.

Once, even, play had to be stopped a minute as a fan — caught in the heat and believing as Newton had earlier on that the match couldn't last too long and having sucked more beer sooner than he might otherwise have, and having friendly nips from the soft sacks around — fell not only asleep, but down as well; fell from the top row of the bleachers to the ground beneath, much to the huge delight of his friends, whose thoroughgoing and hearty laughter disturbed Hoke right as he was about to serve. Though it bothered Hoke — who wasn't about to say anything to them about letting the players be the ones to scream and shout — it didn't seem to bother the fellow who had fallen. He grunted once when he hit, belched, and lay quietly the rest of the day, except for his snoring.

But as the play wore on, it became apparent that Hoke had put the hex sign on Newton, who just couldn't manage to get any sort of real lead again — Hoke had taken the second set seven-six. Newton was still winning his share of games, but he was taking longer and longer to do it, and it appeared to me that he hadn't planned on having to stay out in this August sunshine for as long as we all were. The number of deuce games and the number of deuces in those games was telling on him. How Hoke managed to stay on as long as he did, I don't know. Greed probably. And I suppose a certain amount of pride, too.

But it was not until Hoke tied the third set at six games that I really noticed how much slower on their feet they were. Newton was preparing for the first serve of the 13th game. It was one o'clock in the afternoon and they had been playing steadily since ten that morning. By now about four more people had dropped from the stands, each with a kind of soft thud and grunt. The ones who could stick it out with the beer, and with the air thick enough to chew, it seemed, grew more and more interested in the game, though their outbursts were reserved for the more spectacular plays.

Newton served right to Hoke who returned it — there had come to be a good bit of extended volleying by now rather than the attempts to dominate every point — and after a bit Hoke managed to put the ball out to where Newton had to make a little run for it. Earlier in the day it would have been nothing, but Newton never got to the ball. He had begun making chase and even had his racket extended, his arm and him leaning way out after it, but his legs hadn't been able to follow. It was like his body was outrunning his feet such that he simply fell down. I even wondered, I hate to admit it, how Hoke had gotten over there to weight Newton's shoes like that.

Then I glanced over at Hoke and noticed something about him, too. His fancy sneakers had long, ugly black streaks on them which at first I took for slits, but which I finally realized was tar. Then I looked at the court itself, and there I saw great ripples that hadn't

been there at the start of the game. It was like looking at a relief
map of Appalachia, great crinkles ridging up all over.

Then Hoke, reaching up high after charging the net, fell flat on
his ass. His feet just purely slid out from under him. It was the
court, I realized, even with the stands clapping and whistling happily behind me at Hoke's comic fall. They were playing on what
was quickly becoming a lake of tar.

"Stop," I shouted, and jumped to my feet.

It was too sudden a move in the heat, I suppose, because the
next thing I knew, Hoke was pouring that sticky Crocodile Juice
all over me.

"You all right?" he asked.

"Yes, I think so."

He didn't even say *Good* or anything, but started right back out
to the tar pit to resume the game.

"Wait," I shouted again. "Newton, Hoke, come over here."

"What for?" Newton panted.

"Because I'm the durned referee, Newton, Now get over here.
Hoke, you too."

They approached and I said, "This can't go on. That tennis court
of yours is melting, Hoke."

"What do you mean, 'That tennis court of *yours*'? What do you
mean by that?"

"Hoke, you built the durned thing and it is melting. There is no
proper way to finish this match today. Neither one of you can stand
up." I tried to appeal to their softest spots. "Neither one of you can
play up to your finest capabilities. It's all tied right now. Call it a
draw and each of you keep your money, or finish it up tomorrow
after the court has cooled."

"Tomorrow is Sunday, Lodi," Newton felt inclined to inform
me.

"Sunday Schmundy," Hoke wrinkled up his nose at Newton. To
me he said, "Lodi, durn it, you don't interrupt tennis matches. It
ain't cricket, you know," and he laughed in a labored and wheezy
kind of way.

"But if it rained we'd postpone it until there wasn't any more
rain and until the court was dry, wouldn't we?"

"This ain't rain, Lodi. This here is nothing more than tennis
weather."

Tennis weather? I thought.

"But Hoke . . . Newton . . ." I tried to plead for good sense, but the onlookers started stomping their feet, started shouting questions as to whether or not someone had won and weren't they going to get to see the rest of the thing.

Hoke, his Stratabow in one hand, opened his arms up toward the stands and said, "Lodi, you wouldn't want to disappoint *them,* would you?"

I looked back and saw the soft paper sacks getting softer and softer, and I saw fresh reserves of supplies being carried up from the local markets.

"All right," I said. "But it's dumb."

I sat back down, weary from trying to make fools act sensible. There I was sitting out in God only knew what kind of heat; there they were running around smacking puce and mint green and baby blue balls back and forth at each other for reasons that still remained obscure and suspicious to me; and across the way was a handful of soft gulls, anxious to believe people like Newton Slock, willing to be ashamed of little old hamlets like Ickey Honey that hadn't ever done them any harm by being there, delighted to know nothing of my town's past, perfectly programmed to accept that prior to Residential Communities there had been nothing but Chaos; while to my rear was a surly wad of retards and mean things waiting in a sad and desperate way for some blood to flow.

"Serve it up," I hollered. "Hell on it. Serve it up."

And as they resumed their stances, Poppa reached up from behind me and slapped my arm. I jumped.

"This thang gonna keep on a while?" he asked.

I nodded. "It looks it," I said.

"Then here," he said. "You look to need it," and he slipped a tall can of beer into my hand. I could have kissed him. Instead, I tilted my head back and drank that beer down in gulp after gulp after gulp. God, but it was good. I never took the rim from my lips until it was empty. Then I belched once and felt lots better.

The play went on without me, but I tried to follow what was happening just in case they were to make me decide an issue. The fact is, though, they had begun playing for real and they had too much to worry about just staying on the court without wasting a lot of energy being snippy with each other. In the meantime, I got madder and madder.

They could hardly move any more. Their shoes were clogged

with tar; they slipped constantly; and the natty outfits they looked so prancy in earlier were beyond redemption. Talk about your Deep-Down Dirt, I'd like to see a washing machine get those duds clean. Ha! And there was another beer in my hand.

Soon I even noticed that their rackets were getting gummed up. And the balls would hardly bounce. And the more beer I drank, the angrier I got about it. But I did have to admit that it was funny. Once, Newton just plain could not lift a foot from the court. He was reaching and stretching, and — of course it could have been partly the beer by then — it seemed like slow motion as he fell the length of himself onto the court. The crowd appreciated that as did Hoke, who coughed and wheezed and managed to let out a little bleating laugh of his own.

But on the next play, Newton — not to be outdone or shown up without a fight — caught Hoke prancing slowly along the line of the net, delayed his swing by a fraction, and placed the volley with tremendous drive and accuracy right in Hoke's balls.

Down he went with a squawk like Daffy Duck winged in mid-flight. Oh how my Natives loved that. Poppa pounded me on the back.

"What happened?" he demanded, his face a terrible crimson.

"That air feller he clipped him right in the balls, Poppa," his son answered, "and down he went. See there?"

Hoke was indeed holding himself near the afflicted area, but seemed to be all right, more or less.

"In the balls?" Poppa screamed. "In the balls?" His face cracked into something that must for him have approached a smile, but it was hard to say, because it gave way almost directly to a look of pain and loss.

"Goddamn," he said. "Goddamn. The only thing interesting to happen out there the whole day and I miss it. Goddam it, Boy, whyn't you tell me? Whyn't you *tell* me?" and I thought he was going to clip the boy across the mouth. Instead, he popped two more beers and gave me one.

"Durn," he muttered, by then too heartsore even to curse.

Hoke was back up on his feet ready to go. The games by then were eight and eight.

I think.

Yes, they must have been. Eight and eight with Newton about to serve yet once more. He took his time about it, even managing again to go back to his friend the fence and talk to it a while. Then it was back to the line.

I drank another can of beer. Entire.

It was just like the very first serve of the game. As a matter of fact, I was thinking it *was* the very first serve of the game, because Newton looked exactly as he had, except for the oil and tar he had dredged up from the macadam court, of course. But he wound up the same way, and I finally understood that he was out to win two games in a row so he could put all this madness behind us.

Good luck, Newton, I found myself saying as I chuckled into despair, knowing as I did that he would never be able to do it. This match, I had come to understand, was like the rock of Sisyphus: there was no end. No matter who got an advantage, it would be deuced the next time around. We were all damned. The world had come to an end the night before, only none of us understood it. For reasons unknown to us all, we were here for Eternity to watch Newton Slock and Hoke Warble battle each other in a tar pit with balls that bounced less and less, on feet that stuck more and more, under a pitiless sun that was to grow hotter and hotter with the passing of each millennium until our brains were seared and scorched beyond the redeeming power that any further harrowing could possibly bestow. Me and these careless nine-fingered folk and their children . . . and the beer would get foamier as the air got heavier . . .

Newton served.

. . . and we were all in it together for no reason under the sun except that we had planned our own destruction this way. We had all planned to be doing what we were doing, and the World was stopped right then and we were cursed and damned to keep it up until the very edge of Time itself . . .

Hoke got his racket out with just enough of a push behind it to get the ball back over the net.

. . . and if I had been doing what I was supposed to be doing when God placed his mighty finger on our little spinning ball and said, "Stop. It is enough," I would now be out in the pine groves listening to the cooling breezes soughing through my beloved trees. I would be noting with loving interest the progress of the borers and listening to their little *crunch-crunches* with both the sadness of the Tree Lover as well as the admiration and awe of a True Bug Man. Or I could have taken that trip back to Austria that I had

wanted to take for so long, but for which there simply never had
been the money or the time — or so I had kept telling myself . . .

Newton made a beautiful play on Hoke's return and drove it
deep into the corner.

Instead, here I was with these people I did not love, though I
might have a grudging admiration for their ability to survive; instead, here I was having to watch that which I did not love, though
again I had learned to have a modest admiration for it; instead,
here I was exposed to all, having to judge that which I knew so
little of . . .

But it was higher than he would have preferred, and with the
increasing heaviness of the balls, it bounced stolidly up rather than
skittishly off and out of reach.

Instead, I had not lived my life as we are admonished to do: as
though each moment might be our last and that therefore each
moment should be lived as the moment of greatest good, because
if God wearied of watching us spin and spin and spin . . .

So Hoke got to make a play on it. He returned it. Newton had to
make a run and answer with a high lob.

He could end it all at any time. Which it was more and more
apparent He had already done. He was the Final Arbiter, the Last
Word, the Judge . . .

But it went right to where Hoke was.

The Great Referee in the sky . . .

And he had it played perfectly.

The Great Referee can just say STOP! and it stops . . .

He timed it all, screwed his nerves and wind and Head PBI High
Tensile Aluminum Framed racket all into a single piece of fury,
brought his arm around in his most convincing swing of the afternoon, and smashed it into Newton's court. The ball was more a
projectile hurtling with blind rage and savage speed, but Newton,
knowing he had to take this point to keep himself going, was up to
the moment; he was prepared; his arm was already drawn back to
deliver a telling, highly controlled blow for superior competence,
when the ball hit.

SLUUURCK!

The sound of it echoed, reverberated forward to Eternity and
back into the fastnesses of Pre-history, and forward again to our
own blink of Time. It was an answer to prayer. That's all I could
think of at the time. An answer to prayer. And I remember won-

dering why God had deemed my charred soul worthy of salvaging for yet a little longer. The ball — charged though it was — went slurking directly into a thick, gooey tar bubble, tried to bounce up as is its nature, and though it managed to proceed some two inches on its destined course, remained, finally, where it was, like a fly foolishly buzzing into a spider's web, a captive like the rest of us; a thing caught forever in the wrong place at the wrong time.

Until — with the clarity of Vision we all hope Deity surely must have — I sprang to my feet, beer can clutched in each hand, arms spread in the benediction of salvation, and pronounced: STOP! IT IS ENOUGH.

And with that, I collapsed giddily, face down, eyes wide, my lips spread in a sanctified smile, my brain purged forever of trivia, it now being heavy with the insight and inspiration of Deity; collapsed, I say, into the slick pool of Hoke Warble's rapidly melting tennis court.

My head almost started hurting all over again when I read the weekly paper and looked at that picture of Hoke Warble and Newton Slock grinning like jackanapes, shaking hands, holding out those thousand-dollar checks they were donating to the Ickey Honey Country Club and Recreation Center to have more tennis courts built so all those Residents and nine-fingered folk could come play tennis with each other and spend their hard-earned money in the Pro Shop on expensive rackets and sneakers and alligator shirts and warm-up togs and colored balls and . . .

I spread more goo across my flaking forehead to ease the sunburn which was still pretty uncomfortable, but I had been put to bed for heat stroke. That's what the doctor called it. I suppose he was right as far as he knew, but I'm not so sure that that's what really put me down. I think it was the knowledge that I had been taken in and that the entire Thousand-Dollar-Winner-Take-All-Grudge-Match was a put-up job from the start. To create some lively interest in the sport, is what the paper quoted Hoke as saying. And it was to become an annual thing, Mr. Warble had strongly hinted. It would attract visitors, he said. They would spend lotsa money, they did *not* quote him as saying. It would put us on the map, he *did* add. It would put us on the map.

It was enough to make a grown man sick.

My trouble, I'm sure, is that I try to be straightforward about things. So it seems to me that they could have gotten that interest by fixing up the court they already had and by getting the people who wanted to play to build a new one. But as I say, Hoke always was one to see things on a somewhat grander scale than the rest of us. He always needed a little drama in his life. As for me . . .

Well, I don't mind there being more tennis courts. And I don't mind there being a Club House. And I don't mind them taking the cover off the old swimming pool and fixing it up so it can be used again. That's all nice enough. I guess I don't mind things changing and growing, really. It's just that I like to see things grow where they will grow. Maybe I've been too favored by the natural flow of our small streams and the twists and turns of the gulleys and draws, the odd profile of a mountain face, or the startled explosion of a deer flushed from hiding when you weren't looking for it. I guess I like for streets to follow the natural bend of the land. I guess I still like towns that have kinks in them, kinks and little odd places that are there because there were some kinky and odd people around who put their marks on the place at one time and another. Kinks and odd corners: *that's* what lets people know they are in Ickey Honey — or anyplace else that is still somewhere. Kinks and odd corners on the maps of our hearts.

NATALIE L. M. PETESCH

Main Street Morning

(FROM NEW LETTERS)

> Nor must you dream of opening any door
> Until you have foreseen what lies beyond it.
> — RICHARD WILBUR, *Walking to Sleep*

YOU HAVE COME all this way to find out the truth about yourself, not the self you have carefully devised for over thirty-one years, but the self which split involuntarily into chromosomes, giving you his dark, curled hair but not her fern-green eyes — those mutual gifts which existed before you did, and which subsequently She gave away as if their love had not existed and therefore you, Marie, did not exist either.

A long search and a longer doubt have brought you to this ridiculous point, where you watch through your binoculars like a would-be assassin as *She* (Cecilia Roche née Cecilia Niall) goes to work, the woman who once either hated you or loved you, or both, but could not have been indifferent. She is about to leave Sears Roebuck where she is employed during the evening hours in Drapes & Fabrics, Custommade. She has gone in just now only to collect her check or perhaps to exchange a few words with her fellow employees and emerges, clutching her handbag. She does not trouble to straighten her skirt: perhaps she is indifferent to such matters. A few doors down on Main Street, she pauses at the window of a shoe store where they are offering (you recall) two pairs for five dollars: you wonder if that means she still has no money: for long ago you decided that it was money and only money which could have wrenched you away from her, sobbing. Yes, sobbing: you will not have it any other way.

You'd be the first to admit that this is a crazy way for you to spend your vacation. Cooped up in a room of the Manor Hotel, facing Main Street. Of course, every small town in the U.S. has its Main Street, but only this one has Cecilia Niall Roche in it. She has lived here for thirty years, ever since World War Two, as her generation refers to it — as if World War Three were already included in their plans. She (naturally) has had other children, though none of them could look like you, with that share of your genetic inheritance which belongs to Jules Blaine. Natural though it may be, the fact wrenches from you a spasm of loneliness, reminding you how quickly one's pendulum swings from being glorious Prince Hal to Falstaff snuffling in his bed. The moral of this comparison, Marie, you admonish yourself, is that a woman who plans to spy on her own mother ought to remain calm and not drink too much coffee. Already you're too nervous to handle the binoculars, which bear the sweating imprint of your fingers. But at least since you bought the binoculars you've been able to see her face, clearly framed like an antique portrait, and you accept the fact that she is (as they say) "lovely." (Suddenly you become "love-lier" to yourself.)

It's a round saucer of a face, with smooth puffed-out cheeks, precisely the sort of face you would smile at for its Campbell Soup innocence, if she were someone else. If you were to meet that cherubic face at a party, would you ever imagine that she had lain in a ward, labored thirty-eight hours, and finally given birth to a nameless little gnome (yourself)? That, carefully adjusting her mask, she had gone back to Duluth, Boise, Davenport, Sheboygan — back to this very Main Street, the home of her fathers: absolved, pardoned, excused, by all except the main character of this drama, yourself? Nobody has yet asked your pardon.

Adjusting the binoculars like a telescopic sight, you think: suppose you were now to take the elevator down, walk out the revolving door, and trap her as she emerges from, say, the bakery, and walking toward her, in face to face confrontation you say: "Mother? . . ." You practice it a moment, repeating in various inflections: QUESTION: Mother? . . . EXCLAMATION; SHOCK OF RECOGNITION: Mother!!!! . . . SARDONIC: Mot*herrr!* EXPLETIVE: Mother!

You turn away from the window, understanding very well that what you've tried to do is destroy your feelings. Good: you've

destroyed them, Marie, how clever of you — now what are you
going to do with the bits and pieces? You get up from your aching
knees (you should have placed a pillow in front of the window, but
you were too nervous and you forgot). You decide to go out . . . to
actually *see* her. You'll follow her, till you catch her metaphorically
in the till. You'll then inform her she's under citizen's arrest.
J'accuse, Cecilia Niall Roche . . . So you go down the hall which
smells like a subway urinal: it's that roach killer they use, an
invisible fluid which destroys the nervous system, they paint it
along the baseboards. In the elevator the elevator operator (no
orange-eyed electronic robots in Main Street) looks warily down at
his feet: you're a stranger here, he can tell that, but he doesn't
want to be nosy, you've paid for your privacy and there've been no
big-city habits, no men in your room, no strange activities — unless
the long silences during which you are on your knees at the window
waiting for Her to come out have seemed to him portentous. It is
a small local hotel where people know each other and are friendly;
there's no protocol of deliberate silences separating Each from the
Other, as in big cities. Still, you feel he'd like to penetrate your
mystery. Not *my* mystery, you defend yourself sardonically; *my* life
is a dull and open secret: *her* mystery.

But you think your bitterness may show on your face, so quickly
you cross over the uneven step (he doesn't even say tonelessly,
"Watch your step" — here on Main Street they don't warn you
every time of what's right before your eyes). Out in the sun you're
momentarily blinded. You've left your binoculars upstairs and for
a moment you panic, as if without those defensive shields you'll not
be able to bear the evidence of your eyes.

Out here on the street — so quiet one wonders where all the
population explosion that demographers murmur about has exploded to — there is no possibility you will lose sight of her. There
she is, walking very slowly this Monday morning. Well, if she's not
in a hurry, neither are you. You have the advantage this time,
there's no programmed period of gestation, after which you must
"show," willie-nillie. Now you may show and be damned. The
woman ahead of you is a bit shorter and stouter than the one you
spied upon from the window: you take that in as though it's merely
one more response to a random sample you're doing on Main
Street.

She's gone into a Rexall's. Although it's still early (10:30 A.M.) the three or four booths in the small drug store are already filled except for the one nearest the cash register and lunch counter: she takes it. Across the aisle from her sits an old man, alone and unshaven. He's spread himself around the booth with a newspaper borrowed from the rack, looking as much at ease as if he were in the neighborhood library. She checks the time with the red and black electric clock above the lunch counter which reads, instead of the hours: S U N R I S E   B R E A D.

As for you, Marie, nearly a third of your face covered by wide sunglasses, you head for the lunch counter, your back turned to her. Actually, you see her quite clearly in the round sign facing you which has a mirror finish and a Bicentennial sticker glued like a bull's eye at the center, offering you Homemade Apple Pie. You promptly order pie and coffee, although you can see the bakery label on the pan, and you know it will be too sweet and taste not at all of apples. Still, it's something to shut your mouth on while waiting for the person she is waiting for.

You've not long to wait — they're punctual on Main Street, with no subway hangups or traffic jams to slow them down — there she is. Her appointment is with no Jules Blaine, of course, no dashing young lover in khaki, but only another middle-aged woman like herself (wearing — somewhat to your surprise — real Indian moccasins such as are popular in the Southwest). Her housedress, however, is predictable — a pale blue cotton with some sort of trimming at the sleeves, a starched strand of which is coming loose near the rounded forearm. No matter: she's smiling a warm greeting and already they're into something you can't share, you've no idea what they're talking about. The occasional clink of money, the ring of the cash register or an eruption of news from a small radio on the counter chops up their conversation into secret semaphores and codes: you have to strain to hear them.

The woman in blue greets Cecilia with a sort of calm delight. You're somehow shocked to hear Her addressed so personally yet casually — rather like the *tu* instead of the *vous* coming from a street vendor once as you browsed among the bookstalls along the Seine. It had frightened you, as though someone had meant to insult you: it had in fact been only a boy about ten years old, selling plastic replicas of Notre Dame and Sacré Coeur: he'd stared at you, challengingly, enjoying his own insolence. Still, you'd bought one, pretending not to understand his rudeness . . .

Already Cecilia's begun to pull out some snapshots she's taken somewhere, and her friend of course thinks they're wonderful pictures. She even says it: "These are just wonderful."

"Neil took them. We said he shouldn't have to take pictures at his own wedding, but he insisted. He wanted some done by himself. He said he was the best wedding photographer in the State, he wasn't going to start married life by letting somebody else take pictures of his own wife!"

The woman in blue erupted into a delighted, mischievous laugh.

"But Sandy, he's not at his own wedding!"

Sandy! Somehow you'd never thought of that. But peering into the mirror across from you, you imagine you do see a few faint freckles along the nose, rather like the vein of cinnamon deep in your apple pie. Well: so her hair has not always been corn-colored but rather (you now embellish the antique photo in your mind), a desert color, a sunset color, something Jules would certainly have preferred to his own coarse black hair cropped close by the Army so that one saw the pale olive skin against the hair, curling like knotholes.

". . . so exciting, I thought I'd never make it . . . and not to cost me anything either."

"And what about? . . ." Her friend looks at her tentatively.

Sandy glances around to see if anyone is listening, sees only the rounded indifference of your back, hunched addictively over the apple pie. You hardly notice that in your excitement you have spilled hot coffee over your hand.

"Oh, I guess they'll be all right." Then defensively, "He might have done a lot worse, I guess. He might have married . . ." Her voice lowered, Sandy whispers the unmentionable. Then her tone changes. "But it'll work out, I'm sure. Besides, it's their affair, not mine . . . Why don't you take these and show them to Phil? I've got to do some more errands . . ." She glances again at the red and black clock on the wall. Yourself, you have difficulty with the clock: it reads to you like a concrete poem:

BREAD

READ

AD

Or, if you blur your eyes a second, DAD, or D EAD.

Sandy's friend murmurs something like "not losing a son but gaining a daughter." You strain your ears, you *think* you hear her say she knows what it's like to lose a daughter, but it must be your imagination, you can't pin the words down, Sandy's voice disappears into a kind of murmuring protest or enumeration, you're not sure which. Finally you hear it ". . . getting used to it, you know . . . daughters-in-law and one grandson."

You now experience a totally irrational pride in your sex. But that she does actually have such an Item as a grandson is a bit of a shock to you: it puts her in danger of getting lost again just when you've "found" her, as if she could suddenly disappear at that point where the parallel lines between past and future meet. And now you're experiencing something else. Somehow the fact of her grandson is wrapped up like those Japanese *origami*, a design within a design, with the fact that you will soon be thirty-two years old. You feel suddenly hollow and wasted, as if the long struggle to resist entrapment by your own body (as Sandy was entrapped) has put you exactly there and nowhere else.

But now here she is: bright-yellow hair, and around her eyes criss-crosses, like those on your apple pie: lines so deeply slashed into the cheeks they might have been deliberately grooved there, as on some carefully crafted mask of clay about to be fired in the kiln. You try to imagine what she looked like back then — when you were presenting her with that historic moral choice: reject and survive or accept and be damned. In your now-corrected script of the Forties you see Sandy was "titian-haired": You even enjoy the cliché which at other times would have struck you as laughable.

In your new script Sandy is meeting her lover, your father Jules Blaine, in New York. She has told her parents that she is "taking a holiday" from the government office on Main Street (where several months ago she met Jules Blaine, who came to inquire about a friend of his who is missing in action . . .) Part of Sandy's work at the big government office is typing up casualty reports: it's a job that fills her mind with nightmares, and when Jules enters her office she already sees him as a casualty of the war.

But she has come to New York to be with him, with Jules. Where did she discover the cunning, the duplicity, during The Biggest War on Earth to escape from Main Street to do this? Impossible for you, in the Present, to understand how she managed it. Although for a while you helped run a radio program in New York, and have written television commercials, you've never had to make your audience understand why they should purchase cars, curtains, cough syrups . . . all you had to do was invent a catchy slogan, retain their attention.

Thus, it's difficult for you to imagine what she is saying to Jules as they climb the Fifth Avenue bus. You understand the feeling though: it's summer, they're sitting on "top-of-New York," looking down. There is a slight breeze as they head crosstown toward Riverside. Her hair is not coarse and curled into knotholes like yours, like Jules', but soft and curved around the ears like the mouth of a cream pitcher (they call it a "page boy"). Jules is singing something from *Oklahoma*. If you listen carefully, you can almost hear his voice: *People will say we're in lo-ove* . . . There are tears in Sandy's eyes, perhaps of joy? — no, of grief, because Jules is going down South before being shipped overseas. "No," he says, he "doesn't know which "Theater.' " They smile bitterly at the word *theater*. She begs: won't she be able to be with him again before they send him away? (Sitting in the drug store you almost urge them on: yes, yes, they *must* see each other!)

All is quickly decided — ecstatically, spontaneously, as if no lovers in time of war had ever thought of it before . . . She will join him in a week. Not a word to Sandy's parents waiting on Main Street of course: so far as they know she will still be in New York, visiting Sandy's best friend. "Will Melissa cover for you?" asks Jules. She nods; they are utterly delighted with the conspiracy (oh what a joy it is to fool one's parents, *isn't it? isn't it? isn't it?*). They are as ecstatic as if there were not yet to be endured in this war a Battle of the Bulge, an Iwo Jima, an Okinawa.

They are on their way to Melissa's apartment: during the summer Melissa's family are not there, they are at the Cape, only Sandy is there with Jules — hour after hour, whenever he can escape to her. After which he returns to the barracks, where he becomes again the property of the State. He and Sandy have a special arrangement for calls, so that when the phone rings it can only be him: to the rest of the world the occupants are permanently out of town. In a city of seven million Sandy recognizes only one person. When one evening while they are celebrating Jules' nineteenth birthday at Rockefeller Center they run into some of Jules' relatives, they brazen it out. Jules makes up a story on the spot: he is good at making up stories, as Sandy, obviously, is not.

Indeed Sandy is having trouble right now explaining to her friend in the booth how she feels about it all — about her daughter-in-law, or her former daughter-in-law, it's not clear which. ". . . It breaks my heart, though to see . . ." and she goes on. It has something to do with the way her grandson is being treated or not treated, loved or not loved, ignored or spoiled or both. He's being deprived of something, that's obvious. And Sandy's grief is as keen as if it were her own child being singled out by fate for unjustifiable suffering. (You pause to wonder: is there *justifiable* suffering?) But no, what Sandy is protesting is not her grandson's suffering but her son's, his loneliness . . . You decide it must be the older son, not Neil, since Neil is the boy from whose wedding she's just returned.

While Sandy's present life continues under your ear like a pizzicato, you suck at the rim of your now-empty cup and gaze sideways at the clock which seems to your blurred vision to be reading the hour of D EAD. You continue to watch Sandy and Jules descend the Fifth Avenue bus. They are now returning to Melissa Levin's Riverside apartment. Again, there's an elevator — not much different from the one on Main Street — and they're going up, up, up: with your coffee cup in hand you are transfixed by the vision, which blurs as she steps quickly into the apartment. As they shut the door in your face, you can feel the melting of their bones.

It's been a long cup of coffee and you know you're beginning to look out of place, a young unmarried woman like you, having no job to go to on a Monday morning on Main Street. But you're afraid to get up, afraid your body will reveal how like a shuttlecock it's been tossed between two women, both of them Sandy. You now notice, with a combination of relief and panic, that Sandy's friend has gotten up to leave. That leaves you and her alone (at least from your point of view). Now would be the moment, the sweet and catastrophic moment to say . . . to say . . . Instantly you destroy your impulse by a rescuing gesture of absurdity . . . to say: *Mother come home. All is forgiven.* Love, Marie.

Fortunately for you Sandy has decided it's time to hurry on to her appointment. For a few moments you're too weak to move, you'll have to let her leave without you. But a faint grind of electricity from the B R E A D clock reminds you that if you lose sight of her now you won't see her again till she goes back to work; and there you will be able to observe her only as she measures the fabrics, snipping away at yards of muslin, corduroy or denim like one of the Three Fates cutting away lives. So, leaving some money on the counter, you hurry out to the opposite side of Main Street. Ah, there she is, going into the local bank. So: she lives in the "real" world after all, complete with savings, mortgages, escrows and overdrawn accounts. You follow her inside. The bank is surprisingly crowded for such a small town and there're only two windows open for service. It's obvious that people are just as busy with banks in Main Street as everywhere in America . . . and what's this? Sandy is buying a U.S. Savings Bond for someone's birthday, for the grandson whose neglect she was protesting at the drug store.

You now get into a parallel line, ostensibly to cash a traveler's check and to get some small change for the parking meter. While waiting in line your mind wanders: waiting is for you (and for Sandy) one of the more draining rituals in our still unpredictable technology. It was to avoid Waiting that Sandy got on that train to the army base in Carolina (S.). You glance down at the modest hemline which presently hides her legs, and you contrast it with her appearance on that train in August of 1944. She is going to meet Jules, where she will sit in the sweltering heat (there is no air conditioning) for twenty-eight hours, the perspiration trickling down her back, while the train crawls along with its fantastic overload of servicemen (by this time next year the lists will be in the thousands who will never return).

It is the first train Sandy could get to — as the blue carbon share of her ticket assures her — CAROLINA (S.). There are no seats. All night long Sandy and about six other people sit on the suitcases piled between the cars, guarding their feet as the coupled trains grind again and again to a halt. At these stops a few teenagers called Soldiers climb down, their duffel bags on their shoulders. Always they have this dazed look, as if they do not recognize the town they have come to visit.

Eventually Sandy's train does arrive in Carolina S., late in the afternoon. She is faint with sleeplessness and from the shock of the heat, which is something she has never experienced on Main Street. Jules cannot get away in time to meet her, so there she stands, feeling exhausted and lightheaded but also enjoying an odd excitement at the sight of a mule standing at the train station, its cart loaded with bales of hay. It stands patiently, only its ears flick in protest whenever there's a whoosh of steam from the locomotive (no diesel on this ancient train, though we are not only a year away from Hiroshima).

Sandy takes a cab to the hotel Jules has instructed her to go to. She showers and changes her clothes, but she is too restless either to sleep or read (there is no radio in her room), so she goes out to the street. In spite of her fatigue and her awe at the sun which glowers down like some wrathful Jehovah making good His threat of destruction by fire, she strolls down their Main Street which is only a few blocks from the hotel. She is filled with a romantic curiosity about the town, which is exciting to her because Jules "lives" there. She presently notices a line of black people, extending all the way around the corner: they are waiting at the Colored entrance to see a film with Cary Grant. At the front of the movie house there is another ticket taker, sitting idly, waiting for the First Show to begin.

Sandy does not wish to wander far from the hotel: what if Jules should arrive early and not find her? She begins — somewhat reluctantly, as she is enjoying her first stroll in a Southern town — to trace her steps. She is rewarded for her small sacrifice, because as the hotel comes again into view she sees Jules standing outside, obviously looking up and down the street for a slender girl with bare legs and honey-colored hair. They are at once in each other's arms: through the khaki shirt Sandy can feel the warm sweat of Jules' body.

The bank teller now holds the U.S. Savings Bond tentatively above her typewriter and asks Sandy, "Who should I make it out to?" Sandy replies, "Make it out to Jules B. Roche II."

Jules? You can scarcely believe the effrontery of it. What a cunning hypocrite, to name her firstborn son for her lover — to have this perpetual reminder of her love which is at the same time *her fault, her fault, her most grievous fault* . . . She has managed, apparently, to repress the memory of how she tried to destroy everyone and everything associated with Jules Blaine. How in late March of 1945 she rode out to the Armbruster farm, which is about four miles south of Main Street: that is as far as the municipal bus line will go.

*

March 1945

The bus driver looks at Sandy oddly as she descends — a girl of eighteen, with no shopping bags, no suitcase, no boots or scarf or gloves, nor (he glances down) stockings. And it is snowing, sleeting; a bruising March wind whips about the pools of water left by the boots of previous passengers standing at the driver's change box. He looks again, confirming his first impression: the girl steps down one step at a time, bearing the heavy weight of her curving belly against herself as she grips the edge of the doorway, she makes her way clumsily out of the bus: the driver peers out the window on his side to see where she might be going. He sees only a weathered cowshed for somebody who may have a dairy animal or two and a water pump nobody uses any more. The old Armbruster farmhouse is still in use, though he does not presently see any smoke from their chimney: he has the impression that the Armbrusters are away visiting folks in Canada.

The driver watches while the girl, whose honey-colored hair seems to be darkening as it becomes wet with sleet, makes her way to the farmhouse as if she knows where she's going and why. Certainly she must know the Armbrusters: she has a key and opens the front door easily. The driver is tempted to shrug away the incident, but the curve of the belly haunts him all the way back to the garage where he places a tentative call to the police. Not wanting to be nosy or cruel, "but not everyone who *looks* like a nut is crazy," he apologizes.

In the farmhouse Sandy does not bother to light a lamp or turn on the heat. Instead she goes methodically to the linen closet where she knows she will find all the sheets, dishtowels, bath towels and facecloths (she has been here many times, baby-sitting for the Armbrusters), and begins very expertly to lay the bath towels across the window sills, blocking out the air. She even admires the colorful towels, their creamy texture, towels which the Armbrusters received as a wedding present and which have lasted a decade: now they're soft and flannel-like, suited for swaddling bands . . . Every window plugged, Sandy now lays the folded sheets at the base of the doors, sealing up all drafts: the sheets are very white and glint in the semi-darkness like the eyes of animals. She is beginning to feel cold and at the same time somewhat feverish: yet it is not boring, this final domestic chore, there is even a tidiness about it: she opens the gas jets neatly so that their tiny porcelain arms all extend parallel to one another. Then she goes to a rocking chair where almost at once she achieves a slow rhythmical rock; the wood creaks slightly, gradually shading to a hum like a lullaby, to which she falls quietly asleep . . . When the screaming sirens stop in front of the farmhouse and the firemen smash the windows Sandy is sleeping soundly, her body soft, yielding to unconsciousness. At once she is carried out, given oxygen.

Well: she has made an attempt to get rid of you, Marie, and of herself too. But it's useless. After that fiasco, you grow and grow visibly, invincibly, for good or evil — until at last God repents of his wrath and washes you out with her blood.

You're glad you don't remember the trauma of your birth. It's bad enough reliving her trauma at the Home for Unwed Mothers. There's no such place on Main Street, they don't have unwed mothers on Main Street, so to spare Sandy the pain of neighborly curiosity, Sandy is shipped off to a benevolent institution in Philadelphia, where two months after her failure at the Armbruster farm, you, Marie, are born. Once in a sociology class you took part in a panel, along with three other undergraduates, on "The Unwed Mother." Eventually all four of you decided it would be an excellent idea to visit the local hospital, where you taped interviews with the women there, who made surprisingly fierce statements about the right to keep their child.

Sandy's opinion on this subject, however, is not being asked. Instead, now that she has carried "full term," she has been lying all night covered by a coarse army blanket, her hands on her belly, her eyes closed. She is praying, praying, praying. For this ordeal to be over. For the wisdom and the strength to know what to do. For some word from Jules who is hidden away somewhere in Iwo Jima, hidden so well that he will never be found except by Japanese children looking for relics of the victorious invading army.

Finally a nun enters the room; it is dawn; she pulls the curtains apart, and smiles at Sandy. Impossible to know whether her cruelty is intentional when she says what she says to all her girls every morning, "And how are you feeling today?"

At last you have gotten through the line: it has taken, it seems to you, an incredibly long time. But this is a small town; what would have been a quick and businesslike affair in any other place is here a social event. You clutch your change, pocket the money from your traveler's check and move slowly toward the door.

"Put his father's name on it too, please," says Sandy. "Jules B. Roche. I mean, not his mother's name. His mother —"

"Yes, I know . . ." the teller says sadly. "It nearly broke my heart to hear it. Like your son got to be a father and a widower both at once. Like God didn't know which way to treat him, hardly."

Sandy bows her head, pulls out a handkerchief which she doesn't need but uses to conceal her pain at hearing her life counted out by the teller like so much small change.

The teller goes to type up the U.S. Bond while you loiter nearby, looking over some information about how the government is now insuring your savings up to $40,000.

Sandy now puts her grandson's gift into her handbag: you hear that he is six, going on seven, and the teller adds: "Well, you tell him 'Happy Birthday' for me, will you?" Sandy is perceptibly happier now that her list of woes, like the plagues of Egypt, have been named and numbered and she is momentarily free to forget them, including the one she will never forget and cannot share with anyone — not with the teller, nor with her husband, nor with her sons, nor with anybody but you, Marie. Who now share her sorrow as she leaves by the electronic door.

Outdoors she stands again in the August sun, squinting at the clock which is suitably cloistered in a church steeple. She feels the need to move quickly now, as the moment she has been planning for has arrived, and she must hurry to meet it. Ah . . . you see at once to whom she is hurrying. It is Jules B. Roche II, descending now from a bus, holding a sheet of paper on which you can see as he waves it at her whorled circles of dark blue fingerpaint. "It's a storm! A storm!" he informs her. Diffident, anxious to assure the artist that his success is clear and striking, she says simply, "Oh what a beautiful painting!"

You now apprehend that for Sandy love is always terminal, always something for her life to be lost in . . . Overcome by her failure to express her perfect admiration for his painting, she swoops down, capsizes the artist in her arms, covers him with kisses. "Did you have a nice day?" she asks at last: respectfully.

Your knees are weak as you lean against the freshly painted red, white and blue fire hydrant. Your impulse is to run toward them crying out, *me too! me too!* You can now taste your own long denial;

you want to run and tell her all about your thirty-one years without her and have her cry out with absolving certainty: *Oh what a beautiful daughter you are!* have her insist with incontrovertible passion: *Oh what a beautiful life you have!* Which will give you the courage to go on, to go back into the ugliness of your century where life begins with television commercials and ends with nursing homes. But, as they pass you, Jules is trying to guess what they will do together to celebrate his birthday and Sandy is laughing. *Laughing.* It is the first time in all your imagined scripts that you have heard her laugh and it is real laughter, not something you have projected onto invented memories. Hearing it now for the first time, you lean weakly against the fire hydrant, standing aside to let them pass.

MAX SCHOTT

Murphy Jones: Pearblossom, California

(FROM ASCENT)

SHE'D BEEN IN LOW SPIRITS and I gave her a lot of advice on how to raise them. Didn't help, but she got better. No reason why she shouldn't — nothing wrong with her but some broken ribs, and they'd healed. I remember thinking at the time that she wouldn't learn a damn thing from the accident, and that that was a pity. I couldn't decide whether I thought a harder knock would have done her any more good. The one she got seemed hard enough when it happened.

Just when she'd started feeling fairly good again, a man came along who she hadn't seen for years.

Nice-looking fellow, even yet. Lives way off in some little Nevada town she exiled him to, years back. Had to come this way on business — that's what he said in the note he wrote her.

When Margaret told me Toni'd got the letter, I said: "Did she mention the man's name?"

·"Wendell," Margaret said.

"Wendell? — isn't he the one she bought that old Desert Lass mare from about a century ago?"

"Same one," Margaret said. "She had a romance with him just after her marriage broke up."

"So she tells me one thing and you another."

"Well, they're both true."

"Doesn't surprise me. Lots of buckets dipped in the well since then: wonder she even remembers him."

"It would be a wonder if she didn't. She wants us to have him over here to supper so that she won't have to spend an evening alone with him unless she decides to."

"Doesn't want to see him?"

"She wants to," Margaret said, "if she could do it without his seeing her. She's afraid he'll be struck by the change."

"He'll lie if he is," I said. "He won't turn and run."

Toni came over that night and sat down at the kitchen table with Margaret and me. More color in her cheeks than I'd seen in months and I told her so.

"Old friend of yours coming to town I hear?" She nodded. "How long's it been?"

"Eighteen years," she said, and blushed.

"That's a while. He'll be pleased to see how you've turned out."

"Thanks. He probably won't recognize me."

"I hope he's done as well. Have you heard from him over the years?"

"Not for a long time."

"You're full of curiosity then, I'll bet — only natural."

"A little," she said. She looked down and rubbed the rim of her cup with her thumb and looked up at Margaret. Seemed I was preventing a conversation, so before long I excused myself and carried my coffee into the front room and started looking over my daybook from the auction-yard.

I could hear them jabbering but I couldn't make out the words. "Shut that door," I hollered. Someone shut it, and I opened the heater vent beside my chair and heard every word.

" 'I don't want to see you any more' — I was going to tell him," Toni said.

"Over already," I said to myself, "Damn, they work fast!" But it turned out they were talking about a man named Ben and hadn't even arrived at Wendell yet. One thing on her mind and she'll talk about another.

"So after that I couldn't go up to Ben's stables any more and ride his horses. And after about a month of stewing I decided to buy a horse of my own. That's when I met Wendell. I bought Lass from him and took a few horse training lessons, and I had a real wild affair with him — the first one like that I ever had, where there wasn't a lot of dawdling around. A good thing there wasn't because the whole thing only lasted two weeks. He decided to go back to his wife, not because of me but because of the judge. When I met him they were separated, and he said they were going to get a divorce. But when the judge told him how much he'd have to pay, he decided to go back."

"Oh, Toni, you don't believe that do you? Still?" I heard Margaret say.

"Well, not that that's why he went back, but I believe the judge had a lot to do with the timing. If the hearing hadn't been right then, he wouldn't have gone back right then. Maybe we'd have run through each other, or who knows what might have happened, I don't know. We were both only twenty-two. Anyway, the way it was it was cut off."

"What attracted you so about him?"

"Well, he was big and tall and strong and handsome — and I'd been sitting in my house for a month. It was lust at first sight."

"I don't know about that man Wendell," I said to Margaret later. "Going back to your wife just to keep out of jail — that's a new one."

"That's not all of it," Margaret said.

"I'll bet it isn't," I said, "but it's all I heard because someone closed that heater vent in the kitchen."

"I know they did," she said. "But I'll tell you some of it. His wife wouldn't let him in the house because he'd been with Toni — and he asked Toni to call her and plead his case for him — can you imagine!"

"Did she turn him down?"

"Yes, but it seems to have been just because she didn't know what to say. He took advantage of all her good feelings. He told her she was too big a temptation for him to resist. So she located him a job and loaned him the money to move. I said to Toni that he sounded a little sneaky to me. Maybe I shouldn't have."

"Did he pay back the money?"

"Yes."

"Well, maybe he's all right. He was no more than a kid himself."

When he came to town Toni called me up to say so. I stopped by her barn to meet him, and I don't know if it's to my credit, but the man did make a good first impression on me.

I found them out in the pasture, standing looking at Desert Lass who had her head down grazing. Wendell was curly headed and dark complected. "That's the kind women like all right," I said to myself.

Toni introduced us, and I stood and helped them look at the old mare.

"You know her from way back," I said.

"I'd never have recognized her," he said.

"A colt or two and they get a little dough-bellied," I said.

"Last thing a man would think of when he thought of her was belly," Wendell said. "Moved like a cat."

"A streamlined one will end up more womb-sprung than one who's on the big-bellied side to begin with," I said.

"Stands to reason," he said, "not much room in there for a colt."

"That's right," I said. "Colt has to bang out a nest for himself and the next one will stretch it on out some more."

"Must be so," he said, "from the looks of her."

"Agreeable fellow," I said to myself, "man you can talk to."

"How many's she had, Toni?" he said.

"Six," Toni said.

"My wife had seven, but one died." Toni just looked at him.

"That's too bad," I said. "Where is it you're from, exactly?"

"Gerlach," he said. "Nevada."

"I know the town but I can't place it. Where is that near?"

"Not too near anywhere," he said. "Seventy miles from Fernley."

"Fernley: I've been through there for sure. Fair-sized place, is it?"

"Fernley? About five hundred in the summer. Right on the paved road, sixty miles west of Fallon."

"Fallon: I know that place for a fact. Ate supper there and lost a game of blackjack. Hundred miles east of Reno?"

"That's right. You're up that way again, stop by. All good roads. Dirt from Fernley to Gerlach, but it's good ground and you don't even know you're in a car."

"I will," I said. "Train horses up there, do you?"

"Those boys up there don't care if their horses go crooked or in a straight line, and if they don't I don't."

"I don't blame you a bit," I said.

"I watch over some cattle for a man. Eight hundred mother cows."

"That's a lot. Have some men working under you?"

"No, sir," he said. "No help but two dogs."

"Don't see how you do it," I said.

"I can press my wife into service if I have to," he said.

"Press her into service?" Toni said.

"If I have to," he said.

"Been there long?" I said.

"Gerlach? — Ever since I left Los Angeles."

"You don't strike me like a Los Angeles man."

"How old's old Lass there, Toni?" he said.

"Twenty-three."

"Five when I left. Maybe I've changed some."

"Must be quite a change," I said, "to go away-off to a place like Gerlach from the city."

"I don't live right in downtown Gerlach," he said. "About thirty-five miles out."

"How'd you happen to locate there?"

"This old girl right here saw an ad: 'Cowboy wanted: High desert; school bus service, house, meat and milk furnished (they meant a milk cow); Two hundred dollars a month; Northern Nevada; Apply box xxx Western Livestock Journal.' Remember that?"

"I remember," Toni said. "He wasn't a city person to start with, Murphy. He was pretty much like he is now, come to think of it."

"I believe it," I said, "but they say a person can get spoiled fast, living in town, young country boy especially. Milking that same old cow day in and day out by lantern light might look a little hum-drum after your city."

"Jan milks," he said. "My wife."

"How's she getting along?" Toni said.

"Just right," he said. "Looks good, feels good — for a woman who's shelled out kids like she has and been alive as long, she gets by all right: that's what everyone says that sees her. I don't pay a whole lot of attention myself."

"That's too bad," Toni said. "I'm glad she's well."

"She does all right," Wendell said. "But you, now, you never settled. I thought you might. Once in a while I'd catch a thought floating through that you'd married and settled down — but you never." He turned to me. "Don't you think a person ought to settle down, time you're our age? I understand you're a married man."

"Darned right," I said. "I've been telling her so for years. Just like talking to a log."

"It takes one to know one, Murphy — a log I mean," and she gave me a little push on the shoulder.

"I hadn't seen her for a long time, but she looks fine," he said. "First thing I said to myself when I saw her: 'She looks fine!' Don't you!" And he put his hand on her shoulder and shook her, and I saw her stiffen.

"Yep, I'd have known her on the street anywhere," he said and put his hand back by his side.

Wendell went downtown to get a room for the night.

When I came home from the auction-yard Toni and Margaret were busy talking in the kitchen. Usually if they're like that and I come in, they'll look at me and start to wink and whistle. But this time soon as she saw me she said: "I'm sorry, Murphy, if I'd known what he was like I'd never have imposed him on you and Margaret — or on myself."

"What's he like?" I said. "Seems to be a nice enough fellow from what I saw."

"Uk," she said.

"Oh, you exaggerate — unless he's done something?"

"He hasn't done anything," Toni said.

"He's a good guy," I said to Margaret. "Takes care of eight hundred cows almost by himself."

"He must be all right then," Margaret said.

"Lives up not too far from where I used to," I said.

"He's a jerk, Murphy. He has eight-hundred-and-one cows."

"Eight hundred and a wife and two dogs," I said, "but the cows aren't his, they belong to his boss. Didn't I hear you say he's just like he always was?"

"He sort of is," she said. "It's hard to explain."

"And you used to like him. Have you changed so much?"

"I don't think so. I hope not. He used to be very good looking, I know I'm not wrong about that."

"Good-looking man right today," I said. "You know, I believe she's still carrying a torch."

"Yeah, fat chance," Toni said. "People don't get stupider, do they? I must have had rocks in my head. Poor Jan!"

"My, my, and I have to feed him supper," Margaret said.

"Oh, he's just an ordinary fellow," I said. "Hasn't as much respect for the sex as Toni would like — but I blame his wife for that."

"What's she supposed to do — punch him in the eye?" Toni said. He knocked on the door.

"Shall I let him in?" Margaret said.

"Do we have to?" Toni said. "Let's not!" Then darned if she

didn't clap her hand over her mouth and start to have a fit of schoolgirl giggling.

"Too bad we don't have any arsenic," Margaret said.

"Phaa!" I whispered. "Now you two behave yourself! Where do you think you're going?" I said to Toni.

"The bathroom."

"Act your age, you!"

"Really, Murphy, I have to stop laughing, I'll be back."

"You're as bad as she is," I said to Margaret. "Get out of the way. I'll let him in. Go cook."

I opened the door. He'd shaved and had his hat in his hands. "Poor guy," I thought. "Come in, come in," I said. "Good to see you so soon again." I shook hands with him. "Come into the kitchen and meet my wife."

"Hello," he said to Margaret. "Smells good. Toni here yet?"

"In the bathroom doing some last-minute landscaping," I said.

"Is she?" he said. "Suits me the way she is. Older than she used to be, but looks fine."

"You bet," I said. "She'll probably ruin it."

I took him into the front room, and pretty soon she came out, which I was glad to see, and offered him and me some of my whiskey. I'm famous for not being much of a drinker, but I took a drink.

He took one too, and his flowed straight to his extremities, if I'm not mistaken. Toni was in and out from the kitchen setting the table, and he couldn't keep his eyes off of her. He kept trying to get her to look at him, and she kept trying not to — and I believe she had more success.

When she was in the kitchen I said to him: "I looked at a map a while ago, Wendell, and you know, it wouldn't be a hundred miles from where you live over to where I used to live — if there was a way to get there."

"Where you from?" he said.

"Little town of Wagontire over in Oregon," I said. "Sixty miles north of Likely."

"Uh, huh," he said. "Can't place it. Good smell coming out of there."

"I'll show you on the map," I said. So I brought out a map, though I had a little trouble getting him to look at it. Toni came out of the kitchen and looked over my shoulder.

"Wendell and I were almost neighbors," I said. "Only a hundred miles from my place to his — no roads though — lava rock so thick you can't even ride a horse across. But it's the same country. My old neighbor Sterling Green, he had cattle on both sides." He sat up at the name. "Know him?"

"Know him? — damn him! I work for him."

"Hah! — you see! Margaret, come in here! You women uht — scuse me" (attack the man, I started to say) "and the man works for my neighbor! Here!" And I put out my hand so he had to shake it again.

"Get Murphy another drink," Margaret said.

"Don't pay them any mind, Wendell," I said. "No wonder you take care of eight hundred cows with just a wife and a pair of dogs. He's the shortest-handedest man in the world, that Sterling, damned if he's not!"

Toni went back in the kitchen with Margaret, and I told Wendell a story or two about Sterling. No one could fault me for not being able to talk to a stranger. He didn't have to say a word or even listen.

"That's turned into quite a looking woman, that Toni," he said. "Different from what she was, but they say we most of us change a little. Took me a while to get used to it, but she looks better every time she lifts a leg. It's a wonder no one ever married her."

"She says you're just like you used to be," I said.

"I've had people tell me I haven't changed. One other old girl told me I didn't look a day older than I did twenty years ago. I told her, 'You don't either,' but I lied to her face."

"I don't blame you," I said.

"I never pay them much mind," he said, "but if Toni says I haven't changed, that's good, the way I see it, because she liked me the way I was, and so to reason it on out, that means there's hope."

"Just between you and me, Wendell," I said, "there's no hope. If I understood you correctly, there's not a hope in the world in that direction. For many another man and boy, maybe, but not for you and me."

He'd been watching the kitchen door in case she'd run by, but he turned and looked at me like I'd said something in Greek.

We sat down to eat. Toni told us where to sit, and she put herself across at an angle from Wendell, which with only four of us was as far away as she could get. Still it was close as he'd got so far, so he proceeded to try to talk to her.

"How's business, Toni?" he said. "How're the ponies treating you?"

"Fine," she said.

"You say you had some kind of accident?"

"I'm almost all right now," she said.

"What happened?"

"A horse fell on me."

"Now what'd you go and let him do that for?" Wendell said and laughed, big old horse laugh.

"By god, she's right," I said to myself. "The man is dense and so was I not to see it."

"I shouldn't have," she said.

"I'll say you shouldn't have. I never taught you to do like that, did I?"

"No," she said. Never cracked a smile. That chilled him a little, but he didn't give it up.

"Training those horses is no business for a woman. Don't see why you don't settle down and keep house."

"She has more than that to keep her from settling down, Wendell. She has oats to sow, so we'd better let her be. Pass Wendell those peas, speaking of oats."

Margaret and Toni both looked at me, and I was a little surprised myself, when I'd heard what I said. But it didn't faze Wendell.

"What kind of horse fell on you? Just to make conversation," he said.

"A quarter horse stallion, four-year-old," she said.

"Conversation?" I said to myself. "If you want conversation so bad, I can give it to you." "Shouldn't have been left a stallion but he was," I said. "Man that owns him drove all the way to Texas to buy him, but he's a billy goat just the same. I wouldn't breed a mare of mine to him, I'll tell you that, Wendell!"

Wendell turned and nodded at me. Thought he could get around me with a nod. "Never crossed my mind," he said. "How'd he happen to fall over on you?" he said to Toni. "Slip?"

"No," she said, "he —"

"Slip ha!" I said. (Why should I let her trouble herself to talk?) "He didn't slip, Wendell, I was right there and can vouch for it, you bet he didn't slip!"

"He's really drunk!" Margaret said.

"Phaa — keep quiet," I said. "Pass that meat over to where Wendell can reach it."

"What'd he do?" Wendell said — to me this time — but I wouldn't even look at him.

"Toni," I said, "if you'd shown him that stick before you got on him that day — you know the day I mean — I believe he'd never have done it to you."

"I wish you'd said so at the time."

"I wish it too, sweetheart."

"What stick's that?" Wendell said.

"Wendell," I said, "you ask about that stick, and I'll tell you: it was a green stick, you see, cut from a bush. About yay long." I held up my hands. "At first it was green, but then the sap dried out of it and it shrunk about two inches and turned kind of gray — but it was the same stick and the horse knew it.

"Well, when this horse was first brought to her he had no manners at all. Every time he saw something alive he'd try to fornicate with it: he'd get up and walk around on his hind legs and beller — you know how they do, Wendell — and his old neck would swell up like a bullfrog's." Wendell reached up and rubbed his neck, which had swollen and turned pretty red. "That's right," I said. "The horse's manners were right out of Texas. The owner calls him Golden Son of Yellow Moon or something like that, but Toni and I, we always just called him Tex. (Wendell, you just reach over and help yourself.)

"So the first day, soon as he started in to rear and squeal she stepped off and kicked him in the belly a couple of times and cut that stick from a bush. After that whenever he'd begin to titillate himself she'd pound him on top of the neck, right behind his ears: whack-whack-whack. 'Cut it out, Tex,' she'd say — way you taught her years back, no doubt."

"Darned right," Wendell said.

"Darned right," I said. "That first day it didn't keep him from carrying on, but by the next day he was sore, and by the time two weeks went by she had his attention, and if his mind happened to start to wander she'd just whisper, 'Hey now, Tex' in one of his ears. Or if he was sorely tried — say if a mare walked by winking — you know how they'll do, Wendell — with her tail in the air and maybe pissing a little — why Toni'd just hold the stick up where he could see it with his big right eye."

"Murphy — eat your supper," Margaret said.

"I don't mind," Toni said.

"This will interest Wendell," I said. "She'd hold it up where he could see it and he'd subdue his old gonads.

"She rode him about six weeks — that was last winter. Then they took him home to breed a few mares with and didn't bring him back till August. And before she got on him that first time again, she found that same little old stick thrown back in a corner of the tackroom. Turned gray, but that horse recognized it, you bet he did, been better if he didn't. But at first she didn't show it to him, just clambered up in the saddle with the stick stuck in her belt, that's the pity of it. Because if he'd had a chance to carry that stick along in his mind's eye, there'd never have been any trouble — that's what I think, maybe a little pawing and squealing, but no trouble.

"He had a good picture of that stick registered in his brain and he hadn't forgot what it was used for — but the memory had slipped way back down into his subconscious — that's the way I see it. Wasn't the smartest horse in the world anyway, and darned foolish at times — led astray by his feelings like more beasts than one since the world began —"

"Eat," Margaret said.

"But I'd hesitate to say to a man that he was outright stupid — just thickheaded. Well, we rode along — came to where there was some mares loose in a field. He looked over the fence at them and must have gone to thinking about the good old days back home, tossed his head and puffed his neck up and nickered at those mares. Rattled your jaw, didn't it, Toni?"

"I don't remember."

"That's right: I forgot, she doesn't remember a thing. Anyhow, it had slipped Tex's mind that there's a time and place for everything and such a thing in the world as a stick. And to jog his memory she said, 'Tex, cut it out,' took the stick out from her belt and held it up as of old. He saw it, and it all came back to him, too much all of a sudden, and he threw himself over backwards — landed flat bang on his right side and right on top of her. Darned if I ever saw anything quite like it, Wendell. Looked like he'd been electrocuted."

"And you don't remember a thing?" Wendell said.

"No," she said. "I woke up in the hospital."

"That was unforgiving ground, too — sand, but packed down. When Tex got up and ran off she never wiggled. Scared me."

"Aw," Wendell said, "I hate to think of you lying there like that."
And he laid his big right arm out on the table like a ham. I don't
know if he expected her to reach across and take his hand in hers
or butter it or what. "Sorry I ever got you started training those
horses," he said. "A woman like you doesn't need to be in a business
like that. If I didn't live so far away I'd see to it that you weren't."

"I hope *you're* drunk, too," Margaret said.

"Good thing you live so far away," Toni said. "Just how would
you go about seeing to it?" And she laid down her fork and looked
him right in the eye.

"Ha! Watch out, Wendell, you hound!" I said to myself. "Wendell —" I said.

"I don't know *how*," Wendell said, "but I'd stop you training
those horses, because it's only right."

"Wendell, my friend," I said, "I don't know how it is in Nevada
but in Pearblossom the cats scratch. If you antagonize them, I
mean. Otherwise they won't, I think. So you'll have to bark up
another tree, if you can find any."

"I'll make some coffee," Margaret said.

Toni covered her mouth with her napkin.

"I didn't catch all that," Wendell said. "I haven't seen six trees
since I left home, but if I said something you folks took offense at,
I take it back."

"No, no — no offense, old buddy," I said. I picked his hand up
and shook it. "Toni," I said, "Wendell here said he was sorry to
think of you lying stretched out like that, and I really thought you
were dead for a minute or two there, and it didn't make me feel so
very good, I don't know if I ever told you."

She reached across and ruffled my bit of hair.

As soon after supper as she could get away with it — in fact a
little sooner, she stood up, looking shamefaced: she was going to
leave him with us if she could.

"You going?" Wendell said. (Dumb as he was, he was the first to
see it.)

"I'm sorry to run out on you-all," she said. "I'll see you before
you leave tomorrow, Wendell. Thank you," she said to us, "I'll do
you a favor sometime," and she gave me and Margaret a smile,
friendly but not cheerful.

"I'll give you a ride," Wendell said.

"Thanks, my car's here."

"No need at all for you to run off, Wendell," I said. "It's early. Sit right down there and I'll fix you what you've never had."

"Murphy, it's been good talking to you," he said. "You too, Mrs. Jones. Thanks for the supper."

"Goodbye," Margaret said.

"You're welcome, Wendell," I said, "but I wish you'd stay a few minutes longer."

"Can't," he said. "Where's my hat?"

"Nice to run into a fellow from up there," I said. "You take care of that good wife of yours. Tell Sterling you saw me, and if he doesn't say anything too bad about me give him my best regards. When you planning to go back?"

He winked at me. "I'm supposed to head on back tomorrow, but with luck I might stay around a day or two and see the sights."

Toni was behind him with her hand on the doorknob. She shook her head no and made a face.

"Well, then, with luck we'll see you again," I said. "But you never know about that luck stuff: sometimes a man will bow his head and pray for luck and just wind up with a stiff neck." I rubbed my neck, since he seemed to understand sign language best. Then I shook his hand, I hope for the last time.

I saw them out, and when I went into the front room again, Margaret was sitting over by the window, half in the dark, holding a magazine. "Better turn on the light if you want to read," I said.

"Shh," she said.

I walked over and looked out the window. Toni and Wendell were standing by Toni's car. Toni had her hand on the doorhandle, and he was standing pretty close to her. "Shouldn't eavesdrop," I said to Margaret.

"No," she said. Wendell went to put his arms around Toni, and Toni backed against her car. "Ouch," she said.

"Those ribs," I whispered.

"You may have to go out and pour water on him," Margaret said.

"Goodnight," Toni said, "I'm going home. I'll see you tomorrow before you leave."

"I feel like that horse that fell on you," he said.

"You sure do," she said. "Look: I don't want to. Can't you understand?"

"Don't want to what?" he said.

"I don't want to do anything but go home and go to bed — all by myself."

"Oh. Why don't you want to?"

"I just don't want to."

"No one will ever know, Toni," he said and pressed himself toward her.

"Will he hurt her?" Margaret said.

"No — he just hasn't got the message yet," I said.

"My God! Not yet!?" she said.

"I don't think so."

"It's just between me and you," Wendell said.

"But *I* don't want to," Toni said.

"Oh . . . you just don't want to?"

"No."

"Oh." He backed up a step and she started to open the car door.

"Toni," he said, "I just want to tell you something."

"What?"

"I'll never forget the first time I saw you."

"That's nice of you," she said. "I won't either."

"You were with Shirley."

"I remember."

"And when the two of you came walking up to the barn where I was working I said to myself: 'Now there's two plums,' and I said to you: 'Anything I can do for you girls?' and you said you were looking for a horse to buy."

"I remember," Toni said. "And I asked you if you happened to know Ben Webber. You were both in the same business, and I couldn't think of anything else to say."

"I don't remember that," he said. "I remember I said, 'Now you girls aren't really looking for a horse, are you? I'll bet you're just out joyriding around.' And you said, 'A little of both.' Or maybe Shirley said that. But I know for sure you were the one that couldn't stand still. You kept wiggling. I remember it because I remember saying to myself, 'Now this one's more of a plum than the other one.' It had to have been you because of what happened after. Because it happened with you, or I wouldn't be here now. And we had a good time, didn't we?"

"Yes," she said.

"But now you say you don't want to, without even a reason."

"No, I don't."

"Maybe it's because of that judge?"

"No, I've no hard feelings."

"That judge was enough to chill a man's ardor. I asked him, 'What if I can't pay that much?' 'Then bring your toothbrush next time,' he said. I'll never forget it. But we had a good time right up to then. When I left I at least had a reason." He put his hand on her shoulder and put his face up close to hers, not like he wanted to kiss her but to look in her eyes.

She didn't move a muscle, and he must have read an answer there. (I believe he was a sort of a veterinary psychologist at heart.)

"Then I won't wrestle you for it," he said.

"No, I knew you wouldn't if you ever really understood."

And she said goodnight, got in her car and drove away.

"What an ordeal!" Margaret said. "I was wrong about his being sneaky."

IAN McEWAN

Psychopolis

(FROM THE AMERICAN REVIEW)

MARY WAS A PARTNER in a feminist bookstore in Venice. I met her there lunchtime on my second day in California. That same evening we were lovers, and not so long after that, friends. The following Friday I chained her by the foot to my bed for the whole weekend. It was, she had explained to me, a thing she "had to go into to come out of." I remember her extracting (later, in a crowded bar) my solemn promise that I would not listen if she demanded to be set free. Anxious to please my new friend, I bought a fine chain and diminutive padlock. With brass screws I secured a steel ring to the wooden base of the bed and all was set. Within hours she was insisting on her freedom, and though a little confused I got out of bed, showered, dressed, put on my carpet slippers and brought her a large frying pan to urinate in.

She tried on a firm, sensible voice. "Unlock this," she said. "I've had enough."

I admit she frightened me. I poured myself a drink and hurried out onto the balcony to watch the sun set. I was not at all excited. I thought to myself, If I unlock the chain she will despise me for being weak. If I keep her there she might hate me, but at least I will have kept my promise. The pale orange sun dipped into the haze, and I heard her shout to me through the closed bedroom door. I closed my eyes and concentrated on being blameless.

I returned indoors (the sun now set and the bedroom silent) and wandered from room to room turning on the lights, leaning in doorways and staring in at objects that already were familiar. I set up the music stand and took out my flute. I had taught myself to play years ago and there are many errors, strengthened by habit,

which I no longer have the will to correct. I do not press the keys
as I should with the very tips of my fingers, and my fingers fly too
high off the keys and so make it impossible to play fast passages
with any facility. Furthermore my right wrist is not relaxed, and
does not fall, as it should, at an easy right angle to the instrument.
I do not hold my back straight when I play, instead I slouch over
the music. My breathing is not controlled by the muscles of my
stomach, I blow carelessly from the top of my throat. My embou-
chure is ill-formed and I rely too often on a syrupy vibrato. I lack
the control to play any dynamics other than soft or loud. I have
never bothered to teach myself the notes above top G. My musi-
cianship is poor, and slightly unusual rhythms perplex me. Above
all I have no ambition to play any other than the same half-dozen
pieces and I make the same mistakes each time.

Several minutes into my first piece I thought of her listening
from the bedroom and the phrase "captive audience" came into
my mind. While I played I devised ways in which these words
could be inserted casually into a sentence to make a weak, light-
hearted pun, the humor of which would somehow cause the situation to be elucidated. I put the flute down and walked toward the
bedroom door. But before I had my sentence arranged, my hand,
with a kind of insensible automation, had pushed the door open
and I was standing in front of Mary. She sat on the edge of the bed
brushing her hair, the chain decently obscured by blankets. In
England a woman as articulate as Mary might have been regarded
as an aggressor, but her manner was gentle. She was short and
quite heavily built. Her face gave an impression of reds and blacks,
deep red lips, black, black eyes, dusky apple-red cheeks and hair
black and sleek like tar. Her grandmother was Indian.

"What do you want?" she said sharply and without interrupting
the motion of her hand.

"Ah," I said. "Captive audience!"

"What?" When I did not repeat myself she told me that she
wished to be left alone. I sat down on the bed and thought, If she
asks me to set her free I'll do it instantly. But she said nothing.
When she had finished with her hair she lay down with her hands
clasped behind her head. I sat watching her, waiting. The idea of
asking her if she wished to be set free seemed ludicrous, and
simply setting her free without her permission was terrifying. I did
not even know whether this was an ideological or psychosexual

matter. I returned to my flute, this time carrying the music stand to the far end of the apartment and closing the intervening doors. I hoped she couldn't hear me.

On Sunday night, after more than 24 hours of unbroken silence between us, I set Mary free. As the padlock sprang open I said, "I've been in Los Angeles less than a week and already I feel a completely different person."

Though partially true, the remark was designed to give pleasure. One hand resting on my shoulder, the other massaging her foot, Mary said, "It'll do that. It's a city at the end of cities."

"It's sixty miles across!" I agreed.

"It's a thousand miles deep!" cried Mary wildly and threw her brown arms about my neck. She seemed to have found what she had hoped for.

But she was not inclined to explanations. Later that evening we ate out in a Mexican restaurant and I waited for her to mention her weekend in chains and when, finally, I began to ask her she interrupted with a question.

"Is it really true that England is in a state of total collapse?"

I said yes and spoke at length without believing what I was saying. The only experience I had of total collapse was a friend who killed himself. At first he only wanted to punish himself. He ate a little ground glass washed down with grapefruit juice. Then when the pains began he ran to the tube station, bought the cheapest ticket and threw himself under a train. The brand new Victoria line. What would that be like on a national scale? We walked back from the restaurant arm in arm without speaking. The air hot and damp around us, we kissed and clung to each other on the pavement beside her car.

"Same again next Friday?" I said wryly as she climbed in, but the words were cut by the slam of her door. Through the window she waved at me with her fingers and smiled. I didn't see her for quite a while.

I was staying in Santa Monica in a large, borrowed apartment over a shop which specialized in renting out items for party givers and, strangely, equipment for "sickrooms." One side of the shop was given over to wineglasses, cocktail shakers, spare easy chairs, a banqueting table and a portable discotheque, the other to wheel-chairs, tilting beds, tweezers and bedpans, bright tubular steel and colored rubber hoses. During my stay I noticed a number of these stores throughout the city. The manager was immaculately dressed and initially intimidating in his friendliness. On our first meeting he told me he was "only twenty-nine." He was heavily built and wore one of those thick, drooping moustaches grown throughout America and England by the ambitious young. On my first day he came up the stairs and introduced himself as George Malone and paid me a pleasant compliment. "The British," he said, "make damn good invalid chairs. The very best."

"That must be Rolls-Royce," I said.

Malone gripped my arm. "Are you shitting me? Rolls-Royce make . . ."

"No, no," I said nervously. "A . . . a joke." For a moment his face was immobilized, the mouth open and black, and I thought, He's going to hit me. But he laughed.

"Rolls-Royce. That's neat!" And the next time I saw him he indicated the sickroom side of his shop and called out after me, "Wanna buy a Rolls?" Occasionally we drank together at lunchtime in a red-lit bar off Colorado Avenue where George had introduced me to the barman as "a specialist in bizarre remarks."

"What'll it be?" said the barman to me.

"Pig oil with a cherry," I said, cordially hoping to live up to my reputation. But the barman scowled and turning to George spoke through a sigh.

"What'll it be?"

It was exhilarating, at least at first, to live in a city of narcissists. On my second or third day I followed George's directions and walked to the beach. It was noon. A million stark, primitive figurines lay scattered on the fine, pale, yellow sand till they were swallowed up, north and south, in a haze of heat and pollution. Nothing moved but the sluggish giant waves in the distance, and the silence was awesome. Near where I stood on the very edge of the beach were different kinds of parallel bars, empty and stark, their crude geometry marked by silence. Not even the sound of the waves reached me, no voices, the whole city lay dreaming. As I began walking toward the ocean there were soft murmurs nearby, and it was as if I overheard a sleep-talker. I saw a man move his hand, spreading his fingers more firmly against the sand to catch the sun. An icebox without its lid stood like a gravestone at the head of a prostrate woman. I peeped inside as I passed and saw empty beercans and a packet of orange cheese floating in water. Now that I was moving among them I noticed how far apart the solitary sunbathers were. It seemed to take minutes to walk from one to another. A trick of perspective had made me think they were jammed together. I noticed too how beautiful the women were, their brown limbs spread like starfish; and how many healthy old men there were with gnarled muscular bodies. The spectacle of this common intent exhilarated me and for the first time in my life I too urgently wished to be brown-skinned, brown-faced so that when I smiled my teeth would flash white. I took off my trousers and shirt, spread my towel and lay down on my back thinking, I shall be free, I shall change beyond all recognition. But within minutes I was hot and restless, I longed to open my eyes. I ran into the ocean and swam out to where a few people were treading water and waiting for an especially huge wave to dash them to the shore.

Returning from the beach one day I found pinned to my door a note from my friend Terence Latterly. "Waiting for you," it said, "in the Doggie Diner across the street." I had met Latterly years ago in England when he was researching a still uncompleted thesis on George Orwell, and it was not till I came to America that I realized how rare an American he was. Slender, extraordinarily pallid, fine black hair that curled, doe eyes like a Renaissance princess, long straight nose with narrow black slits for nostrils, Terence was unwholesomely beautiful. He was frequently approached by gays, and once, in Polk Street, San Francisco, literally mobbed. He had a stammer, slight enough to be endearing to those charmed by such things, and he was intense in his friendships to the point of occasionally lapsing into impenetrable sulks about them. It took me some time to admit to myself I actually disliked Terence but by that time he was in my life and I accepted the fact. Like all compulsive monologuists he lacked curiosity about other people's minds, but his stories were good and he never told the same one twice. He regularly became infatuated with women whom he drove away with his labyrinthine awkwardness and consumptive zeal, and who provided fresh material for his monologues. Two or three times now I had seen quiet, lonely, protective girls fall hopelessly for Terence and his ways, but he was not interested. Terence cared for long-legged, tough-minded independent women who were rapidly bored by Terence. He once told me he masturbated every day.

He was the Doggie Diner's only customer, bent morosely over an empty coffee cup, his chin propped in his palms.

"In England," I told him, "a dog's dinner means some kind of unpalatable mess."

"Sit down then," said Terence. "We're in the right place. I've been so humiliated."

"Sylvie?" I asked obligingly.

"Yes, yes. Grotesquely humiliated." This was nothing new. Terence dined out frequently on morbid accounts of blows dealt him by indifferent women. He had been in love with Sylvie for months now and had followed her here from San Francisco. She made a living setting up health food restaurants and then selling them, and as far as I knew, she was hardly aware of the existence of Terence.

Wrapped in a constant, faint blue cloud, cars drifted by at 20 miles an hour, their drivers propped their tanned forearms on the window ledges, their car radios and stereos were on, they were all going home or to bars for happy hour. After a suitable silence I said, "Well . . . ?"

From the day he arrives in Los Angeles Terence pleads with Sylvie over the phone to have a meal with him in a restaurant, and finally she consents. Terence buys a new shirt, visits a hairdresser and spends an hour in the late afternoon in front of the mirror, staring at his face. He meets Sylvie in a bar, they drink bourbon. She is relaxed and friendly, and they talk easily of California politics of which Terence knows next to nothing. Since Sylvie knows Los Angeles she chooses the restaurant. As they are leaving the bar she says, "Shall we go in your car or mine?"

Terence who has no car and cannot drive says, "Why not yours?"

By the end of the hors d'oeuvres they are starting in on their second bottle of wine and talking of books, and then of money, and then of books again. Lovely Sylvie leads Terence by the hand through half a dozen topics; she smiles and Terence flushes with love and love's wildest ambitions. He loves so hard he knows he will not be able to resist declaring himself. He can feel it coming on, a mad confession. The words tumble out, a declaration of love worthy of the pages of Walter Scott, its main burden being that there is nothing, absolutely nothing, in the world Terence would not do for Sylvie. In fact, drunk, he challenges her now to test his devotion. Touched by the bourbon and wine, intrigued by this wan, fin de siècle lunatic, Sylvie gazes warmly across the table and returns his little squeeze to the hand. In the rarefied air between them runs a charge of goodwill and daredevilry. Sylvie's gaze shifts momentarily from Terence's face to the door of the restaurant through which a well-to-do middle-aged couple are now entering. She frowns, then smiles.

"Anything?" she says.

"Yes yes, anything." Terence is solemn now, sensing the real challenge in her question.

Sylvie leans forward and grips his forearm. "You won't back out?"

"No, if it's humanly possible I'll do it." Again Sylvie is looking over at the couple who wait by the door to be seated by the hostess, an energetic lady in a red soldierlike uniform. Terence watches too. Sylvie tightens her grip on his arm.

"I want you to urinate in your pants, now. Go on now! Quick! Do it now before you have time to think about it."

Terence is about to protest, but his own promises still hang in the air, an accusing cloud. With drunken sway, and with the sound of an electric bell ringing in his ears, he urinates copiously, soaking his thighs, legs and backside and sending a small, steady trickle to the floor.

"Have you done it?" says Sylvie.

"Yes," says Terence, "but why . . .?" Sylvie half rises from her seat and waves prettily across the restaurant at the couple standing by the door.

"I want you to meet my parents," she says. "I've just seen them come in." Terence remains seated for the introductions. He wonders if he can be smelled. There is nothing he will not say to dissuade this affable, graying couple from sitting down at their daughter's table. He talks desperately and without a break ("as if I was some kinda bore"), referring to Los Angeles as a "shithole" and its inhabitants as "greedy devourers of each other's privacy." Terence hints at a recent prolonged mental illness from which he has hardly recovered, and he tells Sylvie's mother that all doctors, especially women doctors, are "arseholes" (assholes). Sylvie says nothing. The father cocks an eyebrow at his wife and the couple wander off without farewell to their table on the far side of the room.

Terence appeared to have forgotten he was telling his story. He was cleaning his nails with the tooth of a comb. I said, "Well, you can't stop there. *What happened?* What's the explanation for all this?" Around us the diner was filling up, but no one else was talking. Terence said, "I sat on a newspaper to keep her car seat from getting wet. We didn't speak much and she wouldn't come in when we got to my place. She told me earlier she didn't like her parents much. I guess she was just fooling around." I wondered if Terence's story was invented or dreamed.

There were long pointless days when I thought, Everywhere on earth is the same. Los Angeles, California, the whole of the United States seemed to me then a very fine and frail crust on the limitless, subterranean world of my own boredom. I could be anywhere, I could have saved myself the effort and the fare. I wished in fact I was nowhere, beyond the responsibility of place. I woke in the morning stultified by oversleep. Although I was neither hungry nor thirsty, I ate breakfast because I dared not be without the activity. I spent ten minutes cleaning my teeth knowing that when I finished I would have to choose to do something else. I returned to the kitchen, made more coffee and very carefully washed the dishes. Caffeine aided my growing panic. There were books in the living room that needed to be studied, there was writing that needed completion but the thought of it all made me flush hot with weariness and disgust. For that reason I tried not to think about it, I did not tempt myself. It hardly occurred to me to set foot inside the living room.
    Instead I went to the bedroom and made the bed and took great care over the "hospital corners." Was I sick? I lay down on the bed and stared at the ceiling without a thought in my head. Then I stood up and with my hands in my pockets stared at the wall. Perhaps I should paint it another color, but of course I was only a temporary resident. I remembered I was in a foreign city and hurried to the balcony. Dull, white, box-shaped shops and houses, parked cars, two lawn sprinklers, festoons of telephone cable everywhere, one palm tree teetering against the sky, the whole lit by a cruel white glow of a sun blotted out by high cloud and pollution. It was as obvious and self-explanatory to me as a row of suburban English bungalows. What could I do about it? Go somewhere else? I almost laughed out loud at the thought.
    More to confirm my state of mind than change it, I returned to the bedroom and grimly picked up my flute. The piece I intended to play, dog-eared and stained, was already on the music stand,

Bach's Sonata No. 1 in A minor. The lovely opening Andante, a series of lilting arpeggios, requires a flawless breathing technique to make sense of the phrasing, yet from the beginning I am snatching furtively at breaths like a supermarket shoplifter, and the coherence of the piece becomes purely imaginary, remembered from gramophone recordings and superimposed over the present. At bar 15, four and a half bars into the Presto, I fumble over the octave leaps but I press on, a dogged, failing athlete, to finish the first movement short of breath and unable to hold the last note its full length. Because I catch most of the right notes in the right order, I regard the Allegro as my showpiece. I play it with expressionless aggression. The Adagio, a sweet thoughtful melody, illustrates to me every time I play it how out of tune my notes are, some sharp, some flat, none sweet, and the demisemiquavers are always mistimed. And so to the two minuets at the end which I play with dry, rigid persistence, like a mechanical organ turned by a monkey. This was my performance of Bach's sonata, unaltered now in its details for as long as I could remember.

I sat down on the edge of the bed and almost immediately stood up again. I went to the balcony to look once more at the foreign city. Out on one of the lawns a small girl picked up a smaller girl and staggered a few steps with her. More futility. I went inside and looked at the alarm clock in the bedroom. Eleven-forty. Do something, quick! I stood by the clock listening to its tick. I went from room to room without really intending to, sometimes surprised to find that I was back in the kitchen again fiddling with the cracked plastic handle of the wall can opener. I went into the living room and spent 20 minutes drumming with my fingers on the back of a book. Toward the middle of the afternoon I dialed the time and set the clock exactly. I sat on the lavatory a long time and decided then not to move till I had planned what to do next. I remained there over two hours, staring at my knees till they lost their meaning as limbs. I thought of cutting my fingernails, that would be a start. But I had no scissors. I commenced to prowl from room to room once more, and then, toward the middle of the evening, I fell asleep in an armchair, exhausted with myself.

George at least appeared to appreciate my playing. He came upstairs once, having heard me from the shop, and wanted to see my flute. He told me he had never actually held one in his hands before. He marveled at the intricacy and precision of its levers

and pads. He asked me to play a few notes so he could see how
it was held, and then he wanted me to show him how he could
make a note for himself. He peered at the music on the stand and
said he thought it was "brilliant" the way musicians could turn
such a mess of lines and dots into sounds. The way composers
could think up whole symphonies with dozens of different instru-
ments going at once was totally beyond him. I said it was beyond
me too.

"Music," George said with a large gesture of his arm, "is a sacred
art." Usually when I wasn't playing my flute I left it lying about
collecting dust, assembled and ready to play. Now I found myself
pulling it into its three sections and drying them carefully and
laying each section down like a favorite doll in the felt-lined case.

George lived out in Simi Valley on a recently reclaimed stretch
of desert. He described his house as "empty and smelling of fresh
paint still." He was separated from his wife and two weekends a
month had his children over to stay, two boys aged seven and
eight. Imperceptibly George became my host in Los Angeles. He
had arrived here penniless from New York City when he was 22.
Now he made almost $40,000 a year and felt responsible for the
city and my experience in it.

Sometimes after work George drove me for miles along the freeway in his new Volvo. "I want you to get the feel of it, the insanity
of its size."

"What's that building?" I would say to him as we sped past an
illuminated Third Reichian colossus mounted on a manicured
green hill.

George would glance out of his window. "I dunno, a bank or
temple or something."

We went to bars, bars for starlets, bars for "intellectuals" where
screenwriters drank, lesbian bars and a bar where the waiters, lithe,
smooth-faced young men, dressed as Victorian serving maids. We
ate in a diner founded in 1947 which served only hamburgers and
apple pie, a renowned and fashionable place where waiting customers stood like hungry ghosts at the backs of those seated.

We went to a club where singers and stand-up comedians performed in the hope of being discovered. A man with stooped
shoulders and wild curly hair shuffled onto the stage. He took the
microphone out of its rest, held it close to his lips and said nothing.
He seemed to be stuck for words. He wore a torn, muddied denim
jacket over bare skin, his eyes were swollen almost to the point of

closing and under the right there ran a long scratch that ended at the corner of his mouth and gave him the look of a partly made-up clown. His lower lip trembled and I thought he was going to weep. The hand that was not holding the microphone worried a coin and looking at that I noticed the stains down his jeans, yet, fresh wet vomit clung there. His lips parted but no sounds came out. The audience waited patiently. Somewhere at the back of the room a wine bottle was opened. When he spoke finally it was to his fingernails, a low, cracked murmur.

"I'm such a goddamn mess!"

The audience broke into fallabout laughter and cheering, which after a minute gave way to foot-stamping and rhythmic clapping. George and I, perhaps constrained by each other's company, smiled. The man reappeared by the microphone the moment the last clapping died away. Now he spoke rapidly, his eyes still fixed on his fingers. Sometimes he glanced worriedly to the back of the room and we caught the flash of the whites of his eyes. He told us he had just broken up with his girl friend, and how, as he was driving away from her house, he had started to weep, so much so that he could not see to drive and had to stop his car. He thought he might kill himself but first he wanted to say good-bye to *her*. He drove to a call box but it was out of order and this made him cry again. Here the audience, silent till now, laughed a little. He reached his girl friend from a drug store. As soon as she picked up the phone and heard his voice she began to cry too. But she didn't want to see him. She told him, "It's useless, there's nothing we can do." He put the phone down and howled with grief. An assistant in the drug store told him to leave because he was upsetting the other customers. He walked along the street thinking about life and death, it started to rain, he popped some amyl nitrite, he tried to sell his watch. The audience was growing restless, a lot of people had stopped listening. He bummed 50 cents from a bum. Through his tears he thought he saw a woman aborting a foetus in the gutter and when he got closer he saw it was cardboard boxes and a lot of old rags. By now the man was talking over a steady drone of conversation. Waitresses with silver trays circulated the tables. Suddenly the speaker raised his hand and said.

"Well, see you," and he was gone. A few people clapped but most did not notice him leave.

*

Not long before I was due to leave Los Angeles George invited me to spend Saturday evening at his house. I would be flying to New York late the following day. He wanted me to bring along a couple of friends to make a small farewell party, and he wanted me to bring my flute.

"I really want to sit," said George, "in my own home with a glass of wine in my hand and hear you play that thing." I phoned Mary first. We had been meeting intermittently since our weekend. Occasionally she had come and spent the afternoon at my apartment. She had another lover she more or less lived with, but she hardly mentioned him and it was never an issue between us. After agreeing to come, Mary wanted to know if Terence was going to be there. I had recounted to her Terence's adventure with Sylvie, and described my own ambivalent feelings about him. Terence had not returned to San Francisco as he intended. He had met someone who had a friend "in screen writing" and now he was waiting for an introduction. When I phoned him he responded with an unconvincing parody of Semitic peevishness.

"Five weeks in this town and I'm invited out already?"

I decided to take seriously George's wish to hear me play the flute. I practiced my scales and arpeggios, I worked hard at those places in the Sonata No. 1 where I always faltered and as I played I fantasized about Mary, George and Terence listening spellbound and a little drunk, and my heart raced.

Mary arrived in the early evening and before driving to pick up Terence we sat around on my balcony watching the sun and smoked a small joint. It had been on my mind before she came that we might be going to bed for one last time. But now that she was here and we were dressed for an evening elsewhere, it seemed more appropriate to talk. Mary asked me what I had been doing and I told her about the nightclub act. I was not sure whether to present the man as a performer with an act so clever it was not funny, or as someone who had come in off the street and taken over the stage.

"I've seen acts like that here," said Mary. "The idea, when it works, is to make your laughter stick in your throat. What was funny suddenly gets nasty."

I asked Mary if she thought there was any truth in my man's story.

She shook her head.

"Everyone here," she said, gesturing toward the setting sun, "has got some kind of act going like that."

"You seem to say that with some pride," I said as we stood up. She smiled and we held hands for an empty moment in which there came to me from nowhere a vivid image of the parallel bars on the beach; then we turned and went inside.

Terence was waiting for us on the pavement outside the house where he was staying. He wore a white suit and as we pulled up he was fixing a pink carnation into his lapel. Mary's car had only two doors. I had to get out to let Terence in, but through a combination of sly maneuvering on his part and obtuse politeness on my own, I found myself introducing my two friends from the back seat. As we turned onto the freeway Terence began to ask Mary a series of polite, insistent questions and it was clear from where I sat, directly behind Mary, that as she was answering one question he was formulating the next, or falling over himself to agree with everything she said.

"Yes, yes," he was saying, leaning forward eagerly, clasping together his long, pale fingers. "That's a really good way of putting it." Such condescension, I thought, such ingratiation. Why does Mary put up with it? Mary said that she thought Los Angeles was the most exciting city in the USA. Before she had even finished Terence was outdoing her with extravagant praise.

"I thought you hated it," I interjected sourly. But Terence was adjusting his seat belt and asking Mary another question. I sat back and stared out the window, attempting to control my irritation. A little later Mary was craning her neck trying to find me in her mirror.

"You're very quiet back there," she said gaily.

I fell into sudden, furious mimicry.

"That's a really good way of putting it, yes, yes." Neither Terence nor Mary made any reply. My words hung over us as though they were being uttered over and over again. I opened my window. We arrived at George's house with 25 minutes of unbroken silence behind us.

The introductions over, the three of us held the center of George's huge living room while he fixed our drinks at the bar. I held my flute case and music stand under my arm like weapons. Apart from the bar the only other furniture was two yellow, plastic sag chairs, very bright against the desert expanse of brown carpet.

Sliding doors took up the length of one wall and gave onto a small backyard of sand and stones in the center of which, set in concrete, stood one of those treelike contraptions for drying clothes on. In the corner of the yard was a scrappy sagebrush plant, survivor of the real desert that was here a year ago. Terence, Mary and I addressed remarks to George and said nothing to each other.

"Well," said George when the four of us stood looking at each other with drinks in our hand, "follow me and I'll show you the kids." Obediently we padded behind George in single file along a narrow, thickly carpeted corridor. We peered through a bedroom doorway at two small boys in a bunk bed reading comics. They glanced at us without interest and went on reading.

Back in the living room I said, "They're very subdued, George. What do you do, beat them up?" George took my question seriously and there followed a conversation about corporal punishment. George said he occasionally gave the boys a slap on the back of the legs if things got really out of hand. But it was not to hurt them, he said, so much as to show them he meant business. Mary said she was dead against striking children at all, and Terence, largely to cut a figure I thought, or perhaps to demonstrate to me that he could disagree with Mary, said that he thought a sound thrashing never did anyone any harm. Mary laughed, but George, who obviously was not taking to this faintly foppish, languid guest sprawled across his carpet, seemed ready to move into the attack. George worked hard. He kept his back straight even when he sat in the sag chair.

"You were thrashed when you were a kid?" he asked as he handed round the Scotch. Terence hesitated and said, "Yes." This surprised me. Terence's father had died before he was born and he had grown up with his mother in Vermont.

"Your mother beat you?" I said before he had time to invent a swaggering bully of a father.

"Yes."

"And you don't think it did you any harm?" said George. "I don't believe it." Terence stretched his legs.

"No harm done at all." He spoke through a yawn that might have been a fake. He gestured toward his pink carnation.

"After all, here I am."

There was a moment's pause, then George said, "For example, you never had any problem making out with women?"

I could not help smiling. Terence sat up.

"Oh yes," he said. "Our English friend here will verify that." By this Terence referred to my outburst in the car.

But I said to George, "Terence likes to tell funny stories about his own sexual failures." George leaned forward to catch Terence's full attention. "How can you be sure they're not caused by being thrashed by your mother?"

Terence spoke very quickly. I was not sure whether he was very excited or very angry. "There will always be problems between men and women and everyone suffers in some way. I conceal less about myself than other people do. I guess you never had your backside tanned by your mother when you were a kid, but does that mean you never have any hangups with women? I mean, where's your wife . . . ?" Mary's interruption had the precision of a surgeon's knife. "I was only ever hit once as a kid, by my father, and do you know why that was? I was twelve. We were all sitting round the table at suppertime, all the family, and I told everyone I was bleeding from between my legs. I put some blood on the end of my finger and held it up for them all to see. My father leaned across the table and slapped my face. He told me not to be dirty and sent me up to my room."

George got up to fetch more ice for our glasses and muttered "Simply grotesque" as he went. Terence stretched out on the floor, his eyes fixed on the ceiling like a dead man's. From the bedroom came the sound of the boys singing, or rather chanting, for the song was all on one note. I said to Mary something to the effect that between people who had just met, such a conversation could not have taken place in England.

"Is that a good thing do you think?" Mary asked. Terence said, "The English tell each other nothing."

I said, "Between telling nothing and telling everything there is very little to choose." "Did you hear the boys?" George said as he came back. "We heard some kind of singing," Mary told him. George was pouring more Scotch and spooning ice into the glasses. "That wasn't singing. That was praying. I've been teaching them the Lord's Prayer."

On the floor Terence groaned and George looked round sharply.

"I didn't know you were a Christian, George," I said.

"Oh, well, you know . . ." George sank into his chair. There was a pause, as if all four of us were gathering our strength for another round of fragmentary dissent.

Mary was now in the second sag chair facing George. Terence lay like a low wall between them, and I sat cross-legged about a yard from Terence's feet. It was George who spoke first, across Terence to Mary.

"I've never been interested in churchgoing much but . . ." He trailed off, a little drunkenly, I thought. "But I always wanted the boys to have as much of it as possible while they're young. They can reject it later, I guess. But at least for now they have a coherent set of values that are as good as any other, and they have this whole set of stories, really good stories, exotic stories, believable stories."

No one spoke so George went on. "They like the idea of God. And heaven and hell, and angels and the devil. They talk about that stuff a whole lot and I'm never sure quite what it means to them. I guess it's a bit like Santa Claus, they believe it and they don't believe it. They like the business of praying, even if they do ask for the craziest things. Praying for them is a kind of extension of their . . . their inner lives. They pray about what they want and what they're afraid of. They go to church every week, it's about the only thing Jean and I agree on."

George addressed all this to Mary who nodded as he spoke and stared back at him solemnly. Terence had closed his eyes. Now that he had finished, George looked at each of us in turn, waiting to be challenged. We stirred. Terence lifted himself onto his elbow. No one spoke.

"I don't see it's going to hurt them, a bit of the old religion," George reiterated.

Mary spoke into the ground. "Well, I don't know. There's a lot of things you could object to in Christianity. And since you don't really believe in it yourself we should talk about that."

"OK," said George. "Let's hear it."

Mary spoke with deliberation at first. "Well, for a start, the Bible is a book written by men, addressed to men and features a very male God who even looks like a man because he made man in his own image. That sounds pretty suspicious to me, a real male fantasy . . ."

"Wait a minute," said George.

"Next," Mary went on, "women come off pretty badly in Christianity. Through original sin they are held responsible for everything in the world since the Garden of Eden. Women are weak, unclean, condemned to bear children in pain as punishment for the failures of Eve, they are the temptresses who turn the minds of men away from God; as if women were more responsible for men's sexual feelings than the men themselves! Like Simone de Beauvoir says, women are always the 'other,' the real business is between a man in the sky and the men on the ground. In fact women only exist at all as a kind of divine afterthought, put together out of a spare rib to keep men company and iron their shirts, and the biggest favor they can do Christianity is not to get dirtied up with sex, stay chaste, and if they can manage to have a baby at the same time then they're measuring up to the Christian church's ideal of womanhood — the Virgin Mary." Now Mary was angry, she glared at George.

"Wait a minute," he was saying, "you can't impose all that women's lib stuff onto the societies of thousands of years ago. Christianity expressed itself through available . . ."

At roughly the same time Terence said, "Another objection to Christianity is that it leads to passive acceptance of social inequalities because the real rewards are in . . ." And Mary cut in across George in protest, "Christianity has provided an ideology for sexism now, and capitalism . . ."

"Are you a communist?" George demanded angrily, although I was not sure who he was talking to. Terence was pressing on loudly with his own speech. I heard him mention the Crusades and the Inquisition.

"This has nothing to do with Christianity," George was almost shouting. His face was flushed.

"More evil perpetrated in the name of Christ than . . . this has nothing to do with . . . to the persecution of women herbalists as witches . . . Bullshit. It's irrelevant . . . corruption, graft, propping up tyrants, accumulating wealth at the altars . . . fertility goddess . . . bullshit . . . phallic worship . . . look at Galileo . . . this has nothing to . . ."

Suddenly I heard another voice ringing in my ears. It was my own. I was talking into a brief, exhausted silence. ". . . Driving across the States I saw this sign in Illinois along Interstate 70 which said, 'God, Guts, Guns made America great. Let's keep all three.' "

"Hah!" Mary and Terence exclaimed in triumph.

George was on his feet, empty glass in hand. "That's right," he cried. "That's right. You can put it down but it's right. This country has a violent past, a lot of brave men died making . . ."

"Men!" echoed Mary.

"All right, and a lot of brave women too. America was made with the gun. You can't get away from that." George strode across the room to the bar in the corner and drew out something black from behind the bottles. "I keep a gun here," he said, holding the thing up for us to see.

"What for?" Mary asked.

"When you have kids you begin to have a very different attitude toward life and death. I never kept a gun before the kids were around. Now I think I'd shoot at anyone who threatened their existence."

"Is it a real gun?" I said. George came back toward us with the gun in one hand and a fresh bottle of Scotch in the other.

"Dead right it's a real gun!" It was very small and did not extend beyond George's open palm.

"Let me see that," said Terence.

"It's loaded," George warned as he handed it across. The gun appeared to have a soothing effect on us all. We no longer shouted, we spoke quietly in its presence. While Terence examined the gun George filled our glasses.

Then Terence snapped the safety catch and leveled the gun at George's head. "Raise your hands, Christian," he said dully.

George did not move. He said, "You oughtn't to fool around with a gun." Terence tightened his grip. Of course he was fooling around, and yet I could see from where I was that his finger was curled about the trigger, and he was beginning to pull on it.

"Terence!" Mary whispered, and touched his back gently with her foot. Keeping his eyes on Terence, George sipped at his drink. Terence brought his other hand up to steady the gun, which was aimed at the center of George's face.

"Death to the gun owners." Terence spoke without a trace of humor. I tried to say his name too, but hardly a sound left my throat. When I tried again I said something in my accelerating panic that was quite irrelevant.

"Who is it?"

Terence pulled the trigger.

From that point on the evening collapsed into conventional, labyrinthine politeness at which Americans, when they wish, quite outstrip the English. George was the only one to have seen Terence remove the bullets from the gun, and this united Mary and me in a state of mild but prolonged shock. We ate salad and cold cuts from plates balanced on our knees. George asked Terence about his Orwell thesis and the prospects of teaching jobs. Terence asked George about his business, fun party rentals and sick-room requisites. Mary was questioned about her job in the feminist bookshop and she answered blandly, carefully avoiding any statement that might provoke discussion. Finally I was called on to elaborate on my travel plans which I did in great and dull detail. I explained how I would be spending a week in Amsterdam before returning to London. This caused Terence and George to spend several minutes in praise of Amsterdam, although it was quite clear they had seen very different cities.

Then while the others drank coffee and yawned, I played my flute. I played my Bach sonata no worse than usual, perhaps a little more confidently for being drunk, but my mind ran on against the music. For I was weary of this music and of myself for playing it. As the notes transferred themselves from the page to the end of my fingers I thought, Am I still playing *this*? I still heard the echo of our raised voices, I saw the black gun in George's open palm, the comedian reappear from the darkness to take the microphone again, I saw the silver chain around Mary's ankle, I saw myself many months ago setting out for San Francisco from Buffalo in a drive-away car, shouting out for joy over the roar of the wind through the open windows, "It's me, I'm here, I'm coming . . ." Where was the music for all this? Why wasn't I even looking for it? Why did I go on doing what I couldn't do, music from another time and civilization, its certainty and perfection to me a pretense and a lie, as much as they had once been, or might still be, a truth to others. What should I look for? (I tooled through the second movement like a piano roll.) Something difficult and free. I thought of Terence's stories about himself, his game with the gun, Mary's experiment with herself, of myself in an empty moment drumming my fingers on the back of a book, the vast, fragmented city without a center, without citizens, a city that existed only in the mind, a nexus of change or stagnation in individual lives. Picture and idea crashed drunkenly one after the other, discord battened to bar after bar of implied harmony and inexorable logic. For the pulse of one beat I glanced past the music at my friends where they sprawled on the floor. Then their afterimage glowed briefly at me from the page of music. Possible, even likely, that the four of us would never see each other again, and against such commonplace transience my music was inane in its rationality, paltry in its over-determination. Leave it to others, to professionals who could evoke the old days of its truth. To me it was nothing, now that I knew what I wanted. This genteel escapism . . . crossword with its an-swers written in, I could play no more of it.

I broke off in the slow movement and looked up. I was about to say, "I can't go on any more," but the three of them were on their feet clapping and smiling broadly at me. In parody of concert-goers George and Terence cupped their hands round their mouths and called out, "Bravo! Bravissimo!" Mary came forward, kissed me on the cheek and presented me with an imaginary bouquet. Overwhelmed by nostalgia for a country I had not yet left, I could do no more than put my feet together and make a bow, clasping the flowers to my chest. Then Mary said, "Let's go. I'm tired."

PETER MARSH

By The Yellow Lake

(FROM THE NEW YORKER)

THERE IS no far shore. Where there ought to be a dark tree line, there is only a vacant sky over the endless shallow lake — yellow water no deeper than my waist, stretching out as far as I can see — a lake compressed, the color of heavy sky before a great summer storm, and over it a sky with no color at all. Behind me, across the beach, Suzanne's house stands away from her neighbors' houses, out into the sand, with one old poplar tree beside it. I had to cut through some of the roots of the poplar yesterday to continue my digging under the house. Her basement, what there is of it, lies below the level of the lake. A mixture of coarse beach sand and yellow water seeps there. Under her house the sand has collected and turned gray and musty.

Suzanne bought the place because she liked the location, on the lake, but it is a poorly built house. Only half of the basement was ever completed. Her living room was sinking into the beach when I arrived. She thought the picture window overlooking the lake would shatter from the strain of the house sinking and shifting, so I have jacked the living room from underneath, on braces, until I can lay a proper foundation. There is only a makeshift foundation now: in places a few rows of red clay bricks laid on sand beneath the timbers, and in some places not even bricks, no foundation. The local contractors wouldn't touch the job, and it is no wonder. The only way to remove the sand has been with a wheelbarrow, along a network of boards from the unfinished half of the basement into the old part and up a ramp on the storm-cellar stairs.

I can smell the wet basement sand even here by the water — the smell is in my clothes, follows me home after work, where I have to hang my clothes outside — and back across the beach the wet gray mound I have been piling beside her house shows dark against the morning light.

I often work fourteen hours a day for Suzanne, and now Father Prior has told my mother — I have it from her — that he thinks I perform these long hours each day just for my ego's sake, as if I saw this work as only a test of strength. He should have sensed more here than labor. Indirectly, it was Father Prior who brought us to the yellow lake in the first place. In the beginning, when my mother and I came here, came to Father Prior, came to the Priory, inserted ourselves into this community, it was because of Father Prior's influence over my grandfather and because of my grandfather's influence over my mother. My father had been sent away by then, had gone off to start his life again. He had had no say in family matters for some time. Now Father Prior is failing us. He should have sensed more here than simple labor.

My grandfather was a minister all his life, but during the last years, instead of settling, as one might expect of a churchman, he became distant and troubled. He used to hallucinate and say strange things to people and walk about in the night. Everyone said it was senility. My mother assured me he had lost his faith. Through colleagues he heard about the Priory by the yellow lake, and he began making retreats to see Father Prior. The retreats became a regular part of his life, to the extent that just before he died, there was talk of him retiring to live out his days under Father Prior's care. In the course of things my mother, too, became absorbed into the life of the Priory. She introduced me to the Priory, talked me into living with the monks an entire summer rather than going to summer camp, and shortly after my grandfather's death, almost as if in his place, she bought a house near the yellow lake and we joined the Priory community permanently.

I came with my mother, but she expected me to leave in time. As a young person I was expected to want to leave home. In the end it was suggested that leaving would be a healthy experience. I have been away, not far, and for only a few years. I have no interest in travel, and I am glad to be in my mother's house again. I have been back for just a few months now.

Suzanne offered me the job in her basement not long after my return, and the night she spoke to me of it I had a vivid dream of my grandfather in hiding near the yellow lake, working underground in an elegant chamber. He was covering the walls of the chamber with abstract murals — long, sweeping things — moving about the room engrossed in his painting, painting seriously and with much energy, looking younger than I had ever before known him. He had a firm jaw and a full head of hair, both of which he had lost by the time I was born. He painted with authority, as if he had always been a painter of murals but had kept his art from the world. It was a large chamber, grand in its proportions and furnishings. The room was hung all around with trailing plants and it was filled with a clear green light. It felt deep and very still, like a sacred place. Although I sensed that it was forbidden to cross the threshold to the chamber of murals, I was filled with the power of discovery, and I entered without fear. I realized immediately that my grandfather had hoped I might find him there and would have the courage to come in. Without looking directly at me, dipping his head a little and gesturing with his arm in a motion of offering, he showed me his chair — of white marble inlaid with designs of red and blue. He offered me the chamber of his murals silently, and then he left me there.

I accepted Suzanne's offer of work without consideration, and though I am proud of my long hours — Father Prior is right about that bit of pride — what keeps me at this extraordinary labor is my dream of the chamber of murals.

I got to know Suzanne because she is the only one of my mother's friends who owns a piano. I went to Suzanne at first to play the piano. I still do. I practice for a couple of hours most mornings before work. When I told Father Prior about practicing at Suzanne's — "You play with a great passion," she had told me — he laughed. "You had better watch your step," he said. "That is a widow you are dealing with, you know." I was surprised. As with his thoughts about my working so hard, he was not entirely wrong — Suzanne does encourage my free coming and going in her house, invites more than a casual interest in her life. But, really, she knows nothing about me, nor I about her; she just wants her living room to stop sinking into the beach and she couldn't find a proper contractor to complete such odd work. Father Prior seems most often to be correct about things on a superficial level like that. He sees only the most obvious parts of things — if I am not guilty of the same short sight. My mother continues to think highly of

him and has had him to dinner since I have been back, but despite
the influence of her feelings for him I find Father Prior the way he
has always been — effervescent, bald and shining, with a too
healthy pink glow. He seems to inspire faith in everyone here but
me. Father Prior is one of those leaders who draw people to them
by sheer force of good will; he draws them in with his own strong
pink light. I, for one, could never confide in him. I don't think he
would listen for a moment to my dream of the chamber of murals.

I turn away from the lake to face the crowded line of houses
across the beach. I walk back, smelling the damp-mold smell of the
basement sand on my clothes, watching the house with the big
poplar tree. A hysterical singsong of evangelism comes to me
across the sand: "He washed himself, He washed himself, He
washed himself and He got down to wash the others gathered
. . ." The voice comes on as I close with the houses, comes wafting
out to me across the sand. "He washed himself before them, and
He got down to wash the people gathered there before Him."
Inside the house to the right of Suzanne's, Anna is listening to her
records behind closed window blinds, storing up faith. The few
times I see Anna on the beach, in the evening, or just for a moment
to talk to someone during the day, she is pale. She has an innocent,
puffy face, and she moves like a stranger out toward the lake —
an ungainly foreigner across the sand.

Bothwell, Anna's husband, met me at Suzanne's when I first
went there, and he hired me to lay cement steps and a walk to their
front door. That was my first job here, before I got the job with
Suzanne. In fact, I suspect that it was Bothwell who suggested to
Suzanne that I tackle her basement. Bothwell thinks I am quite a
boy. I have heard him use exactly that phrase in describing me to
his neighbors. He speaks to them while I am present, refers to me
in the third person. Except for me, he is the youngest man in the
neighborhood. He keeps a constant watch on my progress in Suzanne's basement — comes drinking beer at the end of his day and
sits on the cellar stairs beside my ramp to watch me shovel the sand
and wheel it past him. He is small and thin — not pleasantly small
but fighting his smallness — with sharp eyes, and with blond hair
almost white. A trickster. He gets himself into trouble, usually to
do with drinking — trouble with his wife, trouble with his neighbors. The kind of small trouble that is easily avoidable. I respect

Bothwell, because he is older than me and because he goes out of his way, most times, to impress me with his good intentions. He would like to be my friend and I am impressed by that. He is always inviting me to visit him, to use his boat, to drink with him. When I first knew Bothwell he brought his pistol over to my mother's house and bothered me until I went out in the woods with him to shoot at beer cans. I surprised us both by shooting much better than he did, and he left without speaking. He was dark like that sometimes when I worked for him. He used to come out of the house at six-thirty in the morning with a cup of coffee in one hand and a doughnut in the other, step on the forms I had set so carefully with my level, and race on out to his car without so much as a word of greeting. I would guess Bothwell is somewhere in his thirties, but it is hard to think exactly how old he might be. He has a boyishness about him, but he has, too, a disguise of pulled lines about his face, I once met him on the road after work one night. This was some time after I had first met him. I was walking toward him down the road and I heard the cocking of his pistol as I approached — before he knew who it was — and then he passed quickly, muttering "Hello," because he had embarrassed himself.

Anna is always going to the Priory for services, as often as twice a day, and Father Prior tells my mother that Anna is a sick woman and that Bothwell drinks because he is sorry that he married her. Such standard fare coming from Father Prior. I know there is more to Bothwell and Anna than that. I don't think they are sorry in the least that they are together. Anna is Bothwell's own image of himself. She is an inseparable part of him. He can't be sorry. His secret parts searched her out and now cling to her, fill her, until she has no character of her own. He fills her with himself. Anna is Bothwell. How else could she be so pale? Everything of her goes into keeping Bothwell. She is his mother and his servant and his savior. How could Father Prior know, with his pink light a substitute for the dark fire of people like Bothwell? I imagine Father Prior watches Bothwell in complete bewilderment until he is unable to digest his daily bread and passes it in steaming hard black rocks at night and weeps under his bedcovers for understanding, until he is blessed with sleep.

I am making progress in the sand; I have opened a wide hole under the side of the house through which I am now able to toss the shovelfuls of sand, rather than having to wheel them up the ramp. I have burrowed half a dozen yards in under the house as well, so that the hole along the side makes a trench of light above the wall of sand. At the hole Suzanne's children appear from time to time to look down on me. They have nothing to say. Their faces appear over the wall of sand, they watch quietly, and they disappear.

Everyone seems to be watching me in here. The job has taken on heroic proportions as far as the rest of them are concerned. My mother came to see the work. Bothwell considers it a herculean task and brings his drinking friends from around the neighborhood to watch as I heave out the wet sand shovel by shovel. He has taken upon himself the credit for having discovered my talents as an unflagging laborer. I am Bothwell's man, as far as Bothwell is concerned, and he has already arranged for me to paint the house of his neighbor on the other side when I have finished at Suzanne's.

Of those who watch, Suzanne is the only one to express doubts about the success of my work. Her fears grow in proportion to the size of the hole under her living room. The hole does grow large. There will be much filling to do after I have laid a foundation and cemented a block wall in place. Several times now portions of the sand wall have caved in — a foot of murky water covers the area where I am working — and I think Suzanne expects the erosion to continue until her living room, instead of sinking quietly into the beach, ultimately falls into the hole. She sees the water eating away the sand on which the braces I have erected stand. She sees me working on and on, the sand wall collapsing as fast as I can shovel it out, creating more work for myself with each new day.

There are problems. I have admitted problems to her, but I am confident. Father Prior has been suggesting that we accept the aid of a Brother Julius from the Priory. He is reportedly more skilled than I in the construction of such things, but so far I have managed to keep the work to myself. Bothwell vigorously defends my independent progress. I don't know exactly what he sees when he comes to sit on the stairs — me without a shirt, working at the end of my shovel in the damp until by the end of the day, exhausted, I begin to focus on pings of light around me in the darkness and I have to leave — but he is apparently enthralled with the spectacle of my labor, and his attention comforts me.

It had been my impression that the yellow lake would erupt, that it had withdrawn into itself and now seethed underneath. I find this morning that the lake is dead. Though the water is shallow, you can't see the bottom. I have just returned from the lake. I have been out in Bothwell's rowboat in the early morning, under the vacant sky. It is a sunless sky over the lake — too clear, as if there is a vacuum above the water. I pulled myself out into the lake on the oars, poking at the bottom as I went, until Suzanne's poplar tree was in the distance and I was alone on the endless water. I fished alone and I pulled myself back in again to work. The fish I caught were white, bloodless, stunted things.

From Suzanne's house, before I descend for the day into the basement, I see the yellow lake filled by a migration of shadow-men, creatures from ages past — a wide, trailing herd scattered across the lake, stooping naked figures with long arms dangling to the water, passing down the lake in a dead silence — uniformly spaced, knee-deep in the water, and moving together with heads hanging, not seeing. I am reminded of my grandfather's summer house, of sitting on the veranda watching boats pass down on the water, and for just a moment in the early morning I am confused. I hurry down the passage into the basement, sliding down the sand-covered ramp into the comfort of Suzanne's dark cellar.

Suzanne has decided she wants the job finished for the summer solstice. Each year a different member of the Priory community plays host to the summer-solstice celebration, and this year they will come to Suzanne's for Vespers and a barbecue on the beach. She wants my construction site cleaned up by then. She is really pushing to have things finished for her party, and I now have the assistance of Brother Julius, the young mason from the Priory, forced on me. Brother Julius has been sent to help set the foundation and lay the first course of blocks. Now that the heavy work has been completed, Brother Julius has arrived. The mound of sand outside is gone, carted for fill to the shallow swamp under the willow trees in Suzanne's yard. A network of trenches over which we will pour the basement floor has been laid and filled with clay piping to drain away the lake water into a sump pit. Suzanne will have to live with the frequent throbbings of the pump. Bothwell has stopped coming around since Brother Julius's arrival. My only consolation for having Julius here has been the pleasure of keeping him working all one Sunday and into the night because of a rainstorm. The water poured down the sand wall into our work area, breaking away great slides onto our forms. Julius is a tall boy with a brusque, humorless manner. There is little conversation between us. I have been forced to defer to him on all counts.

Since Julius arrived, the closer I come to seeing the work completed, the less there is of my grandfather in it. I find the power of dreams and visions fades with time, and I work simply to finish the job before the summer solstice. I escape any active life within the community. I am separated from the people of Suzanne's neighborhood, separated from Priory life, by my constant labor. The people here are distant from me. I observe them only by chance. I hear Bothwell roaring off to work in the morning and home again at night — his muffler has gone. I listen to Suzanne above me, moving about the house, feeding her children, playing the radio. I think of the Priory grounds, always empty, the brethren hidden away inside the buildings.

My dream of my grandfather is a memory. Sometimes it is strong — vivid for a moment, the way it used to be — and at other times it is little more than nonsense, distant in the climate of daylight hours. I try to realize the days passing, but I am usually lost in the fatigue and the repetition of work. I think of days rather than time. When I was a boy I used to find myself, on the last day of a family vacation at the summer house, seeing for the first time the sharp outline of trees against the sky, the magic light and color of the water I had been swimming in for weeks, and aching to begin again, to have an opportunity to appreciate the things it had taken me the summer to know. If I think hard enough about living to the fullest my days by the yellow lake, I am staggered by the endless memories and fantasies that flow through my head in a continuous river during the course of a day. If I could record every instant of thought . . .

"For you, Holy Father, in fear of being taken at the last without your grace . . ." All of them hunched over before the yellow lake — the light has very nearly left the sky — black mounds, a row of bulky silhouettes before the open water. "We have gathered here by the yellow lake . . ." Father Prior stands, his back to the water, with the community kneeling before him in front of rows of beach chairs in the sand. The brethren are on either side of Father Prior, dispensing holy water in the direction of the congregation, arms swishing back and forth, standing beneath a high, rising trail of incense — a dark line of robes against the barren horizon, a cluster of holy men with their feet sinking into the wet sand near the shoreline and the bottom hems of their robes already wet and covered with grains of the sand climbing.

Anna has managed to drag Bothwell to this service. He sits beside her, his thin legs crossed at the knee, in worn and shining trousers, white socks showing above paint-splattered black oxfords, his head cocked to one side, one hand playing with his pant leg. I expect his head to begin twitching at any moment. I have come late and there is only one chair left, beside Anna and Bothwell, which I would prefer not to take, so I stand to the rear of the aisles and look on. But I am not to be left to myself. A retired Air Force colonel I have seen at the Priory is motioning silently for me to take the empty seat. He is making waving motions with his arm. He has turned in his chair, creating quite a disturbance with his efforts to point out the empty chair, as if I had not already seen it. "The bread was the flesh and the wine was His blood," Father Prior calls back to me, but his voice floats the other way, out over the dead water. They have all come. Suzanne's children sit near the beginnings of what will be the bonfire. They have probably gathered all the wood. My mother and her friends are seated up at the front, near Father Prior. "To the Father, and to the Son, and to the Holy Ghost. As it was in the beginning, is now, and ever shall be, world without end. Amen." World without end. It is the secret of Father Prior to inspire his pink glow of faith. And I am made to feel outside that faith at times, until I remember that if it is real it includes me, whether or not I choose to be included — the all-encompassing faith of a world without end. It is a difficult thing for me to think about. I prefer to let my feelings about their faith slip to me past my thoughts. My mother tells me, when I complain about the people and the atmosphere at the Priory, the pink glow of faith, that she is waiting for the proper changes to come, the merging of thought and feeling into true spirit.

The resounding "amen" from the congregation rises sluggishly above the beach. There is a pause while the congregation stands, and under cover of this break one of Father Prior's older lieutenants I do not recognize skirts around the beach chairs with the intention of aiding the colonel in finding me the empty chair. He looks cautiously annoyed at my standing during Vespers. "Brother," he whispers to me, "there is a chair for you." And he is gone, sweeping off around the other side, a matronly herdsman. There is a sandy shuffling as the congregation stands to receive Communion. The brethren have forgotten their chants, and in-

stead of kneeling at a Communion rail they form a semicircle
around the Father to receive the bread and the wine, a social
gathering of the flock. There are many smiles and low comments
from Father Prior as he makes his way around the Communion
circle. The retired colonel leads the congregation in prayer. "Pray
for our soldiers around the world," he calls out. Anna follows him.
"Lord, help those who will not help themselves." Her pale tones
are almost lost on the beach.

There was no need to hurry to complete the work. We have
gathered down near the water, a hundred yards from the construction site. I have poured the floor and blocked in the walls, and it is
now only a dark place under Suzanne's living room.

Vespers are over, and Father Prior plays his guitar, singing folk
songs popular a decade ago, doing his best to be the guiding spirit
of the party, the spirit of the summer solstice. The brethren join
him. They must sing those songs with him on every holiday. The
rest of us wander about. Bothwell is making an extraordinary show
of laying out a long industrial extension cord from his house — to
play records for dancing, he has announced whenever he thinks
anyone is interested. There are bottles of tequila and everyone is
trying sips of it with lemon and salt, showing each other how to
perform the ritual. Summer solstice is one of the few times each
year when the brethren have the opportunity to mingle with out-
siders, but at first they wander shyly, gathering in clumps, sipping
at their drinks away from the others. A group of energetic men
from the congregation have taken it upon themselves to get the
bonfire started, and as the fire grows I am drawn closer to them
all, isolated with them on the shore inside the circle of light from
the fire. Father Prior goes on with his singing, an oblivious performer, unaware of those still around him, trying to make his
efforts a success. He acts with a forced naturalness, a forced abandon, as if it were hard for him to do; one can almost hear him
thinking: ". . . singing because I love to sing . . . whether it is considered to be good or even adequate . . . I express . . ." He sings:
"And they kissed so sweet and comforten as they clung to each
other . . ."

I allow myself only scattered exchanges with these people during
the course of the night. I see in them only remote parts of myself,
passing before me like the shadow-men passing down the lake. I

am obligated to be here for this short time with them, but they will
not become individuals and I will not have to acknowledge them as
long as I limit myself to watching. Even my mother can't touch me
under these circumstances. It is only odd to see her slightly drunk
and dancing in the sand among her friends.

Bothwell has connected the power line, and his stereo plays in
competition with Father Prior's singing on the far side of the circle
of firelight, the fire between them and its crackling separating their
music. An ant-line of people between the fire and Suzanne's house
enters and leaves the circle of light. There are mock bullfights on
the sand between the brethren and female matadors from the
congregation. Father Prior's songs are no longer heard by anyone.
Suzanne's children are ignored while they dance around the bonfire among the adults' legs. The bravest of my mother's friends are
naked, skinny-dipping, calling out to each other in the dark, but
the water is barely deep enough for them to submerge themselves.
There is no danger of them drowning in the yellow lake.

STANLEY ELKIN

The Conventional Wisdom

(FROM THE AMERICAN REVIEW)

ELLERBEE HAD BEEN having a bad time of it. He'd had financial reversals. Change would slip out of his pockets and slide down into the crevices of other people's furniture. He dropped deposit bottles and lost money in pay phones and vending machines. He overtipped in dark taxicabs. He had many such financial reversals. He was stuck with Superbowl tickets when he was suddenly called out of town and with theater and opera tickets when the ice was too slick to move his car out of his driveway. But all this was small potatoes. His portfolio was a disgrace. He had gotten into mutual funds at the wrong time and out at a worse. His house, appraised for tax purposes at many thousands of dollars below its replacement cost, burned down, and recently his once flourishing liquor store, one of the largest in Minneapolis, had drawn the attentions of burly, hopped-up and armed deprivators, ski-masked, head-stockinged. Two of his clerks had been shot, one killed, the other crippled and brain damaged, during the most recent visitation by these marauders, and Ellerbee, feeling a sense of responsibility, took it upon himself to support his clerks' families. His wife reproached him for this which led to bad feeling between them.

"Weren't they insured?"

"I don't know, May. I suppose they had some insurance but how much could it have been? One was just a kid out of college."

"Whatshisname, the vegetable."

"Harold, May."

"What about whosis? He was no kid out of college."

"George died protecting my store, May."

"Some protection. The black bastards got away with over fourteen hundred bucks." When the police called to tell him of the very first robbery, May had asked if the men had been black. It hurt Ellerbee that this should have been her first question. "Who's going to protect you? The insurance companies red-lined that lousy neighborhood a year ago. We won't get a penny."

"I'm selling the store, May. I can't afford to run it anymore."

"Selling? Who'd buy it? *Selling!*"

"I'll see what I can get for it," Ellerbee said.

"Social Security pays them benefits," May said, picking up their quarrel again the next day. "Social Security pays up to the time the kids are eighteen years old, and they give it to the widow, too. Who do you think you are, anyway? We lose a house and have to move into one not half as good because it's all we can afford, and you want to keep on paying the salaries not only of two people who no longer work for you, but to pay them out of a business that you mean to sell! Let Social Security handle it."

Ellerbee, who had looked into it, answered May. "Harold started with me this year. Social Security pays according to what you've put into the system. Dorothy won't get three hundred a month, May. And George's girl is twenty. Evelyn won't even get that much."

"Idealist," May said. "Martyr."

"Leave off, will you, May? I'm responsible. I'm under an obligation."

"Responsible, under an obligation!"

"Indirectly. God damn it, yes. Indirectly. They worked for me, didn't they? It's a combat zone down there. I should have had security guards around the clock."

"Where are you going to get all this money? We've had financial reverses. You're selling the store. Where's this money coming from to support three families?"

"We'll get it."

"*We'll* get it? There's no we'll about it, Mister. *You'll*. The stocks are in joint tenancy. You can't touch them, and I'm not signing a thing. Not a penny comes out of my mouth or off my back."

"All right, May," Ellerbee said. "I'll get it."

In fact Ellerbee had a buyer in mind — a syndicate that specialized in buying up business in decaying neighborhoods — liquor and drugstores, small groceries — and then put in ex-convicts as personnel, Green Berets from Vietnam, off-duty policemen, ex-

perts in the martial arts. Once the word was out, no one ever
attempted to rob these places. The syndicate hiked the price of
each item at least 20 percent — and got it. Ellerbee was fascinated
and appalled by their strong-arm tactics. Indeed, he more than a
little suspected that it was the syndicate itself which had been
robbing him — all three times his store had been held up he had
not been in it — to inspire him to sell, perhaps.

"We read about your trouble in the paper," Mr. Davis, the lawyer
for the syndicate, had told him on the occasion of his first robbery.
The thieves had gotten away with $300 and there was a four-line
notice on the inside pages. "Terrible," he said, "terrible. A fine old
neighborhood like this one. And it's the same all over America
today. Everywhere it's the same story. Even in Kansas, even in
Utah. They shoot you with bullets, they take your property. Terrible. The people I represent have the know-how to run businesses
like yours in the spoiled neighborhoods." And then he had been
offered a ridiculous price for his store and stock. Of course he
turned it down. When he was robbed a second time, the lawyer
didn't even bother to come in person. "Terrible. Terrible," he said.
"Whoever said lightning doesn't strike twice in the same place was
talking through his hat. I'm authorized to offer you ten thousand
less than I did the last time." Ellerbee hung up on him.

Now, after his clerks had been shot, it was Ellerbee who called
the lawyer. "Awful," the lawyer said. "Outrageous. A merchant
shouldn't have to sit still for such things in a democracy."

They gave him even less than the insurance people had given
him for his under-appraised home. Ellerbee accepted, but decided
it was time he at least hint to Davis that he knew what was going
on. "I'm selling," he said, "because I don't want anyone else to die."

"Wonderful," Davis said, "wonderful. There should be more
Americans like you."

He deposited the money he got from the syndicate in a separate
account so that his wife would have no claims on it and now, while
he had no business to go to, he was able to spend more time in the
hospital visiting Harold.

"How's Hal today, Mrs. Register?" he asked when he came into
the room where the mindless quadraplegic was being cared for.
Dorothy Register was a red-haired young woman in her early
twenties. Ellerbee felt so terrible about what had happened, so
guilty, that he had difficulty talking to her. He knew it would be

impossible to visit Harold if he was going to run into his wife when he did so. It was for this reason, too, that he sent the checks rather than drop them off at the apartment, much as he wanted to see Hal's young son, Harold, Jr., in order to reassure the child that there was still a man around to take care of the boy and his young mother.

"Oh, Mr. Ellerbee," the woman wept. Harold seemed to smile at them through his brain damage.

"Please, Mrs. Register," said Ellerbee, "Harold shouldn't see you like this."

"Him? He doesn't understand a thing. You don't understand a thing, do you?" she said, turning on her husband sharply. When she made a move to poke at his eyes with a fork he didn't even blink. "Oh, Mr. Ellerbee," she said, turning away from her husband, "that's not the man I married. It's awful, but I don't feel anything for him. The only reason I come is that the doctors say I cheer him up. Though I can't see how. He smiles that way at his bedpan."

"Please, Mrs. Register," Ellerbee said softly. "You've got to be strong. There's little Hal."

"I know," she moaned, "I know." She wiped the tears from her eyes and sniffed and tossed her hair in a funny little way she had which Ellerbee found appealing. "I'm sorry," she said. "You've been very kind. I don't know what I would have done, what *we* would have done. I can't even thank you," she said helplessly.

"Oh don't think about it, there's no need," Ellerbee said quickly. "I'm not doing any more for you than I am for George Lesefario's widow." It was not a boast. Ellerbee had mentioned the older woman because he didn't want Mrs. Register to feel compromised. "It's company policy when these things happen," he said gruffly.

Dorothy Register nodded. "I heard," she said, "that you sold your store."

He hastened to reassure her. "Oh now listen," Ellerbee said, "you mustn't give that a thought. The checks will continue. I'm getting another store. In a very lovely neighborhood. Near where we used to live before our house burned down."

"Really?"

"Oh yes. I should be hearing about my loan any time now. I'll probably be in the new place before the month is out. Well," he said, "speaking of which, I'd better get going. There are some fixtures I'm supposed to look at at the Wine and Spirits Mart." He waved to Harold.

"Mr. Ellerbee?"

"Mrs. Register?"

The tall redhead came close to him and put her hands on his shoulders. She made that funny little gesture with her hair again and Ellerbee almost died. She was about his own height and leaned forward and kissed him on the mouth. Her fingernails grazed the back of his neck. Tears came to Ellerbee's eyes and he turned away from her gently. He hoped she hadn't seen the small lump in his trousers. He said good-bye with his back to her.

The loan went through. The new store, as Ellerbee had said, was in one of the finest neighborhoods in the city. In a small shopping mall it was flanked by a good bookstore and a fine French restaurant. The Ellerbees had often eaten there before their house burned to the ground. There was an art cinema, a florist, and elegant haberdasher's and dress shops. The liquor store, called High Spirits, a name Ellerbee decided to keep after he bought the place, stocked, in addition to the usual gins, Scotch, bourbons, vodkas, and blends, some really superior wines, and Ellerbee was forced to become something of an expert in oenology. He listened to his customers — doctors and lawyers, most of them — and in this way was able to pick up a good deal.

The business flourished — doing so well that after only his second month in the new location he no longer felt obliged to stay open on Sundays — though his promise to his clerks' families, which he kept, prevented him from making the inroads into his extravagant debt that he would have liked. Mrs. Register began to come to the store to collect the weekly checks personally. "I thought I'd save you the stamp," she said each time. Though he enjoyed seeing her — she looked rather like one of those splendid wives of the successful doctors who shopped there — he thought he should discourage this. He made it clear to her that he would be sending the checks.

Then she came and said that it was foolish, his continuing to pay her husband's salary, that at least he ought to let her do something to earn it. She saw that the suggestion made him uncomfortable and clarified what she meant.

"Oh, no," she said, "all I meant was that you ought to hire me. I was a hostess once. For that matter I could wait on trade."

"Well, I've plenty of help, Mrs. Register. Really. As I may have told you, I've kept on all the people who used to work for Anderson." Anderson was the man from whom he'd bought High Spirits. "It's not as though you'd be hiring additional help. I'm costing you the money anyway."

It would have been pleasant to have the woman around, but Ellerbee nervously held his ground. "At a time like this," he said, "you ought to be with the boy."

"You're quite a guy," she said. It was the last time they saw each other. A few months later, while he was examining his bank statements, he realized that she had not been cashing his checks. He called her at once.

"I can't," she said. "I'm young. I'm strong." He remembered her fierce embrace in her husband's hospital room. "There's no reason for you to continue to send me those checks. I have a good job now. I can't accept them any longer." It was the last time they spoke.

And then he learned that George's widow was ill. He heard about it indirectly. One of his best customers — a psychiatrist — was beeped on the emergency Medi-Call he carried in his jacket, and asked for change to use Ellerbee's pay phone.

"That's not necessary, Doc," Ellerbee said, "use the phone behind my counter."

"Very kind," the psychiatrist said, and came back of the counter. He dialed his service. "Doctor Potter. What have you got for me, Nancy? What? She did *what*? Just a minute, let me get a pencil — Bill?" Ellerbee handed him a pencil. "Lesefario, right. I've got that. Give me the surgeon's number. Right. Thanks, Nancy."

"Excuse me, Doctor," Ellerbee said. "I hadn't meant to listen, but Lesefario, that's an unusual name. I know an Evelyn Lesefario."

"That's the one," said the medical man. "Oh," he said, "you're *that* Ellerbee. Well, she's been very depressed. She just tried to kill herself by eating a mile of dental floss."

"I hope she dies," his wife said.

"*May!*" said Ellerbee, shocked.

"It's what she wants, isn't it? I hope she gets what she wants."

"That's harsh, May."

"Yes? Harsh? You see how much good your checks did her? And another thing, how could she afford a high-priced man like Potter on what *you* were paying her?"

He went to visit the woman during her postoperative convalescence, and she introduced him to her sister, her twin she said, though the two women looked nothing alike and the twin seemed to be in her seventies, a good dozen years older than Mrs. Lesefario. "This is Mr. Ellerbee that my husband died protecting his liquor store from the niggers."

"Oh yes?" Mrs. Lesefario's sister said. "Very pleased. I heard so much about you."

"Look what she brought me," Mrs. Lesefario said, pointing to a large brown paper sack.

"Evelyn, don't. You'll strain your stitches. I'll show him." She opened the sack and took out a five-pound bag of sugar.

"Five pounds of sugar," the melancholic woman said.

"You don't come empty handed to a sick person," her sister said.

"She got it at Kroger's on special. Ninety-nine cents with the coupon," the manic-depressive said gloomily. "She says if I don't like it I can get peach halves."

Ellerbee, who did not want to flaunt his own gift in front of her sister, quietly put the dressing gown, still wrapped, on her tray table. He stayed for another half hour, and rose to go.

"Wait," Mrs. Lesefario said. "Nice try but not so fast."

"I'm sorry?" Ellerbee said.

"The ribbon."

"Ribbon?"

"On the fancy box. The ribbon, the string."

"Oh, your stitches. Sorry. I'll get it."

"I'm a would-be suicide," she said. "I tried it once, I could try it again. You don't bring dangerous ribbon to a desperate, unhappy woman."

In fact Mrs. Lesefario did die. Not of suicide, but of a low-grade infection she had picked up in the hospital and which festered along her stitches, undermining them, burning through them, opening her body like a package.

The Ellerbees were in the clear financially, but his wife's reactions to Ellerbee's efforts to provide for his clerk's families had soured their relationship. She had discovered Ellerbee's private account and accused him of dreadful things. He reminded her that it had been she who had insisted he would have to get the money for the women's support himself — that their joint tenancy was not to be disturbed. She ignored his arguments and accused him further. Ellerbee loved May and did what he could to placate her.

"How about a trip to Phoenix?" he suggested that spring. "The store's doing well and I have complete confidence in Kroll. What about it, May? You like Phoenix, and we haven't seen the folks in almost a year."

"Phoenix," she scoffed, "the *folks*. The way you coddle them. Any other grown man would be ashamed."

"They raised me, May."

"They raised you. Terrific. They aren't even your real parents. They only adopted you."

"They're the only parents I ever knew. They took me out of the Home when I was an infant."

"Look, you want to go to Phoenix, go. Take money out of your secret accounts and go."

"Please, May. There's no secret account. When Mrs. Lesefario died I transferred everything back into joint. Come on, sweetheart, you're awfully goddamn hard on me."

"Well," she said, drawing the word out. The tone was one she had used as a bride, and although Ellerbee had not often heard it since, it melted him. It was her signal of sudden conciliation, cute surrender, and he held out his arms and they embraced. They went off to the bedroom together.

"You know," May said afterwards, "it *would* be good to run out to Phoenix for a bit. Are you sure the help can manage?"

"Oh, sure, May, absolutely. They're a first-rate bunch." He spoke more forcefully than he felt, not because he had any lack of confidence in his employees, but because he was still disturbed by an image he had had during climax. Momentarily, fleetingly, he had imagined Mrs. Register beneath him.

In the store he was giving last-minute instructions to Kroll, the man who would be his manager during their vacation in Phoenix.

"I think the Californias," Ellerbee was saying. "Some of them beat several of even the more immodest French. Let's do a promotion of a few of the better Californias. What do you think?"

"They're a very competitive group of wines," Kroll said. "I think I'm in basic agreement."

Just then three men walked into the shop.

"Say," one called from the doorway, "you got something like a Closed sign I could hang in the door here?" Ellerbee stared at him. "Well you don't have to look at me as if I was nuts," the man said. "Lots of merchants keep them around. In case they get a sudden toothache or something they can whip out to the dentist. All right, if you ain't you ain't."

"I want," the second man said, coming up to the counter where Ellerbee stood with his manager, "to see your register receipts."

"What is this?" Kroll demanded.

"No, don't," Ellerbee said to Kroll. "Don't resist." He glanced toward the third man to see if he was the one holding the gun, but the man appeared merely to be browsing the bins of Scotch in the back. Evidently he hadn't even heard the first man, and clearly he could not have heard the second. Conceivably he could have been a customer. "Where's your gun?" Ellerbee asked the man at the counter.

"Oh gee," the man said, "I almost forgot. You got so many things to think about during a stick-up — the traffic flow, the timing, who stands where — you sometimes forget the basics. Here," he said, "here's my gun, in your kisser," and took an immense hand gun from his pocket and pointed it at Ellerbee's face.

Out of the corner of his eye Ellerbee saw Kroll's hands fly up. It was so blatant a gesture Ellerbee thought his manager might be trying to attract the customer's attention. If that was his idea it had worked, for the third man had turned away from the bins and was watching the activity at the counter. "Look," Ellerbee said, "I don't want anybody hurt."

"What's he say?" said the man at the door who was also holding a pistol now.

"He don't want nobody hurt," the man at the counter said.

"Sure," said the man at the door, "it's costing him a fortune paying all them salaries to the widows. He's a bood businessman all right."

"A better one than you," the man at the counter said to his confederate sharply. "He knows how to keep his mouth shut."

Why, they're white, Ellerbee thought. They're *white* men! He felt oddly justified and wished May were there to see.

"The register receipts," the man at the counter coaxed. Ellerbee's cash register kept a running total on what had been taken in. "Just punch Total Tab," the man instructed Kroll. "Let's see what we got." Kroll looked at Ellerbee and Ellerbee nodded. The man reached forward and tore off the tape. He whistled. "Nice little place you got here," he said.

"What'd we get? What'd we get?" the man at the door shouted.

Ellerbee cleared his throat. "Do you want to lock the door?" he asked. "So no one else comes in?" He glanced toward the third man.

"What, and have you kick the alarm while we're fucking around trying to figure which key opens the place?" said the man at the door. "You're a cutie. What'd we get? Let's see." He joined the man at the counter. "Holy smoke! Jackpot City! We're into four figures here." In his excitement he did a foolish thing. He set his revolver down on top of the appetizer table. It lay on the tins of caviar and smoked oysters, the imported cheeses and roasted peanuts. The third man was no more than four feet from the gun, and though Ellerbee saw that the man had caught the robber's mistake and that by taking one step toward the table he could have picked up the pistol and perhaps foiled the robbery, he made no move. Perhaps he's one of them, Ellerbee thought, or maybe he just doesn't want to get involved. Ellerbee couldn't remember ever having seen him. (By now, of course, he recognized all his repeat customers.) He still didn't know if he were a confederate or just an innocent bystander, but Ellerbee had had enough of violence and hoped that if he *were* a customer he wouldn't try anything dumb. He felt no animus toward the man at all. Kroll's face, however, was all scorn and loathing.

"Let's get to work," the man said who had first read the tape, and then to Kroll and Ellerbee, "Back up there. Go stand by the apéritifs."

The third man fell silently into step beside Ellerbee.

"Listen," Ellerbee explained as gently as he could, "you won't find that much cash in the drawer. A lot of our business is Master Charge. We take personal checks."

"Don't worry," the man said who had set his gun down (and who had taken it up again). "We know about the checks. We got a guy we can sell them to for — what is it, Ron, seventeen cents on the dollar?"

"Fourteen, and why don't you shut your mouth, will you? You want to jeopardize these people? What do you make it?"

Ellerbee went along with his sentiments. He wished the big-mouth would just take the money and not say anything more.

"Oh, jeopardize," the man said. "How jeopardized can you get? These people are way past jeopardized. About six hundred in cash, a fraction in checks. The rest is all credit card paper."

"Take it," Ron said.

"You won't be able to do anything with the charge slips," Kroll said.

"Oh yeah?" Ron's cohort said. "This is modern times, fellow. We got a way we launder Master Charge, BankAmericard, all of it."

Ron shook his head and Ellerbee glanced angrily at his manager. The whole thing couldn't have taken four minutes. Ron's partner took a fifth of Chivas and a bottle of Lafitte '47. He's a doctor, Ellerbee thought.

"You got a bag?"

"A bag?" Ellerbee said.

"A bag, a paper bag, a doggy bag for the boodle."

"Behind the counter," Ellerbee said hopelessly.

The partner put the cash and the bottle of Chivas into one bag and handed it to Ron, and the wine, checks, and credit charges into a second bag which he held on to himself. They turned to go. They looked exactly like two satisfied customers. They were almost at the door when Ron's partner nudged Ron. "Oh, yeah," Ron said, and turned back to look at them. "My friend, Jay Ladlehaus, is right," he said, "you know too much."

Ellerbee heard two distinct shots before he fell.

When he came to, the third man was bending over him. "You're not hurt," Ellerbee said.

"Me? No."

The pain was terrific, diffuse, but fiercer than anything he had ever felt. He saw himself covered with blood. "Where's Kroll? The other man, my manager?"

"Kroll's all right."

"He is?"

"There, right beside you."

He tried to look. They must have blasted Ellerbee's throat away, half his spinal column. It was impossible for him to move his head. "I can't see him," he moaned.

"Kroll's fine." The man cradled Ellerbee's shoulders and neck and shifted him slightly. "There. See?" Kroll's eyes were shut. Oddly, both were blackened. He had fallen in such a way that he seemed to lie on both his arms, retracted behind him into the small of his back like a yoga. His mouth was open and his tongue floated in blood like meat in soup. A slight man, he seemed strangely bloated, and one shin, exposed to Ellerbee's vision where the trou-

ser leg was hiked up above his sock, was discolored as thunder-
cloud.

The man gently set Ellerbee down again. "Call an ambulance,"
Ellerbee wheezed through his broken throat.

"No, no. Kroll's fine."

"He's not conscious." It was as if his words were being mashed
through the tines of a fork.

"He'll be all right. Kroll's fine."

"Then for *me*. Call one for *me*."

"It's too late for you," the man said.

"For Christ's sake, will you!" Ellerbee gasped. "I can't move. You
could have grabbed that hoodlum's gun when he set it down. All
right, you were scared, but some of this is your fault. You didn't
lift a finger. At least call an ambulance."

"But you're dead," he said gently. "Kroll will recover. You passed
away when you said 'move.' "

"Are you crazy? What are you talking about?"

"Do you feel pain?"

"What?"

"Pain. You don't feel any, do you?" Ellerbee stared at him. "Do
you?"

He didn't. His pain was gone. "Who are you?" Ellerbee said.

"I'm an angel of death," the angel of death said.

"You're —"

"An angel of death."

Somehow he had left his body. He could see it lying next to
Kroll's. "I'm dead? But if I'm dead — You mean there's really an
afterlife?"

"Oh boy," the angel of death said.

They went to Heaven.

Ellerbee couldn't have said how they got there or how long it
took, though he had the impression that time had passed, and
distance. It was rather like a journey in films — a series of quick
cuts, of montage. He was probably dreaming, he thought.

"It's what they all think," the angel of death said, "that they're
dreaming. But that isn't so."

"I could have dreamed you said that," Ellerbee said, "that you
read my mind."

"Yes."

"I could be dreaming all of it, the holdup, everything."

The angel of death looked at him.

"Hobgoblin . . . I could . . ." Ellerbee's voice — if it was a voice — trailed off.

"Look," the angel of death said, "I talk too much. I sound like a cabbie with an out-of-town fare. It's an occupational hazard."

"What?"

What? Pride. The proprietary air. Showing off death like a booster. Thanatopography. 'If you look to your left you'll see where . . . Julius Caesar de dum de dum . . . Shakespeare da da da . . . And dead ahead our Father Adam heigh ho —' The tall buildings and the four-star sights. All that Baedeker reality of plaque place and high history. The Fields of Homer and the Plains of Myth. Where whosis got locked in a star and all the Agriculture of the Periodic Table — the South Forty of the Universe, where Hydrogen first bloomed, where Lithium, Berylium, Zirconium, Niobium. Where Lead failed and Argon came a cropper. The furrows of gold, Bismuth's orchards . . . Still think you're dreaming?"

"No."

"Why not?"

"The language."

"Just so," the angel of death said. "When you were alive you had a vocabulary of perhaps seventeen or eighteen hundred words. Who am I?"

"An eschatological angel," Ellerbee said shyly.

"One hundred per cent," the angel of death said. "Why do we do that?"

"To heighten perception," Ellerbee said, and shuddered.

The angel of death nodded and said nothing more.

When they were close enough to make out the outlines of Heaven, the angel left him and Ellerbee, not questioning this, went on alone. From this distance it looked to Ellerbee rather like a theme park, but what struck him most forcibly was that it did not seem — for Heaven — very large.

He traveled as he would on Earth, distance familiar again, volume, mass, and dimension restored, ordinary. (*Quotidian,* Ellerbee thought.) Indeed, now that he was convinced of his death, nothing seemed particularly strange. If anything, it was all a little familiar. He began to miss May. She would have learned of his death by this time. Difficult as the last year had been, they had loved each other.

It had been a good marriage. He regretted again that they had been unable to have children. Children — they would be teenagers now — would have been a comfort to his widow. She still had her looks. Perhaps she would remarry. He did not want her to be lonely.

He continued toward Heaven and now, only blocks away, he was able to perceive it in detail. It looked more like a theme park than ever. It was enclosed behind a high milky fence, the uprights smooth and round as the poles in subway trains. Beyond the fence were golden streets, a mixed architecture of minaret-spiked mosques, great cathedrals, the rounded domes of classical synagogues, tall pagodas like holy vertebrae, white frame churches with their beautiful steeples, even what Ellerbee took to be a storefront church. There were many mansions. But where were the people?

Just as he was wondering about this he heard the sound of a gorgeous chorus. It was making a joyful noise. "Oh dem golden slippers," the chorus sang, "Oh dem golden slippers." It's the Heavenly Choir, Ellerbee thought. They've actually got a Heavenly Choir. He went toward the fence and put his hands on the smooth posts and peered through into Heaven. He heard laughter and caught a glimpse of the running heels of children just disappearing around the corner of a golden street. They all wore shoes.

Ellerbee walked along the fence for about a mile and came to gates made out of pearl. The Pearly Gates, he thought. There are actually Pearly Gates.

An old man in a long white beard sat behind them, a key attached to a sort of cinch that went about his waist.

"Saint Peter?" Ellerbee ventured. The old man turned his shining countenance upon him. "Saint Peter," Ellerbee said again, "I'm Ellerbee."

"I'm Saint Peter," Saint Peter said.

"Gosh," Ellerbee said, "I can't get over it. It's all true."

"What is?"

"Everything. Heaven. The streets of gold, the Pearly Gates. You. Your key. The Heavenly Choir. The climate."

A soft breeze came up from inside Heaven and Ellerbee sniffed something wonderful in the perfect air. He looked toward the venerable old man.

"Ambrosia," the Saint said.

"There's actually ambrosia," Ellerbee said.

"You know," Saint Peter said, "you never get tired of it, you never even get used to it. He does that to whet our appetite."

"You eat in Heaven?"

"We eat manna."

"There's actually manna," Ellerbee said. An angel floated by on a fleecy cloud playing a harp. Ellerbee shook his head. He had never heard anything so beautiful. "Heaven is everything they say it is," he said.

"It's paradise," Saint Peter said.

Then Ellerbee saw an affecting sight. Nearby, husbands were reunited with wives, mothers with their small babes, daddies with their sons, brothers with sisters — all the intricate blood loyalties and enlisted loves. He understood all the relationships without being told — his heightened perception. What was most moving, however, were the old people, related or not, some just lifelong friends, people who had lived together or known one another much the greater part of their lives and then had lost each other. It was immensely touching to Ellerbee to see them gaze fondly into one another's eyes and then to watch them reach out and touch the patient, ancient faces, wrinkled and even withered but, Ellerbee could tell, unchanged in the loving eyes of the adoring beholder. If there were tears they were tears of joy, tears that melded inextricably with tender laughter. There was rejoicing, there were Hosannahs, there was dancing in the golden streets. "It's wonderful," Ellerbee muttered to himself. He didn't know where to look first. He would be staring at the beautiful flowing raiments of the angels — There are actually raiments, he thought, there are actually angels — so fine, he imagined, to the touch that just the caress of the cloth must have produced exquisite sensations not matched by anything in life, when something else would strike him. The perfectly proportioned angels' wings like discrete Gothic windows, the beautiful halos — There are actually halos — like golden quoits, or, in the distance, the lovely green pastures, delicious as fairway — all the perfectly banked turns of Heaven's geography. He saw philosophers deep in conversation. He saw kings and heroes. It was astonishing to him, like going to an exclusive restaurant one has only read about in columns and spotting, even at first glance, the celebrities one has read about, relaxed, passing the time of day, out in the open, up-front and sharing their high-echelon lives.

"This is for keeps?" he asked Saint Peter. "I mean it goes on like this?"

"World without end," Saint Peter said.

"Where's . . ."

"That's all right, say His name."

"God?" Ellerbee whispered.

Saint Peter looked around. "I don't see Him just . . . Oh, wait. *There!*" Ellerbee turned where the old Saint was pointing. He shaded his eyes. "There's no need," Saint Peter said.

"But the aura, the light."

"Let it shine."

He took his hand away fearfully and the light spilled into his eyes like soothing unguents. God was on His throne in the green pastures, Christ at His right Hand. To Ellerbee it looked like a picture taken at a summit conference.

"He's beautiful. I've never . . . It's ecstasy."

"And you're seeing Him from a pretty good distance. You should talk to Him sometime."

"People can talk to Him?"

"Certainly. He loves us."

There were tears in Ellerbee's eyes. He wished May no harm, but wanted her with him to see it all. "It's wonderful."

"We like it," Saint Peter said.

"Oh, I do too," Ellerbee said. "I'm going to be very happy here."

"Go to Hell," Saint Peter said beatifically.

Hell was the ultimate inner city. Its stinking sulfurous streets were unsafe. Everywhere Ellerbee looked he saw atrocities. Pointless, profitless muggings were commonplace; joyless rape that punished its victims and offered no relief to the perpetrator. Everything was contagious, cancer as common as a cold, plague the quotidian. There was stomachache, headache, toothache, earache. There was angina and indigestion and painful third-degree burning itch. Nerves like a hideous body hair grew long enough to trip over and lay raw and exposed as live wires or shoelaces that had come undone.

There was no handsomeness, no beauty, no one walked upright, no one had good posture. There was nothing to look at — although it was impossible to shut one's eyes — except the tumbled kaleidoscopic variations of warted deformity. This was one reason, Ellerbee supposed, that there was so little conversation in Hell. No one could stand to look at anyone else long enough. Occasionally two or three — lost souls? gargoyles? devils? demons? — of the damned, jumping about in the heat first on one foot then the other, would manage to stand with their backs to each other and perhaps get out a few words — a foul whining. But even this was rare and when it happened that a sufferer had the attention of a fellow sufferer he could howl out only a half-dozen or so words before breaking off in a piercing scream.

Ellerbee, constantly nauseated, eternally in pain, forever befouling himself, longed to find something to do, however tedious or make-work or awful. For a time he made paths through the smoldering cinders, but he had no tools and had to use his bare feet, moving the cinders to one side as a boy shuffles through fallen leaves hunting something lost. It was too painful. Then he thought he would make channels for the vomit and excrement and blood. It was too disgusting. He shouted for others to join him in work details — "Break up the fights, pile up the scabs" — even ministering to the less aggravated wounds, using his hands to wipe away the gangrenous drool since there was no fabric in Hell, all clothing consumed within minutes of arrival, flesh alone inconsumable, glowing and burning with his bones slow as phosphor. Calling out, suggesting in screams which may have been incoherent, all manner of pointless, arbitrary arrangements — that they organize the damned, that they count them. Demanding that their howls be synchronous.

No one stopped him. No one seemed to be in charge. He saw, that is, no Devil, no Arch-fiend. There were demons with cloven feet and scaly tails, with horns and pitchforks — They actually have horns, Ellerbee thought, there are actually pitchforks — but these seemed to have no more authority than he had himself, and when they were piqued to wrath by their own torment the jabs they made at the human damned with their sharp arsenal were no more painful — and no less — than anything else down there.

Then Ellerbee felt he understood something terrible — that the abortive rapes and fights and muggings were simply a refinement of his own attempts to socialize. They did it to make contact, to be friendly.

He was free to wander the vast burning meadows of Hell and to scale its fiery hills — and for many years he did — but it was much the same all over. What he was actually looking for was its Source,

Hell's bright engine room, its storm-tossed bridge. It had no engine room, there was no bridge, its energy, all its dreadful combustion coming perhaps from the cumulative, collective agony of the inmates. Nothing could be done.

He was distracted, as he was sure they all were ("Been to Heaven?" he'd managed to gasp to an old man whose back was on fire and the man had nodded), by his memory of Paradise, his long-distance glimpse of God. It was unbearable to think of Heaven in his present condition, his memory of that spectacular place poisoned by the discrepancy between the exaltation of the angels and the plight of the damned. It was the old story of the disappointment of rising expectations. Still, without his bidding, thoughts of Paradise force-fed themselves almost constantly into his skull. They induced sadness, rage.

He remembered the impression he'd had of celebrity when he'd stood looking in at Heaven from beyond the Pearly Gates, and he thought to look out for the historic bad men, the celebrated damned, but either they were kept in a part of Hell he had not yet been or their sufferings had made them unrecognizable. If there were great men in Hell he did not see them and, curiously, no one ever boasted of his terrible deeds or notoriety. Indeed, except for the outbursts of violence, most of the damned behaved, considering their state, in a respectable fashion, even an exemplary one. Perhaps, Ellerbee thought, it was because they had not yet abandoned hope. (There was actually a sign: "Abandon Hope, All Who Enter Here." Ellerbee had read it.)

For several years he waited for May, for as long, that is, as he could remember her. Constant pain and perpetual despair chipped away at most of the memories he had of his life. It was possible to recall who and what he had been, but that was as fruitless as any other enterprise in the dark region. Ultimately, like everything else, it worked against him — Hell's fine print. It was best to forget. And that worked against him too.

He took the advice written above Hellgate. He abandoned hope, and with it memory, pity, pride, his projects, the sense he had of injustice — for a little while driving off, along with his sense of identity, even his broken recollection of glory. It was probably what they — whoever they were — wanted. Let them have it. Let them have the straight lines of their trade wind, trade route, through street, thrown stone vengeance. Let them have everything. Their pastels back and their blues and their greens, the recollection of gratified thirst, and the transient comfort of a sandwich and beer that had hit the spot, all the retrospective of good weather, a good night's sleep, a good joke, a good tune, a good time, the entire mosaic of small satisfactions that made up a life. Let them have his image of his parents and friends, the fading portrait of May he couldn't quite shake, the pleasure he'd had from work, from his body. Let them have all of it, his measly joy, his scrapbook past, his hope, too.

Which left only pure pain, the grand vocabulary they had given him to appreciate it, to discriminate and parse among the exquisite lesions and scored flesh and violated synapses, among the insulted nerves, joints, muscle and tissue, all the boiled kindling points of torment and the body's grief. That was all he was now, staggering Hiroshima'd flesh — a vessel of nausea, a pail of pain.

He continued thus for several years, his amnesia willed — There's Free Will, Ellerbee thought — shuffling Hell in his rote aphasia, his stripped self a sealed environment of indifference. There were years he did not think the name Ellerbee.

And even *that* did not assuage the panic of his burning theater'd, air raid warning'd, red alert afterlife. (And that was what they wanted, and he knew it, wanting as much as they did for him to persist in his tornado watch condition, fleeing with others through the crimped, cramped streets of mazy, refugee Hell, dragging his disaster-poster avatar like a wounded leg.) He existed like one plugged into superb equipment, interminably terminal — and changed his mind and tried it the other way again, taking back all he had surrendered, Hell's Indian giver, and dredged up from where he had left them the imperfect memories of his former self. (May he saw as she had once been, his breastless, awkward, shapeless childhood sweetheart.) And when that didn't work either — he gave it a few years — he went back to the other way, and then back again, shifting, quickly tiring of each tack as soon as he had taken it, changing fitfully, a man in bed in a hot, airless room rolling position, agressively altering the surfaces of his pillow. If he hoped — which he came to do whenever he reverted to Ellerbee — it was to go mad, but there was no madness in Hell — the terrific vocabulary of the damned, their poet's knack for rightly naming everything which was the fail-safe of Reason — and he could find peace nowhere.

He had been there sixty-two years, three generations, older now as a dead man than he had been as a living one. Sixty-two years of nightless days and dayless nights, of aggravated pain and cumulative grief, of escalate desperation, of not getting used to it, to any of it. Sixty-two years Hell's greenhorn, sixty-two years eluding the muggers and evading the rapists, all the joyless joy riders out for a night on his town, steering clear of the wild, stampeding, horizontal avalanche of the damned. And then, spinning out of the path of a charging, burning, screaming inmate, he accidentally backed into the smoldering ruin of a second. Ellerbee leaped away as their bodies touched.

"Ellerbee?"

Who? Ellerbee thought wildly. Who?

"Ellerbee?" the voice repeated.

How? Ellerbee wondered. How can he know me? In this form, how I look . . .

Ellerbee peered closely into the tormented face. It was one of the men who had held him up, not the one who had shot him but his accomplice, his murderer's accomplice. "Ladlehaus?" It was Ellerbee's vocabulary which had recognized him, for his face had changed almost completely in the sixty-two years, just as Ellerbee's had, just as it was Ladlehaus's vocabulary which had recognized Ellerbee.

"It is Ellerbee, isn't it?" the man said.

Ellerbee nodded and the man tried to smile, stretching his wounds, the scars which seamed his face, and breaking the knitting flesh, lined, caked as stool, braided as bowel.

"I died," he said, "of natural causes." Ellerbee stared at him. "Of leukemia, stroke, Hodgkin's disease, arteriosclerosis. I was blind the last thirteen years of my life. But I was almost a hundred. I lived to a ripe old age. I was in a Home eighteen years. Still in Minneapolis."

"I suppose," Ellerbee said, "you recall how *I* died."

"I do." Ladlehaus said. "Ron dropped you with one shot. That reminds me," he said. "You had a beautiful wife. May, right? I saw her photograph in the Minneapolis papers after the incident. There was tremendous coverage. There was a TV clip on the Six O'Clock News. They interviewed her. She was —" Ellerbee started to run. "Hey," the accomplice called after him. "Hey, wait."

He ran through the steamy corridors of the Underworld, plunging into Hell's white core, the brightest blazes, Temperature's moving parts. The pain was excruciating, but he knew that it was probably the only way he would shake Ladlehaus so he kept running. And then, exhausted, he came out the other side into an area like shoreline, burning surf. He waded through the flames lapping about his ankles and then, humiliated by fatigue and pain, he did something he had never done before.

He lay down in the fire. He lay down in the slimy excrement and noxious puddles, in the loose evidence of their spilled terror. A few damned souls paused to stare at him, their bad breath dropping over him like an awful steam. Their scabbed faces leaned down toward him, their poisoned blood leaking on him from imperfectly sealed wounds, their baked, hideous visages like blooms in nightmare. It was terrible. He turned over, turned face down in the shallow river of pus and shit. Someone shook him. He didn't move. A man straddled and penetrated him. He didn't move. His attacker groaned. "I can't," he panted, "I can't — I can't see myself in his *blisters.*" That's why they do it, Ellerbee thought. The man grunted and dismounted and spat upon him. His fiery spittle burned into an open sore on Ellerbee's neck. He didn't move. "He's dead," the man howled. "I think he's dead. His blisters have gone out!"

He felt a pitchfork rake his back, then turn in the wound it had made as if the demon were trying to pry foreign matter from it.

"Did he die?" Ellerbee heard.

He had Free Will. He wouldn't move.

"Is he dead?"

"How did he do it?"

Hundreds pressed in on him, their collective stench like the swamps of men dead in earthquake, trench warfare — though Ellerbee knew that for all his vocabulary there were no proper analogies in Hell, only the mildest approximations. If he didn't move they would go away. He didn't move.

A pitchfork caught him under the armpit and turned him over.

"He's dead. I think so. I think he's dead."

"No. It can't be."

"I think."

"How? How did he do it?"

"Pull his cock. See."

"No. Make one of the women. If he isn't dead maybe he'll respond."

An ancient harridan stooped down and rubbed him between her palms. It was the first time he had been touched there by a woman in sixty-two years. He had Free Will, he had Free Will. But beneath her hot hands his penis began to smoke.

"Oh God," he screamed. "Leave me alone. Please," he begged.

They gazed down at him like teammates over a fallen player.

"Faker," one hissed.

"Shirker," said another scornfully.

"He's not dead," a third cried. "I told you."

"There's no death here."

"World without end," said another.

"Get up," demanded someone else. "Run. Run through Hell. Flee your pain. Keep busy."

They started to lift him. "Let go," Ellerbee shouted. He rolled away from a demon poking at him with a pitchfork. He was on his hands and knees in Hell. Still on all fours he began to push himself up. He was on his knees.

"Looks like he's praying," said the one who had told him to run.

"No."

"Looks like it. I think so."

"How? What for?"

And he started to pray.

"Lord God of Ambush and Unconditional Surrender," he prayed. "Power Play God of Judo Leverage. Grand Guignol, Martial Artist —"

The others shrieked, backed away from him, cordoning Ellerbee off like a disaster area. Ellerbee, caught up, ignoring them, not even hearing them, continued his prayer.

"Browbeater," he prayed, "Bouncer Being, Boss of Bullies — this is Your servant, Ellerbee, sixty-two-year foetus in Eternity, tot, toddler, babe in Hell. Can You hear me? I know You exist because I saw You, avuncular in Your green pastures like an old man on a picnic. The angeled minarets I saw, the gold streets and marble temples and all the flashy summer palace architecture, all the gorgeous glory locked in Receivership, Your zoned Heaven in Holy Escrow. The miracle props — harps and Saints and Popes at tea. All of it — Your manna, Your ambrosia, Your Heavenly Host in their summer whites. So can You *hear* me, pick out my voice from all the others in this din bin? Come on, come on, Old Terrorist,

God the Father, God the Godfather! The conventional wisdom is
we can talk to You, that You love us, that —"
  "I can hear you."
  A great awed whine rose from the damned, moans, sharp cries.
It was as if Ellerbee alone had not heard. He continued his prayer.
  "I hear you," God repeated.
  Ellerbee stopped.
  God spoke. His voice was pitchless, almost without timbre, almost
bland. "What do you want, Ellerbee?"
  Confused, Ellerbee forgot the point of his prayer. He looked at
the others who were quiet now, perfectly still for once. Only the
snap of localized fire could be heard. God was waiting. The
damned watched Ellerbee fearfully. Hell burned beneath his
knees. "An explanation," Ellerbee said.
  "For openers," God roared, "I made the heavens and the earth!
Were you there when I laid the foundations of the firmament?
When I —"
  Splinters of burning bone, incandescent as filament, glowed in
the gouged places along Ellerbee's legs and knees where divots of
his flesh had flared and fallen away. "An *explanation*," he cried out,
"an *explanation*! None of this what-was-I-doing-when-You-pissed-
the-oceans stuff, where I was when You colored the nigger and
ignited Hell. I wasn't around when You elected the affinities. I
wasn't there when You shaped shit and fashioned cancer. Were
You there when I loved my neighbor as myself? When I never stole
or bore false witness? I don't say when I never killed but when I
never even raised a hand or pointed a finger in anger? Where were
You when I picked up checks and popped for drinks all round?
When I shelled out for charity and voted Yes on the bond issues?
So no Job job, no nature in tooth and claw, please. An explana-
tion!"
  "You stayed open on the Sabbath!" God thundered.
  "I what?"
  "You stayed open on the Sabbath. When you were just getting
started in your new location."
  "You mean because I opened my store on Sundays? That's why?"
  "You took My name in vain."
  "I took . . ."
  "That's right, that's right. You wanted an explanation, I'll give
you an explanation. You wanted I/Thou, I'll give you I/Thou. You

took It in vain. When your wife was nagging you because you
wanted to keep those widows on the payroll. She mocked you when
you said you were under an obligation and you said, 'Indirectly.
G-d damn it, yes. Indirectly.' 'Come on, sweetheart,' you said,
'you're awfully g-d-damn hard on me.' "

"That's why I'm in Hell? *That's* why?"

"And what about the time you coveted your neighbor's wife?
You had a big boner."

"I coveted no one, I was never unfaithful, I practically chased
that woman away."

"You didn't honor your father and mother."

Ellerbee was stunned. "I did. I *always* honored my father and
mother. I loved them very much. Just before I was killed we were
planning a trip to Phoenix to see them."

"Oh, *them*. They only adopted you. I'm talking about your natural parents."

"I was in a Home. I was an *in*fant!"

"Sure, sure," God said.

"And *that's* why? *That's* why?"

"You went dancing. You wore zippers in your pants and drove
automobiles. You smoked cigarettes and sold the demon rum."

"These are Your reasons? *This* is Your explanation?"

"You thought Heaven looked like a theme park!"

Ellerbee shook his head. Could this be happening? This pettiness
signaled across the universe? But anything could happen, everything could, and Ellerbee began again to pray. "Lord," he prayed,
"Heavenly Father, Dear God — maybe whatever is is right, and
maybe whatever is is right isn't, but I've been around now, walking
up and down in it, and *ev*erything is true. There is nothing that is
not true. The philosopher's best idea and the conventional wisdom,
too. So I am praying to You now in all humility, asking Your
forgiveness and to grant one prayer."

"What is it?" God asked.

Ellerbee heard a strange noise and looked around. The damned,
too, were on their knees — all the lost souls, all the gargoyles, all
the demons, kneeling in fire, capitulate through Hell like a great
ring of the conquered.

"What is it?" He asked.

"To kill us, to end Hell, to close the camp."

"Amen," said Ellerbee and all the damned in a single voice.

"Ha!" God scoffed and lighted up Hell's blazes like the surface of a star. Then God cursed and abused Ellerbee, and Ellerbee wouldn't have had it any other way. *He*'d damned him, no surrogate in Saint's clothing but the real McCoy Son of a Bitch God Whose memory Ellerbee would treasure and eternally repudiate forever, happily ever after, world without end.

But everything was true, even the conventional wisdom, perhaps especially the conventional wisdom — that which had made up Heaven like a shot in the dark and imagined into reality halos and Hell, gargoyles, gates of pearl, and the Pearl of Great Price, that had invented the horns of demons and cleft their feet and conceived angels riding clouds like cowboys on horseback, their harps at their sides like goofy guitars. Everything. Everything was. The self and what you did to protect it, learning the house odds, playing it safe — the honorable percentage baseball of existence.

Forever was a long time. Eternity was. He would seek out Ladlehaus, his murderer's accomplice, let bygones be bygones. They would get close to each other, close as family, closer. There was much to discuss in their fine new vocabularies. They would speak of Minneapolis, swap tales of the Twin Cities. They would talk of Ron, of others in the syndicate. And Ladlehaus had seen May, had caught her in what Ellerbee hoped was her grief on the Six O'Clock News. They would get close. And one day he would look for himself in Ladlehaus's glowing blisters.

JOHN GARDNER

Redemption

(FROM THE ATLANTIC)

ONE DAY in April — a clear, blue day when there were crocuses in bloom — Jack Hawthorne ran over and killed his brother, David. Even at the last moment he could have prevented his brother's death by slamming on the tractor brakes, easily in reach for all the shortness of his legs; but he was unable to think, or rather thought unclearly, and so watched it happen, as he would again and again watch it happen in his mind, with nearly undiminished intensity and clarity, all his life. The younger brother was riding, as both of them knew he should not have been, on the cultipacker, a two-ton implement lumbering behind the tractor, crushing new-ploughed ground. Jack was twelve, his brother, David, seven. The scream came not from David, who never got a word out, but from their five-year-old sister, who was riding on the fender of the tractor, looking back. When Jack turned to look, the huge iron wheels had reached his brother's pelvis. He kept driving, reacting as he would to a half-crushed farm animal, and imagining, in the same stab of thought, that perhaps his brother would survive. Blood poured from David's mouth.

Their father was nearly destroyed by it. Sometimes Jack would find him lying on the cow-barn floor, crying, unable to stand up. Dale Hawthorne, the father, was a sensitive, intelligent man, by nature a dreamer. It showed in old photographs, his smile coded, his eyes on the horizon. He loved all his children and would not consciously have been able to hate his son even if Jack had indeed been, as he thought himself, his brother's murderer. But he could not help sometimes seeming to blame his son, though consciously he blamed only his own unwisdom and — so far as his belief held firm — God. Dale Hawthorne's mind swung violently at this time, reversing itself almost hour by hour, from desperate faith to the most ferocious, black-hearted atheism. Every sickly calf, every sow that ate her litter, was a new, sure proof that the religion he'd followed all his life was a lie. Yet skeletons were orderly, as were, he thought, the stars. He was unable to decide, one moment full of rage at God's injustice, the next moment wracked by doubt of His existence.

Though he was not ordinarily a man who smoked, he would sometimes sit up all night now, or move restlessly, hurriedly, from room to room, chain-smoking Lucky Strikes. Or he would ride away on his huge, darkly thundering Harley-Davidson 80, trying to forget, morbidly dwelling on what he'd meant to put behind him — how David had once laughed, cake in his fists; how he'd once patched a chair with precocious skill — or Dale Hawthorne would think, for the hundredth time, about suicide, hunting in mixed fear and anger for some reason not to miss the next turn, fly off to the right of the next iron bridge onto the moonlit gray rocks and black water below — discovering, invariably, no reason but the damage his suicide would do to his wife and the children remaining.

Sometimes he would forget for a while by abandoning reason and responsibility for love affairs. Jack's father was at this time still young, still handsome, well-known for the poetry he recited at local churches or for English classes or meetings of the Grange — recited, to loud applause (he had poems of all kinds, both serious and comic), for thrashing crews, old men at the V.A. Hospital, even the tough, flint-eyed orphans at the Children's Home. He was a celebrity, in fact, as much Romantic poet-hero as his time and western New York State could afford — and beyond all that, he was now so full of pain and unassuageable guilt that women's hearts flew to him unbidden. He became, with all his soul and without cynical intent — though abandoning all law, or what he'd once thought law — a hunter of women, trading off his sorrow for the sorrows of wearied, unfulfilled country wives. At times he would be gone from the farm for days, abandoning the work to Jack and whoever was available to help — some neighbor or older cousin or one of Jack's uncles. No one complained, at least not openly. A stranger might have condemned him, but no one in the family did, certainly not Jack, not even Jack's mother, though her

sorrow was increased. Dale Hawthorne had always been, before
the accident, a faithful man, one of the most fair-minded, genial
farmers in the county. No one asked that, changed as he was, he
do more, for the moment, than survive.

As for Jack's mother, though she'd been, before the accident, a
cheerful woman — one who laughed often and loved telling stories, sometimes sang anthems in bandanna and blackface before
her husband recited poems — she cried now, nights, and did only
as much as she had strength to do — so sapped by grief that she
could barely move her arms. She comforted Jack and his sister,
Phoebe — herself as well — by embracing them ferociously whenever new waves of guilt swept in, by constant reassurance and
extravagant praise, frequent mention of how proud some relative
would be — once, for instance, over a drawing of his sister's, "Oh,
Phoebe, if only your great-aunt Lucy could see this!" Great-aunt
Lucy had been famous, among the family and friends, for her
paintings of families of lions. And Jack's mother forced on his
sister and himself comforts more permanent: piano and, for Jack,
French horn lessons, school and church activities, above all an
endless, exhausting ritual of chores. Because she had, at thirty-
four, considerable strength of character — except that, these days,
she was always eating — and because, also, she was a woman of
strong religious faith, a woman who, in her years of church work
and teaching at the high school, had made scores of close, for the
most part equally religious, friends, with whom she regularly corresponded, her letters, then theirs, half filling the mailbox at the
foot of the hill and cluttering every table, desk, and niche in the
large old house — friends who now frequently visited or phoned
— she was able to move step by step past disaster and in the end
keep her family from wreck. She said very little to her children
about her troubles. In fact, except for the crying behind her closed
door, she kept her feelings strictly secret.

But for all his mother and her friends could do for him — for
all his father's older brothers could do, or, when he was there, his
father himself — the damage to young Jack Hawthorne took a
long while healing. Working the farm, ploughing, cultipacking,
disking, dragging, he had plenty of time to think — plenty of time
for the accident to replay, with the solidity of real time repeated, in
his mind, his whole body flinching from the image as it came, his

voice leaping up independent of him, as if a shout could perhaps drive the memory back into its cave. Maneuvering the tractor over sloping, rocky fields, dust whorling out like smoke behind him or, when he turned into the wind, falling like soot until his skin was black and his hair as thick and stiff as old clothes in an attic — the circle of foothills every day turning greener, the late spring wind flowing endless and sweet with the smell of coming rain — he had all the time in the world to cry and swear bitterly at himself, standing up to drive, as his father often did, Jack's sore hands clamped tight to the steering wheel, his shoes unsteady on the bucking axlebeam — for stones lay everywhere, yellowed in the sunlight, a field of misshapen skulls. He'd never loved his brother, he raged out loud, never loved anyone as well as he should have. He was incapable of love, he told himself, striking the steering wheel. He was inherently bad, a spiritual defective. He was evil.

So he raged and grew increasingly ashamed of his raging, reminded by the lengthening shadows across the field of the theatricality in all he did, his most terrible sorrow mere sorrow on a stage, the very thunderclaps above — dark blue, rushing sky, birds crazily wheeling — mere opera set, proper lighting for his rant. At once he would hush himself, lower his rear end to the tractor seat, lock every muscle to the stillness of a statue, and drive on, solitary, blinded by tears; yet even now it was theater, not life — mere ghastly posturing, as in that story of his father's, how Lord Byron once tried to get Shelley's skull to make a drinking cup. Tears no longer came, though the storm went on building. Jack rode on, alone with the indifferent, murderous machinery in the widening ten-acre field.

When the storm at last hit, he'd be driven up the lane like a dog in flight, lashed by gusty rain, chased across the tracks to the tractor shed and from there to the kitchen, steamy, full of food smells from his mother's work and Phoebe's, sometimes the work of some two or three friends who'd stopped by to look in on the family. Jack kept aloof, repelled by their bright, melodious chatter and absentminded humming, indignant at their pretense that all was well. "My, how you've grown!" the old friend or fellow teacher from the high school would say, and to his mother, "My, what big *hands* he has, Betty!" He would glare at his little sister, Phoebe, his sole ally, already half traitor — she would bite her lips, squinting, concentrating harder on the mixing bowl and beaters; she was forever making cakes — and he would retreat as soon as possible to the evening chores.

He had always told himself stories to pass the time when driving the tractor, endlessly looping back and forth, around and around, fitting the land for spring planting. He told them to himself aloud, taking all parts in the dialogue, gesturing, making faces, abandoning dignity, here where no one could see or overhear him, half a mile from the nearest house. Once all his stories had been of sexual conquest or of heroic battle with escaped convicts from the Attica Prison or kidnappers who, unbeknownst to anyone, had built a small shack where they kept their captives, female and beautiful, in the lush, swampy woods beside the field. Now, after the accident, his subject matter changed. His fantasies came to be all of self-sacrifice, pitiful stories in which he redeemed his life by throwing it away to save others more worthwhile. To friends and officials of his fantasy, especially to heroines — a girl named Margaret, at school, or his cousin Linda — he would confess his worthlessness at painful length, naming all his faults, granting himself no quarter. For a time this helped, but the lie was too obvious, the manipulation of shame to buy love, and in the end despair bled all color from his fantasies. The foulness of his nature became clearer and clearer in his mind until, like his father, he began to toy — dully but in morbid earnest now — with the idea of suicide. His chest would fill with anguish, as if he were dreaming some nightmare wide awake, or bleeding internally, and his arms and legs would grow shaky with weakness, until he had to stop and get down from the tractor and sit for a few minutes, his eyes fixed on some comforting object, for instance a dark, smooth stone.

Even from his father and his father's brothers, who sometimes helped with chores, he kept aloof. His father and uncles were not talkative men. Except for his father's comic poems, they never told jokes, though they liked hearing them; and because they had lived there all their lives and knew every soul in the county by name, nothing much surprised them or, if it did, roused them to mention it. Their wives might gossip, filling the big kitchen with their pealing laughter or righteous indignation, but the men for the most part merely smiled or compressed their lips and shook their heads. At the G.L.F. feedstore, occasionally, eating an ice cream while they waited for their grist, they would speak of the weather or the Democrats; but in the barn, except for "Jackie, shift that milker, will you?" or "You can carry this up to the milk house now," they said nothing. They were all tall, square men with deeply cleft chins and creases on their foreheads and muscular jowls; all Presbyterians, sometime deacons, sometime elders; and they were all gentle-hearted, decent men who looked lost in thought, especially Jack's father, though on occasion they'd abruptly frown or mutter, or speak a few words to a cow, or a cat, or a swallow. It was natural that Jack, working with such men, should keep to himself, throwing down ensilage from the pitch-dark, sweet-ripe crater of the silo or hay bales from the mow, dumping oats in front of the cows' noses, or — taking the long-handled, blunt wooden scraper from the whitewashed wall — pushing manure into the gutters.

He felt more community with the cows than with his uncles or, when he was there, his father. Stretched out flat between the two rows of stanchions, waiting for the cows to be finished with their silage so he could drive them out to pasture, he would listen to their chewing in the dark, close barn, a sound as soothing, as infinitely restful, as waves along a shore, and would feel their surprisingly warm, scented breath, their bovine quiet, and for a while would find that his anxiety had left him. With the cows, the barn cats, the half-sleeping dog, he could forget and feel at home, feel that life was pleasant. He felt the same when walking up the long, fenced lane at the first light of sunrise — his shoes and pants legs sopping wet with dew, his ears full of birdcalls — going to bring in the herd from the upper pasture. Sometimes on the way he would step off the deep, crooked cow path to pick cherries or red raspberries, brighter than jewels in the morning light. They were sweeter then than at any other time, and as he approached, clouds of sparrows would explode into flight from the branches, whirring off to safety. The whole countryside was sweet, early in the morning — newly cultivated corn to his left, to his right, alfalfa and, beyond that, wheat. He felt at one with it all. It was what life ought to be, what he'd once believed it was.

But he could not make such feelings last. *No,* he thought bitterly on one such morning, throwing stones at the dull, indifferent cows, driving them down the lane. However he might hate himself and all his race, a cow was no better, or a field of wheat. Time and again he'd been driven half crazy, angry enough to kill, by the stupidity of cows when they'd pushed through a fence and — for all his shouting, for all the indignant barking of the dog — they could no longer locate the gap they themselves had made. And no better to be grain, smashed flat by the first rainy wind. So, fists clenched, he raged inside his mind, grinding his teeth to drive out thought, at war with the universe. He remembered his father, erect, eyes flashing, speaking Mark Antony's angry condemnation from the stage at the Grange. His father had seemed to him, that night, a creature set apart. His extended arm, pointing, was the terrible warning of a god. And now, from nowhere, the black memory of his brother's death rushed over him again, mindless and inexorable as a wind or wave, the huge cultipacker lifting — only an inch or so — as it climbed toward the shoulders, then sank on the cheek, flattening the skull — and he heard, more real than the morning, his sister's scream.

One day in August, a year and a half after the accident, they were combining oats — Jack and two neighbors and two of his cousins — when Phoebe came out, as she did every day, to bring lunch to those who worked in the field. Their father had been gone, this time, for nearly three weeks, and since he'd left at the height of the harvest season, no one was sure he would return, though as usual they kept silent about it. Jack sat alone in the shade of an elm, apart from the others. It was a habit they'd come to accept as they accepted, so far as he knew, his father's ways. Phoebe brought the basket from the shade where the others had settled to the shade here on Jack's side, farther from the bright, stubbled field.

"It's chicken," she said, and smiled, kneeling.

The basket was nearly as large as she was — Phoebe was seven — but she seemed to see nothing unreasonable in her having to lug it up the hill from the house. Her face was flushed, and drops of perspiration stood out along her hairline, but her smile was not only uncomplaining but positively cheerful. The trip to the field was an escape from housework, he understood; even so, her happiness offended him.

"Chicken," he said, and looked down glumly at his hard, tanned arms black with oat-dust. Phoebe smiled on, her mind far away, as it seemed to him, and like a child playing house she took a dish towel from the basket, spread it on the grass, then set out waxpaper packages of chicken, rolls, celery, and salt, and finally a small plastic thermos, army green.

She looked up at him now. "I brought you a thermos all for yourself because you always sit alone."

He softened a little without meaning to. "Thanks," he said.

She looked down again, and for all his self-absorption he was touched, noticing that she bowed her head in the way a much older girl might do, troubled by thought, though her not quite clean, dimpled hands were a child's. He saw that there was something she wanted to say and, to forestall it, brushed flying ants from the top of the thermos, unscrewed the cap, and poured himself iced tea. When he drank, the tea was so cold it brought a momentary pain to his forehead and made him aware once more of the grating chaff under his collar, blackening all his exposed skin, gritty around his eyes — aware, too, of the breezeless, insect-filled heat beyond the shade of the elm. Behind him, just at the rim of his hearing, one of the neighbors laughed at some remark from the younger of his cousins. Jack drained the cup, brooding on his aching muscles. Even in the shade his body felt baked dry.

"Jack," his sister said, "did you want to say grace?"

"Not really," he said, and glanced at her.

He saw that she was looking at his face in alarm, her mouth slightly opened, eyes wide, growing wider, and though he didn't know why, his heart gave a jump. "I already said it," he mumbled. "Just not out loud."

"Oh," she said, then smiled.

When everyone had finished eating she put the empty papers, the jug, and the smaller thermos in the basket, grinned at them all and said goodbye — whatever had bothered her was forgotten as soon as that — and, leaning far over, balancing the lightened but still awkward basket, started across the stubble for the house. As he cranked the tractor she turned around to look back at them and wave. He nodded and, as if embarrassed, touched his straw hat.

Not till he was doing the chores that night did he grasp what her look of alarm had meant. If he wouldn't say grace, then perhaps there was no heaven. Their father would never get well, and David was dead. He squatted, drained of all strength again, staring at the hoof of the cow he'd been stripping, preparing her for the milker, and thought of his absent father. He saw the motorcycle roaring down a twisting mountain road, the clatter of the engine ringing like harsh music against shale. If what he felt was hatred, it was a terrible, desperate envy, too: his father all alone, uncompromised, violent, cut off as if by centuries from the warmth, chatter, and smells of the kitchen, the dimness of stained glass where he, Jack, sat every Sunday between his mother and sister, looking toward the pulpit where in the old days his father had sometimes read the lesson, soft-voiced but aloof from the timid-eyed flock, Christ's sheep.

Something blocked the light coming in through the cow-barn window from the west, and he turned his head, glancing up.

"You all right there, Jackie?" his uncle Walt said, bent forward, nearsightedly peering across the gutter.

He nodded and quickly wiped his wrist across his cheeks. He moved his hands once more to the cow's warm teats.

A few nights later, when he went in from chores, the door between the kitchen and living room was closed, and the house was unnaturally quiet. He stood a moment listening, still holding the milk pail, absently fitting the heel of one boot into the bootjack and tugging until the boot slipped off. He pried off the other, then walked to the icebox in his stocking feet, opened the door, carried the pitcher to the table, and filled it from the pail. When he'd slid the pitcher into the icebox again and closed the door, he went without a sound, though not meaning to be stealthy, toward the living room. Now, beyond the closed door, he heard voices, his sister and mother, then one of his aunts. He pushed the door open and looked in, about to speak.

Though the room was dim, no light but the small one among the pictures on the piano, he saw his father at once, kneeling by the davenport with his face on his mother's lap. Phoebe was on the davenport beside their mother, hugging her and him, Phoebe's cheeks stained, like her mother's, with tears. Around them, as if reverently drawn back, Uncle Walt, Aunt Ruth, and their two children sat watching, leaning forward with shining eyes. His father's head, bald down the center, glowed, and he had his glasses off.

"Jackie," his aunt called sharply, "come in. It's all over. Your dad's come home."

He would have fled, but his knees had no strength in them and his chest was wild, churning as if with terror. He clung to the doorknob, grotesquely smiling — so he saw himself. His father raised his head. "Jackie," he said, and was unable to say more, all at once sobbing like a baby.

"Hi, Dad," he brought out, and somehow managed to go to him and get down on his knees beside him and put his arm around his back. He felt dizzy now, nauseated, and he was crying like his father. "I hate you," he whispered too softly for any of them to hear.

His father stayed. He worked long days, in control once more, though occasionally he smoked, pacing in his room nights, or rode off on his motorcycle for an hour or two, and seldom smiled. Nevertheless, in a month he was again reciting poetry for schools and churches and the Grange, and sometimes reading Scripture from the pulpit Sunday mornings. Jack, sitting rigid, hands over his face, was bitterly ashamed of those poems and recitations from the Bible. His father's eyes no longer flashed, he no longer had the style of an actor. Even his gestures were submissive, as pliant as the grass. Though tears ran down Jack Hawthorne's face — no one would deny that his father was still effective, reciting carefully, lest his voice should break, "Tomorrow's Bridge" and "This Too Will Pass" — Jack scorned the poems' opinions, scorned the way his father spoke directly to each listener, as if each were some new woman, his father some mere suffering sheep among sheep, and scorned the way Phoebe and his mother looked on smiling, furtively weeping, heads tipped. Sometimes his father would recite a poem that Jack himself had written, in the days when he'd tried to write poetry, a comic limerick or some maudlin piece about a boy on a hill. Though it was meant as a compliment, Jack's heart would swell with rage; yet he kept silent, more private than before. At night he'd go out to the cavernous haymow or up into the orchard and practice his French horn. One of these days, he told himself, they'd awaken and find him gone.

He used the horn more and more now to escape their herding warmth. Those around him were conscious enough of what was happening — his parents and Phoebe, his uncles, aunts, and cousins, his mother's many friends. But there was nothing they could do. "That horn's his whole world," his mother often said, smiling but clasping her hands together. Soon he was playing third horn with the Batavia Civic Orchestra, though he refused to play in church or when company came. He began to ride the Bluebus to

Rochester, Saturdays, to take lessons from Arcady Yegudkin, "the
General," at the Eastman School of Music.

Yegudkin was seventy. He'd played principal horn in the orchestra of Czar Nikolai and at the time of the Revolution had escaped,
with his wife, in a dramatic way. At the time of their purge of
Kerenskyites, the Bolsheviks had loaded Yegudkin and his wife,
along with hundreds more, onto railroad flatcars, reportedly to
carry them to Siberia. In a desolate place, machine guns opened
fire on the people on the flatcars, then soldiers pushed the bodies
into a ravine, and the train moved on. The soldiers were not careful to see that everyone was dead. Perhaps they did not relish their
work; in any case, they must have believed that, in a place so remote, a wounded survivor would have no chance against wolves
and cold weather. The General and his wife were among the few
who lived, he virtually unmarked, she horribly crippled. Local
peasants nursed the few survivors back to health, and in time the
Yegudkins escaped to Europe. There Yegudkin played horn with
all the great orchestras and received such praise — so he claimed,
spreading out his clippings — as no other master of French horn
had received, in all history. He would beam as he said it, his Tartar
eyes flashing, and his smile was like a thrown-down gauntlet.

He was a big-bellied, solidly muscular man, hard as a boulder for
all his age. His hair and moustache were as black as coal except for
touches of silver, especially where it grew, with majestic indifference to ordinary taste, from his cavernous nostrils and large,
dusty-looking ears. The sides of his moustache were carefully
curled, in the fashion once favored by Russian dandies, and he was
one of the last men in Rochester, New York, to wear spats. He
wore formal black suits, a huge black overcoat, and a black fedora.
His wife, who came with him and sat on the long maple bench
outside his door, never reading or knitting or doing anything at all
except that sometimes she would speak unintelligibly to a student
— Yegudkin's wife, shriveled and twisted, watched him as if wor-
shipfully, hanging on his words. She looked at least twice the old
man's age. Her hair was snow white and she wore lumpy black
shoes and long black shapeless dresses. The two of them would
come, every Saturday morning, down the long marble hallway of
the second floor of Killburn Hall, the General erect and imperato-
rial, like some sharp-eyed old Slavonic king, moving slowly, waiting
for the old woman who crept beside him, gray claws on his coat

sleeve, and seeing Jack Hawthorne seated on the bench, his books
and French horn in its tattered black case on the floor beside him,
the General would extend his left arm and boom, "Goot mworn-
ing!"

Jack, rising, would say, "Morning, sir."

"You have met my wife?" the old man would say then, bowing
and taking the cigar from his mouth. He asked it each Saturday.

"Yes, sir. How do you do."

The old man was too deaf to play in orchestras anymore. "What's
the difference?" he said. "Every symphony in America, they got
Yegudkins. I have teach them all. Who teach you this? *The General!*" He would smile, chin lifted, triumphant, and salute the ceiling.

He would sit in the chair beside Jack's and would sing, with
violent gestures and a great upward leap of the belly to knock out
the high B's and C's — *Tee! Tee!* — as Jack read through Kop-
prasch, Gallay, and Kling, and when it was time to give Jack's lip a
rest, the General would speak earnestly, with the same energy he
put into his singing, of the United States and his beloved Russia
that he would nevermore see. The world was at the time filled with
Russophobes. Yegudkin, whenever he read a paper, would be so
enraged he could barely contain himself. "In all my age," he often
said, furiously gesturing with his black cigar, "if the Russians would
come to this country of America, I would take up a rifle and shot
at them — *boof!* But the newspapers telling you lies, all lies! You
think they dumb fools, these Russians? You think they are big, fat
bush-overs?" He spoke of mile-long parades of weaponry, spoke of
Russian cunning, spoke with great scorn, a sudden booming laugh,
of Napoleon. Jack agreed with a nod to whatever the General said.
Nevertheless, the old man roared on, taking great pleasure in his
rage, it seemed, sometimes talking like a rabid communist, sometimes like a fascist, sometimes like a citizen helplessly caught between mindless, grinding forces, vast, idiot herds. The truth was,
he hated both Russians and Americans about equally, cared only
for music, his students and, possibly, his wife. In his pockets, in
scorn of the opinions of fools, he carried condoms, dirty pictures,
and grimy, wadded-up dollar bills.

One day a new horn he'd ordered from Germany, an Alexander,
arrived at his office — a horn he'd gotten for a graduate student.
The old man unwrapped and assembled it, the graduate student

looking on — a shy young man, blond, in a limp gray sweater —
and the glint in the General's eye was like madness or at any rate
lust, perhaps gluttony. When the horn was ready he went to the
desk where he kept his clippings, his tools for the cleaning and
repair of French horns, his cigars, photographs, and medals from
the czar, and pulled open a wide, shallow drawer. It contained
perhaps a hundred mouthpieces, of all sizes and materials, from
raw brass to Lucite, silver, and gold, from the shallowest possible
cup to the deepest. He selected one, fitted it into the horn, pressed
the rim of the bell into the right side of his large belly — the horn
seemed now as much a part of him as his arm or leg — clicked the
shining keys to get the feel of them, then played. In that large,
cork-lined room, it was as if, suddenly, a creature from some other
universe had appeared, some realm where feelings become birds
and dark sky, and spirit is more solid than stone. The sound was
not so much loud as large, too large for a hundred French horns,
it seemed. He began to play now not single notes but, to Jack's
astonishment, chords — two notes at a time, then three. He began
to play runs. As if charged with life independent of the man, the
horn sound fluttered and flew crazily, like an enormous trapped
hawk hunting frantically for escape. It flew to the bottom of the
lower register, the foundation concert F, and crashed below it, and
on down and down, as if the horn in Yegudkin's hands had no
bottom, then suddenly changed its mind and flew upward in a
split-second run to the horn's top E, dropped back to the middle
and then ran once more, more fiercely at the E, and this time burst
through it and fluttered, manic, in the trumpet range, then lightly
dropped back into its own home range and, abruptly, in the middle
of a note, stopped. The room still rang, shimmered like a vision.

"Good horn," said Yegudkin, and held the horn toward the
graduate student, who sat, hands clamped on his knees, as if in a
daze.

Jack Hawthorne stared at the instrument suspended in space
and at his teacher's hairy hands. Before stopping to think, he said,
"You think I'll ever play like that?"

Yegudkin laughed loudly, his black eyes widening, and it seemed
that he grew larger, beatific and demonic at once, like the music;
overwhelming. "Play like *me?*" he exclaimed.

Jack blinked, startled by the bluntness of the thing, the terrible
lack of malice, and the truth of it. His face tingled and his legs went

weak, as if the life were rushing out of them. He longed to be away from there, far away, safe. Perhaps Yegudkin sensed it. He turned gruff, sending away the graduate student, then finishing up the lesson. He said nothing, today, of the stupidity of mankind. When the lesson was over he saw Jack to the door and bid him goodbye with a brief half-smile that was perhaps not for Jack at all but for the creature on the bench. "Next Saturday?" he said, as if there might be some doubt.

Jack nodded, blushing.

At the door opening on the street he began to breathe more easily, though he was weeping. He set down the horn case to brush away his tears. The sidewalk was crowded — dazed-looking Saturday-morning shoppers herding along irritably, meekly, through painfully bright light. Again he brushed tears away. He'd be late for his bus. Then the crowd opened for him and, with the horn cradled under his right arm, his music under his left, he plunged in, starting home.

LYNNE SHARON SCHWARTZ

Rough Strife

(FROM THE ONTARIO REVIEW)

> Now let us sport us while we may;
> And now, like am'rous birds of prey . . .
> . . . tear our pleasures with rough strife
> Thorough the iron gates of life.
> — ANDREW MARVELL

CAROLINE AND IVAN finally had a child. Conception stunned them; they didn't think, by now, that it could happen. For years they had tried and failed, till it seemed that a special barren destiny was preordained. Meanwhile, in the wide spaces of childlessness, they had created activity: their work flourished. Ivan, happy and moderately powerful in a large foundation, helped decide how to distribute money for artistic and social projects. Caroline taught mathematics at a small suburban university. Being a mathematician, she found, conferred a painful private wisdom on her efforts to conceive. In her brain, as Ivan exploded within her, she would involuntarily calculate probabilities; millions of blind sperm and one reluctant egg clustered before her eyes in swiftly transmuting geometric patterns. She lost her grasp of pleasure, forgot what it could feel like without a goal. She had no idea what Ivan might be thinking about, scattered seed money, maybe. Their passion became courteous and automatic until, by attrition, for months they didn't make love — it was too awkward.

One September Sunday morning she was in the shower, watching, through a crack in the curtain, Ivan naked at the washstand. He was shaving, his jaw tilted at an innocently self-satisfied angle.

He wasn't aware of being watched, so that a secret quality, an essence of Ivan, exuded in great waves. Caroline could almost see it, a cloudy aura. He stroked his jaw vainly with intense concentration, a self-absorption so contagious that she needed, suddenly, to possess it with him. She stepped out of the shower.

"Ivan."

He turned abruptly, surprised, perhaps even annoyed at the interruption.

"Let's not have a baby anymore. Let's just . . . come on." When she placed her wet hand on his back he lifted her easily off her feet with his right arm, the razor still poised in his other, outstretched hand.

"Come on," she insisted. She opened the door and a draft blew into the small steamy room. She pulled him by the hand toward the bedroom.

Ivan grinned. "You're soaking wet."

"Wet, dry, what's the difference?" It was hard to speak. She began to run, to tease him; he caught her and tossed her onto their disheveled bed and dug his teeth so deep into her shoulder that she thought she would bleed.

Then with disinterest, taken up only in this fresh rushing need for him, weeks later Caroline conceived. Afterwards she liked to say that she had known the moment it happened. It felt different, she told him, like a pin pricking a balloon, but without the shattering noise, without the quick collapse. "Oh, come on," said Ivan. "That's impossible."

But she was a mathematician, after all, and dealt with infinitesimal precise abstractions, and she did know how it had happened. The baby was conceived in strife, one early October night, Indian summer. All day the sun glowed hot and low in the sky, settling an amber torpor on people and things, and the night was the same, only now a dark hot heaviness sunk slowly down. The scent of the still-blooming honeysuckle rose to their bedroom window. Just as she was bending over to kiss him, heavy and quivering with heat like the night, he teased her about something, about a mole on her leg, and in reply she punched him lightly on the shoulder. He grabbed her wrists, and when she began kicking, pinned her feet down with his own. In an instant Ivan lay stretched out on her back like a blanket, smothering her, while she struggled beneath, writhing to escape. It was a silent, sweaty struggle, interrupted with outbursts of wild laughter, shrieks and gasping breaths. She tried biting but, laughing loudly, he evaded her, and she tried scratching the fists that held her down, but she couldn't reach. All her desire was transformed into physical effort, but he was too strong for her. He wanted her to say she gave up, but she refused, and since he wouldn't loosen his grip they lay locked and panting in their static embrace for some time.

"You win," she said at last, but as he rolled off she sneakily jabbed him in the ribs with her elbow.

"Aha!" Ivan shouted, and was ready to begin again, but she quickly distracted him. Once the wrestling was at an end, though, Caroline found her passion dissipated, and her pleasure tinged with resentment. After they made love forcefully, when they were covered with sweat, dripping on each other, she said, "Still, you don't play fair."

"I don't play fair! Look who's talking. Do you want me to give you a handicap?"

"No."

"So?"

"It's not fair, that's all."

Ivan laughed gloatingly and curled up in her arms. She smiled in the dark.

That was the night the baby was conceived, not in high passion but rough strife.

She lay on the table in the doctor's office weeks later. The doctor, whom she had known for a long time, habitually kept up a running conversation while he probed. Today, fretting over his weight problem, he outlined his plans for a new diet. Tensely she watched him, framed and centered by her raised knees, which were still bronzed from summer sun. His other hand was pressing on her stomach. Caroline was nauseated with fear and trembling, afraid of the verdict. It was taking so long, perhaps it was a tumor.

"I'm cutting out all starches," he said. "I've really let myself go lately."

"Good idea." Then she gasped in pain. A final, sickening thrust, and he was out. Relief, and a sore gap where he had been. In a moment, she knew, she would be retching violently.

"Well?"

"Well, Caroline, you hit the jackpot this time."

She felt a smile, a stupid, puppet smile, spread over her face. In the tiny bathroom where she threw up, she saw in the mirror the silly smile looming over her ashen face like a dancer's glowing grimace of labored joy. She smiled through the rest of the visit, through his advice about milk, weight, travel and rest, smiled at herself in the window of the bus, and at her moving image in the fenders of parked cars as she walked home.

Ivan, incredulous over the telephone, came home beaming stupidly just like Caroline, and brought a bottle of champagne. After dinner they drank it and made love.

"Do you think it's all right to do this?" he asked.

"Oh, Ivan, honestly. It's microscopic."

He was in one of his whimsical moods and made terrible jokes that she laughed at with easy indulgence. He said he was going to pay the baby a visit and asked if she had any messages she wanted delivered. He unlocked from her embrace, moved down her body and said he was going to have a look for himself. Clowning, he put his ear between her legs to listen. Whatever amusement she felt soon ebbed away into irritation. She had never thought Ivan would be a doting parent — he was so preoccupied with himself. Finally he stopped his antics as she clasped her arms around him and whispered, "Ivan, you are really too much." He became unusually gentle. Tamed, and she didn't like it, hoped he wouldn't continue that way for months. Pleasure lapped over her with a mild, lackadaisical bitterness, and then when she could be articulate once more she explained patiently, "Ivan, you know, it really is all right. I mean, it's a natural process."

"Well I didn't want to hurt you."

"I'm not sick."

Then, as though her body were admonishing that cool confidence, she did get sick. There were mornings when she awoke with such paralyzing nausea that she had to ask Ivan to bring her a hard roll from the kitchen before she could stir from bed. To move from her awakening position seemed a tremendous risk, as if she might spill out. She rarely threw up — the nausea resembled violent hunger. Something wanted to be filled, not expelled, a perilous vacuum occupying her insides. The crucial act was getting the first few mouthfuls down. Then the solidity and denseness of the hard unbuttered roll stabilized her, like a heavy weight thrown down to anchor a tottering ship. Her head ached. On the mornings when she had no classes she would wander around the house till almost noon clutching the partly eaten roll in her hand like a talisman.

Finishing one roll, she quickly went to the breadbox for another; she bought them regularly at the bakery a half-dozen at a time. With enough roll inside her she could sometimes manage a half-cup of tea, but liquids were risky. They sloshed around inside and made her envision the baby sloshing around too, in its cloudy fluid. By early afternoon she would feel fine. The baby, she imagined, claimed her for the night and was reluctant to give up its hold in the morning: they vied till she conquered. She was willing to yield her sleeping hours to the baby, her dreams even, if necessary, but she wanted the daylight for herself.

The mornings that she taught were agony. Ivan would wake her up early, bring her a roll, and gently prod her out of bed.

"I simply cannot do it," she would say, placing her legs cautiously over the side of the bed.

"Sure you can. Now get up."

"I'll die if I get up."

"You have no choice. You have a job." He was freshly showered and dressed, and his neatness irritated her. He had nothing more to do — the discomfort was all hers. She rose to her feet and swayed.

Ivan looked alarmed. "Do you want me to call and tell them you can't make it?"

"No, no." That frightened her. She needed to hold on to the job, to defend herself against the growing baby. Once she walked into the classroom she would be fine. A Mondrian print hung on the back wall — she could look at that, and it would steady her. With waves of nausea rolling in her chest, she stumbled into the bathroom.

She liked him to wait until she was out of the shower before he left for work, because she anticipated fainting under the impact of the water. Often at the end she forced herself to stand under an ice cold flow, leaning her head way back and letting her short fair hair drip down behind her. Though it was torture, when she emerged she felt more alive.

After the shower had been off a while Ivan would come and open the bathroom door. "Are you O.K. now, Caroline? I've got to go." It made her feel like a child. She would be wrapped in a towel with her hair dripping on the mat, brushing her teeth or rubbing cream into her face. "Yes, thanks for waiting. I guess this'll end soon. They say it's only the first few months."

He kissed her lips, her bare damp shoulder, gave a parting

squeeze to her toweled behind, and was gone. She watched him walk down the hall. Ivan was very large. She had always been drawn and aroused by his largeness, by the huge bones and the taut legs that felt as though he had steel rods inside. But now she watched with some trepidation, hoping Ivan wouldn't have a large, inflexible baby.

Very slowly she would put on clothes. Selecting each article seemed a much more demanding task than ever before. Seeing how slow she had become, she allowed herself over an hour, keeping her hard roll nearby as she dressed and prepared her face. All the while, through the stages of dressing, she evaluated her body closely in the full-length mirror, first naked, then in bra and underpants, then with shoes added, and finally with a dress. She was looking for signs, but the baby was invisible. Nothing had changed yet. She was still as she had always been, not quite slim yet somehow appearing small, almost delicate. She used to pride herself on strength. When they moved in she had worked as hard as Ivan, lugging furniture and lifting heavy cartons. He was impressed. Now, of course, she could no longer do that — it took all her strength to move her own weight.

With the profound sensuous narcissism of women past first youth, she admired her still-narrow waist and full breasts. She was especially fond of her shoulders and prominent collarbone, which had a fragile, inviting look. That would all be gone soon, of course, gone soft. Curious about how she would alter, she scanned her face for the pregnant look she knew well from the faces of friends. It was far less a tangible change than a look of transparent vulnerability that took over the face: nearly a pleading look, a beg for help like a message from a powerless invaded country to the rest of the world. Caroline did not see it on her face yet.

From the tenth to the fourteenth week of her pregnancy she slept, with brief intervals of lucidity when she taught her classes. It was a strange dreamy time. The passionate nausea faded, but the lure of the bed was irresistible. In the middle of the day, even, she could pass by the bedroom, glimpse the waiting bed and be overcome by the soft heavy desire to lie down. She fell into a stupor immediately and did not dream. She forgot what it was like to awaken with energy and move through an entire day without lying down once. She forgot the feeling of eyes opened wide without effort. She would have liked to hide this strange, shameful perversity from Ivan, but that was impossible. Ivan kept wanting to go

to the movies. Clearly, he was bored with her. Maybe, she imagined, staring up at the bedroom ceiling through slitted eyes, he
would become so bored he would abandon her and the baby and
she would not be able to support the house alone and she and the
baby would end up on the streets in rags, begging. She smiled.
That was highly unlikely. Ivan would not be the same Ivan without
her.

"You go on, Ivan. I just can't."

Once he said, "I thought I might ask Ruth Forbes to go with me
to see the Charlie Chaplin in town. I know she likes him. Would
that bother you?"

She was half-asleep, slowly eating a large apple in bed and
watching *Medical Center* on television, but she roused herself to
answer. "No, of course not." Ruth Forbes was a divorced woman
who lived down the block, a casual friend and not Ivan's type
at all, too large, loud and depressed. Caroline didn't care if he
wanted her company. She didn't care if he held her hand on his
knee in the movies as he liked to do, or even if, improbably, he
made love to her afterwards in her sloppy house crawling with
children. She didn't care about anything except staying nestled in
bed.

She made love with him sometimes, in a slow way. She felt no
specific desire but didn't want to deny him, she loved him so. Or
had, she thought vaguely, when she was alive and strong. Besides,
she knew she could sleep right after. Usually there would be a
moment when she came alive despite herself, when the reality of
his body would strike her all at once with a wistful throb of lust,
but mostly she was too tired to see it through, to leap towards it, so
she let it subside, merely nodding at it gratefully as a sign of
dormant life. She felt sorry for Ivan, but helpless.

Once to her great shame, she fell asleep while he was inside her.
He woke her with a pat on her cheek, actually, she realized from
the faint sting, a gesture more like a slap than a pat. "Caroline, for
Christ's sake, you're sleeping."

"No, no, I'm sorry. I wasn't really sleeping. Oh, Ivan, it's nothing.
This will end." She wondered, though.

Moments later she felt his hands on her thighs. His lips were
brooding on her stomach, edging, with expertise, lower and lower
down. He was murmuring something she couldn't catch. She felt
an ache, an irritation. Of course he meant well, Ivan always did.

Wryly, she appreciated his intentions. But she couldn't bear that excitement now.

"Please," she said. "Please don't do that."

He was terribly hurt. He said nothing, but leaped away violently and pulled all the blankets around him. She was contrite, shed a few private tears and fell instantly into a dreamless dark.

He wanted to go to a New Year's Eve party some close friends were giving, and naturally he wanted her to come with him. Caroline vowed to herself she would do this for him because she had been giving so little for so long. She planned to get dressed and look very beautiful, as she could still look when she took plenty of time and tried hard enough; she would not drink very much — it was sleep-inducing — and she would not be the one to suggest going home. After sleeping through the day in preparation, she washed her hair, using something she found in the drugstore to heighten the blond flecks. Then she put on a long green velvet dress with gold embroidery, and inserted the gold hoop earrings Ivan bought her some years ago for her twenty-fifth birthday. Before they set out she drank a cup of black coffee. She would have taken No-Doze but she was afraid of drugs, afraid of giving birth to an armless or legless baby who would be a burden and a heartache to them for the rest of their days.

At the party of mostly university people, she chatted with everyone equally, those she knew well and those she had never met. Sociably, she held a filled glass in her hand, taking tiny sips. She and Ivan were not together very much — it was crowded, smoky and loud; people kept moving and encounters were brief — but she knew he was aware of her, could feel his awareness through the milling bodies. He was aware and he was pleased. He deserved more than the somnambulist she had become, and she was pleased to please him. But after a while her legs would not support her for another instant. The skin tingled: soft warning bells rang from every pore. She allowed herself a moment to sit down alone in a small alcove off the living room, where she smoked a cigarette and stared down at her lap, holding her eyes open very wide. Examining the gold and rose-colored embroidery on her dress, Caroline traced the coiled pattern, mathematical and hypnotic, with her index finger. Just as she was happily merging into its intricacies, a man, a stranger, came in, breaking her trance. He was a very young man, twenty-three, maybe, of no apparent interest.

"Hi. I hear you're expecting a baby," he began, and sat down with a distinct air of settling in.

"Yes. That's quite an opening line. How did you know?"

"I know because Linda told me. You know Linda, don't you? I'm her brother."

He began asking about her symptoms. Sleepiness? Apathy? He knew, he had worked in a clinic. Unresponsive, she retorted by inquiring about his taste in music. He sat on a leather hassock opposite Caroline on the couch, and with every inquisitive sentence drew his seat closer till their knees were almost touching. She shifted her weight to avoid him; tucked her feet under her and lit another cigarette, feeling she could lie down and fall into a stupor quite easily. Still, words were coming out of her mouth, she heard them; she hoped they were not encouraging words but she seemed to have very little control over what they were.

"I —" he said. "You see —" He reached out and put his hand over hers. "Pregnant women, like, they really turn me on. I mean, there's a special aura. You're sensational."

She pulled her hand away. "God almighty."

"What's the matter? Honestly, I didn't mean to offend you."

"I really must go." She stood up and stepped around him.

"Could I see you some time?"

"You're seeing me now. Enjoy it."

He ran his eyes over her from head to toe, appraising. "It doesn't show yet."

Gazing down at her body, Caroline stretched the loose velvet dress taut over her stomach. "No, you're right, it doesn't." Then, over her shoulder, as she left their little corner, she tossed, "Fuck you, you pig."

With a surge of energy she downed a quick Scotch, found Ivan and tugged at his arm. "Let's dance."

Ivan's blue eyes lightened with shock. At home she could barely walk.

"Yes, let's." He took her in his arms and she buried her face against his shoulder. But she held her tears back, she would not let him know.

Later she told him about it. It was three-thirty in the morning, they had just made love drunkenly, and Ivan was in high spirits. She knew why — he felt he had her back again. She had held him close and uttered her old sounds, familiar moans and cries like a

poignant, nearly forgotten tune, and Ivan was miraculously restored, his impact once again sensible to eye and ear. He was making her laugh hysterically now, imitating the eccentric professor of
art history at the party, an owlish émigré from Bavaria who ex-
pounded on the dilemmas of today's youth, all the while pronouncing "youth" as if it rhymed with "mouth." Ivan had also
discovered that he pronounced "unique" as if it were "eunuch."
Then, sitting up in bed cross-legged, they competed in making up
pretentious scholarly sentences that included both "unique" and
"youth" mispronounced.

"Speaking of 'yowth,' " Caroline said, "I met a weird one tonight,
Linda's brother. A very eunuch yowth, I must say." And giggling,
she recounted their conversation. Suddenly at the end she unex-
pectedly found herself in tears. Shuddering, she flopped over and
sobbed into her pillow.

"Caroline," he said tenderly, "please. For heaven's sake, it was
just some nut. It was nothing. Don't get all upset over it." He
stroked her bare back.

"I can't help it," she wailed. "It made me feel so disgusting."

"You're much too sensitive. Come on." He ran his hand slowly
through her hair, over and over.

She pulled the blanket around her. "Enough. I'm going to sleep."

A few days later, when classes were beginning again for the new
semester, she woke early and went immediately to the shower,
going through the ritual motions briskly and automatically. She
was finished and brushing her teeth when she realized what had
happened. There she was on her feet, sturdy, before eight in the
morning, planning how she would introduce the topic of the dif-
ferential calculus to her new students. She stared at her face in the
mirror with unaccustomed recognition, her mouth dripping white
foam, her dark eyes startled. She was alive. She didn't know how
the miracle had happened, nor did she care to explore it. Back in
the bedroom she dressed quickly, zipping up a pair of slim rust-
colored woollen slacks with satisfaction. It didn't show yet, but
soon.

"Ivan, time to get up."

He grunted and opened his eyes. When at last they focused on
Caroline leaning over him they burned blue and wide with astonishment. He rubbed a fist across his forehead. "Are you dressed
already?"

"Yes. I'm cured."

"What do you mean?"

"I'm not tired anymore. I'm slept out. I've come back to life."

"Oh." He moaned and rolled over in one piece like a seal.

"Aren't you getting up?"

"In a little while. I'm so tired. I must sleep for a while." The words were thick and slurred.

"Well!" She was strangely annoyed. Ivan always got up with vigor. "Are you sick?"

"Uh-uh."

After a quick cup of coffee she called out, "Ivan, I'm leaving now. Don't forget to get up." The January air was crisp and exhilarating, and she walked the half-mile to the university at a nimble clip, going over her introductory remarks in her head.

Ivan was tired for a week. Caroline wanted to go out to dinner every evening — she had her appetite back. She had broken through dense earth to fresh air. It was a new year and soon they would have a new baby. But all Ivan wanted to do was stay home and lie on the bed and watch television. It was repellent. Sloth, she pointed out to him more than once, was one of the seven deadly sins. The fifth night she said in exasperation, "What the hell is the matter with you? If you're sick go to a doctor."

"I'm not sick. I'm tired. Can't I be tired too? Leave me alone. I left you alone, didn't I?"

"That was different."

"How?"

"I'm pregnant and you're not, in case you've forgotten."

"How could I forget?"

She said nothing, only cast him an evil look.

One evening soon after Ivan's symptoms disappeared, they sat together on the living-room sofa sharing sections of the newspaper. Ivan had his feet up on the coffee table and Caroline sat diagonally, resting her legs on his. She paused in her reading and touched her stomach.

"Ivan."

"What?"

"It's no use. I'm going to have to buy some maternity clothes."

He put down the paper and stared. "Really?" He seemed distressed.

"Yes."

"Well, don't buy any of those ugly things they wear. Can't you get some of those, you know, sort of Indian things?"

"Yes. That's a good idea. I will."

He picked up the paper again.

"It moves."

"What?"

"I said it moves. The baby."

"It moves?"

She laughed. "Remember Galileo? *Eppure, si muove.*" They had spent years together in Italy in their first youth, in mad love, and visited the birthplace of Galileo. He was a hero to both of them, because his mind remained free and strong though his body succumbed to tyranny.

Ivan laughed too. "*Eppure, si muove.* Let me see." He bent his head down to feel it, then looked up at her, his face full of longing, marvel and envy. In a moment he was scrambling at her clothes in a young eager rush. He wanted to be there, he said. Caroline, taken by surprise, was suspended between laughter and tears. He had her on the floor in silence, and for each it was swift and consuming.

Ivan lay spent in her arms. Caroline, still gasping and clutching him, said, "I could never love it as much as I love you." She wondered, then, hearing her words fall in the still air, whether this would always be true.

Shortly after she began wearing the Indian shirts and dresses, she noticed that Ivan was acting oddly. He stayed late at the office more than ever before, and often brought work home with him. He appeared to have lost interest in the baby, rarely asking how she felt, and when she moaned in bed sometimes, "Oh, I can't get to sleep, it keeps moving around," he responded with a grunt or not at all. He asked her, one warm Sunday in March, if she wanted to go bicycle riding.

"Ivan, I can't go bicycle riding. I mean, look at me."

"Oh, right. Of course."

He seemed to avoid looking at her, and she did look terrible, she had to admit. Even she looked at herself in the mirror as infrequently as possible. She dreaded what she had heard about hair falling out and teeth rotting, but she drank her milk diligently and so far neither of those things had happened. But besides the grotesque belly, her ankles swelled up so that the shape of her own legs was alien. She took diuretics and woke every hour at night to go to the bathroom. Sometimes it was impossible to get back to sleep so she sat up in bed reading. Ivan said, "Can't you turn the light out? You know I can't sleep with the light on."

"But what should I do? I can't sleep at all."

"Read in the living room."

"It's so cold in there at night."

He would turn away irritably. Once he took the blanket and went to sleep in the living room himself.

They liked to go for drives in the country on warm weekends. It seemed to Caroline that he chose the bumpiest, most untended roads and drove them as rashly as possible. Then when they stopped to picnic and he lay back to bask in the sharp April sunlight, she would always need to go and look for a bathroom, or even a clump of trees. At first this amused him, but soon his amusement became sardonic. He pulled in wearily at gas stations where he didn't need gas and waited in the car with folded arms and a sullen expression that made her apologetic about her ludicrous needs. They were growing apart. She could feel the distance between them like a patch of fog, dimming and distorting the relations of objects in space. The baby that lay between them in the dark was pushing them apart.

Sometimes as she lay awake in bed at night, not wanting to read in the cold living room but reluctant to turn on the light (and it was only a small light, she thought bitterly, a small bedside light), Caroline brooded over the horrible deformities the baby might be born with. She was thirty-one years old, not the best age to bear a first child. It could have cerebral palsy, cleft palate, two heads, club foot. She wondered if she could love a baby with a gross defect. She wondered if Ivan would want to put it in an institution, and if there were any decent institutions in their area, and if they would be spending every Sunday afternoon for the rest of their lives visiting the baby and driving home heartbroken in silence. She lived through these visits to the institution in vivid detail till she knew the doctors' and nurses' faces well. And there would come a point when Ivan would refuse to go anymore — she knew what he was like, selfish with his time and impatient with futility — and she would have to go alone. She wondered if Ivan ever thought about these things, but with that cold mood of his she was afraid to ask.

One night she was desolate. She couldn't bear the loneliness and
the heaviness anymore, so she woke him.

"Ivan, please. Talk to me. I'm so lonely."

He sat up abruptly. "What?" He was still asleep. With the dark
straight hair hanging down over his lean face he looked boyish and
vulnerable. Without knowing why, she felt sorry for him.

"I'm sorry. I know you were sleeping but I —" Here she began
to weep. "I just lie here forever in the dark and think awful things
and you're so far away, and I just —"

"Oh, Caroline. Oh, God." Now he was wide awake, and took her
in his arms.

"You're so far away," she wept. "I don't know what's the matter
with you."

"I'm sorry. I know it's hard for you. You're so — everything's so
different, that's all."

"But it's still me."

"I know. I know it's stupid of me. I can't —"

She knew what it was. It would never be the same. They sat up
all night holding each other, and they talked. Ivan talked more
than he had in weeks. He said of course the baby would be perfectly all right, and it would be born at just the right time, too, late
June, so she could finish up the term, and they would start their
natural childbirth group in two weeks so he could be with her and
help her, though of course she would do it easily because she was
so competent at everything, and then they would have the summer
for the early difficult months, and she would be feeling fine and be
ready to go back to work in the fall, and they would find a good
person, someone like a grandmother, to come in, and he would try
to stagger his schedule so she would not feel overburdened and
trapped, and in short everything would be just fine, and they would
make love again like they used to and be close again. He said
exactly what she needed to hear, while she huddled against him,
wrenched with pain to realize that he had known all along the right
words to say but hadn't thought to say them till she woke him in
desperation. Still, in the dawn she slept contented. She loved him.
Every now and then she perceived this like a fact of life, an ancient
tropism.

Two weeks later they had one of their horrible quarrels. It happened at a gallery, at the opening of a show by a group of young
local artists Ivan had discovered. He had encouraged them to apply

to his foundation for money and smoothed the way to their success. Now at their triumphant hour he was to be publicly thanked at a formal dinner. There were too many paintings to look at, too many people to greet, and too many glasses of champagne thrust at Caroline, who was near the end of her eighth month now. She walked around for an hour, then whispered to Ivan, "Listen, I'm sorry but I've got to go. Give me the car keys, will you? I don't feel well."

"What's the matter?"

"I can't stop having to go to the bathroom and my feet are killing me and my head aches, and the kid is rolling around like a basketball. You stay and enjoy it. You can get a ride with someone. I'll see you later."

"I'll drive you home," he said grimly. "We'll leave."

An awful knot gripped her stomach. The knot was the image of his perverse resistance, the immense trouble coming, all the trouble congealed and solidified and tied up in one moment. Meanwhile they smiled at the passers-by as they whispered ferociously to each other.

"Ivan, I do not want you to take me home. This is your event. Stay. I am leaving. We are separate people."

"If you're as sick as you say you can't drive home alone. You're my wife and I'll take you home."

"Suit yourself," she said sweetly, because the director of the gallery was approaching. "We all know you're much bigger and stronger than I am." And she smiled maliciously.

Ivan waved vaguely at the director, turned and ushered her to the door. Outside he exploded.

"Shit, Caroline! We can't do a fucking thing anymore, can we?"

"You can do anything you like. Just give me the keys. I left mine home."

"I will not give you the keys. Get in the car. You're supposed to be sick."

"You big resentful selfish idiot. Jealous of an embryo." She was screaming now. He started the car with a rush that jolted her forward against the dashboard. "I'd be better off driving myself. You'll kill me this way."

"Shut up," he shouted. "I don't want to hear any more."

"I don't care what you want to hear or not hear."

"Shut the hell up or I swear I'll go into a tree. I don't give a shit anymore."

It was starting to rain, a soft silent rain that glittered in the drab dusk outside. At exactly the same moment they rolled up their windows. They were sealed in together, Caroline thought, like restless beasts in a cage. The air in the car was dank and stuffy. When they got home he slammed the door so hard the house shook. Caroline had calmed herself. She sank down in a chair, kicked off her shoes and rubbed her ankles. "Ivan, why don't you go back? It's not too late. These dinners are always late anyway. I'll be O.K."

"I don't want to go anymore," he yelled. "The whole thing is spoiled. Our whole lives are spoiled from now on. We were better off before. I thought you had gotten over wanting it. I thought it was a dead issue." He stared at her bulging stomach with such loathing that she was shocked into horrid, lucid perception.

"You disgust me," she said quietly. "Frankly, you always have and probably always will." She didn't know why she said that. It was quite untrue. It was only true that he disgusted her at this moment, yet the rest had rolled out like string from a hidden ball of twine.

"So why did we ever start this in the first place?" he screamed.

She didn't know whether he meant the marriage or the baby, and for an instant she was afraid he might hit her, there such compressed force in his huge shoulders.

"Get the hell out of here. I don't want to have to look at you."

"I will. I'll go back. I'll take your advice. Call your fucking obstetrician if you need anything. I'm sure he's always glad of an extra feel."

"You ignorant pig. Go on. And don't hurry back. Find yourself a skinny little art student and give her a big treat."

"I just might." He slammed the door and the house shook again. He would be back. This was not the first time. Only now she felt no secret excitement, no tremor, no passion that could reshape into lust; she was too heavy and burdened. It would not be easy to make it up — she was in no condition. It would lie between them silently like a dead weight till weeks after the baby was born, till Ivan felt he could reclaim his rightful territory. She knew him too well. Caroline took two aspirins. When she woke at three he was in bed beside her, gripping the blanket in his sleep and breathing heavily. For days afterwards they spoke with strained, subdued courtesy.

They worked diligently in the natural childbirth classes once a week, while at home they giggled over how silly the excercises were, yet Ivan insisted she pant her five minutes each day as instructed. As relaxation training, Ivan was supposed to lift each of her legs and arms three times and drop them, while she remained perfectly limp and passive. From the very start Caroline was excellent at this routine, which they did in bed before going to sleep. A substitute, she thought, yawning. She could make her body so limp and passive her arms and legs bounced on the mattress when they fell. One night for diversion she tried doing it to Ivan, but he couldn't master the technique of passivity.

"Don't do anything, Ivan. I lift the leg and I drop the leg. You do nothing. Do you see? Nothing at all," she smiled.

But that was not possible for him. He tried to be limp but kept working along with her; she could see his muscles, precisely those leg muscles she found so desirable, exerting to lift and drop, lift and drop.

"You can't give yourself up. Don't you feel what you're doing? You have to let me do it to you. Let me try just your hand, from the wrist. That might be easier."

"No, forget it. Give me back my hand." He smiled and stroked her stomach gently. "What's the difference? I don't have to do it well. You do it very well."

She did it very well indeed when the time came. It was a short labor, less than an hour, very unusual for a first baby, the nurses kept muttering. She breathed intently, beginning with the long slow breaths she had been taught, feeling quite remote from the bustle around her. Then, in a flurry, they raced her down the hall on a wheeled table with a train of white-coated people trotting after, and she thought, panting, No matter what I suffer, soon I will be thin again, I will be more beautiful than ever.

The room was crowded with people, far more people than she would have thought necessary, but the only faces she singled out were Ivan's and the doctor's. The doctor, with a new russet beard and his face a good deal thinner now, was once again framed by her knees, paler than before. Wildly enthusiastic about the proceedings, he yelled, "Terrific, Caroline, terrific," as though they were in a noisy public place. "O.K., start pushing."

They placed her hands on chrome rails along the table. On the left, groping, she found Ivan's hand and held it instead of the rail.

She pushed. In surprise she became aware of a great cleavage, like a mountain of granite splitting apart, only it was in her, she realized, and if it kept on going it would go right up to her neck. She gripped Ivan's warm hand, and just as she opened her mouth to roar someone clapped an oxygen mask on her face so the roar reverberated inward on her own ears. She wasn't supposed to roar, the natural childbirth teacher hadn't mentioned anything about that, she was supposed to breath and push. But as long as no one seemed to take any notice she might as well keep on roaring, it felt so satisfying and necessary. The teacher would never know. She trusted that if she split all the way up to her neck they would sew her up somehow — she was too far gone to worry about that now. Maybe that was why there were so many of them, yes, of course, to put her back together, and maybe they had simply forgotten to tell her about being bisected; or maybe it was a closely guarded secret, like an initiation rite. She gripped Ivan's hand tighter. She was not having too bad a time, she would surely survive, she told herself, captivated by the hellish bestial sounds going from her mouth to her ear; it certainly was what her students would call a peak experience, and how gratifying to hear the doctor exclaim, "Oh, this is one terrific girl! One more, Caroline, give me one more push and send it out. Sock it to me."

She always tried to be obliging, if possible. Now she raised herself on her elbows and, staring straight at him — he too, after all, had been most obliging these long months — gave him with tremendous force the final push he asked for. She had Ivan's hand tightly around the rail, could feel his knuckles bursting, and then all of a sudden the room and the faces were obliterated. A dark thick curtain swiftly wrapped around her and she was left all alone gasping, sucked violently into a windy black hole of pain so explosive she knew it must be death, she was dying fast, like a bomb detonating. It was all right, it was almost over, only she would have liked to see his blue eyes one last time.

From somewhere in the void Ivan's voice shouted in exultation, "It's coming out," and the roaring stopped and at last there was peace and quiet in her ears. The curtain fell away, the world returned. But her eyes kept on burning, as if they had seen something not meant for living eyes to see and return from alive.

"Give it to me," Caroline said, and held it. She saw that every part was in the proper place, then shut her eyes.

They wheeled her to a room and eased her onto the bed. It was past ten in the morning. She could dimly remember they had been up all night watching a James Cagney movie about prize-fighting while they timed her irregular mild contractions. James Cagney went blind from blows given by poisoned gloves in a rigged match, and she wept for him as she held her hands on her stomach and breathed. Neither she nor Ivan had slept or eaten for hours.

"Ivan, there is something I am really dying to have right now."

"Your wish is my command."

She asked for a roast beef on rye with ketchup, and iced tea. "Would you mind? It'll be hours before they serve lunch."

He brought it and stood at the window while she ate ravenously. "Didn't you get anything for yourself?"

"No, I'm too exhausted to eat." He did, in fact, look terrible. He was sallow; his eyes, usually so radiant, were nearly drained of color, and small downward-curving lines around his mouth recalled his laborious vigil.

"You had a rough night, Ivan. You ought to get some sleep. What's it like outside?"

"What?" Ivan's movements seemed to her extremely purposeless. He was pacing the room with his hands deep in his pockets, going slowly from the foot of the bed to the window and back. Her eyes followed him from the pillow. Every now and then he would stop to peer at Caroline in an unfamiliar way, as if she were a puzzling stranger.

"Ivan, are you O.K.? I meant the weather. What's it doing outside?" It struck her, as she asked, that it was weeks since she had cared to know anything about the outside. That there was an outside, now that she was emptied out, came rushing at her with the most urgent importance, wafting her on a tide of grateful joy.

"Oh," he said vaguely, and came to sit on the edge of her bed. "Well, it's doing something very peculiar outside, as a matter of fact. It's raining but the sun is shining."

She laughed at him. "But haven't you ever seen it do that before?"

"I don't know. I guess so." He opened his mouth and closed it several times. She ate, waiting patiently. Finally he spoke. "You know, Caroline, you really have quite a grip. When you were holding my hand in there, you squeezed it so tight I thought you would break it."

"Oh, come on, that can't be."

"I'm not joking." He massaged his hand absently. Ivan never complained of pain; if anything he understated. But now he held out his right hand and showed her the raw red knuckles and palm, with raised flaming welts forming.

She took his hand. "You're serious. Did I do that? Well, how do you like that?"

"I really thought you'd break my hand. It was killing me." He kept repeating it, not resentfully but dully, as though there were something secreted in the words that he couldn't fathom.

"But why didn't you take it away if it hurt that badly?" She put down her half-eaten sandwich as she saw the pale amazement ripple over his face.

"Oh, no, I couldn't do that. I mean — if that was what you needed just then —" He looked away, embarrassed. "Listen," he shrugged, not facing her, "we're in a hospital, after all. What better place? They'd fix it for me."

Overwhelmed, Caroline lay back on the pillows. "Oh, Ivan. You would do that?"

"What are you crying for?" he asked gently. "You didn't break it, did you? Almost doesn't count. So what are you crying about. You just had a baby. Don't cry."

And she smiled and thought her heart would burst.

TIM McCARTHY

The Windmill Man

(FROM THE COLORADO QUARTERLY)

WHAT WAS the premonition? It had been with him at least since the day old Clayton Hobbs fell off the mill and killed himself. Nearly a month ago now. Clayton had been astride the tail pouring fresh oil into that gear case. The simplest of jobs. But Clayton was over seventy years old and had vowed never to climb another windmill tower. "Hang it all. I ain't going to drag Justus across forty miles of desert just to pour a few quarts of oil into a gear case." Those might have been his words, talking to himself in the way of the lonely, tobacco juice bubbling at his lip, bursting, staining his mustache. The simplest of jobs, yet something went wrong. The old man lost his balance, or his heart kicked up on him — something! He fell sixty feet to the ground. No one found him for three days, after the ravens and the coyotes had got to him, an oil can crushed in his fist. Justus sent flowers: "Condolences. Justus Knight." And that night he crept out of bed while his wife slept, went out and leaned against the windmill down by the corral, and cried.

For fifty years Clayton had been a windmill man in that part of the state and clear over into Arizona. He had been one of many to begin with. But gradually the others had died off or been killed or crippled, and no one had showed up to fill their shoes. Clayton was alone. In those last years he taught Justus everything he knew about mindmills — including how to fear and love them, if such things can indeed be taught. Justus had the ten sections his father left him, but they were mostly sand and creosote bush and they wouldn't carry fifty head without feeding extra. He also had two daughters and a wife who wanted her slice of the American pie, so he had to find some other way to earn money. The neighbors laughed at him when he finally went into the windmill business on his own. Windmills were on the way out; he would never make a living. That was six years ago. Clayton had referred his dwindling trade to Justus and now the younger man had more work than he could handle. Six years had brought changes that were astonishing to most people. Gas was short, electricity threatened or curtailed. You couldn't buy anything when you wanted it, and what you did get hold of cost twice what it was worth. The country was going to pot, and some of its people were turning back to the things they could more or less rely upon. Things like the windmill, a machine as simple as it was old upon the earth. And the wind to drive it, which for all its capriciousness was free and full of power. Now Clayton was dead, and Justus was the only good windmill man for a long way around.

He should have been content, and he supposed that for the most part he was. Until a month ago at least. He was keeping his wife happy. She had a new pickup, and they had recently moved from the adobe ranch house his father had built into a shiny, air-conditioned mobile home that had arrived in two sections and was designed to look like a house. It almost succeeded, too, when it was set on a concrete foundation and surrounded by a trim lawn. A year of work and watering had turned the place into a regular oasis, with the towering antenna for the colored television filling in for a palm tree. Justus was glad that his wife liked the place, and he always felt cool and clean there himself. But there were days when he still preferred the corral and pens and old adobes down across the arroyo to the rear. Usually such things didn't trouble him one way or the other. He was on the road most of the time. He had his work and he liked it. There was a solid, straightforward satisfaction in building a windmill from the ground up — lowering the drop pipe, cylinder, and sucker rod two, three, or even four hundred feet toward the bowels of the earth, cementing the anchor posts, and coaxing the tower up stage by stage until the stub tower clamped into its peak and you could set the gin pole to haul the mill up. Then before long he could throw the furl lever and watch that towering creation groan to life. Those first strokes never failed to pump up an edge of tension, of anticipation, that drew his belly a little tight. For after all those years, all those windmills, he had not overcome the wonder, the sudden thrill he felt every time that first jet of water spurted from the lead pipe. That was the kind of satisfaction a man could stand upon, could build his life upon from the ground up.

If anyone had ever succeeded in getting Justus to talk seriously about his work, he probably would have told him something of the sort. Yet even that much was unlikely. Justus was a reserved man, a little shy in his ways. He thought he knew himself pretty well. He was small and trim, with light brown eyes and a straight look. His round chin bulged from a squarish face and he kept his sandy hair cropped so close that from a distance he appeared bald. On the ground his manner was tight, even stiff at times. He didn't smoke, swear, or drink. His voice was an even drawl, subdued, almost a hush, as if there were something deep within himself that he feared to awaken. But once up on a windmill tower his whole body and bearing seemed to relax, to run with life. He swung out free as a wild thing, silent and sure, and often those who watched from below clamped their awe-hung jaws for fear of giving themselves away. What most men found dangerous Justus experienced as a kind of liberation.

That was his secret. He was hardly conscious of it himself, but even if he had been able to articulate it down to its last wind-torn detail, he never would have done so. Justus was not the kind of man to give so precious a thing away. He kept what was his to himself and let others think what they would. There was a kind of sideways satisfaction even in that. Anyway it all held for him until the day Clayton Hobbs fell off the mill. What was the premonition? At first it was only a shadow, a certain darkness that he could all but feel in his chest, as if a cloud had come between him and his heart. Then he got the job of erecting what he had come to call the Royal Don windmill, and the shadow began to take shape. It was as if that windmill were the voice of his premonition, an articulation of it shaping itself girt by girt, angle brace by angle brace into the sky.

The Royal Don windmill fought him from the start. Clayton had warned him that might happen. "Cussed things can get so ornery they might as well as be human," he said. The mill was to pump a domestic well on a newly purchased piece of land up off the old Royal Don Mine road. Once you left the shade of the giant cotton-woods along the Mimbres there was nothing up there but rocks and hills, rugged arroyo-slashed rangeland, flood-heaved, wind-dried, and sun-cracked. Oak, juniper, mesquite. No one had ever lived on it before — no white man at any rate — then along came

Jesse Pruit and drilled a well on an impossible hill. Why in God's name would anyone ever want to live out here? That was Justus's first reaction as he turned off the mine road onto Pruitt's track. But the place had its pull. Even Justus felt it, and he was a man who usually saw land only in terms of wind, water, and grazing potential. There was a subdued, even subtle grandeur to it, if you can imagine such a thing. It stretched north to the brooding Black Range, west and south along the coppery Santa Rita hills, then past the granite jut of Cooke's Peak and clear into Mexico. A long, lonely landscape that could tumble your heart and in the next breath ache low in your belly with the spirit of a half-forgotten place, an old memory you could not quite catch and conquer. Justus hopped out of his pickup, turned a quick circle, then let his gaze come to rest on the rough, raw pyramid called Cooke's Peak, monumental, anchoring the Mimbres Range to the plain. "Nice place you got here," he said. Jesse Pruit seemed to ponder this. He looked sideways at the ground, shoved his hands in his jeans with his thumbs thrusting free, hunched his hulking shoulders, spit, shifted his plug, lurched Justus a straight look, and said, "Yup." Jesse had come over from Texas, but Justus didn't hold that against him. He liked the man from the start. Though Jesse was over fifty, you could tell at a glance that he was still a working fool. He looked to have been carved from oak, the whole of him, from his salted sideburns to his down-at-the-heel boots. Solid. You would have had to roast him an hour to get an ounce of fat off of him. His cap was the only whimsical touch. He favored the same floppy, polka-dotted affair that Justus liked to wear on the job. Justus had a sign reading "I work alone" taped to the toolbox in the back of his truck. But when Jesse offered to give him a hand, he did not hesitate to accept. Good thing he did, too! He needed all the help he could get with the Royal Don windmill.

It wasn't just the windmill, either. The land itself seemed to resent the intrusion. It offered them about a foot of stony topsoil, then crumbled to a rock-ribbed grainy substance that looked more like ashes than dirt. It was like digging into the record of some primordial conflagration deep as the earth. The more you dug, the more there was to dig; the hole never got any deeper. They finally had to drench it with river water so they could take the anchor holes down to four feet. From there the first two sections of the tower went up easily. Justus began to feel better. But the ground around the well sloped two ways, and they had a devil of a time squaring and leveling those sections so they could cement them down. They'd get one leg right only to throw another one off. Round and round they wrestled it through an afternoon of ninety-degree heat, a vicious circle that brought them both to the edge of cursing. They kept looking to the west for wind but none came, and they counted themselves lucky on that score. At five they got it leveled and went down to Jesse's trailer for a drink of cold water. Suddenly — out of a sky so calm that even the ravens had forsaken it — a fierce wind gusted up, rocked into the hill, snapped sotol stalks, swooshed like sixty through the juniper, and died. In the silence that whirled like a second, soundless wind into its wake both men turned to face the hill, knowing full well what they would see. For a moment, neither could draw a breath. There was no air! Up there on the hill the tower lay on its side like the skeleton of some prehistoric beast. Jesse spit and looked sideways at the ground. Justus yanked off his polka-dotted cap and swabbed his glistening pate.

And that's the way it went with the Royal Don windmill. Two anchor posts were bent beyond use. Parts were hard to find. There was a delay of three days before they could heave the tower back into place. Then they took it up, section by section, girt by girt, fighting, it seemed, for every bolt and nut they could punch or hammer home. After what seemed a month of Sundays, Justus pried the ill-fitted stub tower close enough to clamp, then worked the wooden platform down over it. The tower was up! Justus looked down at the other man and almost smiled. Jesse had been watching every move, shading his eyes with a big brown hand, one cheek bulging with tobacco. Now he looked aslant and rotated his shoulders, the way a boxer does sometimes to loosen up, spat, then knelt by one corner post to chain a block into place. With luck they would haul the mill up before quitting time. But the first time Justus swung up onto the platform he knocked a wrench off. "Watch it!" The shout was too late. Jesse's forearm was gashed to the bone, the wrench bloody by his knee. Justus had to drive him into Silver for stitches. Another day shot. He began to hate that windmill the way he would never have allowed himself to hate another man. He'd already lost money on it. Now it had cost him his helper. Next thing he knew he would be losing his temper — something no windmill man could safely allow himself to do.

The next day they got the tailbone, vane, and motor assembled and the whole works onto the tower — Justus handling the tackle and a somewhat wan Jesse backing the pickup with one hand. But of course the wind had gusted up at the very moment Justus was anchoring the block on top of the gin pole. He rocked there forty feet in the air, fighting for balance, clinging like a lover to that wavering plastic pole, his heart punching into his throat. And then the motor wouldn't slip plump onto the mill pipe. Justus wrestled it every which way until his belly burned with anger and the blood surged hot into his head. He could barely see for the sweat smarting his eyes. Finally he gripped the rim of the gear case, braced both feet against the motor and wrenched his whole weight into it, time after time, hunched parallel to the ground like some lesser primate raging at the mesh of his cage, heaving, twisting, until Jesse heard him screech something that sounded like shhee-at! and the motor clunked home. Jesse smiled, looked sideways at the ground, and spat.

The wheel went on without undue trouble, arm after arm, tediously but true, which for this windmill was something of a small miracle. By sunset the sucker rod was bolted to the pump pole, the connection made between the towering mill and the short brass cylinder three hundred feet into the earth. The wind was still up. Justus threw the furl lever, but for the first time that he could remember he did not keep watch for that first jet of water. He put his ear to the drop pipe, and as soon as he heard that both check valves were working properly, he turned his back on the clicking, clanking mill, hopped into his pickup and began to make out Jesse's bill. For all he cared that windmill could spin itself off the face of the earth — even if he would have to replace it under his usual guarantee.

What was the premonition? It weighed heavy in him again as he crossed the divide into Silver City that afternoon. Jesse had caught up with him by phone at the Carlton ranch outside of Lordsburg: "That windmill of yours has gone crazy. Furl wire's broken, storm's coming, tank's full, and the water's wasting all over the ground."

My windmill. The protest rose in Justus's throat but he forced it down. His heart fell, quaked. In a small, quiet voice he said, "I'm real busy right now. Can't you climb up there and brake it?"

There was a long silence. For a moment he thought Jesse had hung up. Then he pictured him looking slantwise at the floor, one hand holding the phone, the other stuffed in his pocket, thumb thrusting free. He waited, fought to gird his heart for what he knew he was about to hear. Finally Jesse spoke: "I could . . . but I'm not about to. Not the way that thing's turning . . . You *do* guarantee your work, don't you?"

"I'll be there directly."

Now he had crossed the Santa Ritas and was heading down the valley. He drove mechanically, watching the road but not really seeing it. He tried not to think, to imagine. The few thoughts that forced themselves upon him seemed to come from somewhere outside his head. Echoes. But always it was there. The premonition. Towering into a roiling sky. A runaway windmill. He hadn't realized until that afternoon how hard he had been fighting to put the Royal Don windmill behind him. Now it was there. A runaway. A premonition.

It hadn't rained for nearly a year. The grass was burned beyond feeding, the ground cracked like a dead skin. Today the first rain of the season was brewing over the Black Range. A runaway windmill was bad enough. But a runaway with lightning, a shifting wind . . . Justus shrugged and felt a little better. It would be, *had* to be that way with the Royal Don windmill.

He was almost through the village before he realized where he was. Haphazard adobes, most of them unplastered, rusted tin roofs, mud walls bellying above crumbling stone foundations, a rickety store with a single gas pump in front, a squat bar, its one small window bright with a neon beer sign. Only two miles to the turn. Not a soul in sight. Newspapers blowing down a dirt street. An election poster on a fence post, half the candidate's head flapping in the wind. A dying place. Yet up there in the hills a few miles above the valley Jesse Pruit was staking a claim on life. With a pick and shovel, some rocks and mud, he was starting the whole circle all over again. A man ought to take hope from that. Justus could not. His belly turned with dread.

Water was running in the Mimbres. First time in months. Justus took note as he crossed the bridge. Must have been raining in the mountains for hours. As he crossed the first cattle guard up from the valley the wind nearly tore the steering wheel from his hand, jolting him from his daze. He had to pull himself together. Get this job done. Go home and watch TV from a big chair, with the first rain clicking on the trailer roof. The image settled him somewhat. And then he caught sight of it. The Royal Don windmill. About a mile to the west across that humping time-slashed land. Barely visible against the lowering day, the roiling blackness of the sky. He looked away, his stomach tightening again, as he turned onto Jesse's track.

Jesse was waiting at the foot of the tower, beneath the whir of the great wheel, in the swift fourbeat click-click-clank-click of the mill, the wind beating his yellow slicker about his legs. The moment Justus hopped from the pickup it began to rain. Cooke's Peak had vanished in the storm. Lightning jagged in a sudden simultaneous row of four across the Black Range. All the land — the hills, the canyons, the arroyos, and the valley — between the Emory Pass and Caballo Blanco in the Santa Rita range was wind-rocked and thundered, heaving with sound. The wind tore at Jesse's hill, wrenched the junipers nearly flat to the rocks. Justus was soaked in the ten steps it took him to reach the tower. "Where's it broke at?" he shouted in response to Jesse's nod.

Jesse spat, the wind smearing his tobacco spit against the storage tank behind. He seemed to consider the question for a moment then shouted his response. "Right at the furl lever. Only way you can hitch it is from the platform."

"We'll see," said Justus setting his jaw. But as he spoke the wind shifted, gusted south, violently. The great wheel heaved round, its tail thrashing, wind-whipped, as if the mill were some monstrous sea creature beached in the storm. Justus stared at it, rain drilling his face, and he realized that what he felt swelling into his heart from the very pit of him was fear.

With a quick, slashing motion he turned and stepped to the pickup, dug a short iron bar from the jumble in back. Maybe he could pry the furl lever home from below the platform, brake the wheel. Supporting the bar like a stubby lance against his hip, he advanced on the tower. "We'll get her," he said with a glance toward Jesse. But the wind snatched his words, smashed them back past his own ear, and Jesse, unhearing, spat and looked aslant. Justus's polka-dotted cap was smeared to his head and pulled so far down over his ears that nothing could blow it off. He tugged at it one last time, then shoved the heavy bar into his belt and scampered up the corner post ladder.

The wind seemed to redound, redouble as he climbed the shuddering tower. The upper cross braces hummed and rattled. The four-beat rhythm of the mill, louder, more immediate, click-click-clank-click. And the wheel, always the wheel, whirring louder, fiercer, until those whirling arms cleaved just above his head. He wrapped his legs around the stub tower and hitched himself around beneath the platform until he could arch the bar up over and probe for a hold on the furl lever. The bar, the tower, everything was slick and slippery in his hands. There! He'd almost had it. Again. Again. But no. It was no good. The wheel was going too fast. He'd never be able to brake it with the bar. Damn this windmill anyway. Damn it all to hell. He would have to attach the furl wire then have Jesse brake the mill from below. Lightning thundered onto the valley, blazing, blinding deep behind his eyes — a cold, white heat. *Rising.* Damn you! Damn you! He heaved himself up and beat at the furl lever with the bar. Beat at it. Beat at it. Damn you! Damn you! But nothing. He could barely hear the iron strike home. He was breathless, exhausted, trembling. He hurled the useless bar out into the blackness of the storm and inched back to the ladder. For a few moments he clung there, motionless, feeling foolish and afraid, despising himself to the edge of tears, breathless, gathering strength. He would have to go up.

His breath was returning. He raised his head above the platform, so close to the raging wheel that its breath felt more powerful than the wind itself. He gauged his move, concentrating so hard that for a moment both the windmill and the storm faded to the recesses of his hearing. If the wind didn't decide to shift he would be all right. He turned his attention to the wind, gauging it, feeling it out. But that voice howling out of the black was dumb, deep as madness, and he could not hear its intent. Now, Justus! He heaved himself onto the platform and in almost the same motion caught the furl lever with one boot and from that foothold swung up onto the tail. At first he merely held on for dear life, straddling that cold, ribbed giant as if it were some towering, insensible mutation of the horse. Then he gradually got his bearings. The wind clubbed and ripped at him, rain stung his face, but he felt he had firm hold. The wheel couldn't touch him here. He was on top! He had been there before, a thousand times, wind or no wind. Here the wheel's whir was a fiercesome roar. Its twelve-foot span whirled so fast that the curving, cleaving blades were one. No. Faster yet! There was a tail of speed, of motion, an aureole of velocity ringing the wheel, making it appear larger than life. But suddenly he was not afraid. His cap was planted firmly, safely upon his ears. He felt light, almost happy

— the way he used to feel in the old days, when Clayton was alive. He glanced confidently down at Jesse. The other man's face was in shadow, his slicker a yellow blur. Only his hands stood forth. They looked huge and very white on the corner post. Even from that height Justus could see that their grip was hard, immovable, as if Jesse alone were holding up the tower. Justus clucked his tongue and twisted his upper body down toward the furl lever, the toe of one boot snagged in the ribbing for support. His heart thrilled to the whir and race of the wind. He had been here before! He had the wire hitched in a jiffy. "Brake the wheel!" he shouted as he arched himself back onto the tail. Then a blast of lightning, thunderous blaze. For a blink of time Justus felt himself burned black against the jagging light. His arms were already flailing, as if he sensed the shift before it came. It came. A clubbing crosswind out of the black. Whipping the tail round, flipping the man off like so much jetsam. He turned once in the air, his body loosely awry, as if it were already limp and lifeless. Yet he landed on his hands and knees — at the last trying to rise even as he fell. The shock was tremendous. His insides seemed to explode against his spine, then collapse into his belly in a mush. Only the polka-dotted cap held true.

What was the premonition? He felt it looming there in the descending black, heard it above the storm in the four-beat rhythm of the mill, in the great wheel whirring as if it would turn forever. He had been there before. He puked a blackish gob, smearing his mouth, the darkening earth, dying, dying out, the windmill man.

L. HLUCHAN SINTETOS

Telling the Bees

(FROM PRAIRIE SCHOONER)

I LEFT THE PICTURE hanging over the kitchen table, though it's a sad, faded scene to look on — with that dark woman in her old-time dress and veil walking down the alley between the hives. It's the only thing that Wendell ever gave me, and secondhand at that, still spotted with fly specks when he brought it in.

He didn't know that the title, "Telling the Bees," meant anything in particular, and I explained to him that when someone in the house dies, you have to tell the bees right away or else they will take sick and die off, too. I don't know if I hold with these old superstitions, even though my Dad swore this one was true. I never found out that it wasn't, for I promised Dad that I'd tell them when he died, and I kept my word. Same as when I got back from the hospital the other time, the night my husband was killed. The house was so hot and still that I went outside and walked up and down in the bee yard, saying "Dick's dead . . . Dick's dead . . ." until it seemed the words were coming out of the boxes. Maybe that was to be on the safe side or maybe it was because saying it made it a fact. But I didn't tell Wendell I'd done any bee-telling myself, because I'd have been embarrassed to have him think I was super-stitious.

Now that I think on it, he'd have eaten up those stories as he was crazy to hear anything that had to do with the bees. I wondered if it would have been the same to him if I'd raised chickens. He never called me Nancy after the first afternoon — always "honey" or "honey-pot" or sometimes, as if he were talking to someone else in the room, "my honey lady." Around here, people sometimes call me "the honey lady" the way they call old Mrs. Purdie "the egg lady," but Wendell didn't pick it up from them because he wasn't from here. He was from Willowdale, thirty miles north, where he taught sociology in the college. Later I started wishing he'd say my real name now and then, though at first I liked being "honey" as Dick had never bothered to sweet-name me. Mostly he didn't bother to name me at all. With just the two of us here, there hadn't been any doubt that he was talking to me. Even when there had been other people around, his voice for me was different — flat and edged with a secret hatefulness. He'd never seemed as if he'd cared too much for me; still he was always accusing me of giving the eye to other men. Not that I ever really did.

Later, after he was dead, I wondered if he hadn't seen something in me that I didn't know was there. Because then I found that I couldn't seem to think of a good reason for saying "no" to a man if he wanted me. It might have been different if we could have had children, but I don't know. I really can't figure out what it is that makes me want a man. In one of my library books there was a woman who went around having affairs, and the other people in the book said that she was looking for love. That made me stop and think. Not that I had affairs like the ones in books; I just had sex with a lot of different men — sometimes no more than once or twice. Sometimes regularly in a way that didn't count, like the way it is with Brady. He's the county agricultural agent, and he comes by every six months, but it doesn't mean much, since he's married. No one's ever really said anything much about love or looking for it.

Once in a while someone would say that he loved me — just at the wrong time, when we were lying still together afterward. And sometimes I'd feel squeezed inside as if I were loving, but I was only *wanting*. Like the way I'd watch Brady's heavy, official hands checking off boxes on his county forms and I'd be looking at the hairs on his wrists, feeling tender and weak as a sick kitten. Then later when I was lying next to his ordinary, naked body and he was sighing and saying foolish things, my head would seem to clear all of a sudden. I'd realize that there was nothing special about him once I'd had him again and seen him spent and addled. Which is pretty much the way of it. A man in bed can't be trusted for telling the way he feels, and a woman out of bed can't trust herself to know what she's feeling. Anyway, I know well enough that you don't go looking for love between the sheets, so I don't expect that

it's that bringing me there. I never was one to put much stock in
love as a reason for much of anything.

I never expected love from Dick though I did think that we
could get along married as well as anyone. After my folks died, I
was worn out trying to run the place by myself and it seemed as if
Dick might be handy. He was a Patterson — nine of them on four
acres — and he'd never have had so much as a hen coop if he
hadn't got it any easy way, like marrying it. He didn't care to work
for another man and set his mind on truck-farming, even though
all the Pattersons ever knew was walnuts. Whatever I or anyone
else said, he had to go contrary to it. By the time we'd been married
eight years, we'd sold off all but these three acres, and he was
planning on selling off these last to go partners in a gas station in
Willowdale just before he got drunk that night he drove the truck
off the levee road. I wouldn't have minded moving to town in spite
of knowing that Dick didn't know any more about gas stations than
he did about truck farms. In a year we would have been high and
dry, but I'd almost have liked to take the chance. Probably his
killing himself was for the best. Either way, you have to take things
as they come.

I suppose I even took Wendell as he came. I didn't go out
looking for him; he came after me. He drove up one June afternoon when I was out by the road, hanging a board that says "Comb
Honey." (Some winter I mean to paint a new one, for the sign's
just my Dad's lettering on raw wood, with an "e" like a loop of
thread drawn up as an afterthought between the "n" and the "y".)
A white Volkswagen pulled up alongside with a man at the wheel
who looked like the devil might look if he came from Willowdale.
He looked foreign, dark and peaked; his eyebrows slanted down
the middle of his forehead like a broken fence rail. His black
moustache and little beard were clipped close like the ones in
pictures of old Russian counts. When he smiled, his teeth showed
up like new whitewash. I felt peculiar meeting his eyes, so I just
stared past his head and waited for him to say whether he wanted
honey or just directions. I was sure he wasn't a salesman or one of
those fellows with the finicky voices who come around every so
often wanting to buy up old furniture.

He looked from me to the sign and asked, "You sell honey?"

"That's right." I said.

His eyes lit on the mailbox. "Are you Mrs. Patterson?"

"That's right."

"That sign looks heavy," he told me, not stirring from his car. "Your husband ought to put it up for you."

"He can't. He's dead." I lifted the last piece of chain into the screw hook and brushed my hands on my skirt. "You have much trouble finding the place?"

"I wasn't actually looking for it," he said. "I just saw you hanging your sign, and it came to me that I haven't tasted fresh honey in years." He pulled over to the shoulder of the road then and got out of his car.

I liked the way he was dressed — very distinguished in a white shirt and dark blue, knitted vest, even though the weather had turned hot. He made conversation about how much better fresh honey was than store honey — which is sort of silly since most of my honey goes right to the Willowdale markets. But that's the kind of thing town people always say, and I'm so used to it that I can agree with them without even having to think about it. Which was a blessing in this case as I couldn't have said anything that took any sense; I was feeling hot and dizzy as if I'd been working in the sun with no hat.

He asked for a look around. By the time I'd taken him through the bee yard and honey house and had shown him how I scraped the combs, I was more used to his looks and not feeling so nervous. He had me wrap up a couple of sections for him, and I took him to the house for his change and a cup of coffee. He had three cups of coffee and he stayed until noon the next day. I liked him first of all for staying because most men will leave as soon as it's over. And I liked him because I'd never really seen anything like him before. I stayed awake most of the night, watching him in what light came through the window and thinking how pretty he was. Once he halfway woke up and smiled at me before he closed his eyes again. The sight of his teeth gleaming in the dark made me feel that I could cut my heart out for him if he asked me to just then. I wanted to watch over him all night, a way I never felt about anyone — not even Dick when we were first married. I couldn't believe it when Wendell came back the next weekend — as he'd said he would — and every weekend after that.

I never really got used to his being there. I'd sneak a glance over at him while he was reading the newspaper (the one from New York that he used to bring with him) and think he looked like a diplomat. I felt almost as if I could be in a book. He'd talk about himself so I came to know a lot about him. He was thirty-two, four years younger than I am, and had been born and raised in Chicago. He'd been to school in New York and had been to Europe twice. When he divorced, his wife got custody of their two girls. Some men lie to you about not being married when they are, but Wendell was telling me the truth because he couldn't have put that much spirit into griping about alimony and child support if he had been making up a story. He said that his ex-wife was an artist and a bitch. The kind of artist that she was, she made sculptures out of cloth — I didn't understand exactly how she did that. I didn't exactly understand why she was a bitch unless it was that she talked too much for Wendell.

When he talked about his job, he didn't say much about his classes, but told me mostly about the people he worked with. I had him describe how they looked and I got so I could imagine them almost as well as if I'd met them. The woman who taught Women's History looked like Cardinal Richelieu he said — I looked the cardinal up in the library encyclopedia and couldn't stop imagining her with a mare's-tail moustache over a sour mouth. "She's got it in for me," Wendell said. When I asked why, he told me that she was a neurotic who hated men. There were other people in the department who didn't get along with Wendell as they were afraid of boat-rockers. I'd never realized what complicated things went on in a college.

I liked hearing about everyone and especially about the parties that Wendell had to go to every so often. He said they were boring, but I don't think I would have been bored. I've always thought it would be wonderful to go to a cocktail party like the ones in magazine ads where all the people are dressed to kill and look as if they don't even know it. I couldn't help hoping that Wendell would take me to a college party some time, but he never did. Once in a while I'd take a cigarette from the packs he'd leave behind him, and I'd practice smoking and holding it just so and pretend I was elegant. It was a harmless piece of foolishness that never came to anything.

Only once did I ever meet any of the people who worked with him. In August he came out just for the afternoon, bringing another professor and his wife to meet me. Ray, the husband, smoked a pipe and talked in a low, rumbling voice — he looked much more like a professor than Wendell did. At first I was disappointed in Barbara because she didn't look at all like the way

I'd imagined a professor's wife, but looked more like a middle-aged woman pretending to be a hippie. I suppose that was all right since I found out later that she was an artist, just like Wendell's ex-wife, and made rugs that people hung on their walls instead of laying on the floor.

Wendell had me show them around. As I was in the middle of extracting, I took them into the honey house and explained the difference between preparing comb honey and extracted honey. Knowing better, I let Barbara have the electric knife to try taking the cappings off a section. Of course, she ruined the comb, but I didn't really mind because she seemed so nice and interested in everything.

Afterward we went back to the house and sat on the porch, the others drinking the red wine they'd brought with them and me drinking a beer. While Wendell and Ray were talking together, Barbara asked me questions about myself, then told me that she and Ray wanted to get back to the land. It turned out that they were both from Los Angeles and that what she had meant by getting back was that they wanted to buy a farm. That surprised me because I thought that college professors made pretty good money and could afford to live in town. Although she seemed willing to talk about it, I changed the subject so that she wouldn't think I was nosing into their money affairs.

I like to remember that afternoon. Though we were in the dog days, a cool breeze was blowing in off the river. The air was filled with smells: apples from the tree in the sideyard, marigolds and tomatoes from the kitchen garden, alfalfa from down the road. Not too many trucks passed on the highway; if you sat still, you could hear just the bees. Wendell came close to spoiling the day just once when he caught my arm as I was going by and said to Ray, "I sometimes think that the honey lady here is the only *real* person I've ever known."

He was a little drunk, but that didn't excuse his saying it. It was an unkindness to Ray and Barbara, and it embarrassed me by making me into something more than I am. The truth is that living out here alone makes me feel as if I've been made-up and forgotten about. And it's the same with everything around me. Sometimes, when my work's caught up, I sit on the porch for an hour, staring at the pasture across the road as if I've never seen it before. Even though I've looked at it all my life, it seems as if I can't really settle

my eyes on it and fix it down. The longer I look, the less real it gets
— as if I could wear a thing down by just staring. Pretty soon it
seems as if I could see through everything, like glass — the trees
are glass and the cows are glass and the fence is glass and the sky is
glass. And I think I must be turning to glass, too. As soon as I close
my eyes when I'm alone at night, I feel myself getting thin and
transparent. Sometimes that feeling goes away, and sometimes I
have to lie awake with my eyes open, breathing hard and prickling
all over with sweat. The made-up people in books, Ray and Barbara — all seem more real to me than I am.

Wendell made a change for me. At night I pressed myself up
against him to feel the hardness of his bone, and the sound of his
breathing made me able to hear my own. He'd say, "I love holding
you, honey," and then I was a woman to hold. When I didn't use
my body except to carry me around, I'd start to forget I had it —
Wendell kept the flesh on my bones.

During the week while he was away, I'd think about him coming
back and it was almost as good as having him there. I'd make up
conversations with him when I was scrubbing or hoeing in the
vegetables. I'm in the habit of making up conversations anyway,
because I don't see too many people to talk to. Salesmen, county
agents, the Willowdale distributor who buys most of my honey. I
make my real living from wholesaling the honey, but I keep my
sign out just so customers will stop in and talk. In spite of what you
hear about them, the hippies are usually respectful and friendly
and have a lot of interesting questions and opinions. As far as my
neighbors go, they are all decent and civil; however, the women
don't care to visit with me because they think I've been carrying on
since Dick died. I'm not complaining about that as you have to lie
with the lumps when you've made your own bed. Even if I'd
stopped to think of the consequences of the way I was acting, I
would have gone ahead and done it anyway. So, most of the company I get I've had to make up. Sometimes I'd pretend I was
talking to Dad or to one of the customers or maybe to someone out
of a book I'd been reading. After I met Wendell, I'd pretend it was
him or one of the people he told me about. Barbara and Ray never
came again as Wendell had words with Ray, but I'd still imagine
being friends with Barbara and talking to her in the kitchen in
woman-talk. I'm not crazy enough to think that these made-up
people were here; I just like to pretend that so that I could talk.

It's a funny thing that a woman who likes to talk as much as I do has had to spend pretty much her whole life with her mouth shut. Staying quiet hasn't made a bit of difference in my wanting to talk. I can feel the words inside me like pop in a shook bottle, just fizzing to get out. I want to tell someone what I'm thinking and feeling; I can't look at a thing without wanting to put into words how it is. When I first married Dick, I saw right off that half of what I said rubbed him wrong and the other half he wouldn't pay mind to, so I learned not to say anything. Most of the men I ever knew said they couldn't stand what they called "yackey women."

Since Wendell was a college professor, I thought that he'd be different. He was and he wasn't. One evening I called him out to the porch to look at the sky, and I tried to tell him how it made me feel sad in a queer, soft way. He said, "Honey, there are different kinds of sensitivity in people. Responsiveness to nature is fine, but when you distort what should be a purely visceral reaction into language, then you're transforming a pure experience into a counterfeit one. Words are essentially the material of travesty." He went on like that for a while so I didn't say any more. It was the same at night when we were in bed just after sex and I'd feel like talking about just anything that crossed my mind; then he'd say, "Hush, don't spoil it, honey"; and would kiss me to stop my mouth. He told me that I was a Valkyrie (the encyclopedia said these were supernatural maidens in Scandinavian mythology, but had no pictures) and that my style was to be strong and beautiful and dignified. I suppose he got the idea from my being blond and big-boned.

I decided not to say too much so he would be pleased with me. He didn't mind my asking questions about him or talking about things around the farm — the bees, the kitchen garden, and neighbors like the egg lady. But he only once asked me how I felt about anything. The second time we were in bed he wanted to know if I'd been in love with my husband or any of the men I'd had sex with. I said I guessed I hadn't. Then he told me, "You're still really a virgin. You've never learned how to love. If you'll let me, I'd like to teach you." I had nothing against that. All he could tell me, though, was that I had to learn to surrender myself completely. I couldn't be sure how he meant it because I couldn't see how I could surrender myself any more than I had. If he'd explained more what he meant, maybe I could have. The only thing

I could think of that I hadn't given him was all the words stored up inside me, but he didn't want that.

I tried to give him everything else. I only said "no" to him once, the time he wanted to have sex with me outside under the fig tree one afternoon. Children are always cutting through the back pasture to get from the highway to the lane and could come by at any time. When I gave my reason, he answered that love was a very natural thing and that it wouldn't hurt children to see it. I wouldn't budge. It may be natural for children in some places, but I don't think it is around here. Anyway, I think innocence is pretty natural, too, and children will find out soon enough what the rest of that's about. I don't think he could have held that time against me because I gave in everywhere else whenever he wanted me. I even let him do it in the honey house although no one in his right mind would care to — the temperature's kept around eighty, the floor's sticky, and the walls are lined with tubs and pails that we kept banging into.

Maybe he thought I was too strong. He was always talking about that, but saying he liked it. He would say, "I love how strong you are; your legs are so strong, your back is so strong — you're a tree, you're a horse, you're an acre of wheat . . ." Not all of it made sense; it was just a way of talking he had when he was running his hand over me in bed. Sometimes it embarrassed me for its foolishness, but sometimes it was kind of nice. He would tell me, "You're wonderful. You're the only self-sufficient person I've ever known. You don't need anyone." I never figured out what he saw in me to make him say that.

I suppose he only saw what he wanted to see; I must have done the same, for it took me a while to catch on that he was a lot like other men, even when he was so different. When he said he loved me, he was lying; that made me sad as I saw it and he didn't. He really loved someone else. I could look into his eyes and see him moving me around inside his head the way I've seen them moving dummies in store windows — trying to make them look lifelike. That's what he'd do to me. He'd want me to do queer things — not nasty things, just foolish things. When we sat in the yard, he'd push my skirt up high and say that he wanted my legs all brown and that I should lie in the sun with no clothes on. He didn't mind if I read romance novels, but if I read a book about history or true events, he'd joke that it was a pack of lies and take it out of my hands. He wanted me to always wear my apron or to wait until the weekend to put up fruit even though I'd have more customers to interrupt me then than during the week. Things like that. And always saying, "Hush, don't spoil things, honey."

It came to me that I didn't love him at all, and that made me feel as if I had a secret from him. But the real secret was me. I knew that he'd never know in a million years what I was thinking because he just didn't care to know. We went on sitting on the porch in the afternoon — him with his wine and newspaper, me with my busy-work, towels to mend or fruit to cut up. I'd be thinking about the book that I was reading or imagining talking to Barbara about what was on my mind. Wendell would catch my eye and smile and I'd smile back, saying to myself, "You poor soul, you're like some dumb dirt-farmer with his cabbage crop when he's sitting on a good lode of silver." I guess that was pretty smug of me, but it was how I felt. Yet I didn't want him to leave me, because I knew what it would be like when he was gone.

We could have gone on like that for a long while if Wendell hadn't opened his mouth at the wrong time. Having to work in the heat always makes me a little nervy, and that day was so hot that it hummed. I'd waited until late afternoon, hoping for a breeze, and then went out behind the honey house to fumigate the supers for wax worms. Wendell came along to watch. I was already cross at having had to stop him from absent-mindedly lighting up a cigarette even though I'd warned him that the carbon disulphide was explosive.

He was talking just because he liked the sound of his own voice. Talking about how lousy the college was, talking about how rotten his marriage had been, talking about how I was the only good thing that had ever happened to him. Then he said, "I wonder how much longer this can last. I wonder when you're going to get sick of me and tell me to go away and stop bothering you."

I was making a new stack of supers with my back to him so I couldn't see his face. I heard myself like someone else saying, "How about right now?" I felt very calm and peaceful and went on straightening the stack.

I heard him say, "No, I meant I wondered when you were going to tell me to completely clear out of here."

I just repeated, "How about right now?" with my voice still even. Then I turned around and saw that his face was flushed — tight with anger, not with hurt. He didn't say another word, just wheeled around and strode off to the house as if he wished his feet were hatchets.

I measured out the C.D. into a little dish in the top super, then covered the stack with a tarp. I saw Wendell come out of the house with his jacket and the briefcase he used for his shaving gear. As he got closer to his car, he slowed down as if to give me time to catch up to him. But I just stood there. The oat grass between me and the road was high and yellow, and the light hit the husks so that it looked like a swarm of golden locusts. I kept my eyes on the grass until I heard the car roaring down the road.

The day after he left, I found foulbrood in one of the end hives. The dead larvae had already turned to sticky, stinking jellies at the bottoms of some of the cells. The bees must have robbed a wild hive and brought it in. Taking care of that kept me too busy to think too much on Wendell. He left me a phone number once, but I never used it and I know I never will — even though I have a feeling, a bone-knowing, that that was as real as I was ever going to get, that he was the best and last thing that would ever happen to me out here. But it couldn't have been done any different. "Wendell's gone," I kept saying to myself as I was working, "and that's the end of it." You take what comes and do what has to be done. I only had to burn the one colony and treat the rest of the hives; that stopped the foulbrood spreading. So things could have been much worse.

JOY WILLIAMS

Bromeliads

(FROM THE CORNELL REVIEW)

JONES'S GRANDCHILD is eight days old. He and his wife have not been sent a picture of the baby and although they have spoken with their daughter several times on the telephone they do not have a very good idea of what the child looks like. It seems very difficult to describe a new baby. Jones has seen quite a few new babies in his years of serving a congregation and he has held them and gazed into their large sweet eyes. These experiences, however, cannot help him picture *this* child, his only grandchild, this harmonious and sweet thought that he carries in his mind, green and graceful as a fern.

Jones and his wife had no idea that their daughter was going to have a baby. They had seen her six months ago and she had mentioned nothing about a baby. Several days after the birth, her husband had called them with the news.

Jones lies awake in the night, troubled by this. His wife twists restlessly beside him. She has been having great difficulty sleeping lately. Sleep is full of impossible chores, unending labors. She is so tired but her body cannot find any rest. She feels cold. She gets up and goes into the bathroom and runs hot water over her hands. She pats her cheeks with the hot water. While she is in the bathroom, Jones goes down to the kitchen and boils water for two cups of tea. He makes up a tray of tea and lemon peel and peanut butter cookies. He and his wife sit in bed and sip the tea. She does not feel so cold now. She feels better. They talk about the little baby. Their daughter has told them that the baby has a nice mouth and pale brown hair.

"Pale brown," Jones says enthusiastically.

His wife wants very much to travel down and see the baby even though the trip is over a thousand miles. She wants to leave as soon as possible, the next day. She is very insistent about this.

Jones walks with his daughter in the woods behind her small house. She is pointing out the various species of bromeliads that flourish there. The study of bromeliads is his daughter's most recent enthusiasm. She is a thin, hasty, troubling girl with exact and joyless passions. She lopes silently ahead of Jones through the dappled lemon-smelling woods. The trees twist upwards. Only the tops of them are green. She is wearing a faded brief bikini, and there are bruises on her legs and splashes of paint on the bikini. There is a cast to the flesh, a slender delicate mossy line on her flat stomach, extending down from the navel. It is a wistful, insubstantial line.

The baby is napping back in the little cypress cottage that Jones's daughter and her husband are renting. Jones's wife is napping too. Earlier that morning Jones had gone to the supermarket and bought food for his wife that was rich in iron. Perhaps she is tired because of an iron deficiency. Jones had gone through the aisles, pushing a cart. There was an arrangement in the front of the cart which could be pushed back into a seat, two spaces through which a child could put his legs. Many children were in the store, transported in these carts. Some of them smiled at Jones with their small prim teeth. Jones had bought eggs, green vegetables, liver, molasses and nuts. When he returned, his wife had wanted nothing. She sat in her slip, on a cot in the baby's room.

Jones fanned his face with a roadmap. "I'd like to treat us all to a strawberry soda later," he said.

"Oh that would be very refreshing," his wife replied. "That would be very nice, but right now, I think I'd just like to watch the baby while she sleeps." She had moved her lips in a gesture for Jones.

Jones had kissed her forehead. He had gone outside. His daughter is walking there, padding through the rich mulch of oak leaves with her bare feet.

"Neoregelia spectabilis." his daughter says. *"Aechmea fulgens."* There are hundreds of bromeliads, some growing in the crotches of trees, others clinging epiphyticly to the branches of themselves. His daughter identifies them all. *"Hohenbergia stellata,"* she says.

They are thick glossy plants with extraordinary flowers. Their rosettes of leaves are filled with water.

"Perhaps mother should drink some of this," she says, waggling her finger in the cups of a heavily clustered bromel. The water is brown and acrid. Jones stares at his daughter. She shrugs. "They call it 'tea,' " she says. Her face is remote and bony. "I don't know," she says, and begins gnawing on her nails.

The sunlight falls down through the branches of the cedars and the live oaks as though through measured slats in a greenhouse.

"Aren't bromeliads fascinating," she says abruptly. "No other plant has such versatility in adaptation. They live on nothing. Just the air and the wind. The rain brings dust and bird excrement to feed them. Leaves from trees fall into their cups and break down into nutrients. They must be one of God's favorites. One doesn't have to do anything for them. They take no care whatsoever."

Jones had been saddened by her words.

Jones's daughter is preparing dinner. She darts from kitchen to porch, nursing the baby as she lays out the silverware. The cottage is dark and hot. Everyone is very hot. The dog drinks continually from a large bowl set on the floor. Jones fills it when it is empty and the dog continues to drink. The dog's tongue seems impossibly long and unwieldy. Jones stands in the kitchen, by the refrigerator, filling a glass with ice cubes. His daughter is at the stove, stirring the white sauce with a whisk. The baby has fallen alseep, her cheek riding on her mother's tanned breast, her mouth a lacy bubble of milk. Jones would like to hug them both, his daughter and her child. He does. The baby wakens with a squeak.

"Daddy," Jones's daughter says. She hunches her shoulders.

"What are you thinking about, love?" Jones asks.

"The white sauce," she says. She holds the back of the spoon to her lips. Her lower lip is split and burnt by the sun. She has brushed her brown hair straight back from her forehead and a rim of skin just below the hairline is burnt raw too. Jones stands beside her.

"It's too hot in the kitchen, Daddy, please," she says.

Jones walks to the porch with the glass of ice and gives it to his wife. She has a craving for ice. She chews it most of the day. "What is it that my body wants?" she asks, her teeth grinding the ice.

Jones's son-in-law arrives with a bottle of gin and makes everyone a gimlet with fresh limes from a tree which is visible from the

house. The tree is in bloom and bud and blossom all at the same
time.

"Isn't that peculiar," Jones remarks.

"It's wonderful!" his wife says. "I understand that. It's beautiful!"
For a moment, Jones fears that she will cry.

Jones's daughter has prepared a very nice meal. The sun has
vanished, leaving the sky cerise. The color pouring through the
porch, however, is yellow. Jone's wife wears a gay yellow silk blouse.
It is the shade of the tropical south, of the summer sundown, a
color that brings no light. They all prepare to sit down. Jones's
son-in-law looks concernedly at his hands.

"Excuse me," he says, "I must wash my hands."

He turns them over in a vague offertory gesture. He is a blond,
affable young man, very composed. He recognizes everyone in
some way. There is in him a polite and not too inaccurate recognition of everything. He is a somnolent, affectionate young man.

Jones and his wife and daughter sit down at the table.

"Every time he has to take a leak, he gives me that crap about his
hands," Jones's daughter says.

Jones is uncorking the wine. He coughs.

"Every time," his daughter says. "It drives me crazy."

Her hands knock angrily against the plates. Her husband returns. She won't look at his face. Her eyes are fixed somewhere on
his chest. She thrusts her face forward as though she is going to
fall against his chest.

Jones's wife says, "I hope you take photographs of the baby.
There can never be enough pictures. When one looks back, there
are hardly any pictures at all."

The night before Jones and his wife are to return home, Jones
wakes abruptly from a sound sleep. He hastily puts on his bathrobe
and moves through the strange room. He does not stumble on its
basic unfamiliarity, although he does feel that he has fallen, into
this room, into, even, his life. He feels very much the weight of this
moment which he feels is without resolution. He is in the present,
perfectly reconciled to the future but cut off from the past. It is
the present that Jones has fallen into.

He walks to the baby's crib and she is fine, she is there, sleeping.
Jones moves a chair up beside the crib. The baby wakes when the

morning comes. She begins to cry. Jones's daughter does not come into the room. She has been gone from them now for hours.

Jones can no longer think about his daughter with any confidence. His head sweats. The sweat runs down his cheeks. *That things so extreme and scattering bright . . .* a line from Donne, those are the words which murmur in his mind. There are no other words in his mind.

A letter from Jones's daughter arrives several days later. It is mailed from a little town in the west and the postmark is so large that it has almost obliterated the address. His daughter writes, "I am not well but I will get better if I can only have some time." She does not mention the baby.

Everyone agrees that Jones and his wife should care for the baby. She is weaned easily. She is a healthy, good baby.

Jones's son-in-law is very apologetic. He folds his hands behind his back and bends slightly when he looks at the baby. He hums softly, abstractly, a visiting relative.

Months pass. The baby is five months old now. She is wearing bright blue overalls and a red turtleneck shirt. She is sitting on the floor and wants to take off one of her shoes. She struggles with the shoe. She cannot think of requesting or demanding assistance in this. She tugs and tugs.

Jones and the baby sit with Jones's wife in the hospital where she has been recently committed for tests. There is something wrong with her blood it seems. She is not in a ward. She is just here for tests and she is in a stylish wing where she is allowed to wear her own clothes and even make a cup of tea on the hotplate. She bends now and unties the baby's shoe and holds it in her hand. The baby isn't wearing socks. Jones had just done a washing and none of the socks was dry. His wife feels the baby's toes to find out if they are warm. They seem warm.

Jones wiggles the baby's largest toe. "That's Crandlehurst," he says. He invents silly names for the baby's toes.

The baby looks severely at the toe and then stops looking at it without moving her eyes. Jones cannot think of names for all the baby's toes. No fond and foolish names flower in his brain. No room! His brain, instead, hums hotly with weeds, the weedy metaphors of doctors. *The white cells may be compared to the defending foot soldiers who engage the attacking enemy in mortal hand-to-hand combat and either destroy them or are themselves destroyed.*

Jones presses his fingers as unobtrusively as possible against his temples. He looks at the carpeting. It is red as a valentine, redder than the baby's jersey, certainly more red than his wife's blood.

Jones tells his wife how nice she looks. She is wearing a dress that he likes, one for which he has happy memories. It is very warm in the hospital. She has entered this hospital and is in another season. Outside it is winter. But the memory is one of summer, his wife in this dress with tanned pretty arms. Jones can share this with her. He shares his heart with her, all that there is. As Rilke said . . . where was it where Rilke said? LIKE A PIECE OF BREAD THAT HAS TO SUFFICE FOR TWO. His heart, Jones's love. He looks at the dress. It is a trim blue and white check, slightly faded.

It is summer. They are in a little cottage, on holiday. There is a straw rug on the floor, in a complex petal pattern through which the sand falls. When the rug is lifted, the design remains, perfectly with the sand. There is a marsh. There is a row of raisins on the porch sill for the catbirds.

Jones remembers. In the mornings, the grass seemed polished with a jeweler's cloth. And Jones's wife is in this dress, rubbing the face of their daughter with the hem of this dress. Yet it cannot be this dress, surely, everything was too long ago . . .

But now the visiting hours are over. A buzzer goes off in each of the rooms. Jones and the baby return home. Jones undresses her and then dresses her again for bed. He stays in her room long after she has fallen asleep. Then he goes downstairs and builds a fire in the fireplace and searches through the bookshelves for his collection of Rilke's work. The poems have been translated but the essays have not. He takes out his German grammar and begins to search for the phrase that came to him so magically earlier in the evening. Jones enjoys the feel of the grammar. He enjoys the words of another language. He needs another language, other words. He is so weary of the words he has. He enjoys the search. Is not everything the search? An hour later he comes across the passage. It is not as Jones had thought, not as he expected. Rilke is speaking not of women but of *Dinge*. He is speaking not of lovers and life, but of dolls and death. Each word rises to Jones's lips. WAS IT NOT WITH A THING THAT YOU FIRST SHARED

YOUR LITTLE HEART, LIKE A PIECE OF BREAD THAT
HAD TO SUFFICE FOR TWO? WAS IT NOT WITH A THING
THAT YOU EXPERIENCED, THROUGH IT, THROUGH ITS
EXISTENCE, THROUGH ITS ANYHOW APPEARANCE,
THROUGH ITS FINAL SMASHING OR ENIGMATIC DEPAR-
TURE, ALL THAT IS HUMAN, RIGHT INTO THE DEPTHS
OF DEATH?

Jones's wife had brought the baby a toy from the hospital gift
shop. It is a soft, stuffed blue elephant, eight inches high. Inside it
is a music box which plays the Carousel Waltz. While the waltz
plays, the elephant's trunk rotates very slowly. It is a pretty toy.
Jones's wife is happy that she has at last found something here that
she can give the baby. For the last several days she has walked
down the corridor to the gift shop. Every day, like a bird, in the
warmest, strongest hour of the day, she has ventured out. When at
last she saw something she wanted to buy, she felt relieved, unam-
biguous. She is in control, a woman buying a toy for her grandchild. There have been so many tests. She has been here for days;
they will not release her. They do not know what is wrong, but it is
not the worst! The first tests have been negative. It is bad but it is
not the worst. What can the worst have been? She no longer needs
to fear it.

She returns this day with the toy, panting a little, the veins on
either side of her eyes throbbing. She sits on her bed very quietly.
She can almost see the veins. Often, they seem to hover outside her
head. They are out and they want to get in. They are coiled there,
almost visible, knotted, stiff, a mess, tangled like a cheap garden
hose. These veins, this problem, is something she could take care
of, something she is certainly capable of correcting, of making tidy
and functional again, if only she had the strength. She is quiet
now. The noises in her face have stopped. She looks at the toy
elephant. The girl who runs the gift shop has put it in a bag. A
brown paper bag, crumpled as though it has been used over and
over again.

Jones's wife wraps the toy in tissue paper and waits for the
evening visiting hours. Jones and the baby arrive. The baby smiles
at her new plaything. She is not surprised. She is too little. She
raises her face to the overhead light as though it were the sun and
closes her eyes.

JANE BOWLES

Two Scenes

(FROM ANTAEUS)

The Iron Table

THEY SAT in the sun, looking out over a big new boulevard. The waiter had dragged an old iron table around from the other side of the hotel and set it down on the cement near a half-empty flower bed. A string stretched between stakes separated the hotel grounds from the sidewalk. Few of the guests staying at the hotel sat in the sun. The town was not a tourist center, and not many Anglo-Saxons came. Most of the guests were Spanish.

"The whole civilization is going to pieces," he said.

Her voice was sorrowful. "I know it." Her answers to his ceaseless complaining about the West's contamination of Moslem culture had become increasingly unpredictable. Today, because she felt that he was in a very irritable mood and in need of an argument, she automatically agreed with him. "It's going to pieces so quickly, too," she said, and her tone was sepulchral.

He looked at her without any light in his blue eyes. "There are places where the culture has remained untouched," he announced as if for the first time. "If we went into the desert you wouldn't have to face all this. Wouldn't you love that?" He was punishing her for her swift agreement with him a moment earlier. He knew she had no desire to go to the desert, and that she believed it was not possible to continue trying to escape from the Industrial Revolution. Without realizing he was doing it he had provoked the argument he wanted.

"Why do you ask me if I wouldn't love to go into the desert, when you know as well as I do I wouldn't. We've talked about it over and over. Every few days we talk about it." Although the sun was beating down on her chest, making it feel on fire, deep inside she could still feel the cold current that seemed to run near her heart.

"Well," he said. "You change. Sometimes you say you *would* like to go."

It was true. She did change. Sometimes she would run to him with bright eyes. "Let's go," she would say. "Let's go into the desert." But she never did this if she was sober.

There was something wistful in his voice, and she had to remind herself that she wanted to feel cranky rather than heartbroken. In order to go on talking she said: "Sometimes I feel like going, but it's always when I've had something to drink. When I've had nothing to drink I'm afraid." She turned to face him, and he saw that she was beginning to have her hunted expression.

"Do you think I *ought* to go?" she asked him.

"Go where?"

"To the desert. To live in an oasis." She was pronouncing her words slowly. "Maybe that's what I should do, since I'm your wife."

"You must do what you really want to do," he said. He had been trying to teach her this for twelve years.

"What I really want . . . Well, if you'd be happy in an oasis, maybe I'd really want to do that." She spoke hesitantly, and there was a note of doubt in her voice.

"What?" He shook his head as if he had run into a spiderweb. "What is it?"

"I meant that maybe if you were happy in an oasis I would be, too. Wives get pleasure out of making their husbands happy. They really do, quite aside from its being moral."

He did not smile. He was in too bad a humor. "You'd go to an oasis because you wanted to escape from Western civilization."

"My friends and I don't feel there's any *way* of escaping it. It's not interesting to sit around talking about industrialization."

"What friends?" He liked her to feel isolated.

"Our friends." Most of them she had not seen in many years. She turned to him with a certain violence. "I think you come to these countries so you can complain. I'm tired of hearing the word *civilization*. It has no meaning. Or I've forgotten what it meant, anyway."

The moment when they might have felt tenderness had passed, and secretly they both rejoiced. Since he did not answer her, she went on. "I think it's uninteresting. To sit and watch costumes disappear, one by one. It's uninteresting even to mention it."

"They are not costumes," he said distinctly. "They're simply the clothes people wear."

She was as bitter as he about the changes, but she felt it would be indelicate for them both to reflect the same sorrow. It would happen some day, surely. A serious grief would silence their argument. They would share it and not be able to look into each other's eyes. But as long as she could she would hold off that moment.

Lila and Frank

FRANK PULLED HARD on the front door and opened it with a jerk, so that the pane of glass shook in its frame. It was his sister's custom never to go to the door and open it for him. She had an instinctive respect for his secretive nature.

He hung his coat on a hook in the hall and walked into the parlor where he was certain he would find his sister. She was seated as usual in her armchair. Next to her was a heavy round table of an awkward height which made it useful for neither eating nor writing, although it was large enough for either purpose. Even in the morning Lila always wore a silk dress, stockings and well-shined shoes. In fact, at all times of the day she was fully dressed to go into the town, although she seldom ventured from the house. Her hair was not very neat, but she took the trouble to rouge her lips.

"How were the men at The Coffee Pot tonight?" she asked when her brother entered the room. There was no variety in the inflection of her voice. It was apparent that, like him, she had never tried, either by emphasis or coloring of tone, to influence or charm a listener.

Frank sat down and rested for a while without speaking.

"How were the men at The Coffe Pot?" she said again with no change of expression.

"The same as they always are."

"You mean by that, hungry and noisy." For an outsider it would have been hard to say whether she was being critical of the men at

The Coffee Pot or sincerely asking for information. This was a question she had asked him many times, and he had various ways of answering, depending upon his mood. On this particular night he was uncommunicative. "They go to The Coffee Pot for a bite to eat," he said.

She looked at him. The depths of her dark eyes held neither warmth nor comfort. "Was it crowded?" she asked.

He considered this for a moment while she watched him attentively. He was near the lamp and his face was raspberry-colored, an even deeper red than it would have been otherwise.

"It was."

"Then it must have been noisy." The dropping of her voice at the end of a sentence gave her listener, if he were a stranger, the impression that she did not intend to continue with the conversation. Her brother of course knew this was not the case, and he was not surprised at all when a minute later she went on. "Did you speak with anyone?"

"No, I didn't." He jumped up from his chair and went over to a glass bookcase in the corner. "I don't usually, do I?"

"That doesn't mean that you won't, does it?" she said calmly.

"I wouldn't change my habits from one night to the next," he said. "Not sitting at The Coffee Pot."

"Why not?"

"It's not human nature to do that, is it?"

"I know nothing about human nature at all," she said. "Nor do you, for that matter. I don't know why you'd refer to it. I do suspect, though, that I at least might change very suddenly." Her voice remained indifferent, as though the subject were not one which was close to her. "It's a feeling that's always present with me . . . here." She touched her breast.

Although he wandered around the room for a moment feigning to have lost interest in the conversation, she knew this was not so. Since they lied to each other in different ways, the excitement they felt in conversing together was very great.

"Tell me," she said. "If you don't expect to experience anything new at The Coffee Pot, why do you continue to go there?" This too she had often asked him in the past weeks, but the repetition of things added to rather than detracted from the excitement.

"I don't like to talk to anybody. But I like to go out," he said. "I may not like other men, but I like the world."

"I should think you'd go and hike in the woods, instead of sitting at The Coffee Pot. Men who don't like other men usually take to nature, I've heard."

"I'm not interested in nature, beyond the ordinary amount."

They settled into silence for a while. Then she began to question him again. "Don't you feel uneasy, knowing that most likely you're the only man at The Coffee Pot who feels so estranged from his fellows?"

He seated himself near the window and half smiled. "No," he said. "I think I like it."

"Why do you like it?"

"Because I'm aware of the estrangement, as you call it, and they aren't." This too he had answered many times before. But such was the faith they had in the depth of the mood they created between them that there were no dead sentences, no matter how often repeated.

"We don't feel the same about secrets," she told him. "I don't consider a secret such a great pleasure. In fact, I should hesitate to name what my pleasure is. I simply know that I don't feel the lack of it."

"Good night," said Frank. He wanted to be by himself. Since he very seldom talked for more than ten or fifteen minutes at a time, she was not at all suprised.

She herself was far too excited for sleep at that moment. The excitement that stirred in her breast was familiar, and could be likened to what a traveller feels on the eve of his departure. All her life she had enjoyed it or suffered from it, for it was a sensation that lay between suffering and enjoyment, and it had a direct connection with her brother's lies. For the past weeks they had concerned The Coffee Pot, but this was of little importance, since he lied to her consistently and had done so since early childhood. Her excitement had its roots in the simultaneous rejection and acceptance of these lies, a state which might be compared to that of the dreamer when he is near to waking, and who knows then that he is moving in a dream country which at any second will vanish forever, and yet is unable to recall the existence of his own room. So Lila moved about in the vivid world of her brother's lies, with the full awareness always that just beyond them lay the amorphous and hidden world of reality. These lies which thrilled her heart seemed to cull their exciting quality from her never-failing consciousness of the true events they concealed. She had not changed at all since childhood, when to expose a statement of her brother's as a lie was as unthinkable to her as the denial of God's existence is to most children. This treatment of her brother, unbalanced though it was, contained within it both dignity and merit, and these were reflected faithfully in her voice and manner.

GILBERT SORRENTINO

Decades

(FROM ESQUIRE)

BEN AND CLARA STEIN were made for each other. I won't go so far as to say that they were meant for each other, but it all comes out the same way. It is impossible for me, even now, after these fifteen or so years since I first met them, to think of them as anything but "the Steins."

I have no idea how and where they met, but it might have been at a party during the Christmas vacation — this would have been back in 1955 or thereabouts. Clara was a Bard student at the time, having gone there from Bennington, to which she had gone from Antioch, to which she had gone from Brooklyn College. All this moving about had something to do with art, i.e., she went where art was "possible." All right, I don't know what it means, either. She published some poems in various student magazines, and in one of them an essay on Salinger's *Nine Stories,* which won her a prize of twenty-five dollars' worth of books. She was a dark, slender, hypernervous girl, whose father thought that she was going to be a teacher. He comforted himself with this, although I assure you that he would have sent her to school no matter what he thought she wanted to be, for, to her father, school was good, it was sunshine and bananas with cream. He had plenty of money from his business, which had something to do with electronic hospital equipment, and Clara was denied nothing.

Ben was an English major at Brooklyn College when he met Clara at this party. I will put their meeting at this party since all college parties are essentially the same and I am saved the trouble of describing it. But they met, conversation in the corner, coffee at Riker's, and so on. Ben wore blue work shirts, tweed jackets with leather elbow patches, long scarfs wound around his neck and thrown over the shoulder. His father did something. Whatever your father does, that's what he did: the years shuffling by, marked by decaying Chevys and fevered vacations, the World Series and Gelusil. Ben's minor was French, and he read Apollinaire and Cocteau, His reading of French anglicized him in a Ronald Firbank kind of way, and he affected a weariness and sensitivity that, on Flatbush and Nostrand, was something to see. He had a darting, arcane mind, of a kind that made Clara forever obscure the fact that she had once admired Salinger. Somewhere they found a place to be alone, and in two months Clara was pregnant. Ben married her, after a long, serious talk with her father and mother, during which Ben shook his foot nervously, flashed his compulsive smile at them, and made bewildering jokes about W. H. Auden. Clara's father shook Ben's hand and they both stood there, in wordless misery, laughing cordially. The father couldn't understand how Clara had allowed this silly boy into her slim, straight body.

I first met Ben in a class in classical civilization at Brooklyn College. At the time, I was attending school on the Korean War G.I. Bill, and my school friends were other ex-soldiers like myself, a penurious and shabby bunch indeed. Ben was the first non-veteran I had come across who seemed to have something to do with what I then thought of as reality. We sat in the back of the room, composing obscene sonnets, to which we wrote alternate lines, while the rest of the class relentlessly took notes. Why I was going to school I really can't tell you in any clear way: let's say that I wanted to learn Latin. All right.

Ben and I failed that course, but Ben, who was being supported by Clara's father, panicked. He was afraid that their monthly stipend would be cut off and that he might have to drop out of school or go to work. The reader must know that in the Fifties, Ben was a member of a large minority of young people that thought that life was somehow nonexistent outside of the academy, that is, life within the university was real life — outside were those strange folk who spoke ungrammatical English and worshiped the hydrogen bomb. God knows what has happened to those scholars; I know only what has happened to Ben and Clara. In any event, I myself didn't care about my F, but it was interesting to see Ben's reaction to the failing grade: he begged, he pleaded, he took a makeup exam and wound up with a C for the course. When I say it was interesting, I mean that I saw that Ben was not that romantic Byronesque figure I had taken him to be. He somehow had a goal, a — what shall I call it? — "stake in life." On the other hand, I am more or less still searching for myself, if you can stomach that phrase. Well, let that be; this is the Steins' story.

I suppose it was at about this time that I met Clara, Ben's other half — the banality of that expression is, in this case, perfection itself. The scene: a hot day in June. Ben had received permission to take his makeup exam. I was invited to their apartment to have a drink and some supper and "see the baby," Caleb. At the time, I was going with a girl who regularly contributed to the Brooklyn College literary magazine, and whose father was a shop steward in what used to be a Communist local. She read *The Worker,* and pressed on me the novels of Howard Fast. If she has followed the pattern of her generation, she has married a pharmacist and lives in Kips Bay — but in those days she was my mistress: or, let me write it, My Mistress. How flagrantly serious we were! Lona carried her diaphragm in her bag and we discovered that John Ford was a great artist. We went together to see the Steins in their apartment in Marine Park.

The most exquisite tumblers, tall and paper-thin, filled with icy Medaglia d'Oro topped with whipped cream. Hennessy Five Star. Sliced avocados with lime wedges. Crisp, salty rye and Brie. In my faded khaki shirt, the shoulder ripped where I had fumbled in removing the patch that had once identified me, I ate and drank and understood why Ben had been concerned with his grade. Clara made it clear that the Hennessy was a gift from her father, who apparently was good for little else. "In his freaking air-conditioned Cadillac!" she said. "What else?" Ben said. "De gustibus." Lona was into her harangue on the symmetrical beauties of *Barbary Shore,* Ben was depleting the Cognac, the baby was crying. We spoke of Charles Olson, of whom I was then scarcely aware. Clara thought he was "pure shit," a fake Ezra Pound: she knew about him from Bard or Bennington or someplace. Norman Mailer was also "shit," as was the Communist party, Adlai Stevenson, peace, war, and Ben. Ben would twitch slightly and say Cla-ra, Claa-ra, Claa-rr-aa? Lona and I soon left. At the door, Ben showed me a split in the sole of his shoe, to demonstrate his penury. I soon came to realize that Ben was always broke — I mean that that was his mask. His life, financially speaking, was remarkably stable — but he was always broke. The attainment of this attitude was a talent of Ben's class, which attitude has persisted, and even refined itself. At the time, I was naïve enough to think that one had to be without money to be broke.

Lona and I separated soon after. I remember taking a ferry ride that afternoon and, later in the day, going to Luigi's, a bar near the college, where I got drunk on 2-for-35 Kinsey and beer chasers. Sad, sad, I wanted to be sad. It was delicious.

Some time passed and I lost track of the Steins. Ben had graduated and he and Clara and the baby had left town, Ben gone to some assistantship in the Midwest. I had left school and was working in a factory on Pearl Street, operating a punch press that stamped out Teflon gaskets and couplings. The work exhausted me, but I took comfort in the fact that it left my mind free to write. Of course, if one's mind is too free while working a punch press, one can part with a finger or two. But I was caught in the mythology of the struggling writer in America; in retrospect, I see that I contributed some small part to the myth myself. It is not a comfort — but then, what is? At night, I was slogging through a gigantic and unwieldy novel, *From Partial Fires,* which had long before got completely out of control, but which I persisted in thinking would make my name. I don't know what else I did. I did have an affair with a girl who worked in the factory office, who regarded my manuscript with awe; we saw a lot of movies together and afterward would go to my apartment on Coney Island Avenue and make love. She would leave at midnight; I would walk her to the subway, then return to stare at the thick prose I had last composed. I don't think I have ever been closer to despair.

Suddenly the Steins were back, just for the summer. Ben was going to work in some parks program to bring culture to somebody in the guise of demotic renderings of Restoration comedy. Almost every Saturday we all went to the beach in Ben's car. June, my lover, could not understand the Steins, and they thought of her as an amusing yahoo. Clara delighted in asking June questions like which of "the Quartets" she preferred most. Ben drank vast quantities of vodka and orange juice, as did I. One day I was fired for having taken off three Mondays in a row, and was lucky enough to get on unemployment. June hit me with her beach bag the next Saturday when I called her my "little Polack rose," and she walked off to the bus, crying. Clara seemed delighted and cheerful the rest of the day, and toward twilight we swam together far out into the ocean. Ben seemed to me then the luckiest of men.

Toward Labor Day, Ben became entangled in an affair with a girl named Rosalind, a flautist who attended Juilliard. He would spend the afternoons with her in her loft on East Houston Street. Clara said nothing, but began to take Dexedrine in large amounts, and to comment on my sexual attractiveness whenever Ben was paying attention. Ben would grimace, and say Claa-r-aa, Claa-rr-aaa? One day, when Rosalind had come to the beach with us, and she and Ben had gone walking along the water's edge, hand in hand — innocent love! — collecting shells, I leaned over and kissed Clara and she slapped me, then scratched my face. She was trembling, and flushed. "You rotten son of a bitch! You rotten bastard son of a bitch!" But she said nothing to Ben — as if he would have heard her.

When the Steins left in September for their Midwestern life, Rosalind went with them. I heard that Ben had jumped the island on some eight-lane highway in Indiana and almost killed them all. I can't imagine that it was anything other than an accident; he had Rosalind, he had Clara, he had money. I think I got another job at just about that time, dispatching trucks for a soap company located on the North River. The foreman kept telling me stories about how he used to screw his wife every night so that she wept in hysterical joy. It would be nice if I could say that I thought the foreman was telling the truth, but he was not. He lied desperately, almost gallantly, watching the sun go down over the ugliness of north Jersey each evening as we waited for the trucks to return.

Occasionally, one of these old coffeepots would break down outside of Paterson or Hackensack, and we would have to wait some hours into the evening for it to come in before we could leave. At these times, the foreman would send out for sandwiches and coffee, and tell me about some terrific broad's legs and ass and "everything else" that he had seen somewhere, anywhere. His eyes would widen in his remarkably precise nostalgia for something that had never happened. Once I invented and told him about a wild bedroom scene I had had with a "crazy hot broad" who was the wife of a good friend of mine. As I spun out the details of this lie,

I realized that I was envisioning Clara Stein. So you will see the pass to which I had come.

My novel was completed, and I began the process of retyping the ragged manuscript to which I liked to think I had given my best. I began to frequent the bars I had gone to before beginning work on the book, and in them heard various reports of the Steins. Ben, Clara, and Rosalind had tried to keep their ménage going, but it was hopeless, and Ben left with Rosalind for Taos, where she left him for an Oklahoma supermarket-chain owner who had controlling interest in two of the Taos galleries. "Mountains, mountains, bring me more mountains!" the gallery directors would indubitably command their stables of rustic hacks. Then the Steins were back together again and Ben got Clara pregnant, to prove his love or his manhood or his contempt. At just about the time I heard this story, the Steins came back into New York for Clara's abortion. Her father didn't like the idea, but abortion, in its place . . . it was something like school and the sun, it was good. Their visit was a flying one, and I didn't get to see them, but I did speak briefly with Ben on the phone. He despised the doomed fetus almost as much as he despised Clara and himself. At least that was my impression. But perhaps I was wrong, perhaps Ben was just nervous.

I had finished my novel and sent it to an editor at one of the big houses, a man whom I had met some years before at one of my English professors' "teas." The editor was heavy and shambling, and vodka martinis had kept him from a brilliant career. We had lunch at one of those boozy little French restaurants in the East Fifties, which I remember quite clearly because two women and a man at the table next to ours drunkenly, but seriously, talked over their sexual adventures of the previous weekend. In any event, *From Partial Fires* was too long, too cluttered plot-wise, it was really two novels, the characters were undeveloped and not really convincing except for the woman who was married to Jerry, what was her name? Perhaps if I rewrote? I went home, fuzzily drunk, and tore the manuscript up. My sense of relief was almost as great as it had been the day that my Polack rose had walked out of my life. I felt free now to — do things. To do things.

One of the first things I did was to meet, at a party for somebody's reading at the Y, a really lovely girl who studied yoga and wrote poems that were a marvel of abstract nouns, all counted off in the most meticulous measure this side of John Betjeman. She lived on St. Marks Place in a beautifully appointed apartment, into which I moved with her soon after our first lust had passed. Just before I quit my job at the soap company, I asked her to pick me up there one day after work, so that I could show her off to the foreman. Such small cruelties often return to plague me now. I like to think of them as aberrations, or deviations from a true path.

So Lynn supported me. While she worked at her job — let's say it was in a publishing house where her intelligence would soon be revealed — I walked around a lot, drank coffee, and went to the movies. Occasionally, I wrote poems on her Olivetti, a machine that has the knack of making all poems look amateurish, or I took Lynn's poems and tried to rework them in different rhymes. She was a demon for rhyming.

In my restless peace, after I had done my walking or my typing for the day, and while I was waiting for Lynn to come home, I often thought of the Steins, and wondered how Clara would like Lynn, or, I should say, I wondered how much Clara would dislike her. Lynn would come in around five-thirty or six, with something to make the place "cheery," as if such things could fend off New York, lying in wait outside the windows. She would bring in some flowers, or a tiny Japanese vase; perhaps a cake from Sutter's; a paper lantern to illuminate the late supper of linguini and clam sauce, the Chablis and Anjou pears. We would talk about art and movies and her poems. She had almost put together a first collection and was thinking of publishing it privately in a small offset edition. One of the men in the art department (that is a remarkable phrase) at the office would do a cover drawing for her — he was really good. What else would he be? Does anyone know a bad artist?

One afternoon I got very drunk at Fox's Corner, a bar — now gone — on Second Avenue frequented by gamblers and horse-players. The reason I remember it is because that was the day Kennedy was shot in Dallas. When I got home, Lynn was waiting for me, the TV and radio both on, her face serious and white, and the ashtray filled with her half-smoked Pall Malls. She looked at me, stricken, as if someone who had loved her had died. For some reason, I was sexually aroused and knelt in front of her, then began to work her skirt up over her thighs, opening them with exquisite care. She slapped at my hands, and stood up. "My God!

You're *drunk!* You're drunk and can't you see? Don't you know what's happened? They shot Kennedy! Kennedy is dead!" She was in a rage, and she annoyed me more than I can say — she annoyed me past reason. Smiling in a vague imitation of Ben's compulsive rictus, I chose to be light — ah, light, gay, and facetious. "Ah, well, but what has Kennedy ever done for the novel?"

I suppose that Lynn was right to strike me — even fools can rise to what I suppose they consider to be dignity. So that was the end of that affair. It is only our own deaths that we are allowed to ridicule. I left the next day, while Lynn was at work, placing my key in the mailbox, wrapped in a piece of paper on which I had written: *Ars gratia artis.*

I got another job as a clerk/typist in a small printing house, and settled into a new place on Avenue B, near the Charles movie theater. At a party one night, a drunk told me that Ben and Clara and some art student had set up housekeeping together. Ben was working toward his doctorate, a study of the relation between the songs in Shakespeare's plays and the choruses of Greek drama, and they were in Cambridge. Their son, Caleb, was at boarding school — too late to matter, of course — Ben studied and wrote and drank, the art student painted and drank, and Clara — I couldn't imagine anything that Clara did. My only picture of it all was of Clara and the art student, arms around each other's waists, stumbling into the bedroom while Ben groaned Claa-ra, Claa-rr-aaa? his nose in the sauce.

Soon after, I met a girl who had known Clara from high school, and she said that Clara often spoke of me in her letters; I was touched. We went, later that week, to the New Yorker, and saw *La Grande Illusion* for the seventh time, then took a cab to my place. The following Friday, she called and asked me if I'd like her to come over for the weekend, and I said it was fine with me. When she came in, she had a Jon Vie cake and a teal-blue candle that had been "handcrafted." I kept still. Making love that night, she began to cry, and I thought of the foreman and his fantastic wife. Perhaps he had been telling the truth, after all.

The next few years are a blur of the most disparate things, all of them, however, very much the same in essence. My Jon Vie girl left me one night in a bar when I began to insult her because she had been talking incessantly about Saul Bellow. "Fuck you and your mocky writers," I said, or words to that effect. "Them Jew writers don't speak for us proletariats and blue-collar woikers." I don't know why I said this; I have nothing against Saul Bellow; I've never even read him.

At about the time of this unpleasantness, I began to write again, but found it unsatisfying, both as act and product. I thought that I might write a detective story and get enough money to leave my job and go somewhere, but I couldn't get past the first chapter. What made me quit the whole thing was coming across a magazine one day in the 8th St. Bookshop; in it, there was a poem by Benjamin Stein. I can't remember all of the poem, but it was cast in a curious and affected language, a kind of modernist cant then abounding. The first few lines ran:

> *I touch ya. ya touch*
> *me. yer bellie an mine.*
> *ole catullus wuz rite*
> *1,000,000 kisses . . .*

On the contributors' page, it said that Mr. Stein was an "ex-professor of English now living in the Bay Area with his wife and son." I can't express the feeling of defeat that this little poem carried into my very spirit. I did understand, however, that my own aborted "return to writing" had the closest affinities to this ridiculous trash of Ben's.

I didn't go back to work the next day, nor the next, and then I went in to collect my pay and tell the boss that I had to leave for Chicago because of a family emergency. I lived frugally on some money I had saved, supplemented by occasional free-lance proofreading jobs, looked out the window, and mentally composed hundreds of letters to Ben and Clara. But they were impossible to write, filled, as they would have to be, with no facts at all. I suppose I was vaguely ashamed of myself.

About six weeks before the last of my savings ran out, I got into a silly conversation with some idiot I had known for years. He was buying the drinks and I, in a sponger's honesty, kept telling him, as we got drunk, that I could not buy back. Somehow, we made plans to collaborate on a play that would exploit the ludicrous side of the flower children. "A winner, man, a winner! Maybe we could get a goddamn grant and do it in the parks even!" So we became collaborators, and I moved in with him after explaining my wretched financial status. Oh, well, not to go into it, but I began to carry on with his girl, who was always conveniently at home when he was not. She was a true Miss Post Toasties, white teeth, blue eyes, sunny California hair — ah, dear God. She, of course, told him of our indiscretions after we had had a bitter argument one night over the ultimate artistic value of the Beatles. The Beatles! You can see that I had gone beyond foolishness.

He threw me out, and I took a room by the week in the Hotel Albert until I could get up the nerve to write Ben and ask him for enough money to put down as security and the first month's rent on a shotgun flat on Avenue C. It struck me as I wrote him that I had no one else to write to. I didn't expect him to send me the money, but two weeks later he did, a money order for a hundred and fifty dollars, and a note: *Peace.* The letter was postmarked from Venice, California, another outpost of the lost battalion. I moved into the new place, started working temporary office jobs, and recovered some of my solvency. I even managed to send Ben ten or fifteen dollars a week to pay off the debt. Some months passed, during which time I heard no more from Ben, nor from Clara, either. My experience had got me another truck-dispatching job with a direct-mail company on Fourth Avenue, a few blocks north of Klein's. I handled the trucks that made the daily post-office runs, and acted as a kind of foreman over the constantly changing personnel. Since I despised the management as much as the laborers despised me, the job was a nightmare, and I began to drink my lunches in a Fourteenth Street bar. My afternoons were passed in a boozy haze of sweat, curses, and shouts. For this, I got eighty-five dollars a week.

One afternoon, Clara called me on the job. She wanted to know if I'd like to have a drink with her after work — someone had told her where I was working and she thought . . . Her voice was gentle, almost gentle, and, I thought, resigned. Ben was doing what he wanted to do, write. He was happy. Did it matter to him or to Clara that he wrote badly? Did it matter to anyone? We made a date to meet at a little bar on University Place at five-thirty.

When I got there, Clara was already at the bar, working on what seemed to be, from her manner, her third Gibson. She was cool and brown in a yellow dress and yellow sandals, her hair drawn back from her face. I ordered a bourbon and soda and sat on the barstool next to her, giving her wrist what I hoped she would take to be a friendly squeeze. How I despised myself. What could I possibly have said? It is amazing that I am utterly unable to recall our conversation. Well, you must remember that I was half drunk when I got there, and the bourbons that I subsequently drank did nothing to make me less drunk. It is odd that this should be, that I can't remember anything of what was said, since this was surely one of the most important conversations of my life — that is, if you are willing to accept that my life is of any importance at all. On the way to the bar, I had determined to ask Clara if she would consider "being" with me during her stay in the city. Then we would see — we would see what would happen. God knows, I was no worse than Ben; in some ways, I was better. I had stayed in the city, I had stuck it out, I hadn't fooled myself that I was a writer. I had, in short, faced the music. I don't think that I thought of myself as a failure; not that I do now, of course. But I have come to realize that there are certain options, let us say, that are closed to me. The fashionably grubby artistic circles in New York are filled with people like me, people who are kind enough to lie about one's chances in the unmentioned certitude that one will lie to them about theirs. Indeed, if everyone told the truth, for just one day, in all these bars and lofts, at all these parties and openings, almost all of downtown Manhattan would disappear in a terrifying flash of hatred, revulsion, and self-loathing.

Well, we spoke of Ben, that's for certain. Ah, how marvelously drunk we were getting, gazing at each other through those rose-colored glasses all drinkers wear. Ben had left Clara again and gone to a commune in Colorado with some young girl he had met at a rock concert in Los Angeles. I must have subtly inquired as to Clara's feelings on the matter; I mean, I wanted to know if she cared, I wanted to know if she wanted him back. I clearly remember her facing me, her legs crossed, one of them brushing my calf as she swung it back and forth, the fragile glass to her mouth. Oh, I don't know. I don't know how I said it, said anything. Probably something like, "Why don't we just give it a try for a while? For a few days?" What I wanted to say was: "Your yellow dress. Your yellow sandals. Your dark and sweet skin. Your legs. I don't care about Ben or anything else but you." But I do remember her saying, "Let's go to my hotel. That's what you want, isn't it? Isn't that what you want?" And I said something like — oh, I was determined to force her to spoil our chances, if chances they were — "Is it all right? I mean, with Ben?"

I bought a bottle of Gordon's on the way to the Fifth Avenue Hotel, and we started to drink as soon as we got to her room — no ice, no soda, just the harsh, warm gin out of the bottle. I held the bottle to her mouth as she let her dress and half-slip fall around her feet.

We made love under the shower, weaving and thrusting and shuddering in the drenching spray of hot water that seemed to make me drunker. Clara was leaning against the porcelain tiles of the stall, bent over, and I behind her, my eyes blinded by the streams of water, my mouth open to its metallic heat. "Ben!" she laughed. "Oh, Ben! You rotten son of a bitch! Split me apart, you rotten bastard! Rotten son of a bitch!" I didn't care. I didn't care.

After I dried myself and her, she lay on the bed, smiling at me. "I'm here for two days," she said. "You're not mad at me? Am I all right?" "Why should I be mad at you?" "Come and sleep," she said, "and when we wake up I'll show you some funny things I can do." "Sure," I said, and then she closed her eyes and was asleep in a minute. I dressed and left, and walked aimlessly for an hour, wanting to go back to the hotel. She could call me Ben again. She could show me the funny things she knew how to do. I finished my drunk in a bar on Sixth Avenue, just off Fourteenth Street, and lost my wallet in the cab that took me home.

The next day I called Mrs. Stein at the hotel, and the desk clerk told me that she had checked out very early. It strikes me now that I never even knew why she had come in, that she might have come in for no other reason than to see me. But if I know Clara, she came in to see her mother and father, or to have her teeth checked, or to buy some clothes. She wouldn't come all the way from California just for old times' sake. I know Clara.

I'm living now in a very decent apartment in an old, rather well-kept building on Avenue B and Tenth Street, with the estranged wife of a studio musician. She makes a very good salary as a buyer for Saks, so I have quit my job. Outside, Tompkins Square Park and the streets reel under the assaults of the hordes of mindless consumers of drugs. But in here we are safe behind our triple locks and window gates. About once a month my girl, who is really quite

brilliant — she graduated magna cum laude in political science
from Smith — and I invite a young film maker and his wife over,
and we watch blue movies that they shot in a commune in Berkeley.
We drink wine and smoke a great deal of marijuana and what
happens happens. Each time they come over, we all pretend horror
that "something" may happen, what with the wine and the grass
and the movies. We laugh and make delicately suggestive remarks
to each other. It seems clear that the young film maker's wife likes
me a great deal. Each time they come is a new time, and no one
speaks of the last time.

I've begun to write poems again, or let me be honest and say that
they are attempts at poems. But they seem sincere to me. They
have a nice, controlled flow. My girl likes them.

This morning I got a letter from Ben. It had taken three weeks
to reach me because it had been sent to the Avenue C address. I
don't really know what I'm going to do about it.

I'm reading it again now. Somewhere in the building a young
man is singing a song, accompanying himself on the guitar. I can't
make out the words, but I know that they are about freedom and
love and peace — perfect peace, in this dark world of sin.

dere ole pal —
    you wuz alwaze crazee not to be into life. out here in colorado — the
country will *bring us peace — we are together, all together, suzanne, a*
sweet luvles thing an clara too. come out an see us. good bread an good
head aboundin. a commune for all us lost -ists. dig on it!
    ah jeezus! we all wuz sikk or wounded but now we're gunna get healed.
come on! you aint so g/d old.

                                                        luv,
                                                        ben

JAMES KAPLAN

In Miami, Last Winter

(FROM ESQUIRE)

THE FIRST TIME I saw Harry Urbanic, he was hustling chess for quarters, standing with his arms spread and his hands on the table at the corners of the board, his head flicking back and forth like a serpent about to strike. He was sixteen years old. I was a little younger. It was between rounds of my first tournament, in the ballroom on the third floor of the Henry Hudson Hotel in Manhattan. This was not Harry's first tournament, nowhere near it. At that age he was already nearly a master. Chess players being what they are, though, the fact was not scaring off customers. Harry had a pile of quarters by his left hand. I had just won my first round against a balding, unshaven, unpleasant young man named Levkowitz, and my relief and joy had been so intense that having nobody to tell it to, I'd fled to the lobby drugstore, and wondered, over a tuna sandwich and a chocolate shake, whether I might be a genius. The food tasted like ambrosia. I paid the check, overtipped, went back upstairs to wait for the second round. And walked in and saw Harry.

He was skinny and intense looking, with high cheekbones and slitty eyes. He was rather handsome, for a chess player. A small crowd had gathered around the table, and it was Harry they were watching. His opponent was fat, bearded, middle-aged. I stood off to the side and looked on, fascinated, knowing, as everyone else did, that the fat man was going to get it. Harry really rapped down the pieces when he moved, and the fat man was standing, leaning on the back of a chair, squinting his eyes and pretending not to notice this. He was doing all the talking; Harry wasn't saying a thing.

"You think you've got me, don't you?" the fat man said. "There's life in this old horse yet."

Bang.

"It's good, it's good, it's good. The young man is very good. What can an old geezer do against such talent? This maybe?"

Bang.

"Ouch. Ouch, ouch, ouch. Hot stuff. Too hot. *Tooo* hot. What can I do? This Harry Urbanic is quite a young star. Oh, Jesus. Well, I'm not dead yet. Check."

Bang.

"Best. He defends and attacks simultaneously. I only have one move. Is this the sorry truth? One move only. Ah, dear —"

Bang.

"It's it, isn't it? Well, I won't let you do it to me, sonny. I'll do it meself." The fat man turned over his king and reached into his baggy pants for a quarter. "Take my money, you little snotface." He turned and left the room very quickly.

"A fish is a fish," Harry said. "Who's next?"

I considered for a second, but another taker stepped up first.

My friend down the street, Artie, taught me. Artie was the sort of boy who was good at games; he was always confident he could beat me at anything, and he always did; but it was more than that. Someone who's good at games needs someone who's bad at them — I was Artie's pigeon. He had a small, round, metal chess table. I still remember exactly how those sharp little pieces felt, and how it felt to realize suddenly that I had made an idiotic, fatal mistake; how I lost, infuriatingly and inexorably, to something that was as mysterious as sleight of hand. We always played at his house, as we watched television — Artie didn't even have to give the game his full attention.

Then I found out that Artie wasn't much. The game he had taught me was not the game that Fischer's book talked about. Artie knew nothing about castling. He had never heard of capturing en passant. And his habit of opening the game by pushing his rook pawns was just plain stupid: you had to control the center of the board. It was nearly everything, Fischer said.

I studied the Fischer book, and when I finished it, I took another chess book out of the library. This one was more complicated. The paper was yellowed and the printing was small, and it was full of games played long ago by men with strange names: Bogoljubov, Alekhine, Philidor, Tartakover, Znosko-Borovsky. I repeated the names to myself like an incantation.

Mr. Sipper's chess club met every afternoon at three. Mr. Sipper taught trigonometry, an unpopular subject to begin with, and everyone who had him for a teacher hated him. The desks in his homeroom were bolted down, and the players had to sit on top of them to face each other. The view out the towering, dirty windows was of the school parking lot. The room smelled of chalk dust, varnish, and iron, and, when the boys of the chess club were there, of B.O.

The first time I walked into that room, I saw that there was something odd about those six boys. Even now, I can't tell you exactly what it was, but I could tell right away that they weren't boys who had anything to do with girls — not that I had anything to do with girls, but I wasn't sure if I wanted to give up on them for good, as these boys apparently had. It wasn't just that these boys were ugly or dirty. It was that chess seemed to mean more to them than a mere after-school amusement. They were dressed, all of them, in out-of-fashion clothes, but it wasn't poverty I sensed — only detachment. None of them looked up when I came into the room. Mr. Sipper came over and talked to me, and matched me with the winner of one of the games. I was very nervous and serious and attentive, and I beat the boy.

I was in.

Every afternoon at three, the school would empty through that parking lot outside the window. In the hall outside Mr. Sipper's room, crowds passed, then smaller groups; sometimes girls, cradling their books against their chests, would tap by and stare into the doorway. Jesus, how odd we must've looked, sitting till all were gone, until the parking lot and hallway were quiet and the only sound was the loud tick, once a minute, of the clock over Mr. Sipper's door and, when it got colder, the clicking of the radiator. The afternoons grew short, and I would play until the clock showed times I had never seen in school. Often I walked home in the dark.

I was the best player in the club. The other boys took the game quite seriously, but they were overfond of the attack for its own sake, and of swindles and symmetries — they didn't understand the simple, driving logic of the game: *Develop knights and bishops; control the center.* They would play the same gambits over and over, while I continued to take books out of the libary, books like Nimzovich's *My System.* I was going at it at a different level now. But my game didn't approach genius yet; it was merely studied and effective. My weakness was the end game, when only a few pieces are left on the board — a realm in which chess approaches pure art, where you need the foresight and timing of a composer, where the board is so empty, the possibilities so many, that only a masterful mind can excel. No one in the chess club could take me that far.

One afternoon in December, Mr. Sipper announced that a state-wide junior tournament would be held during Christmas vacation at a local Y. Who proposed to enter?

I remember the silence of the other boys. I felt sorry for them.

Bogoljubov, Alekhine, Philidor, Tartakover, Znosko-Borovsky, as I have mentioned. Also Steinitz, Anderssen, Euwe, Capablanca, Morphy, Nimzovich, Tal, Botvinnik, Fischer, Marshall, Lasker, Pillsbury, Petrosian. Many more. The names rang, of strangeness, of *genius.* Almost every one of the great players was crazy. Misanthropy, eccentric habits, early death. They had created masterpieces. The great moves were taken down and immortalized in books: Steinitz vs. Amateur, Baden-Baden, 1874: 23. P-N7!! Lasker vs. Amateur, Paris, 1903: 15. NxQch!! The exclamation marks indicated overwhelming surprise and mastery. Poor Amateur would have just made his twenty-second move against Steinitz, or his fourteenth against Lasker, would have just rested his chin on his fingers and begun to stare out the windows of the spa, would have just begun to doze in the late-afternoon funk of the stuffy café, when — *BOOM!!* — came immortal move 15 or 23, like the clashing of cymbals next to his ear. He had been sentenced to lose, spectacularly, throughout eternity — NxQch!! P-N7!!

I would be Steinitz and Lasker, I thought, in the days preceding the tournament; my opponents would be Amateur.

I read and reread my chess books, and then the Saturday came. It was snowing lightly, and when I stepped out to the car, the cold, dry air felt as light and quick as my mind. My father drove me to the Y. I don't even know if I said good-bye to him as I got out of the car. The lobby was filled with boys.

Upstairs, in the tournament room, a number of tables had been pushed together to make two giant, parallel surfaces that ran the length of the room; on either side of these were lines of folding chairs. The tabletops were a brown substance, like Masonite. The chessboards were green-and-cream-colored oilcloth. The pieces were large, plastic, heavy, and very worn. The rooks' battlements were chipped and rounded; on the white pieces, you could see the dirt in the niches of the bishops' miters, in the rims of the crowns of the kings and queens, in the eyes and manes of the knights. Next to each board was a specially printed piece of paper for annotating the game, and a chess clock. I had seen a clock before, but never used one. My first opponent, as listed on the draw board, was named Kroll. Who could Kroll be? A melancholy Eastern European boy, newly arrived? An irritable, asthmatic, fat, bespectacled genius with a handkerchief? It turned out that Kroll was a short, friendly, blond, conventional-looking boy. My fears were not allayed: his play might be casual and brilliant. We shook hands, and wound and set the clocks. With much swallowing, I moved my king's pawn two squares forward, pushed the plunger on my side of the clock, and wrote down 1. P-K4 on my score sheet. Kroll thought for a few heart-slowing minutes, and then moved his queen's rook's pawn ahead two spaces. It was Artie's game.

The friendly, conventional boys were soon eliminated from the tournament. There were three rounds that day and two on Sunday. I won my first two games easily, then almost lost the third one through cockiness. I made a spectacular blunder in the opening, losing my queen, and was forced to play on the edge of my seat until my opponent made an even more spectacular error in the end game. I smiled and took back, with a smugness that now amazes me, rightful possession of the game. I hadn't really learned yet to be afraid.

My father came back that evening to pick me up, and I hardly said a word to him, for fear of jinxing myself somehow. I remember that drive home, going slowly because the streets were glazed with ice. I was so full of myself and what I had done that I could barely hold it, yet I didn't say a word or make a superfluous movement: all I had to do in order to win the tournament was get to bed without upsetting the balance. Of course, I couldn't fall asleep for hours; then I had terrible dreams, and overslept in the morning. The roads were still bad, and when I finally got back to the Y, my opponent's piece was moved forward, my clock was ticking, twenty minutes gone. I made my move and pushed the clock plunger before I took off my coat. My opponent replied and started my clock again before I could sit down. He was agressive, but he was weak. I had arrived late, showing an automatic, if unintended, nonchalance, which I held to because I saw that it nettled him. I sat back in my chair and stared at the ceiling while it was his turn to move. It worked. I found a chink, and cracked him like a lobster.

God, I thought this nonchalance was clever and new, but in a few weeks I was to see Harry Urbanic sitting across from his nail-biting opponent in the ballroom of the Henry Hudson Hotel, reclining in his chair and reading a magazine.

I'd like to say a brief word here about my social life at the age of fifteen. I had none. There was the chess club at school; naturally, we had a certain corny, pun-making camaraderie, but even though I was one of them, I didn't want to admit that those boys, with their brown shoes and flannel shirts buttoned up to the neck, were my friends. My friendship with Artie had been dying fast ever since the day I'd slaughtered him in chess. We nodded at each other in the halls at school, but that was all. And as for girls, they were another species. There were pretty ones in my classes, but they only made me feel confused, so I stayed away from them. I had sexual thoughts — I even sneaked home dirty magazines a couple of times — but this was not the main concern in my life. After the tournament at the Y.M.C.A., I started getting a chess magazine whose slick pages were far more titillating to me than *Playboy* could ever be. Each issue had biographical articles about players, analyses of recent grand-master games, and, in the back pages, listings of current tournaments. When I saw the ad for the New Year's Open, at the Henry Hudson Hotel, I didn't have to think twice.

The air on the third floor of the Henry Hudson Hotel was thick with the odors of fresh paint and cigarette smoke, and my reaction was deep pleasure: *Oh, this is it. This is the real stuff.* The hall was packed with every conceivable size and shape of chess player, but they all had two things in common: they were all male, and they all reminded me of the boys in Mr. Sipper's chess club. But here the range was wider. This was a very encyclopedia of quirks. The

players, many of whom seemed to be in various stages of adoles-
cence, had bad teeth, bad posture, bad skin, strange eyes, odd
clothes, or any combination of these. They milled and smoked and
talked and talked as they stood before the bulletin boards on which
the first-round ladder sheets were posted.

"Jeez, I'm glad I don't have to play Matera."

"Howie has Urbanic! Howie has Urbanic! Where's Howie?
Howie, didja see?"

"Who'dja get? Who'dja get?"

"Fishman? Fishman is a fish! No prawblem!"

"A *patzer!*"

"A fish!"

A boy with black-rimmed, smudgy-lensed glasses held together
by rubber bands noticed my bewilderment. "Who a' you?" he
said.

"Paul Stein."

"No, dummkopf, on the sheet, on the sheet. Where are you?" I
looked and looked. "Here you are," he said. "*Paul* Stein, right?
Fourteen twenty-five. Pretty good, pretty good. How'd you get
rated fourteen twenty-five? New Jersey? Jersey doesn't count.
J'ever play in one of these tournaments here before? No? Good
luck, it's a bitch. It's not so bad. Here, you play Levkowitz. He's got
white. He's thirteen ninety-eight. You got thirty points on him —
you should win. I never heard of Levkowitz. How ya play? You
really worth a fourteen twenty-five?"

"Pretty well."

"Pretty well? So does everybody. You're Class C; it's not so great;
it's not so bad, either. I'm in D. My first tournament, they put me
against a master first round! It psyched me out."

"What class is Matera?"

"What's Matera! Hey, Arthur, this guy wants to know what
Matera is!"

Arthur was a tall black boy wearing a leather coat and glasses
that seemed about to come off the end of his nose. "Matera's a
machine, man," he said to me.

"He's only a master," the first boy said. "He'll probably win, or
maybe Urbanic. Cheesh, what's Matera!" the boy said scornfully.

What was wrong with them? Why were they in the tournament
if they were giving up from the start? I wasn't giving up, Matera or
Urbanic or anybody.

I went in. The room was filled with the familiar Masonite tables in rows; on the tables were the familiar green and cream chessboards, the heavy, worn plastic pieces.

I was to play Levkowitz on board 48. At the head of the room was a dais on which there were four small tables: boards 1, 2, 3, and 4. The best players, I sensed, would be assigned to the dais; I knew that I would eventually play there.

The first round was to begin precisely at two. At a few minutes of, I sat down at board 48, wound the chess clocks, set them both to twelve, and wrote my name under "Black" and Levkowitz's under "White." There was a small "vs." printed on the score sheet between the two names. Levkowitz vs. Stein. I thought, *Stein vs. Amateur.*

"Stein?" I looked up and saw a stubble-faced young man with a receding hairline. There had been something hostile in the way he'd said my name. We shook hands (his was sweaty, I noticed with contempt) and began to play. The large room was silent now, except for the ticking of sixty or so clocks. I looked down the long table at the various games in progress: people thinking, people moving pieces, people writing down moves, people punching clock plungers. Somewhere in the room, in front of me, someone said "Check." In the first three minutes! There was a general murmuring and turning of heads. Then I looked and realized my clock was ticking. Levkowitz had brought out a knight.

He played aggressively and with sophistication — we were soon enmeshed in a complex position — and I could see this tournament would be different from the one at the Y. When I carefully sneaked up and feinted and trapped his bishop, Levkowitz acted as if it had been a sudden blunder on his part: he threw up his hands in condescending disgust. A few moves later, when I came back from the bathroom, I found his king turned over. On the score sheet he had written "Resigns."

I've already told you how I floated downstairs to the lobby, and then floated back from the drugstore. The first round — with its silent tension and ticking of clocks — was over, and the ballroom was relaxed and noisy. Some players were milling, gossiping, going over their first-round games with sharp, leisurely hindsight ("And I had him, I *had* him, until guess what I did?" "Not bishop takes?" "Can you believe it? What a schmuck I was. A poisoned pawn!"

"You woulda had more play if you pushed the pawn." "More play! I had a win! I push the pawn, and what can he do? I push it again, and what can he do? Knight here, and what can he do? I had mate in five!"). Others were playing interim games of chess. What does a chess player do in his spare time? Play more chess.

And then I heard pieces rapping sharply, and went to have a look, and saw Harry Urbanic playing his fish trade.

The second round began at five. My game was to be — I couldn't believe my luck — on board 4, on the dais, against someone named Martinez, ranked 1809, Class A. This was it. They were moving me up. They wanted to get a look at me. Why else would they have put me on the dais?

"Mr. Stein? Raul Martinez." I was standing, as I had never done before but as the occasion seemed to dictate, shaking hands with a courtly, kind-faced man with a black moustache and silver hair. He was wearing a suit of an old-fashioned cut, a perfectly ironed white shirt, a tie with a discreet pattern; he smelled faintly of cologne. We sat down; slowly, with an elegant motion of his hand, he moved his king's pawn ahead two spaces, and slowly, quietly, pushed down the clock's plunger.

It was more fun beating Levkowitz. Perhaps out of deference to Mr. Martinez, I played a Ruy Lopez, an ancient and stately defense. I played more calmly and carefully than I ever had, seeing farther ahead than I ever had, so that after a while I had an edge; then I won a pawn, then I played through a long, subtle end game (feeling as if I were advancing through a minefield); and then, on the forty-second move, with my extra pawn unavoidably about to become a queen, Martinez resigned.

"Congratulations, sir," he said, rising to shake my hand. He smiled without rancor.

I killed an hour in the lobby, with its gaudy red carpet, drugstore, newsstand, and somehow disreputable-looking health club (*Olympic Pool/Steam Room/Massages*), and then I held my breath, got into the elevator and rose again to the third floor, where I finally let go of my breath and inhaled, deeply, the cigarette smoke, the stale coffee.

I looked at the score sheets. Matera had won two. Urbanic had won two. I had won two. Then I looked at the draw sheet to see who I was playing next, and I panicked. My name wasn't there! I looked around for the tournament director, somebody to tell about the awful mistake. Maybe, I thought for an instant, I had dreamed the first two rounds. I looked again, and my name appeared. "12. Urbanic-Stein," the sheet said.

I would try very hard to win. What else was there? If he slammed down the pieces when he moved, I would tell the tournament director. Silence was enforceable. I would not let him psych me out. I set up the pieces, filled out my score sheet, and waited. I was black. The time for the beginning of the round went by, and I started Urbanic's clock. Five, ten minutes passed. Maybe I could beat him on time. I stared at the green and cream squares, thinking nothing.

"You're Stein."

When I looked up, the first thing I noticed was his eyes. They were a very light greenish yellow, and the pupils were tiny. Frightening eyes. I nodded. "Yeah," I said.

"Okay," he said. Without sitting down, he slid a pawn forward, very quickly, pushed his clock, turned, and left the room.

I replied, pressed my clock, noted my move, and waited. Five minutes later, he returned, sipping from a Styrofoam cup. He looked at the board, pressed his lips together, nodded a little bit, and brought out another pawn.

"How olda you?" he said.

I told him.

"Oh, yeah?" he said. "That's pretty good, all those games you won."

Somebody shushed him.

"That's a fish," Harry whispered loudly. "They always want it quiet, so they can lose in peace. It's very quiet unda wata."

I smiled, liking him; then I realized my clock was running.

Harry never stayed in the room for more than a few minutes. He never sat down, either. He would stand above me with his hands on the back of his chair, those eyes clicking back and forth; then he would move and leave. It was an effective tactic. It gave me less opportunity to get used to his alarming presence. Whenever he returned, it was a small shock. And his absence gave his moves a final, inhuman aura. Leaving was a form of disdain. But in the end game, things got tight for both of us, and he stayed — stood — for over an hour. The position was dead even. Only a gross error could decide it one way or the other: Urbanic was playing perfectly, it seemed, if without inspiration, and waiting for me to blow it; I was playing at the top of my form, and praying that I wouldn't falter. I sat on my hands, didn't jump at anything, and concentrated. When it was apparent that the game was frozen, we both relaxed a little.

"Congradulations, pal. You got yourself a draw," Urbanic said.

"Well, you did, too," I said, a bit testily.

"Uh-uh. I had the win if I hadn't been a moron on the fifteenth move." And he rapidly rearranged the pieces to their position at that stage. "I coulda won the exchange if I'da done this."

He showed me what he could have done, and he was perfectly right: he had had an easy win. I wondered how I would have felt if I had known this then.

"So why didn't you?" I asked.

"Just stupid. I blew it. You're lucky, boy. I don't make mistakes very often. Now you can go say you drew Harry Urbanic. What's your rating? It'll go up a hundred points. Good luck in your chess korea, kiddo." He smiled sardonically and left the room.

I was unreasonably angry for hours after that, knowing how close I'd come to humiliation. I had found something out playing Harry, and I didn't like it.

My performance in the rest of the tournament leveled off. I was still fuming after playing Urbanic, and I blew the next round; then on Saturday night I won a colossally long game — some eighty moves — that lasted until the early hours of Sunday morning. I was unable to get out of bed five hours later, and I forfeited my first Sunday game; then I came back, ashamed and determined to recoup, in however small a way, and I won the final round from another Class C player, playing so aggressively that I surprised myself. It was after I finished this short game that I saw Harry reclining in his chair, reading while his opponent fretted. This opponent, however, was a Class A player; Urbanic had never felt the need to sit down in his game with me.

Harry took the game, and second place in the tournament. Matera came in first. I received a small trophy, for Best Player, Class C.

My parents decided that I should spend no more time studying chess than I could spare from my schoolwork, but now I was play-ing in tournaments every two weeks or so, and my night table was piled high with volumes of chess literature. Under my arm at all times was *Modern Chess Openings,* ripped strips of paper that served as bookmarks flapping from between the pages. I quit Mr. Sipper's club. I had gone back a couple of times after my first tournaments, as an acknowledged celebrity, but this wore thin quickly, both for me and for the other boys. I was an outcast from the outcasts. To put it more favorably, I was in a league by myself. At school I became known as a character. I liked being a character, and did nothing to change my reputation: if my clothes clashed, or my fingernails were dirty, I saw no particular reason to change. I pretended not to notice stares and whispers. When a newspaper article about me was posted on the bulletin board, the reaction was not a widening of my fame but a grim decision, on most everyone's part, not to notice me at all. Math teachers would stop me in the hall to chat; kids would have nothing to do with me. I was alone — alone on the train to New York, alone on the subway, alone when the elevator door opened on the third floor of the Henry Hudson, alone when I sat down to fight. My parents were worried; but I could tell that they were proud of me, too, and this undercut their seriousness when they came into my room to "chat" — to try to convince me to broaden my life.

But I had developed resources with which to fend them off: I could stare; I could be silent. I could intimidate. After all, I had skill and power. At sixteen, I could cause a riffle by walking into a room full of tournament chess players. Chess was the world, and my power in it was heady. I practiced my stare while looking sideways into the black train window at night — my chin on my palm, my index and middle fingers pointing at my ear — or scowling into the bathroom mirror, my forehead lowered, my eyes menacing.

When I wasn't playing, I was commuting — pushing through a disordered, distracting, superfluous world to arrive at the central, logical, real one.

God alone knows where Harry Urbanic came from, and went to. The articles about him in the chess magazines made only the briefest references to his personal life, time and time again noting the sparse, intriguing facts that he had been born behind the Iron Curtain and that he was a dual — Canadian-American — citizen, a teenager with a clouded past and two passports. Apparently, he didn't live anywhere for very long. The word was that he had left his parents behind somewhere and supported his older brother and himself by gambling. He played chess, checkers, poker, golf, and bridge for money. He would play anything for money, and he would win. Harry's brother, who seemed a little slow, accompanied him everywhere; they lived like gypsies, probably like rich gypsies. In any case, the irregularity of his life often kept Harry off my turf, and I was able to become a metropolitan champion, with a rating nearly as high as his.

I worked at chess; I studied; I was good and I was strong, and frightening to most players. I could bull a win or a draw against nearly anyone, given an even position. Harry probably never touched a chess book until he was twenty — and yet, the same way he never wrote his games down but knew them move for move, he knew all the recorded openings and variations by heart. He didn't have room enough for books in his suitcase. Besides, he was too busy to study. He sat up late playing poker, with hard-bitten businessmen who needed to lose, for thousands of dollars. The money paid for air fares so that Harry and his brother could go to golf tournaments in Florida, so that they could milk the suckers at bridge in the Caribbean. I believe he had an aunt in Queens, which was why he played chess for part of the year in Manhattan.

Harry could look at a chess position with those hooded eyes of his and quickly, instinctively, pull out the perfect move: it was eerie. To my parents, to the kids and teachers at my school, I was great. But the fact is, in the honest and ruthless mill of tournament play, I was shown to be merely very good. Harry Urbanic was the genius.

Something happened in the spring of my junior year. I had just been rated 2000 — I was well on my way to becoming a master. I was sixteen and a half. My shelf at home was lined with large trophies. I was an acknowledged younger power in New York chess, which is some of the strongest chess anywhere. My name was mentioned, as a matter of course, in lists of the up-and-coming. I was skinny; I only shaved once a week, though three times would have looked better. I had my own chess clock, which I brought with me to tournaments; I had a necktie with rooks on it, and one with knights. My parents had given up on trying to change me. I lived in a sort of apartment in the attic of our home, an inviolable den. There was a large poster of Alekhine — the most brilliant and frightening player of modern times — over my bed: Alekhine in a stiff collar, his chin resting on his palm, his middle and index fingers pointed at his ear, Alekhine staring from beneath pale eyebrows. I was going to school about three days a week: through spoken and unspoken agreements with my teachers, nobody gave me any trouble. I was special.

I concentrated on studying the dragon variation of the Sicilian defense for the spring invitational at the Henry Hudson — all the big New York masters would be there, my most important tournament to date. My opponent for the first round was Irving Weinfeld, who had won his first tournament as a boy in knee socks sixty years before. We were in the center of the dais. Our game was shown, at the same time it was being played, on the display board; the large, flat, magnetic pieces were moved by the tournament director himself. Weinfeld was old, fat, bald; he barely spoke English; he wheezed when he breathed, and smiled constantly in what seemed to be an ingratiating manner. He was a master, but he was way past his prime; I couldn't imagine him wanting anything, wanting to win. He was merely a creaky machine that produced good chess moves. I was a body pulsing ambition. But something was wrong. My concentration kept fading in and out.

Weinfeld, playing white, was phlegmatic and correct. I forgot to play the Sicilian, and found myself instead in the middle of a strange, uncataloged variation, a hybrid, which normally would have been rather humorous, like a cartoon animal that is half cat, half dog, but which, tonight, was a real animal — disorienting, frightening. I looked out over the ballroom, at the neat array of tables and the players hunched and thinking, and suddenly everything was strange. What was chess? I remember thinking: Idiot, your clock is running. Weinfeld was breathing wheezily. What, I thought, had this old man devoted his life to? I thought of him going home to his little apartment after the tournament, and it was unbearably sad. I thought of him putting on his silk socks in the morning. He was such an ugly old man. I got a grip on myself, and looked at the board, without an idea in the world of what to do. I became acutely conscious of the sound of my clock. I shifted in my chair; I reached down and scratched my ankle; I felt a draft on the back of my neck. One of the windows to the street was open, and the breeze was blowing the curtains in. It was spring. I looked at the board, and it seemed to be lit strangely, harshly. There was a safe, passive move, and there was an attacking move, of which I was less sure. I had thought too long, and I was angry at Weinfeld. I put my knight down, attacking, with a loud rap.

It was then that I began to feel very afraid, unreasonably afraid. The tournament director moved my corresponding knight into place on the display board, and a couple of players who were standing and watching the board murmured and whispered to each other. I wasn't sure, but I felt that I had blown everything. Weinfeld shifted in his seat and sat up a little straighter. He cleared his throat several times. "I had not anticipated this," he muttered, more to himself than to me. "You have perhaps won with this." I stared and stared at the position, looking for my error. Perhaps I had stumbled onto a brilliancy. At the same instant I saw the mistake, Weinfeld said, "But no. No. Not at all. I play *this*." He moved his bishop all the way across the board, from the corner where it had been lurking, quite invisibly, and he won the game. I simply hadn't seen the bishop. The players watching the display board nodded as the director made Weinfeld's move; Weinfeld looked at me, taking me into account for the first time, and smiled. It was the smile of a ghastly little boy. I could see he was smiling, but I refused to look up at him; I was staring straight down at the board, seeming to think of a rejoinder, realizing that there was nothing. "I think you have nothing," Weinfeld said, in a kindly voice.

"Nothing," I heard the spectators whisper.

"This is a stupid game," I said, with clenched teeth. "This is a *stupid* game," I said, loudly this time.

I got up and walked off the dais and out of the room. I pushed the elevator button, but the elevator didn't come right away, so I ran down the fire staircase. I went through the lobby and out the glass door. The night air was cool. A car honked.

It was the world.

I stopped playing, completely, for a week, then two weeks, then a month. I even stopped reading my chess magazine — I would throw each issue, still in its brown wrapper, on a pile in the corner of my room. At first my days seemed empty — as airy and spacious as a room from which all the furniture has been removed. But then I started spending time in the school library, reading dictionaries and encyclopedias. I had missed a lot, playing chess, I began to listen to music. I spent all my time up in my attic.

For my seventeenth birthday, at the beginning of senior year of high school, my father took me out to buy a stereo and some records. Driving back home, he cleared his throat and asked me if there was anything I wanted to know about sex. I thanked him and told him I felt I knew what I had to know.

Then I went off to college.

I was living in the city. I awakened every morning to that uncomfortable surprise — the swish of cars on Broadway, the whining of garbage trucks, the smell of the air — undeniable. Every morning, my rented sheets were in knots.

My classes were full of smart boys, from all over the country. I, who had always been able to feel myself special, was now surrounded by all kinds of wiseacres and wizards. Even the graffiti in the bathroom seemed frighteningly sophisticated. The bathroom was always crowded and noisy; there seemed to be no privacy anywhere. My classmates were coarse and horny; they had water fights, food fights, they ran through the halls at night, screaming with laughter. I took long walks down Broadway, reciting to myself, to the meter of my footsteps. "I have been acquainted with the night."

Occasionally on these walks, I would pass, on Broadway in the lower hundreds, a place called the House of Chess. It occupied an entire floor above a Chinese restaurant. There was a gaudy sandwich-board sign on the sidewalk in front of the restaurant, inviting anyone to come up and play. I thought of it all going on without me — up there in the House of Chess, back at the Henry Hudson. I thought of the people I'd beaten, and wondered if I could still win. A couple of times, when I walked by the House of Chess, I came very close to going upstairs and kicking some ass. But I didn't.

Then one night I saw a poster stapled to the sign in front of the Chinese restaurant: *Master Harry Urbanic will take on 50 players in a simultaneous exhibition Friday night. Entrance fee: $10. Come one, come all!*

I walked back downtown the next afternoon, pretending to myself I had an errand to do, but really to see if, in broad daylight, the sign would still be there. It was. What did I want? Did I think I could beat Harry? Well, maybe in a simultaneous match I could.

He'd have fifty games to think about, I only one. But what was I doing? I saw myself, older and wiser, moving up the ranks . . . to what? To be a master at the age of thirty? I wasn't any genius, I knew that by now. I wondered what had made me give up in the middle of the Weinfeld game, and then I thought: Giving up in the middle of a tournament and quitting for a year and a half — wasn't that a quirk? The mark of genius?

I turned around and walked back to the House of Chess.

It was a large room, lit brightly, and full of cigarette smoke. The curtains were drawn against the daylight. There was a glass case at the head of the room behind which a man stood next to a cash register. Among other things, in and on the case, were potato chips, candy, cigarettes, chess sweat shirts, chess equipment, and chess magazines. The man was smoking a cigar and reading a gun magazine. I asked him if there were any openings left for the Urbanic exhibition. He said yes, and I paid the fee. For my ten-dollar bill, I received a large blue ticket, which I carefully put in my pocket.

"Could I get a game now?" I asked, trying to sound indifferent.

"How ya play? Beginner? Innermediate? Advanced?"

"Oh, intermediate, I guess."

"Steve," he said. A terrifically bored-looking young man, with heavy eyelids and a drooping moustache, appeared to my right.

"You wanna play?" the young man asked me.

"Sure," I said.

"You wanna clock?" the manager asked me.

"I think so." He handed me one. It was a perfectly ordinary little chess clock, but it frightened me. I hadn't used one in a year and a half, not since the Weinfeld game, when I'd pushed the plunger and blown my game.

"You pay me after," the manager said.

We sat down at a board and I wound the clocks. "Half hour all right?" I asked Steve.

"Whatever you want."

We set up the pieces — the old, bulky plastic pieces — and we began to play.

He read a chess magazine while my clock was running, but as a tactic it didn't impress me: I had seen it often. I paid attention to the game, and I went along for a while, playing a known line, realizing it made him comfortable. Then I made a problematic move, one that would appear, at first and second glances, to be a stupid mistake. He pursed his lips and put aside the magazine.

It was an unsatisfying win.

"How about another?" I said.

"If you want."

This infuriated me. This time I went all out from the beginning, and I took him apart.

I thought of nothing else all week. On the way down Broadway I stopped in at a deli and bought a quart of orange juice, and downed it on the spot. I threw a few punches in the air as I skipped across the street.

The House of Chess was crowded, noisy, vibrating with anticipation. Since I'd come in from the dark, the fluorescent light seemed even more painfully white than usual, and the clouds of smoke made my eyes tear. Fifty boards were on the tables. I sat down at one of them, where there was a place card with my name on it. I felt as awkward as a boy about to pose for his school photograph. The spectators, standing behind a rope at one end of the room, stared and pointed at us. Then I looked around at the other players. I saw that although I didn't know anybody, the men and adolescent boys at the boards next to me looked completely familiar. Suddenly I was special again. For the first time in what seemed like years and years, I was in my element. There was applause to my right, and Harry Urbanic, followed closely by his brother, walked into the room.

Harry was plumper now, and meaner looking: he had grown a Fu Manchu moustache. He was wearing a powder-blue body shirt, through which showed an aggressive belly. He was looking around, casing the opposition: the eyes were the same.

"Any ringuhs heah?" he said, and looked directly at me. Everyone laughed. I went cold. He looked away, and walked to the end of the room, where there was a display board. He gave a brief lecture, a rundown of a game in which he had encircled and massacred a grand-master opponent. He sounded more like a prizefighter than a chess master, calling out *zap* and *wham* as he moved the display pieces.

"Any questions?" he asked when the final position showed his adversary cracked and scattered. He rubbed his hands together. "No? Okay, let's go."

The way it worked was: Urbanic had the white pieces on fifty boards; he would also play one game of Scrabble, against a girl wearing glasses. We sat around the outside of the rectangle, and he was to walk around the inside, taking only seconds for each move, going counterclockwise from board to board. We would each have the time of one Urbanic revolution to consider our next move. This, plus the fact that we each had to play only one game rather than fifty, was supposed to be in our favor. That he was Harry was in his.

With the rap of a pawn, he began. Starting at the far left-hand corner of the room, he began to rumble down the line, at whose approximate midpoint I sat. His first move was easy — king's pawn ahead two spaces on some boards, queen's pawn on others — and Harry moved like a speeded-up film, snapping each piece forward, *bang, bang, bang,* coming closer to me. And then he snapped the white pawn on my board forward, and was gone.

There was a lot of time. I felt almost leisurely. I watched Harry's back, his right shoulder going up and down, as he moved up the opposite side of the rectangle. I decided to move my queen bishop's pawn ahead two spaces — the Sicilian, an aggressive defense. I sat back to wait. Like a train, Urbanic came around again; at my stop, he slammed a second white piece forward. Soon we were all involved in complicated positions. I walked around a little bit on the perimeter of the rectangle, and saw that some players were already losing; some, myself included, were giving him a harder time. But who knew what Harry had in mind? How long would he tolerate an even position before striking? And who would have the power and the presence of mind to strike back or, better yet, not strike back but absorb the blow quietly and proceed insidiously on another flank? The temptation was to retaliate directly to Harry's provocation. Most never got the chance; from the beginning, the train accelerated away, and then bore down on you from behind. And those who did make a clever play of some sort were quickly shown the hollowness of their wit. I held, penetrating his defenses now faster than, now at the same rate as, he penetrated mine. It seemed to me I had a slight advantage. Yes. In my stomach I felt it, what I would do here, what I would do there, five moves from now.

Harry was now taking up to fifteen seconds per move at a couple of boards; leaning his hands on the corners of the table, tapping his foot, and turning his head from side to side, he would look at the situation and finally pick up a piece, smack it down, and move on to the next board. In his wake he left perplexity; in his path there was fear. I looked down the line to my left and saw twenty chins resting on hands, and inexorable Urbanic on the way. The man to my left, whose defense was being split by a wedge of knights and bishops, sighed. "Here comes the truck," he said. He looked at me for commiseration, but I wouldn't reply. My game was going well; what did I care for his? My center was strong, and I had attacking chances. Perhaps Harry would make a merely good move rather than a perfect one. And then? Well, I had a knight I very much wanted to give him.

He wouldn't take it, though, goddamn him — and everything changed. He was amazing. Six hours after we had begun, forty players were defeated. The grim proprietors, like battlefield scavengers, were walking around collecting the chess pieces of the eliminated players. And Urbanic was now *running*, from board to board, smashing down the pieces, and smashing them down in just the right places. His moves were unexpected, pointed, and entirely correct.

My game with Harry had simplified down to a point where there only a few pieces left on the board, but of course the situation had grown much more complex. In a crowd of pieces, slack can be taken up; every move on an empty board reverberates. I had, in a rook-and-pawn end game, what I thought was a small winning edge, a pawn that might break free and run, if and if and if.

It was two in the morning, seven hours past starting time, and my eyes were nearly closed against the smoke and glare, and with fatigue. There were just five of us still playing him. In the bright light, in my exhaustion, everything seemed an illusion. I had sat for so long that I had no more sense of my body. I sat with my elbows on the table and my hands on my forehead, shielding my eyes, furiously trying to decide between two variations before Urbanic came around. It was a question of timing, always my weakness: I had to extrapolate ten, fifteen moves into the future: if I did this and then that, or that and then this, could my pawn get to the last row and become a queen before — ?

My brain just would not work. I had reached the ceiling of my intelligence. Urbanic's back was turned; he was lingering at a board across from me. He would be on me any second; I had to come up with something. He was lifting his head. I pushed a pawn forward.

Harry turned. He came to me. He held on to the corners of my table for minute after minute, head bobbing, reasoning out the alternatives. Several times he reached his hand forward, then pulled it back. He grumbled to himself. Then there was silence. I was looking down at the position, but I felt that he was staring at me. I looked up and into his eyes.

He was no longer considering the position, but was squinting at me, his forehead wrinkled.

"What?" I said.

He continued to stare at me, and I was helpless to do anything but stare back.

"What?" I repeated.

"Wait a second," he said. "Wait a second. Is your name Green, Greenfeld?"

"No," I said wearily. "Stein. My name is Paul Stein."

"Paul Stein, Paul Stein . . . *Paul Stein!* That's right! You used to play in all the metropolitan tournaments, right? I *knew* I knew you from someplace. How ya doin'?"

"Tired," I said, smiling.

"Yeah, it's tough night for everybody." He looked around at the empty chairs. "Well, listen, pal, I don't mean to spoil your evening, but you got a hopeless position there. I have a mate in nine." He moved a piece, raised his eyebrows, and walked away.

I looked at the board and counted the moves out loud, my scrotum tightening.

I looked and looked at the position. Maybe he's wrong, I thought; I shouldn't let him hypnotize me into anything. Sometimes, at the very brink of death, a startling reverse was possible. But no, it was he who had reversed me, and I wasn't even sure where he had done it. It was like sleight of hand: the nut was not under the shell. Maybe I had been deluding myself the whole time.

But I would not concede. I pushed my useless pawn ahead. Harry came around quickly this time, smiling: he had just polished off another opponent. He took a glance at my position and shrugged. He didn't even look me in the face this time; he had forgotten me already.

"It's ridiculous," he said, and moved — and walked away.

A crowd had gathered around the board where Harry was playing his last game. For some reason, I didn't feel like leaving the place — I had been there too long, the night seemed unfinished.

My mind was still racing. *Something was incomplete.* I picked up my score sheet and walked over to the edge of the crowd, where, over shoulders, I was able to see the familiar scene: Harry standing, his adversary sitting, head on hands. The last opponent was a thin young man with bony shoulders and a high forehead in which a thick vein was beating. It was apparently his move, and it was apparently a very difficult move to make. The people massed around the table were murmuring to one another, guessing what might happen. Suddenly, Harry whirled around.

"Hey!" he shouted. "Do I have to clear this room, or what?" He glared around the circle. He shook his head and turned back to the game; his opponent sat in exactly the same attitude as before, except that his face was bright red, and the vein pulsed harder than ever. He reached out and very gently, as if the piece might break, moved a pawn ahead. Harry immediately slapped down a knight. *"Check!"* he barked. The opponent grabbed for the pawn, as if to take his move back, but his hand stopped and fell to the board. He turned his king over, and the crowd around the board burst into applause. Harry reached down and shook the young man's hand, and then began to shake the hands offered all around. People were clapping him on the back; he was smiling. Harry's brother stood over against the wall, arms folded, watching without expression.

I stood on the periphery of the crowd, wondering what to do. I didn't want to be just one of the people congratulating Harry. I was special; I wanted *him* to say something to *me.* Harry broke away from them, gesturing that it was enough. He was moving toward his brother. I sensed my opportunity, and walked up to him.

I tapped him on the shoulder. "Hi," I began.

"Yeah?" Harry said.

"Good game," I said. I meant mine as well as his. Our game.

"Oh, yeah," he said, recognizing me. "How ya doin'?"

"I'm okay. Pretty good, really. But tired. Jesus, you must be *really* tired."

Harry looked at me blankly, and then looked at his brother, who shrugged. "Nah, I'm all right," Harry said. "So, what're we doin'?" he said to his brother. His brother shrugged again.

"So, what're ya up to these days?" Harry asked me. "You live around here, or what?"

"Well, I go to school," I said.

"School!" he nodded. "That's good, that's very good. I introduce you to my brother? This is my brother, Carl. Carl, this is, uh —" Harry snapped his fingers three times, quickly.

"Paul —"

"*Paul.* Listen, Paul, you doing anything? You going home? You wanna go out and get some coffee? I need some coffee."

"Sure," I said.

"Terrific," he said. "Carl, you got the cheese?"

I looked at Carl to see what on earth this could mean; but Carl gave no indication, and instead of waiting for a reply, Harry started moving toward the exit, and Carl and I fell in behind him.

It was almost three in the morning, and Broadway was very quiet. We were walking south, away from school, Harry stepping out ahead of his brother and me at racing speed, and not encouraging us to catch up.

He picked one of those Greek places, gold-vein mirrors, dark hairy countermen wearing short-sleeve shirts. We sat down in a booth, Carl and I on one side, Harry on the other. A waiter came over, his hands on his hips, and lifted his chin inquiringly.

"Three coffees," Harry told him, then turned to me. "You want coffee, right?"

"I just think I'd like a glass of milk, please," I told the waiter.

"Danish," Carl said.

"A Danish, too," Harry called to the waiter, then sat there looking in turn at his brother and me, his eyebrows raised, his head nodding as if affirming a truth, and his fingers drumming on the table. Had he forgotten who I was again?

"So, uh, how many games did you win? Tonight?" I asked him.

"What'd I do, Carl? How many were there? Fifty? That's right, fifty. Forty-seven I took. Three draws, no losses."

"That's amazing," I said.

"Yeah, well, I can't win 'em all — doesn't look right," he said. "Ay, waituh! How about some coffee over here!" Harry shook his head. "Fuckin' Greeks. I gotta get downtown in a little bit."

The waiter put the coffees in front of Carl and me, and the milk and Danish in front of Harry, "Hey, did I order this?" Harry said, shoving the orders into correct position.

"You don't mean to say you drew on purpose?" I said.

"Sure. Why not? Ugh, this coffee is piss."

Carl sipped his coffee, looking straight ahead.

"How's the cheese?" Harry said, and Carl, still looking straight ahead, reached into his jacket pocket and pulled out a thick wad of bills, Harry took it from him.

"Eight hundred sixty," Carl said.

Harry counted the bills, pocketed most of them, and gave the rest to Carl, who put them back in his jacket.

"So. You stopped playing," Harry said to me, "and you went to college. Very smart. Coupla years you'll be married, right? Have a nice job, a kid, maybe? Am I right?"

I was smiling, unwillingly. "Yeah, well, I'm not sure," I said. "You know? I mean, sometimes I think about starting to play again."

"Play? Starting to play what? Chess?"

I nodded.

"Listen, pal, let me save you a lot of grief. You don't have it. You know what I mean? And even if you did, it wouldn't be enough. I was carrying you out there tonight, you know? I had your numba right from the start."

Was I going crazy? I had sensed the edge throughout our game, the tide going back and forth. I had thought he was straining. Then I thought of moves — several where he had played just adequately instead of sharply. Something turned and careened away inside me.

"Hey, fella, don't take it so hard," Harry said. "Carl, you got the tickets, right?"

Carl tapped his coat.

"Terrific," Urbanic said. "Terrific, terrific." Harry hit his palm with his fist. "Miami. You would not fucking *believe* what happened in Miami last wintuh," he said to me.

I tried to smile. Was it true? Was I a *patzer*? Was that all I ever was and ever would be? I felt as I had often felt before I started to play chess, or when I lost a game to Artie, or when I was chosen last for a team. Things were going on and I would never understand. What had happened in Miami last winter? Did women have something to do with it?

"So what time you got?" Harry said. "Jesus, we better cut out." He slurped down the rest of his coffee and pulled out a couple of bills. "Forget about chess, pal," he said. "Play it with your college friends. You can hustle 'em." He winked at me. "Carl, my man, what say? Are we outta here?" He slid out of the booth, stood up, and dropped the bills on the table.

I stood and let them go.

"See ya, pal!" Harry Urbanic called from the door, pushing his brother ahead of him.

"Sure," I called back, my voice suddenly repugnant to me, my hand raised in a childish wave.

JONATHAN BAUMBACH

The Return of Service

(FROM THE AMERICAN REVIEW)

I AM IN A TENNIS MATCH against my father. He is also the umpire and comes to my side of the court to advise me of the rules. "You have only one serve," he says. "My advice is not to miss." I thank him — we have always been a polite family — and wait for his return to the opposing side. Waiting for him to take his place in the sun, I grow to resent the limitation imposed on my game. (Why should he have two serves, twice as many chances, more margin for error?) I bounce the ball, waiting for him — he takes his sweet time, always has — and plan to strike my first service deep to his forehand. And what if I miss, what if ambition overreaches skill? The ordinary decencies of a second chance have been denied me.

"Play is in," says the umpire.

The irreversibility of error gives me pause. It may be the height of folly to attempt the corner of his service box — my shoulder a bit stiff from the delay — and risk losing the point without a contest. The moral imperative in a challenge match is to keep the ball in play. If I aim the service for the optical center of his box, margin for error will move it right or left, shallow or deep, some small or remarkable distance from its failed intention. Easily enough done. Yet there is a crowd watching and an unimaginative, riskless service will lower their regard for me. My opponent's contempt, as the night the day, would follow.

I can feel the restiveness of the crowd. The umpire holds his pocket watch to his ear. "Play is in," he says again. "Play is in, but alas it is not in."

It is my father, the umpire, a man with a long-standing commitment to paradox.

Paradox will only take a man so far. How can my father be in the judge's chair and on the other side of the net at the same time? One of the men resembling my father is an imposter. Imposture is an old game with him. No matter the role he takes, he has the trick of showing the same face.

I rush my first serve and fault, a victim of disorientation, the ball landing two perhaps three inches deep. I plan to take a second serve as a form of protest — a near miss rates a second chance in my view — and ready myself for the toss.

The umpire blows his whistle. "Over and done," he says. "Next point."

This one seems much too laconic to be my father, a man who tends to carry his case beyond a listener's capacity to suffer his words. (Sometimes it is hard to recognize people outside the context in which you generally experience them.) I indicate confusion, a failed sense of direction, showing my irony to the few sophisticates in the audience, disguising it from the rest.

My latest intuition is that neither man is my father, but that both, either by circumstance or design, are stand-ins for him, conventional surrogates.

I protest to the umpire the injustice of only being allowed a single service.

"I'm sorry life isn't fair," he says.

I can tell he isn't sorry, or if he is, it is no great burden of sorrow.

The toss is a measure low and somewhat behind me. Concentrated to a fine degree, I slice the ball into the backhand corner of my father's box. The old man, coming out of his characteristic crouch, slides gracefully to his left and though the ball is by him, he somehow manages to get it back. A short lob, which I put away, smashing the overhead at an acute angle, leaving no possibility of accidental return.

A gratifying shot. I replay it in the imagination. The ball in the air, a lovely arc. The player, myself, stepping back to let it bounce, then racket back, waiting for the ball to rise again, uncharacteristically patient, feeling it lift off the ground, swelling, rising, feeling myself rise with the ball. My racket, that extension of myself, meets the ball at its penultimate height as if they had arranged in advance to meet at that moment and place, the racket delivering the message, the ball the message itself. I am the agent of their coming together, the orchestrator of their perfect conjunction.

I didn't want to leave that point to play another, hated to go on to what, at its best, would be something less. I offered to play the point again. There was some conversation about my request, a huddle of heads at the umpire's chair. The crowd, in traditional confusion, applauded.

The decision was to go on. My father advised, and I appreciated his belated concern, against living in the past.

What a strange man! I wondered if he thought the same about me, and if he did — strange men hold strange opinions — was there basis in fact for his view of my strangeness?

We were positioned to play the third point of the first game. It was getting dark and I expected that time would be called after this exchange or after the next. If I won the first of what I had reason to believe would be the last two points, I was assured of at least a draw. Not losing had always been my main objective. Winning was merely a more affirmative statement of the same principle. I took refuge in strategy, thought to tame the old man at his own game. (I kept forgetting that it wasn't really him, only somebody curiously like him.)

I took a practice toss which drew a reprimand from the umpire's chair. I said I was sorry, mumbled my excuses. It's not something, the toss of a ball, you have any hope of undoing when done. "This is for real," I said.

My credibility was not what it had been. I could feel the murmurs of disbelief whistling through the stands, an ill wind.

"Let's get the road on the show," said the umpire.

My service, impelled by anger, came in at him, the ball springing at his heart, requiring a strategic retreat.

I underestimated his capacity for survival. His return, surprising in itself, was forceful and deep, moving me to the backhand corner, against my intention to play there, with disadvantageous haste. "Good shot," I wanted to say to him, though there wasn't time for that.

There's hardly ever time, I thought, to do the graceful thing. I was busy in pursuit of the ball (my failure perhaps was compliment enough), staving off defeat. Even if I managed the ball's return, and I would not have run this far without that intention, the stroke would not have enough arm behind it to matter. It would merely ask my opponent for an unforced error, a giving up of self-interest.

There were good reasons, then, not to make the exceptional effort necessary to put the ball in my father's court, and if I were a less stubborn man (or a more sensible one), I would not have driven myself in hopeless pursuit. My reutrn was effected by a scooplike shot off the backhand, an improvised maneuver under crisis conditions. Wherever the ball would go, I had done the best I could.

My father tapped the ball into the open court for the point. His gentleness and restraint were a lesson to us all.

I was more dangerous — my experience about myself — coming from behind. Large advantages had always seemed to me intolerable burdens.

The strain of being frontrunner was beginning to tell on my father. His hair had turned white between points, was turning whiter by the moment, thinning and whitening. I perceived this erratic acceleration in the aging process as another one of his strategies. He was a past master in evoking guilt in an adversary.

The umpire was clearing his throat, a means of attracting attention to himself. "Defecate or desist from the pot," he said, winking at the crowd.

Such admonishments were intolerable. He had never let me do anything at my own time and pace. As if in speeded-up motion, I smashed the ball past my opponent — he seemed to be looking the wrong way — for the first service ace of the match.

There was no call from the umpire, the man humming to himself some private tune. We looked at each other a moment without verbal communication, a nod of understanding sufficient. I was readying the toss for the next serve when he called me back. "Let's see that again," he said.

Why again?

"Didn't see it. P'raps should. However didn't. 'Pologize." He wiped some dampness from the corner of his eye with a finger. I could see that he was trying to be fair, trying against predilection to control all events in his path, to perceive history as if it were the prophecy of his will.

I said I would play the point over, though under protest and with perceptible displeasure.

"I will not have this match made into a political spectacle," the umpire said. He gestured me back to the deuce court, world weary and disapproving, patient beyond human forbearance.

I would only accept the point, I said, if it were awarded to me in the proper spirit. I had already agreed to play it again and would not retract that agreement.

The umpire, my father, crossed his arms in front of him, an implacable figure. "Are we here to argue or play tennis?" he asked no one in particular.

I started to protest, then said, "Oh forget it," and returned to the court he had gestured me to, embarrassed at getting my way. I was about to toss the ball for the serve when I noticed that my opponent was sitting cross-legged just inside his own service box.

I asked the umpire if time had been called and he said, "Time calls though is almost never called to account," which made little sense in my present mood. My father, I remembered, tended to treat words as if they were playthings.

"Are you ready?" I shouted across the net. "I'm going to serve."

My opponent cocked his head as if trying to make out where the voice was coming from.

"I'm going to count to five," I said, "and then put the ball into play. One . . ."

There was no point in counting — the old man had no intention of rousing himself — though I was of the mind that one ought to complete what one started. I wasn't going to be the one to break a promise.

I finished counting in a businesslike way and served the ball.

"Indeed," said my father as it skittered off his shoe. The point was credited to my account.

My father stood in the center of the court, arms out, eyes toward the heavens, asking God what he had done to deserve ingratitude.

I would not let him shame me this time, not give him that false advantage.

The umpire coughed while my father got himself ready, dusting off the seat of his shorts, combing his hair.

I hit the next serve into the net cord, the ball catapulting back at me. I caught it with a leap, attracting the crowd's applause.

"Deuce," said the umpire with his characteristic ambiguity.

I had lost count, thought I was either ahead or behind, felt nostalgic for an earlier time when issues tended to have decisive resolutions.

I suspected the umpire not of bias, not so much that, no more than anyone's, but of attempting to prolong the match beyond its natural consequence.

The umpire spoke briefly, and not without eloquence, on the need to set our houses in order. "Sometimes wounds have to be healed in the process." He spoke as if the healing of wounds was at best a necessary evil.

My opponent said the present dispute was a family matter and would be decided at home if his prodigal son returned to the fold.

What prodigal son? I was too old, too grown up, to live with my parents. I had in fact a family of my own somewhere which, in the hurly-burly of getting on, I had somehow misplaced. "Why not stop play at this point," I said, "and continue the match at a later date under more convivial circumstances. Or . . ."

"What alternative, sir, are you proposing?" said my father from the umpire's chair, a hint of derision in the query.

I had planned to say that I would accept a draw, though thought it best to let the suggestion emerge elsewhere.

"I will not be the first one to cry *enough*," said my father. "Don't look to me for concessions. On the other hand . . ."

The umpire interrupted him. "The match will continue until one of the contestants demonstrates a clear superiority." His message was announced over the loud speaker and drew polite applause from the gallery.

My plan was to alternate winning and losing points. There was nothing to be gained, I thought, in beating him decisively and no need to take the burden of a loss on myself.

If I won the deuce point, I could afford to give away the advantage. I could afford to give it away so long as I created the illusion that it was being taken from me.

"Can't win for losing," I quipped after the second deuce.

"Deuces are wild," I said after the fourth tie.

These remarks seemed to anger my adversary. He spat into the wind, sending some of it my way, swore to teach me a lesson in manners. When he lost the next point after an extended rally he flung his racket and threw himself to the ground, lamenting his limitations and the blind malignity of chance.

I turned my back, embarrassed for him, kicked a few balls to show that I was not without passion myself.

I had served the last ad point into the net and assumed a

repetition of that tactic would invite inordinate suspicion among an ordinarily wary and overbred audience. My inclination was to hit the serve wide to the backhand, an expression of overreaching ambition, beyond reproach.

A poor toss — the ball thrown too close — defeated immediate intention. I swung inside out (as they say in baseball when a batter hits an inside pitch to the opposite field), a desperation stroke whose only design was to go through the motions of design. (Perhaps this is rationalization after the fact. The deed of course manifests the intention.) The ball, which had no business clearing the net, found the shallow corner of his box, ticking the line. As if anticipating my accidental shot, he came up quickly. He seemed to have a way of knowing what I was going to do — perhaps it was in the blood — even before I knew myself. He was coming up, his thin knotted legs pushing against the artificial surface as he drove himself forward. There was a small chance that he might reach the ball on its first bounce, the smallest of chances.

His moment arrived and was gone.

My father swung majestically and connected with space, with platonic delusion, the ball moving in its own cycle, disconnected from his intention.

Game and match to the challenger. My father came to the net on the run as is the fashion, hand outstretched. We never did get to shake hands, our arms passing like ships in the night. "I was lucky," I said. "That serve had no business going where it did."

He looked through me, said in the iciest of voices, "I'm grateful for your lesson," and walked off.

Murmurs went through the gallery, an ominous buzzing sound. I asked one of the linesmen, a sleepy old man with thick glasses, what the murmurs signified.

"Well, sir," he wheezed, "this may be out of line, my saying this, but there's some feeling among the old heads that your final service was not in the best traditions of fair play."

I was perfectly willing to concede the point, I said, an unintentional ambiguity. "Why don't we call the match a stalemate."

The old linesman said that it was not within his authority to grant such dispensation. He suggested that I talk directly to my father.

"If I could talk directly to my father, if either of us could talk to the other, we would never have gotten into this match." (That wasn't wholly true. Sometimes you said things because they had a pleasant turn to them.)

"Sir," said the linesman, "a broken heart is not easily repaired."

I walk up and down the now deserted corridors of the stadium, looking for the old man. He is, as always, deceptively difficult to find.

Someone comes up to me in the dark and asks if I'd be interested in a match against an aggressive and skillful opponent.

I say that I am looking for my father, perhaps another time.

"Hold on," he says, holding me by the shoulder. "What's this father of yours look like? An old dude passed here maybe ten minutes ago, tears running down his ancient face."

"The old man was crying?"

"Crying! Jesus, the falls of Niagara were nothing to those tears. I mean, it was not a good scene."

I try to get by, but my companion, a younger man with a viselike grip, holds fast. "Excuse me," I say.

"After we play, we'll talk," says my companion. "I want to show you my new serve."

I am in no mood to look at serves and say so in a kind way, not wanting to hurt his feelings or not wanting to hurt them to excess.

"I may be your last chance, pal," the kid says in his brash way. "To count on chances beyond the second is to live a life of unreproved illusion."

His remark, like most nonsense, has a ring of truth.

I return to the playing area alongside my insinuating companion. We take our places on opposing sides of center court, though I have not at any time, by word or sign, agreed to play him.

My father, or someone like him, is again in the umpire's chair and announces, after a few preliminary hits, that the match is begun.

It is the moment I've been waiting for. "I have not agreed to play this young man a match," I say. "This is not a contest for which I feel the slightest necessity."

My refusal to play either comes too late or goes unheard. My opponent has already tossed the ball for his service, a brilliant toss rising like a sun to the highest point of his extension. The meeting of racket and ball resounds through the stadium like the crash of cymbals.

The ball is arriving. Before I can ready myself, before I can coordinate arm and racket, before I can coordinate mind and arm, the ball will be here and gone, a dream object, receding into the distance like a ghost of the imagination. The first point is lost. And so the game. And so the match. Waiting for the ball's arrival — it is on the way, it has not yet reached me — I concede nothing.

MARY ANN MALINCHAK RISHEL

Staus

(FROM THE HUDSON REVIEW)

MARTHA DIED on a Friday, in his arms. She just walked over to him and said she thought she had the flu and he held her and then she died. No pain, no fear. Like it was nothing. For her.

After that Staus didn't know how he should act. At the funeral he wanted to cry harder, but of all his brothers, he was the oldest and strongest so he had to act right. And he didn't know how to thank the people because Martha always did the thanking and he just didn't know how to say it, so he stood there, awkward, his hands folded below his stomach, nodding his head at the people who passed. Later at the Firehall, where they all went afterwards for coffee and something to eat, he kept staring at the firetruck, red and silver, in the middle of the room, at the light from the fenders, and the steel bars, at the black wheels with their zigzagged heights and hollows, and he said he was sorry they had to sit on the truck to find a place to eat.

Kate said don't worry, that nobody cares, but some of the people gave them mean looks that they had to eat and not sit right.

And then saying goodbye to Father Matey, not staying long, him being Irish and them Slovak, everybody stopping talking until he left.

After that, Staus went to the center of the men. Hose nozzles, sticking out, dropped towards the floor. Heavy black boots, toes pointing in all directions. The long line of table against the back wall. And people eating and laughing and watching him, and the bright bouquets of food clustered around the room, an edge of the paper tablecloth torn off, and the kids throwing it at each other, playing spud and rubbing it over their noses, making masks of their play. People with powdered sugar over their lips and teeth who handed him money and said they didn't know what else to do.

Everything was too scattered and he couldn't stay looking at any one thing. And the red firetruck in the center of the room.

Because of the war they married late — both were past forty. When he was drafted, he was already thirty-two and fought in every campaign across Africa and up the boot.

"Her hair turned grey at nineteen. And she was never ashamed of it. Always kept it grey."

And after the war they dated and he wanted her to marry him right away, but things take long to get settled and so it was a while before they decided. A good hunkie wedding. Plenty of kielbasa, halusky zos kapusta, bobalky, pirohe, nut rolls, whiskey. They had been married twenty years.

"He can still find another wife. It would be a good thing."

Staus used to spend a lot of time fixing his car before the war and when he and Martha got married and moved into her mother's house that she inherited, he practically rebuilt the whole thing, tearing out a wall to make the parlor bigger, making round arches instead of square for the doorways, putting in a bathroom, laying down wider sewer pipes. He redid the outside, too, piling up a high bank from the road and sodding it. He taught himself a lot about fixing things and he was good at it.

And since Kate and Irene were widows, he used to put in or take out their storm windows or work on their toasters and the kids of his sisters would come and ask him to fix their houses since they weren't as good as he was, so he was busy and even his three brothers would come and ask. Only his sister Marcie didn't ask because she had a husband who could do for himself so Staus didn't go much there.

Sometimes Martha used to yell that he was spending too much time doing other people's work and what about his wife, so then the family would call a regular worker to take care of things and Staus and Martha would go to a drive-in movie or something. But nobody ever got mad because they knew Martha was right.

"Wife comes before family."

The first few days after the funeral were busy and Staus ate and slept wherever he was at the moment, but after the Wilkes-Barre people went home, and the ones from Clairton, and Monessen, he didn't know where to go so when his sister Kate called him and said to come and eat, he walked the twenty-five yards down the hill from his home to hers and they had supper and she said don't worry because I'll cook for you and you can sell your house and come and live with me. He said no, his house belonged once to Martha's folks and he wouldn't sell it and he knew how to clean it — but he'd come to her house to eat.

Two weeks after the funeral he took an early retirement. He was getting too old to lift meat onto trucks, he thought, and working turns wasn't worth it. He decided he would just like to live evenly, getting up in the morning and going to bed at night.

The first morning after he quit his job, he got up early and cried for a while then Kate called him to come to breakfast so he went and his sister Irene was there too and they talked too loud and talked about the funeral and he was glad he went even though they gave him a headache and he drank too much coffee.

Later that day he fixed a television antenna on Yancey's roof because Yancey, the baby, never learned how to do a thing around the house and then he went home and slept until Kate called him and told him it was time again for supper.

His sister Irene came over again, although she always said she wasn't going to because it was too noisy, she came and stayed and they argued about which neighbor paid for the stuffed cabbage at the funeral. Kate was sure it was Mary Novak but Irene said that Mary Novak never did a thing for them, all she cared about was working and making a lot of money, and it was probably Joe Kobelnicki, who always helped them out ever since she used to clean for him.

Staus said he'd check his bills, that he thought it was charged to him, but he didn't care as long as everybody had plenty to eat. He had to see Andy about the coffin anyway.

"You'd better check, Staus. He can cheat you, you know. You have to think about those things."

And that's the way it went. Kate would cook for Staus and Irene would always come to sit and watch them eat and they would talk about the price of tomato soup and the best way to drill a hole in a wall to hang a picture and somehow Irene always got things mixed up and Staus would finish eating and go home tired.

Sometimes he would wonder how he had spent his time when Martha was alive and what it was like to have a quiet afternoon when they used to watch the football games — even though she didn't understand the forms — and when he used to come home from work and she would tell him the afternoon story so far.

And since Kate did the cooking for him, it was only right that he should buy the food and each Saturday he and Irene would go shopping, sometimes to four or five different stores to use up all the coupons. Kate didn't like to leave the house much. It was a lot of trouble to get dressed because she couldn't reach around to her back to zipper her dresses and Irene wouldn't help her because she said that Kate should grow up being sixty-seven years old, and learn to dress herself — she always had her daughters dress her when they were still at home — so Kate didn't go and Staus and Irene would shop and compare prices and go from one end of town to the other to get the best bargains and check the sales.

And because Staus wanted to buy the best food, and a lot of it, so that Kate wouldn't think he was cheap, it cost Staus money, and Kate tried to cook it all so that Staus wouldn't think she was cheating him and because it helped slow her embarrassment at having a man in the house again.

And in Monessen Irene's dead husband's sister, Sara, wondered how Staus was.

"Staus, you're going't need more dirt for the grave pretty soon. It's about time for it to sink again." Irene sat hunched in her corner at Kate's kitchen, squeezed against the wall that divided the cellar steps from the door that led to the outside. The afghan she was crocheting for the kids hung over the edge of the table. "And those flowers you put on it keep dying. Maybe you should get some ivy or some kind of fern."

"I'll take a look at it."

"Just plain grass with some sort of outline for the grave is nice, too."

Staus moved closer against his wall to make room for Kate who blocked his chair as she reached across the table for the bread. Kate's hands kept going numb on her and she tapped her fingers against the table to bring back the feeling. She worked hard for him, he knew, and it took her a long time to do things.

"We're goin't have to cut the grass on Bubba's and Zedos' graves, too," said Kate.

Staus saw that the door on the left cupboard didn't close all the way. The kids slam doors and then make the hooks bent, he thought. Maybe he could straighten it out without taking the whole lock apart.

"Well, I just can't do them, Kate. I have to take care of Joe's. Somebody else'll have to do it. I can't do everybody's. You don't go up there so you don't know how much work there is."

"Don't worry, Irene. Staus'll cut the grass. You'll just have to dig around."

"Well, I'll dig, but I'm not doin' the heavy work."

Staus stood up. He could see shades of red behind the darkness of the uneven cupboard door. He stepped over Kate's feet as he left the room. It felt good to stretch.

"They just made a new grave for Johnnie Pozzo's son. Only thirty-five," said Kate.

"Where's it at?"

Irene's voice carried through him as he tried to think above their sounds. He could see her stretch out her bad leg, her foot wrapped in a crushed bedroom slipper.

"Across from Minski — you know, catty corner from Rahovchiks — down about four plots."

"That's kind of swampy."

"Well, the cemetery's getting crowded. Everybody wants to be buried in it and there's no place left."

Staus picked up the paper and sat in the chair by the picture window. He could see all the way down the hill to Roozie's new house on the edge of the dump, past the Christy Park Bridge over to Kelsey Hayes. Back up over the hill, closer towards Ridge Vue stood the old schoolhouse with its three-story fire escape winding right up to the belfry window. And on the second floor, in the two small front rooms was the borough office where Martha worked as the water clerk before they were married.

He could hear Irene counting to herself as she tore out some stitches from the afghan. "They should go to the American one in Versailles. They don't have to be buried in the Slovak one. It's just for people from Holy Trinity. Everybody wants to steal our cemetery property."

Martha was the best water clerk Ridge Vue ever had.

Irene counted. "Thirteen, fourteen, fifteen . . . and, if they wanted to be buried there, they're just goin't have to be buried in the swampy area. They'll just have to have a sinking grave, that's all."

The next month Sara from Monessen called to see how Irene's phlebitis was. They talked for a minute about Staus. Irene said that he was getting along pretty good and he gave a lot for Masses for Martha but that he kept busy. Sara said that things were slow at Irwin Works and that she was taking up beautician work. She would get her certificate soon. Yes, she was dating somebody, a nice fellow from Buena Vista who came up to see her sometimes, but she wouldn't like to live in his town. She said everybody from Monessen would try to come up soon, probably when the weather got cooler, and she hoped Staus was O.K.

The days were slow ones for Staus. He went to Mass on First Friday, then cancelled out of going to a Pirates' baseball game with the Senior Citizens. He didn't like to go out much anymore and, besides, it was mostly women who went. The following Sunday he went over to Betty Ann's and played with her kids for a while then they talked about how to put a patio in. That night he ate out at Pete's Boxcar. Kate didn't feel good — her blood pressure again — and it was too hot to cook. Irene was over at her kids.

Monday he got up early and cut the grass. After showering, he went up to see Martha's sister, Liz. They talked about the funeral and both of them cried. Going back home, he found himself driving past the cemetery. He knew he should check Martha's grave again, but today he wasn't ready. It seemed that somehow her death just didn't want to settle into him.

The next day he took Irene shopping. They went to Loblaws for the meat sale, then to Old Lady Roma's for vegetables. Afterwards, Staus carried everything into Kate's place where she would sort out their food.

It was hot and he had a headache and his body moved slower than it used to.

"I think my awning is goin' to need painted pretty soon. It's rusty underneath and you have to look at it when you sit."

Irene sat down by the kitchen table and began sipping coffee from a white mug that Kate handed her. Staus went into the parlor to read the paper; Kate began putting away the food.

"Ask Staus to fix it, if you want. My awning is pretty bad, too, but I don't complain." There was no room in the refrigerator for the milk and she was tugging at a rack, trying to pull it out without taking off all the food.

"Kate, I'm not complaining. I just said it was goin' bad." Irene took a mouthful of coffee. "I don't have to ask Staus to fix it. I can do it myself."

"Don't be silly. You can't do it yourself. How you gonna take it down. It's ten times heavier than you."

Staus shook the paper, hoping the noise would put some energy into the hot room. Irene pushed her cup to the edge of the table and Kate dropped it into the dishwater.

"I can do it. I've done heavier work than that. I had to. When my husband died, I had to learn how to do everything. Nobody helped me then."

Kate shifted the food rack down two notches then put two jars of hot peppers inside the refrigerator door. Dried pickle juice coated the bars of the rack and a sour cumin-seed odor covered the room.

"You can't lift that awning down. Staus will do it for you."

"No, I'm not asking him to do nothin' for me. If he wants to, he can, but I'm not asking."

Staus got up from the chair. He could finish the paper at his house. It was late, anyway.

"I'll take a look at your awning next week, Irene. I still have to finish the cupboard for Yancey."

Kate closed the refrigerator door. "You don't have to hurry, Staus. You've got plenty of work to do. Irene's awnings ain't that bad. It can wait. My awning's bad, too, but I don't let it get to me."

Staus felt his breathing get heavy. A roll of fat hung below his chest and he couldn't get used to the idea that it belonged to him. It doesn't take long for an old man's belt to feel tight.

"It can't wait, Kate. My awning's worser than yours. How do you know how bad mine is? Do you ever come over to see? No, you don't."

"Irene, I was just over your house a couple of days ago. Sunday."

"Yeah, to get one of my good recipes. For five minutes. But you don't come over to visit."

"I came to visit Tuesday."

"Kate, you wasn't over Tuesday. I was in town Tuesday."

Staus walked out. Irene's would be a job because he would have to take it off the poles to get at all the rust spots. Kate's was newer so he would just have to give it one coat. But they would both take time and he wanted to paint the trim on his house, too, before the cold weather set in.

He should do Kate's first. It was easier and besides, she cooked for him. He didn't want her to think he didn't like her cooking. Her food was okay, if just she didn't talk so much when they ate. He liked it quiet.

It rained all that week and then it got hot again. August hot, and the mills let out their sulfur smoke so that a settled orange mist groped among the Ridge Vue houses and made his chest heavy.

When he began to put an undercoating on Kate's roof, he noticed that the steel was more rusted than he thought and he had to call Zeppi to help him. They worked two days and since it was a high porch, it took him a long time because he kept getting dizzy and his neck hurt from bending his head back so much.

When it was done, Kate said thanks a lot and he went home tired. Later she woke him and told him to come to dinner.

The next two days he had to fix his car and he promised himself that he would do Irene's awnings next week for sure. The rest of that week was so nice he went swimming every day, by himself, where it was quiet and where he and Martha would go every Sunday when she was alive. He liked to fall back onto the water and let it cover him, pretending that she was sitting there on the side, watching him. Martha didn't know how to swim.

Monday of the next week, for some reason, he decided it was time to check on Martha's grave. Mostly nothing new happened inside him, but it was just that he knew he had to finish things, to show himself that what had come about was so.

He was a little late because he slept in, but he figured that he could be at the cemetery by nine. He called Kate, said that he wasn't going for breakfast and that Irene shouldn't come with him since he wouldn't be long. Then he put the fresh dirt, bricks, tools, and an old bag of lime he was storing in the cellar into the trunk of his car.

*

There was a lot between them. Martha had always known that, too.

He drove the two miles down Myer Avenue, past Olie's, the mailman, and Olie's retarded sister's house, onto the dirt road that led to the cemetery and the old iron gate. The gate was still locked but you could get in by squeezing through a split in the wall near where the stone arch over the entrance said "Calvary." He got himself through, then unlatched the splintered wooden bar. Old Man Vosak was getting old. He kept forgetting to open up the place.

After stopping for water, Staus drove his car past the gates and down the narrow road to the bottom of the hill below the main crucifix. The air was clean from the rain and the sky a pale blue, about as blue as it ever got in Ridge Vue except for one or two days a year, mostly in winter.

The grave was on the side of a slope, an irregular rocky section of land with hard clusters of pig leaves growing in pale, almost white, soil. He should have tried to get a better plot, he thought, maybe down by the chapel, or up at the top, but Andy said this was a good one and the funeral was so fast. He stuffed his pockets with the hand tools, then carried the first bushel of dirt up the two hills, slowly, stopping often, breathing hard.

Everything had sunk again from the rains, and the uneven mud falling over the grave boundary made a twisted outline. He focused his eyes to see what the grave would look like when he brought up the extra dirt and began raking the top soil of the grave even. This grave would always sink sideways, being on the side of the hill. Nothing he could do about it. In some places the grass was overgrown and in others nothing but bare spots marked where they all had stood that day she was buried.

Martha.

He hurried back down to the car to get more dirt. It was good rich soil that he held, and it left its dark trail from the car to the grave as it seeped out of the sides of the bushel and onto his shoes. Returning, he said a Hail Mary, then started to work, trying not to think of her underneath his feet, dead.

He was getting old, he thought, as he pushed the grass cutter over the plot and felt it stick against the stones, a jam against his chest. These were extra rocks that had come down from the top of the hill from the last rain. He stopped to clean the blades of the broken grass and dirt, aware that he had eaten too much yesterday and his movements were slow.

He scraped around the grave's edges to remake the outlines, sometimes bringing up traces of white sand and pebbles, and poured the dirt inside of his design. No High Mass. Father Matey said he should say it the same as for all the others, as there'd be hard feelings that he was doing something special. First pew, aisle. Communion. The dry host bearing down on the pain of his throat. Just watching little Stumpy Meskovak hold the yellow candle slanty, the flame shake through the air. And a lid down over her. . . . He sprayed some water on the grave to firm and shape the mound and etched it into a rectangle. Returning to the car, he loaded the bushel with the bricks. They were actually half bricks he got at cost from Unger's Construction, because somebody didn't bake them right. But they were what he wanted. The regular bricks were too big.

He again climbed the two hills to her grave. The day was getting warmer and he wanted to take off his shirt, but he thought it wouldn't be respectful in a cemetery. Kneeling down slowly, he rubbed his hands along the soft soil, allowing himself to feel only the slightest touch against his palms. He set the bricks one by one, around the grave, even in size except for four slightly larger ones at each point of the four corners.

In the center of the grave he placed the last four bricks in the shape of a cross, then he took a whisk broom and brushed each one carefully so that no dirt would hide the whitewash. He checked the design twice. Everything was even.

You could see that grave, he thought, even when you're still inside your car, driving up the road.

It looked good. It was a shame that Casey didn't come to her funeral after all she did for his kids. And that black and white striped dress that hit her behind the knees so nice. Her finger tips touching her head, gently pressing against where it hurt . . .

He should dig around the headstone a little, too. He looked up at the sky. It was about 11:00, he figured. Someone was working around Sopanski's grave. Looked like the old lady's daughter, but somebody else was with her. He didn't know who. His eyes continued beyond the two hills towards the old chapel with the broken windows where his mother and all the women from the old country used to come to say the rosary every Wednesday.

And beyond that, along the road, he saw a stooped figure moving quickly, someone in a pink dress.

He straightened up his back. It ached inside his shoulders and along his waist. He could remember Martha's laugh — a loud giggle that everybody teased her about and the way she turned her head to the side. They liked being married.

He ran his hand along the dry spots in the grass. They felt harsh against his fingers when he touched them — unlike the velvet soil on the grave. He reached for the bag of lime and sprinkled it wherever the grass was weak or sparse. Everything looked strange — all decorated with the white streaks scattered through the grass contrasting with the ordered white of the bricks, tight in their firm rectangle.

As he stood there, rubbing his back, he looked down the road again. The hunched figure was moving closer, the arms pushing against the air, looking up at him. His eyes were getting bad. He couldn't see who it was. Somebody was in a hurry.

He stared. The woman seemed to be going to Sopanski's grave. He watched for a few minutes more and, as he thought, the woman stopped and began gesturing to the two women who came to the side of the road to meet her. Staus bent down and began clipping the sharp grasses at the end of the plot. Maybe if he got all the trim done, everything would look better. He and Irene could bring up fresh flowers next week.

He snipped each leaf sharp, a sense of exactness falling through him as he tried to make the cut level with the others. When he reached the tombstone, he stopped to look at it close.

Martha.

The blue-grey veins of its marble twisted through her name.

"Staus!"

Suddenly he was jarred back to where he was. He lifted himself up and some of the ache in his muscles went away. Then he saw. Down at the bottom of the two hills — it was Kate.

He stood and watched her walk up the first hill before he realized that he should go to meet her.

"Irene's taking down her awning herself."

Staus swore, then dumped all the tools into the bushels. He carried the heaviest one to the car and Kate dragged the two others behind her. When they got back to Romine Avenue, Irene was out in the yard in a striped housedress and a pair of bedroom slippers.

"What the hell you doin'? You can't do that awning."

Irene had three large pieces of it on the ground and she leaned over a can of paint, her body bent.

"I can't wait all year to paint this. I want to sit on my porch before winter sets in."

"I told you I'd do it."

He watched her tear at the aluminum, moving it into sections around the yard. Sixty-four years old but strong. Her heavy body swayed as she lifted a steel bar, her wrapped leg shaking with the weight.

"Never you mind. I want to get it done."

Staus could feel the heat rush through his arms and face. He wished he had done her awning first. Kate would have waited. He would do a good job if she would wait for him to get in the mood.

"Here, give me that. The trouble with you, Irene, is that you're too damn independent. You're goin' to kill yourself yet."

"Don't think, Staus, that you have to do things for me. You ain't my husband. You're not obliged."

"Irene, just shut up and let me handle that." Staus carried the two slats into the shade.

"I don't want you to have to drag yourself to my house to do things."

"I don't drag myself. It's just sometimes I have things to do for myself."

He turned on the electric sander and ran it over the rusty underside of the awning strips. Irene was standing there, watching him hard, too mad to do anything. He knew she didn't want him finishing her work now, being stubborn like she was. But he sanded and she watched from the steps of the porch.

"Staus, you're getting awful grouchy. We don't ask for too much — one or two times a year we ask. Mostly, we let you do what you want." Irene put her hands under her apron. "Who knows. Maybe you're tired of us. Maybe you should live your own life."

Staus pried up the lid of a paint can, smearing green over his fingers. He saw her walk around the yard slow, favoring her weak leg, filling up two buckets with paint brushes and rags she found scattered over the grass. She wasn't a bad woman. Martha always liked her. She was poor but she always thought of her kids. Martha used to say that they were always better dressed than Kate's kids and Kate had three sons and a husband working.

"I just want to do what I'm doin'."

Irene walked closer, lowering her voice to a whisper. "In Monessen, Sara Antonszik." She waited for a truck to pass. "She's a nice girl. Single all these years. She's a good cook, too."

Staus turned and stared full into her face. "Irene — why you mentioning her?" He saw that she got scared but he didn't want to be bothered with things like that. Irene became quiet. She walked back to the porch and sat on a step, her legs stretched out before her, crossed at the ankles, her arms resting against her lap. He could feel her watching him.

"Staus. I wasn't saying nothin'. I was just talkin'."

When Staus was done, Irene said thanks but you didn't have to because I could have finished it myself and do you want something to eat. Staus said O.K. and they sat there, drinking coffee, Irene's silence hovering over the clinks and thuds of the cups against the table. Irene swallowed hard, her eyes looking at the stove. Finally, Staus got up and said he was going home and the hill was a heavy climb this time.

Staus didn't say anything to Kate the next day when he went for breakfast, but she knew Staus and Irene had fought and later that afternoon she went across the street to Irene's and asked her for a recipe. Irene told her that Staus doesn't do much for her and when the one time she asks him, it takes him a year to come and then he looks like he doesn't want to do it. Kate said that she, Irene, was always his and Martha's favorite and he didn't mean not to come. Irene gave Kate the recipe and went over for a cup of coffee the next day. Staus gave her a section of the newspaper he was reading and they talked a little, but didn't say much. When Irene was sitting on her porch the next day, Staus came over to see how the roof was holding up. Irene said it was a good job. And that was that.

Now for sure Irene didn't want to push the matter, but when Sara from Monessen called again and asked how things were, Irene wished that something really could happen between her and Staus since all the families wanted it to and, in a way, they were all a little

disappointed that Staus married Martha instead of Sara. Not that
none of them didn't like Martha. But Sara was already in the family, being the sister of Irene's husband Joe.

Anyway, they didn't even tell him that Sara called.

Then on Labor Day Sunday, the whole gang from Monessen
came — Yush and Beatrice, Steve and Mary, their kids — and
Sara.

Everybody sat around Irene's table and talked a lot and Mary
had a corsage on that her only son George bought her and that
everybody all thought was silly, especially Irene, but they said it
was real pretty. And Beatrice told about her job at the Quick Fish
Fry and how busy they were on Friday and how she hated it but
what could she do since Yush lost his job at the Monessen mill and
he didn't make much doing odd jobs. And Irene sat on the stairs
behind Sara and wished she could do something for her. Staus was
a stubborn man and they didn't know whether or not he would
come over to say hello, even though it wouldn't be very nice if he
didn't.

But he came, right before supper. Irene was cooking by the stove
and Sara was sitting at the table telling how nice everything was.
Staus looked overdressed, the ties of his shoes too tight, making his
legs look swollen, his steps too small and dainty, the feet too centered underneath his chair.

"Staus, you wanna stay for supper? It's fried chicken."

"Nah, I just come over to say hello. Kate's got supper for me
over there."

"How's she doin'?"

"Ah — you know Kate — she don't like to go no place."

"Staus, you want a cup of coffee?"

"Yeah — I'll take a cup of coffee."

And Sara, her hands tucked into the folds of her orange dress,
Staus not looking at her, the side of the refrigerator in front of
him, not wanting to see the grey figure fading and forming itself
again in the enamel. He followed Irene's body as she moved across
the room, serving coffee and cookies before the supper. His deep
brown eyes over the people around him, going a little faster past
the place where Sara set.

"Staus — we're goin' to eat pretty soon. You want to stay and
eat?"

"No, Irene, I said. Kate's over there waiting for me."

Sara, who worked sorting tin during the war, her fingers shaking from the arthritis, searching for something to hold — an edge of the tablecloth, wrapping and unwrapping its edge around her fingers. Sara, the salt and pepper shakers circling each other in a dance of things.

And the kids began to slide on the linoleum and mark off the blue and yellow squares into good sections and bad ones and Irene told them over and over to go play in the other room, that they were making too much noise, but they didn't listen and since they weren't hers, she couldn't say too much.

Then supper was ready and the first shift was ready to eat — all the kids and Sara — because she was in charge of feeding them. But the others wouldn't move from the table so they still ate in two shifts, but with everybody seated at the table at once.

And Staus stayed until the first shift ate, then left to go back to Kate's to eat with her.

After supper and the dishes were done, everybody except the kids walked across the street to say hello to Kate and then they all helped Staus carry old paint cans up to his house. The garbage man didn't take stuff like that and he would have to drive it down to the dump the next day. Later they sat on Staus' porch, looking out over the whole of Ridge Vue and the mills below them, the fire coming from a smoke stack, and Staus asked them if they wanted a ginger ale or a beer.

The women took the ginger ale and the men the beer, and they all sat and watched Mrs. Povac empty her garbage and she had to walk it up the hill to the alley. Her house needed painting, too. It was still hot out and Staus put his feet on the banister to rest them.

"Not too many lights on in the hollow tonight."

They watched the Hungarian refugee get into her car, sliding easily onto the vinyl seat. She was thin, not like the Slovak women, with short cropped hair.

"I heard Thelma Kinesky married a divorced man."

"Ahy — she don't know what she's doin'. Just a smart alec, leaving the church like that. I heard his first wife threw him out."

"Mrs. Sush put those iron bars in front of her house but there never was a car who run into them, was there?"

"No, once I think. Come right down the hill, slid on the ice and dented them. Boy, was she mad. Wanted the Boro Council to pay for straightening out the bend."

And everybody stared over the banister at the town below them at the lights among the dark and the early night-shift of trucks going up and down.

Sara. Staus could feel her presence two people beyond him. Her head was resting against the front wall of the house, and he could smell her perfume, like sweet oil covering his skin. She had a quiet voice, not loud and playful like Martha's and she was nice — but mostly Staus just wanted to talk to Yush and Steve about work in the mills and Sara's being on his porch made him restless and he didn't breathe the same as when he was with only his family.

Sara. He could see her brown shoe resting against the porch step, so balanced that the slightest move would make her foot fall off.

Then everybody from Monessen went home and Kate and Irene didn't say anything.

The next day Staus invited Irene to go to the cemetery. They cut away weeds and dug up the dirt a little and Staus polished the tombstone. Irene had had a hard life, Staus thought, Joe dying so young, and it was good to see her old now, her kids raised, and nothing to worry about, just herself.

He watched her pile dirt on the grave, scraping it up from the washed out overflow, packing it tight, bending her whole body over the grave. Staus could feel her strength as she pounded the soil, smoothed and scraped the dirt. Her grey hair curled in a bun, in places still blond from her younger days. When they were kids, Staus thought, the two of them used to ride in the back of the firetruck on their way to Tunziebok's picnics. With the others and the kegs of beer. Kate was married then and didn't go, she married at eighteen, and Martha was still too young. Him and Irene, though. And their brothers Roozie and John. And the guys from Clairton and Duquesne, some as far away as New Kensington. The girls from Ridge Vue and McKeesport. Everybody came from all over for those picnics. Sometimes as much as fifty of them and then the firetruck had to make two trips for the ones who didn't have cars, and that was most of them. But it didn't matter. They got around.

And the time they took the firetruck to Altoona to surprise the guys up there — it was the old one then, the blue one — only Ridge Vue had a *blue* firetruck — and it broke down on Route 22 right by Rainbow Gardens — and they had to walk the twenty miles back to Ridge Vue, all of the guys singing, and it was two weeks before they could get someone to drive them back out there to fix it so they could drive it home.

And that's when Irene started dating Joe from Monessen only he didn't have a car either so she was right where she started with the Ridge Vue guys. But nobody cared except when Mike Orzslak showed up with his coupe and they would all fight to ride in the rumble seat waving at everybody during their turn around the block.

"How much longer you gonna be, Staus?"

Staus could see that Irene was tired already. She couldn't stay with any one thing long, he thought. He helped her to stand up, waiting to see that she caught her balance. She put on her sweater, resting before she slid her arms through the sleeves, then gathered the hand tools in her apron.

There was still a cool breeze on the hill, but by ten o'clock it would be hot. They had an hour. Staus felt like finishing.

Irene looked around to see that she had all her things — "You can stay more if you want, Staus, but I have other dead people I have to do for, too" — then left him standing on the side of the hill while she went to cut Joe's grass.

Afterwards they went over to Kate's to tell her what they did on the graves. She was baking cookies for her grandson's birthday — they were having a party for him this Sunday, but only relatives. The kitchen was warm and she wanted to finish before the noon heat set in and her nerves got to her. Irene told them how John Supchak, the druggest, got pulled in for giving drugs without a doctor's okay, but he was just doing some old people a favor because how could they afford to always pay doctors just to tell them what pills to take and John knew what was wrong with them because he took care of all the people in Ridge Vue for years now. And Staus watched Kate put sprinkles over the sugar cookies. Bits of the glitter stuck to her fingers then flashed through the air as she rubbed her fingers together to release the flakes. She sprinkled sugar, then glitter.

"Kate, you should make different designs. Don't make them all the same." Irene sat down at the table.

Kate put a cherry in the center of some of the cookies with pieces of mint jelly candy around the edge. Irene took a few cookies and made star and snow flake designs with coconut.

Staus watched. Bits of color pushed into beige dough. Sugar tumbling over the edges of cookies onto torn waxpaper.

"Staus, you'll stay and eat some of these for dinner time," said Kate. She bent over and put a tray into the oven.

Irene gave Staus some of the dough and they began rolling the next group of cookies. Staus put nuts on his, Kate was mostly for chocolate chips and Irene worked with the colored bits of candy.

It was getting along to noon and they would be eating lunch soon. Staus was hungry today even though lately he didn't usually have much of an appetite. Afterwards they would sit on Kate's patio and it would be cooler outside and maybe later he would work on his car. He began rolling more dough into balls, but he wasn't as fast as Irene or Kate.

"Make as many different ones as you can," said Irene.

And for almost an hour they all sat around the table and watched the sugar drop from their hands.

Biographical Notes

Biographical Notes

JONATHAN BAUMBACH has published nine books, including the novels *A Man to Conjure With, What Comes Next, Reruns,* and *Babble.* He is co-Director of the Fiction Collective, writes film criticism for *Partisan Review,* and teaches fiction writing at Brooklyn College.

HAROLD BRODKEY was born in Staunton, Illinois, grew up in the Midwest, and now lives in New York City. His stories have been published in *The New Yorker, Esquire,* and *American Review,* among other magazines, and have been widely anthologized. He is the author of *First Love and Other Sorrows,* a collection of stories. A novel, *Party of Animals,* will be published by Farrar, Straus and Giroux in 1978.

JANE BOWLES was born in New York City in 1917 and educated in the United States and Switzerland. She wrote her first novel in French, married Paul Bowles in 1938, and published *Two Serious Ladies* in 1943. Her play, *In the Summer House,* was produced in New York in 1953. She spent most of her life outside the United States and died in Spain in 1973.

ELIZABETH CULLINAN was born in New York City in 1933. After graduating from college, she went to work at *The New Yorker* magazine, and her first story was published there in 1959. She has published a novel, *House of Gold,* and two collections of short stories, *The Time of Adam* and *Yellow Roses.* From 1960 to 1963 she lived in Dublin and she now lives in New York City.

STANLEY ELKIN teaches in The Writing Program at Washington University in St. Louis. He is the author of two collections of stories and four novels. Currently he is at work on a new novel, *George Mills.*

LESLIE EPSTEIN is the author of the novel *P. D. Kimerakov* and a collection of novellas and stories, *The Steinway Quintet Plus Four*. A new novel, on the Holocaust, will appear early in 1979. After completing the current year on a Guggenheim Fellowship, Mr. Epstein will take up the position of Director of the Graduate Creative Writing Program at Boston University. He has been a Rhodes Scholar and Fulbright Fellow and was recently granted the award in Literature from the American Academy and Institute of Arts and Letters. He lives with his wife, Ilene, and children, Anya, Theo, and Paul.

JOHN GARDNER is the author of *Grendel, The King's Indian, The Sunlight Dialogues, Nickel Mountain* and *October Light* and, most recently, *Moral Fiction*. His stories have appeared widely, in *Esquire, The Atlantic* and other magazines. He is currently teaching and lecturing and working on a new novel.

MARK HELPRIN is the author of *A Dove of the East and Other Stories* and *Refiner's Fire: The Life and Adventures of Marshall Pearl, A Foundling*. He is a frequent contributor to *The New Yorker* and other magazines. He has served in the British Merchant Navy, the Israeli infantry, and the Israeli Air Force. Since writing "The Schreuderspitze," he has become proficient in Alpine mountaineering.

JAMES KAPLAN was born in 1951 in New York City and grew up in Pennsylvania and New Jersey. His stories have been published in *The New Yorker, The Atlantic,* and *Esquire.* A painter as well as a writer, Mr. Kaplan is currently living in upstate New York where he is at work on a new story.

TIM MCCARTHY grew up in Vermont and attended Columbia University, Goddard College, and the University of New Hampshire. Some of his work — short stories and an excerpt from one of his unpublished novels — has appeared in several magazines, including *The Colorado Quarterly* and *The Carolina Quarterly*. He is working on a new novel inspired in part by St. Francis of Assisi. He lives in a small Christian community in New Mexico which, he says, "hasn't done much for my writing output over the last couple of years, but I am learning how to love and to let myself be loved. Happiness and peace have become real, have come alive for me. And that, God knows, is a work of art."

IAN MCEWAN was born in 1948 and at present lives in London. His short stories have appeared widely in both English and American periodicals. He is the author of two collections of stories, *First Love, Last Rites* and *In Between the Sheets,* and of a novel, *The Cement Garden,* which will be published this year.

PETER MARSH, whose "By The Yellow Lake" is his first published story, has subsequently had other work appear in *The New Yorker.*

JOYCE CAROL OATES has published a number of works of fiction, among them the novels *A Garden of Earthly Delights,* which was given the Rosenthal Foundation Award of the National Institute of Arts and Letters, and *Them,* which won the National Book Award in 1970. In recent years she has published the novels *Childwold* and *Son of the Morning* and several short story collections, including *Night-Side* and *All the Good People I've Left Behind.* She was elected to the American Academy and Institute of Arts and Letters in 1978 and is Writer-in-Residence at Princeton for the academic year 1978–79.

NATALIE L. M. PETESCH was educated at Brandeis University and the University of Texas at Austin. In 1974 her collection of short stories, *After the First Death, There Is No Other,* was awarded the University of Iowa School of Letters Award for Short Fiction. She is the author of a novel, *The Odyssey of Katinous Kalokovich.* She has received a *Kansas Quarterly* Fiction Award and recently received First Prize in *The Louisville Review* Fiction Competition for 1978. This year, *New Letters,* in cooperation with The Swallow Press, will publish her *Two Novels: The Long Hot Summers of Yasha K.* and *The Leprosarium.*

MARY ANN MALINCHAK RISHEL was born and raised near the steel mills outside Pittsburgh. After receiving her BA and MA degrees from the University of Pittsburgh, she taught public school in Pennsylvania, New York, and Nova Scotia. "Staus" is one of a dozen short stories about Slovak-Americans she is writing for her MFA thesis at Cornell.

MAX SCHOTT, a former horse trainer, now teaches in the literature program of the College of Creative Studies at the University of California at Santa Barbara. "Murphy Jones: Pearblossom, California" was the first of his stories to be published in an "other-than-local" periodical. Since its appearance, more of his stories have been published in *Ascent* and *Massachusetts Review* and the University of Illinois Press will bring out a collection of his stories, *Up Where I Used to Live,* in the fall of 1978.

LYNN SHARON SCHWARTZ was born and educated in New York City where she still lives. She has worked in many capacities related to writing and literature — as editor for *The Writer,* public relations writer for the New York Urban League, and teacher of English at Hunter College. Her fiction and criticism have appeared in a great range of American magazines and her translations of Italian poetry, in several literary journals. She has had stories selected for inclusion in two recent anthologies, *Pushcart Prize III* and *Banquet: 5 Short Stories,* and is at present working on a collection of her stories and a novel.

L. HLUCHAN SINTETOS, born in 1947 in Ohio, was raised in California and lives now in Santa Cruz. A previous story, published in *Transpacific,* was listed by Martha Foley in her 1971 Roll of Honor, and Ms. Sintetos has,

since then, continued to contribute fiction to smaller California periodicals. (She has said of her writing, "I seem to have the knack for writing
one cohesive and working story every eight years . . . keep me in mind
for 1986.") She is a member of a collective of women writers called The
Group, to which she assigns much credit for the success of "Telling the
Bees."

ROBERT T. SORRELLS received BA and MA degrees from Vanderbilt University and his MFA degree from the Writer's Workshop at the University of Iowa. His fiction has appeared, among other places, in *American
Review, Penthouse, Playgirl,* and the L.S.U. Press anthology *Southern Writing in the Sixties.* He has also written an educational TV film script on
land use and conservation called "South Carolina: Growing, Ready or
Not." Mr. Sorrells has taught at Murray State College in Kentucky and
at the University of Arkansas. A recipient of a grant from the National
Endowment for the Arts, he now lives in Clemson, South Carolina, with
his wife and two children.

GILBERT SORRENTINO was born and raised in Brooklyn, New York, and
educated at Brooklyn College. His poems and stories have appeared in
many periodicals and magazines and he has published several collections
of each. A new novel, *Mulligan Stew,* will be brought out by the Grove
Press in 1979. At present he is at work on another new novel and
collaborating on a short opera based on his novel *Steelwork.* Mr. Sorrentino is the recipient of a Guggenheim Fellowship, a grant from the
National Endowment for the Arts, and a Creative Artists Public Service
(CAPS) grant.

PETER TAYLOR was born in Tennessee in 1917. He was educated in schools
in Nashville, Memphis, and St. Louis. He later attended Kenyon College
and Vanderbilt University. He now lives in Charlottesville, Virginia, and
teaches at the University of Virginia, where he has the Henry Hoynes
Chair of Creative Writing. He is married to the poet Eleanor Ross Taylor. They have two children. His most recent collection of short stories,
published by Alfred A. Knopf, is entitled *In the Miro District and Other
Stories.*

JOY WILLIAMS' first novel, *State of Grace,* was nominated in 1973 for the
National Book Award. Her second novel, *The Changeling,* was published
in June 1978 by Doubleday. Her stories have appeared in *The Paris
Review, Esquire,* and elsewhere, and she has been the recipient of a Gug-
genheim Fellowship and a grant from the National Endowment for the
Arts. She, her daughter Caitlin, and her husband, Rust Hills, live on the
Gulf Coast of Florida as well as in Stonington, Connecticut, and New
York City.

The Yearbook of the American Short Story

January 1 to December 31, 1977

100 Other Distinguished
Short Stories of the Year 1977

FLYNT, CANDACE
Best Friend. Carolina Quarterly, Fall.

GARDINER, JOHN ROLFE
A Prior Claim. The New Yorker, December 19.
Going on Like This. The New Yorker, August 29.
GASS, WILLIAM
Koh Whistles Up a Wind. Tri-Quarterly, Winter.
GILLIATT, PENELOPE
Fleeced. The New Yorker, May 2.
GILMAN, JANET
Boxes. The Massachusetts Review, Spring.
GIVENS, JOHN
The Burning House. Fiction International, Nos. 6/7.
GOODFELLOW, ROBIN
A Grappling of Light. The Massachusetts Review, Summer.
GURGANUS, ALLAN
Condolences to Every One of Us. American Review, #26.
GUSEWELLE, C. W.
Horst Wessel. The Paris Review, Summer.

HEATH, MARY
Grace Abounding. The Virginia Quarterly Review, Summer.
HEDIN, MARY
Tuesdays. Shenandoah, Spring.
HJORTSBERG, WILLIAM
Conquistador. Cornell Review, Spring.
HOFFMAN, WILLIAM
Amazing Grace. The Sewanee Review, Winter.
HOLLAND, BARBARA
The Day's Work. Ms., August.
HOLLINGSHEAD, GREG
Two Stories You Never Know. The Capilano Review, Winter.

IRVING, JOHN
Vigilance. Ploughshares, Vol. 4, No. 1.

JACOBSEN, JOSEPHINE
Jack Frost. Epoch, Spring.
JONES, JAMES
Million-Dollar Wound. Esquire, November.
JUST, WARD
Journalism. The Virginia Quarterly Review, Fall.

KAPLAN, JAMES
Love and Painting. The New Yorker, May 16.
KEILLOR, GARRISON
Don: The True Story of a Young Person. The New Yorker, May 30.
KRANES, DAVID
Slot Queen. Ascent, Vol. 2, No. 3.

LA SALLE, PETER
Argentina? Portugal? Western Humanities Review, Autumn.
LEFFLAND, ELLA
The House of Angels. Harper's, February.
L'HEUREUX, JOHN
Roman Ordinary. Harper's, March.
Success. Harper's, March.

MARSH, PETER
Our Last Breakfast on St. Augustine's Farm. The New Yorker, December 5.
MARSHALL, JOYCE
Paul and Phyllis. The Tamarack Review, Fall.
MATANLE, STEPHEN
The Bureaucracy of Ballroom Dancing. The Georgia Review, Spring.
MERWIN, W. S.
The Ford. The New Yorker, March 28.
METCALF, JOHN
Girl in Gingham. The Fiddlehead. Summer.

MEYERS, LOU
A Summer with No End. The New Yorker, July 18.

MORGAN, BERRY
The Head Rag. The New Yorker, August 8.
The Christmas Bush. The New Yorker, October 17.

MINOT, STEPHEN
Once Upon a Time It Was 1937. The North American Review, Winter.

MUNRO, ALICE
Privilege. The Tamarack Review, Winter.
Royal Beatings. The New Yorker, March 14.

OZICK, CYNTHIA
Puttermesser: Her Work History, Her Ancestry, Her Afterlife. The New Yorker, May 9.

PANCAKE, B. D. J.
Trilobites. The Atlantic Monthly, December.

PETROSKI, CATHERINE
Rings. The North American Review, Spring.
The Deposition. The University of Windsor Review, Fall/Winter.

POVERMAN, C. E.
Retour du Sahara. Fiction International, Nos. 6/7.

RACKHAM, JEFF
Junk. Northwest Review, Vol. 16, No. 3.

REIFLER, SAMUEL
Vimraj H. Denver Quarterly, Spring.

ROBERTSON, MARY ELSIE
Mothers. Mississippi Review, Vol. 4, No. 3.

ROBINSON, MARGARET A.
Pictures and the Possibility of Love. The Saturday Evening Post, September.

ROSE, DANIEL ASA
Small Family with Rooster. The New Yorker, December 19.

SADOFF, IRA
The Last Beatnik. The Mississippi Review, Vol. 4, No. 3.

SAYLES, JOHN
Hoop. The Atlantic Monthly, March.

SANTOS, BIENVENIDO N.
Immigration Blues. New Letters, Summer.

SCHOTT, MAX
The Horse Breaker. Ascent, Vol. 2, No. 3.

SHELNUTT, EVE
Feet. Hawaii Review.
Grace. The Greensboro Review, Spring.

SINGER, ISAAC BASHEVIS
Exes. Confrontation, Fall/Winter.

SKILLINGS, R. D.
The Plymouth Boat. Ploughshares, Vol. 3, Nos. 3&4.

SMITH, C. W.
The Plantation Club. Southwest Review, Winter.

SMITH, LEE
from Black Mountain Breakdown. Carolina Quarterly, Winter.

SONTAG, SUSAN
Unguided Tour. The New Yorker, October 31.

SPENCER, ELIZABETH
Port of Embarkation. The Atlantic Monthly, January.

STEINBACH, MEREDITH
The Foxglove Is a Delicate Flower. CutBank, Fall/Winter.

STONE, ROBERT
A Hunter in the Morning. American Review, #26.

STUART, GABY
The Magic, the Prize, the Lie. The Gramercy Review, July.

THEROUX, PAUL
Reggie Woo. TriQuarterly, Fall.

THORNBURG, THOMAS R.
Yamaha. Forum, Winter.

TROW, GEORGE W. S.
I Cover Carter. The New Yorker, July 25.

TYLER, ANNE
Average Waves in Unprotected Waters. The New Yorker, February 28.

UNGERER, KATHRYN
La Marquesa in Solitary. Esquire, January.
Red Dress, Yellow Dress. Esquire, March.

UPDIKE, JOHN
Guilt Gems. The New Yorker, September 19.

VALGARDSON, W. D.
A Place of One's Own. The Tamarack Review, Summer.

VICTOR, CINDY
Nieces. South Dakota Review, Summer.

VIRGO, SEAN
White Lies. The Malahat Review, No. 43, July.

VIVANTE, ARTURO
The Chest. The New Yorker, March 7.

WATSON, LAWRENCE
Where I Go, What I Do. Quarry West, No. 7.

WETHERELL, W. D.
Narrative of the Whale Truck Essex. Michigan Quarterly Review, Fall.

WHITE, ELLINGTON
The Children Come Home at Christmas Time. The Southern Review, Summer.

WILDMAN, JOHN HAZARD
A House in Arabia. The Sewanee Review, Spring.

Editorial Addresses of American and Canadian Magazines Publishing Short Stories

Adena, Kentucky Metroversity, Garden Court, Alta Vista Road, Louisville, Kentucky 40205

Agni Review, P.O. Box 349, Cambridge, Massachusetts 02138

Americas, Organization of American States, Washington, D.C. 20006

Antaeus, 1 West 30th Street, New York, New York 10001

Antioch Review, P.O. Box 148, Yellow Springs, Ohio 45387

Apalachee Quarterly, P.O. Box 20106, Tallahassee, Florida 32304

Aphra, RFD, Box 355, Springtown, Pennsylvania 18081

Ararat, 628 Second Avenue, New York, New York 10016

Argosy, 420 Lexington Avenue, New York, New York 10017

Arizona Quarterly, University of Arizona, Tucson, Arizona 85721

Ark River Review, English Department, Wichita State University, Wichita, Kansas 67208

Arlington Quarterly, Box 366, University Station, Arlington, Texas 76010

Ascent, English Department, University of Illinois, Urbana, Illinois, 61801

Aspen Anthology, The Aspen Leaves Literary Foundation, Box 3185, Aspen, Colorado 81611

Atlantic Monthly, 8 Arlington Street, Boston, Massachusetts 02116

Aura, Box 348 NBSB, University Station, Birmingham, Alabama 35294

Bachy, 11317 Santa Monica Boulevard, Los Angeles, California 90025

Boston University Journal, 775 Commonwealth Avenue, Boston, Massachusetts 02215

Canadian Fiction, Box 46422, Station G, Vancouver, British Columbia V6R 4G7, Canada

Canadian Forum, 3 Church Street, Suite 401, Toronto, Ontario M5E 1M2, Canada

Canto, 11 Bartlett Street, Andover, Massachusetts 01810

Capilano Review, Capilano College, 2055 Purcell Way, North Vancouver, British Columbia, Canada

Carleton Miscellany, Carleton College, Northfield, Minnesota 55057

Carolina Quarterly, P.O. Box 1117, Chapel Hill, North Carolina 27514

Chariton Review, Division of Language & Literature, Northeast Missouri State University, Kirksville, Missouri 63501

Chelsea, P.O. Box 5880, Grand Central Station, New York, New York 10017

Chicago Review, Faculty Exchange, Box C, University of Chicago, Chicago, Illinois 60637

Cimarron Review, 208 Life Sciences East, Oklahoma State University, Stillwater, Oklahoma 74074

Colorado Quarterly, Hellems 134, University of Colorado, Boulder, Colorado 80309

Commentary, 165 East 56th Street, New York, New York 10022

Confrontation, English Department, Brooklyn Center for Long Island University, Brooklyn, New York 11201

Connecticut Fireside, Box 5293, Hamden, Connecticut 06518

Cornell Review, 108 North Plain Street, Ithaca, New York 14850

Cosmopolitan, 224 West 57th Street, New York, New York 10019

CutBank, Department of English, University of Montana, Bainville, Montana 59812

Dalhousie Review, Dalhousie University, Halifax, Nova Scotia

Dark Horse, % Barnes, 47A Dana Street, Cambridge, Massachusetts 02138

December, 4343 North Clarendon, Apartment 615, Chicago, Illinois 60613

Denver Quarterly, University of Denver, Denver, Colorado 80210

Descant, P.O. Box 314, Station P, Toronto, Ontario M5S 2S8, Canada

Dogsoldier, East 2933 Queen Street, Spokane, Washington 99207

Ellery Queen's Mystery Magazine, 229 Park Avenue South, New York, New York 10003

Epoch, 245 Goldwin Smith Hall, Cornell University, Ithaca, New York 14853

Esquire Fortnightly, 488 Madison Avenue, New York, New York 10022

Event, Douglas College, P.O. Box 2503, New Westminster, British Columbia V3L 5B2, Canada

Falcon, Mansfield State College, Mansfield, Pennsylvania 16933

Family Circle, 488 Madison Avenue, New York, New York 10022

Fault, 331515 Sixth Street, Union City, California 94587

Fiction, Department of English, City College of New York, 138th Street and Convent Avenue, New York, New York 10031

Fiction International, Department of English, St. Lawrence University, Canton, New York 13617

Fiddlehead, The Observatory, University of New Brunswick, Fredericton, New Brunswick E3B 5A3, Canada

Forum, Ball State University, Muncie, Indiana 47306

Four Quarters, LaSalle College, 20th and Olney Avenues, Philadelphia, Pennsylvania 19141

Gallimaufry, 807 North Daniel Street, Arlington, Virginia 22201

Georgia Review, University of Georgia, Athens, Georgia 30602

Gone Soft, Salem State College, Salem, Massachusetts 01970

Good Housekeeping, 959 Eighth Avenue, New York, New York 10019

GPU News, % The Farwell Center, 1568 North Farwell, Milwaukee, Wisconsin 53202

Graffiti, Box 418, Lenoir Rhyne College, Hickory, North Carolina 28601

Grain, Box 1885, Saskatoon, Saskatchewan S7K 3S2, Canada

Gramercy Review, P.O. Box 15362, Los Angeles, California 90015

Green River Review, SVSC, Box 56, University Center, Mississippi 48710

Greensboro Review, Department of English, University of North Carolina at Greensboro, Greensboro, North Carolina 27412

Harper's Bazaar, 312 Fifth Avenue, New York, New York 10022

Harper's Magazine, 2 Park Avenue, New York, New York 10016

Hawaii Review, 2465 Campus Road, University of Hawaii, Honolulu, Hawaii 96822

Hudson Review, 65 East 55th Street, New York, New York 10022

Hustler, 40 West Gay Street, Columbus, Ohio 43215

Intellectual Digest, 110 East 59th Street, New York, New York 10022

Iowa Review, EPB 321, University of Iowa, Iowa City, Iowa 52242

Jeffersonian Review, P.O. Box 3864, Charlottesville, Virginia 22903

Jesture Magazine, Thomas More College, Box 85, Covington, Kentucky 41017

Kansas Quarterly, Department of English, Denison Hall, Kansas State University, Manhattan, Kansas 66506

Ladies' Home Journal, 641 Lexington Avenue, New York, New York 10022

Laurel Review, West Virginia Wesleyan College, Buckhannon, West Virginia 26201

Literary Review, Fairleigh Dickinson University, Madison, New Jersey 07940

Mademoiselle, 350 Madison Avenue, New York, New York 10017

Malahat Review, University of Victoria, Box 1700, Victoria, British Columbia, Canada

Massachusetts Review, Memorial Hall, University of Massachusetts, Amherst, Massachusetts 01002

Matrix, Box 510, Lennoxville, Quebec J0B 1Z0, Canada

McCall's, 230 Park Avenue, New York, New York 10017

MD, MD Publications, 30 East 60th Street, New York, New York 10022

Michigan Quarterly Review, 3032 Roakham Building, University of Michigan, Ann Arbor, Michigan 48109

Minnesota Review, Box 211, Bloomington, Indiana 47401

Mississippi Review, Department of English, Box 37, Southern Station, University of Southern Mississippi, Hattiesburg, Mississippi 39401

Moment, 150 Fifth Avenue, New York, New York 10011

Mother Jones, 607 Market Street, San Francisco, California 94105

Ms., 370 Lexington Avenue, New York, New York 10017

Nantucket Review, P.O. Box 1444, Nantucket, Massachusetts 02554

National Jewish Monthly, 1640 Rhode Island Avenue N.W., Washington, D.C. 20036

New, Beyond Baroque Publications, 1639 W. Washington Boulevard, Venice, California 90291

New Directions, 333 Sixth Avenue, New York, New York 10014

New Letters, University of Missouri–Kansas City, 5346 Charlotte, Kansas City, Missouri 64110

New Orleans Review, Loyola University, New Orleans, Louisiana 70118

New Renaissance, 9 Heath Road, Arlington, Massachusetts 02174

New River Review, Radford College Station, Radford, Virginia 34142

New Voices, P.O. Box 308, Clintondale, New York 12515

New Yorker, 25 West 43rd Street, New York, New York 10036

Nimrod, University of Tulsa, Tulsa, Oklahoma 74104

North American Review, University of Northern Iowa, Cedar Rapids, Iowa 50613

Northern Minnesota Review, Bemidji State College, Bemidji, Minnesota 56601

Northwest Review, University of Oregon, Eugene, Oregon 97403

Occident, Eshleman Hall, University of California, Berkeley, California 94720

Ohio Journal, Department of English, Ohio State University, 164 West 17th Avenue, Columbus, Ohio 43210

Old Hickory Review, P.O. Box 1178, Jackson, Tennessee 38301

Ontario Review, 6000 Riverside Drive East, Windsor, Ontario N8S 1B6, Canada

Paris Review, 45–39 171 Place, Flushing, New York 11358

Partisan Review, Rutgers University, 1 Richardson Street, New Brunswick, New Jersey 08903

Pathway Magazine, P.O. Box 1483, Charleston, West Virginia 25325

Penthouse, 909 Third Avenue, New York, New York 10022

Pequod, P.O. Box 491, Forest Knolls, California 94933

Phylon, Atlanta University, Atlanta, Georgia 30314

Playboy, 919 North Michigan Avenue, Chicago, Illinois 60611

Ploughshares, P.O. Box 529, Cambridge, Massachusetts 02139

Prairie Schooner, 201 Andrews Hall, University of Nebraska, Lincoln, Nebraska 68588

Present Tense, 165 East 56th Street, New York, New York 10022

Prism International, University of British Columbia, Vancouver, British Columbia, Canada

Quarry West, College V, University of California, Santa Cruz, California 95060

Quarterly West, 312 Olpin Union, University of Utah, Salt Lake City, Utah 84112

Quartet, 1119 Neal Pickett Drive, College Station, Texas 77840

Queens Quarterly, Queens University, Kingston, Ontario, Canada

Redbook, 230 Park Avenue, New York, New York 10017

Remington Review, 505 Westfield Avenue, Elizabeth, New Jersey 07208

Response, Box 1496, Brandeis University, Waltham, Massachusetts 02154

Roanoke Review, Box 268, Roanoke College, Salem, Virginia 24513

Rocky Mountain Review, Box 1848, Durango, Colorado 81301

Salmagundi Magazine, Skidmore College, Saratoga Springs, New York 12866

San José Studies, San José State University, San José, California 95192

Saturday Evening Post, 1110 Waterway Boulevard, Indianapolis, Indiana 46202

Saturday Night, 80 Richmond Street E., Toronto, Ontario M5C 2P1, Canada

Seneca Review, Box 115, Hobart and William Smith Colleges, Geneva, New York 14456

Seventeen, 850 Third Avenue, New York, New York 10022

Sewanee Review, University of the South, Sewanee, Tennessee 37375

Shenandoah, Box 722, Lexington, Virginia 24450

South Carolina Review, Department of English, Clemson University, Clemson, South Carolina 29631

South Dakota Review, University of South Dakota, Vermillion, South Dakota 57069

Southern California Review, Bauer Center, Claremont, California 91711

Southern Humanities Review, Auburn University, Auburn, Alabama 36830

Southern Review, Drawer D, University Station, Baton Rouge, Louisiana 70893

Southwest Review, Southern Methodist University, Dallas, Texas 75275

Spectrum, Box 14800, Santa Barbara, California 93107

St. Andrews Review, St. Andrews Presbyterian College, Laurinsburg, North Carolina 28352

St. Louis Literary Supplement, 3523 Itaska Street, St. Louis, Missouri 63111

Story Quarterly, 820 Ridge Road, Highland Park, Illinois 60035

Sumus, The Loom Press, 500 West Rosemary Street, Chapel Hill, North Carolina 27541

Sun & Moon, 4330 Hartwick Road, College Park, Maryland 20740

Tamarack Review, Box 159, Station K, Toronto, Ontario M4P 2G5, Canada

Texas Quarterly, Box 7517, University Station, Austin, Texas 78712

TriQuarterly, 1735 Benson Avenue, Northwestern University, Evanston, Illinois 60201

Twigs, Hilltop Editions, Pikeville College Press, Pikeville, New York 41501

University of Windsor Review, Department of English, University of Windsor, Windsor, Ontario N9B 3P4, Canada

Virginia Quarterly Review, 1 West Range, Charlottesville, Virginia 22903

Vis à Vis, Division of Library Science, California State University–Fullerton, Fullerton, California 92634

Viva, 909 Third Avenue, New York, New York 10022

Vogue, 350 Madison Avenue, New York, New York 10017

Wascana Review, Wascana Parkway, Regina, Saskatchewan, Canada

Webster Review, Webster College, Webster Groves, Missouri 63119

Western Humanities Review, University of Utah, Salt Lake City, Utah 84112

Western Review, Western New Mexico University, Silver City, New Mexico 88061

Wind/Literary Review, RFD Route #1, Box 809K, Pikeville, Kentucky 41501

Woman's Day, 1515 Broadway, New York, New York 10036

Yale Review, 250 Church Street, 1902A Yale Station, New Haven, Connecticut 06520

Yankee, Yankee, Inc., Dublin, New Hampshire 03444